Ivor Allchin lives on the Susse
disputed area - neither county wants it - with his patient and
understanding family.   Having so far survived a career in
graphic design and IT, he writes novels for a dose of reality.
Occasionally he is to be found holding a guitar and does not,
contrary to popular belief, have a Welsh accent.

"Out of the crooked tree of Humanity, no straight thing can ever be made"

- IMMANUEL KANT

Thursday
18th July, 2002

1

In his mind, she was screaming.

In reality, she was sitting at the front of the classroom as if she belonged there, defying him. Reality, however, was not a problem to Jacob Morgan. He already knew that if you stayed strong, and if you believed in it enough, reality could be changed. One day, he would punish her for her presumption.

"So, why couldn't he make the right decision?"

Her words were irrelevant to him.

"Jacob? I just asked you a question."

She had spoken softly, but with authority. Jacob's classmates twisted in their seats and looked back at him across the room, amplifying the supply teacher's baleful gaze. None of this intimidated Jacob, however. She was an Imposter; she had no authority. In reality he remained silent, and returned her stare. In his mind, he could feel her throat between his hands.

Kate Berridge put down her copy of 'Great Expectations', and sagged back into her chair despondently.

"Jacob, why don't you help yourself out a bit here?" A raised eyebrow accompanied her question. "I've been taking this class for three days, and you've not opened your mouth once. I have to say I'm disappointed. I'll take it personally if you don't live up to your troublesome reputation, you know. Go on; answer just one question for me, at least to show that you've done the reading. Let's end the term on a high note."

Jacob did not acknowledge her. He continued to sit stiffly behind his desk, with his hands resting on his knees beneath it, his eyes cold with contempt. Another Sixth Former at the front of the room turned away and sniggered at this, and the moment passed. Then a different student held their hand in the air. Miss Berridge addressed the eager pupil.

"Yes, Richard?"

"Because he was in love with Estella, Miss?" offered Richard.

The teacher nodded. "Spot on. Or at least that's what's implied by Dickens." The normal flow of the class started to return. "Because Pip's upbringing was so harsh, it's no surprise that he…"

Suddenly, Jacob spoke.

"Tell me where she is."

Miss Berridge stopped mid-sentence and frowned.

"I beg your pardon, Jacob?"

"Tell me where she is, or things will happen. Bad things."

He said it with a cold certainty.

Once again the business of academia came to a halt, and once again there were only two people in the room, staring each other down like duellists at dawn.

Eventually Kate Berridge sighed and rose from her chair. "Excuse me, everybody," she said, and slowly walked the five paces to Jacob's desk. In addition to Jacob's own, twenty pairs of male, teenage eyes followed her. With Miss Berridge being barely ten years older than her students, she had already drawn the admiration of both pupils and faculty alike in her few days at Harkham Grammar. Each boy was prepared to suffer her sarcastic discipline if it meant they spent time in her company. She folded her arms and perched on the corner of Jacob's desk.

"Ever seen 'Groundhog Day'?" she asked. The class laughed.

For the first time, Jacob broke eye contact. He looked away and out of the window to his left. Sunlight and shadow drifted across his gaunt features, making him look old and weary, and out of place in his school uniform. His expression remained arrogant, however.

Jacob's silence compelled Miss Berridge into filling it.

"Look, Jacob. You don't like me. I get it. Message received. Your loyalty to Mrs Cole is touching, and I appreciate that I'm probably a poor substitute, if you pardon the pun. But you and I are just plain stuck with each other for the rest of the week, I'm afraid."

"Didn't you know, Miss?" piped up another class member. "Jacob's pining! He and Mrs Cole are an item. Always having lovers' tiffs, they are!"

There was another wave of laughter, and Jacob's anger silently boiled inside him. His fist tightened. He was holding something within it, something sharp, and it was starting to dig into his skin. In an attempt to subdue his rage, Jacob turned his attention to the window again. The school courtyard and the grounds beyond were as before, but now something else was different. A dark green car had just come through the gates. Jacob watched the summer sun glinting on the car's mirrors as it rumbled up the gravel driveway, and he imagined the feel of throwing the Imposter under its wheels.

"Yes, thank you Andrew, for that gem of information," Miss Berridge raised her voice slightly over the subsiding laughter. "Jacob, you know full well that Mrs Cole has taken an early holiday. It's not as if she's emigrated. And it's end of term, so you wouldn't have seen her for another six weeks anyway…"

Apparently ignoring Berridge, Jacob watched as the green car parked in one of the visitors' bays. Gravel crunched and doors slammed shut. He saw two men in suits emerge from the vehicle: one of the men was ordinary in appearance, but the other stuck in his mind. He was shabby and overweight, and wore a grey raincoat despite the warm July weather. His features were familiar, and Jacob's eyes lingered on him.

Miss Berridge was losing her patience. "Jacob! I expect you to look at me when I'm talking to you."

Jacob's eyes remained fixed on the events outside. They darted down to the right as he spied a third figure exiting the main building and walking eagerly out to greet the two visitors. It was Mr Brooks, the Headmaster. The three of them shook hands, and then Jacob spotted the pale flash of police warrant cards.

At this, his pulse quickened.

His grip upon the pewter crucifix drew in tighter still.

A single red tear welled from the spiral of his fist.

"Young man," admonished Miss Berridge, "if you do not snap to it and make an effort in this class, I promise you that, end-of-term or no end-of-term, I will have you in detention and writing essays all summer."

"They don't have the authority," Jacob suddenly cried out, the tension in his voice rising, "and neither do you!" Tearing his gaze away from the detectives in the courtyard, Jacob leapt to his feet.

Blood was mottling his pure white shirt.

The rest of the class began to mutter in alarm, and shuffled their chairs nervously away from him with a howl of scraping metal.

Jacob kicked out savagely at his desk. Miss Berridge, caught by surprise, stood up and stumbled backwards as it crashed over onto its edge, sending Jacob's unopened books skidding across the floor. By now the rest of the class were out of their seats, instinctively clearing a circle around Jacob and retreating from danger. They milled around anxiously, uncertain whether to flee.

Jacob's hand pulsed as he repeatedly squeezed the bloodied crucifix. He glared at his enemies like a cornered beast, his features tense and showing no pain.

"Oh my god," Miss Berridge's voice was unstable with shock. "Jacob, please; sit down and let me get that hand seen to." She circled the upturned desk, heading towards the centre of the room, while keeping her arms extended towards Jacob in a placatory gesture. "Andrew…," she kept her eyes on Jacob while she addressed another student, "Andrew, please go and get Mr Greaves, and the Nurse. The rest of you; leave the room slowly, and wait in the corridor."

The students began to take tentative steps towards the door.

Jacob let out an ungodly scream of rage, and they froze again.

"Andrew!" urged Miss Berridge. "I said go!"

The student called Andrew jerked into life, bewildered and alarmed, and turned to run out of the room.

With unnaturally quick reflexes, Jacob left his desk and rushed to intercept Andrew's escape. Two bounds took him halfway along the back wall, where he wrapped his thin, powerful arms around the oak bookcase that dominated it. His roar of effort startled the disarrayed students into further whimpers of fright, and they looked on helplessly as the bookcase toppled over. The fleeing Andrew saw it too and, with a desperate burst of speed, he hurled himself forward, landing awkwardly on his knees. The gigantic shelves crashed down just inches from his heel, splintering but not breaking, their payload of dog-eared textbooks scattering outwards. A dust cloud billowed from beneath.

The only exit was now blocked, but Andrew was on the correct side of it. He got awkwardly to his feet, limping, wincing when putting weight onto his left leg. Then, after a last, anxious glance, he lumbered into the corridor and was gone.

Jacob's hateful eyes turned slowly to Miss Berridge.

"It's your fault!" he scolded her. "If too many people find out, if too many people know, then she'll never come back!"

Miss Berridge's eyes narrowed in confusion.

"Who'll never come back?" she asked, adrenaline making her question sound desperate. "Mrs Cole?"

Jacob did not answer her. He ran forward and vaulted the bookcase barricade with ease, his cowering classmates parting to let him through. Pausing by the door, Jacob carefully unravelled the blood-smeared chain in his palm, parting it gently into a loop, before lowering it over his head and hanging the crucifix around his neck. It settled into his shirt, staining it with a scarlet outline.

"Things will happen now," he repeated. "Bad things."

And the doorway was empty again.

2

As headmaster of Harkham Grammar, Robert Brooks prided himself on his school's reputation in the local community, its sporting conquests and, above all, its academic achievements. These he attributed to unstinting devotion, hard work, and a high calibre of student. Reality, however, rarely lived up to Mr Brooks' expectations and occasionally he found himself having to turn a blind eye to the odd indiscretion. In this way, he endured the imperfections of those around him, for the greater good of the school. He didn't have to like it, just to get on with it.

Nevertheless, desperate circumstance demanded desperate measures.

Before Brooks escorted the visiting officers out of the sunshine, and into the main hallway, he checked first to make sure that only suitable persons were in the area. So far, Brooks had curbed his anger. Had they really needed to flaunt their warrant cards like that just now? It wasn't as if Brooks hadn't known who they were. He'd asked them to come here. And what had happened to his request that a male and a female officer attend, discreetly, so that onlookers would assume they were merely some visiting parents? Their attire alone gave them away.

The three men entered the grand and academic reception area, which rose into the full height of the building. Massive sash windows sat in lustrous, century-old panelling, and the beamed roof was lofty and spacious. Ahead and to the right, an oak-bannistered staircase swept upwards to a bookshelf-lined mezzanine, which then led on to the first-floor corridors. Incongruous sunshine fluttered down through the glass dome at the building's apex, and was absorbed into the marble floor.

From behind the reception desk, a waspish, middle-aged woman started whispering intently to Mr Brooks around a vase of fresh flowers.

The detectives waited patiently. The younger, more slender man of the two used the time to review entries in his notebook. The elder man paced the chequered floor thoughtfully, with his hands deep inside his raincoat, and listened to the distant murmurs of lessons in progress. Before long he paused, and his eyes lingered on a longhaired janitor just beyond the main staircase, who was buffing the floor to a shine with a very quiet and respectful waxing machine.

As if sensing the attention, the janitor looked up and made eye contact with the older detective, briefly, before resuming his work.

Eventually Mr Brooks re-joined the officers, and smiled in a manner he judged to be polite. His desire to get them behind closed doors was now all too obvious. Gesturing for them to follow him, he said, "Shall we proceed to my office, gentlemen? Classes will be breaking for luncheon soon, so these halls won't stay tranquil for long…"

As she hurried along the corridor in pursuit, Kate Berridge stabbed frantically at her mobile phone. Her employers had briefed her about Jacob Morgan, and trained her in countermeasures, but nothing had prepared her for the unexpected ferocity of his outburst. Her head darted up and down as she dialled, keeping an eye out for the boys that had fled her classroom.

She heard the phone ringing, but nobody was answering it.

Panic clawed at her chest.

A glance over her shoulder revealed that the rest of her class, usually eager to eavesdrop, had indeed stayed put as commanded. That was one small blessing. Maintaining a brisk pace, she hung up the phone and jogged down the steps that marked the boundary between the new block and the older main building. Part of her hoped that she would catch up with Jacob and Andrew soon, but part of her also feared it.

The only thing she feared more were the people who had started this.

The same people who now weren't answering her calls.

Andrew's knee gave way just as he collapsed, panting, against the nearest classroom door. Pain gnawed at his leg. Through the glass he could see Mr Greaves' geography lesson underway as normal, a snapshot of the mundane.

Andrew banged on the door with both hands, and screamed at the top of his voice. The students on the other side were startled out of their daydreams, and then Andrew saw Mr Greaves' mouth forming an expletive. Scowling, the teacher made his way to the classroom door, with Andrew urging him to hurry.

Just then, a cry of rage rolled down the corridor.

Andrew risked a look back, and saw Jacob Morgan come careering into view, his feet skidding on the waxed floor. At the sight of his quarry, Jacob smiled and began running straight for him.

Instinctively backing away, Andrew stumbled. His arms flailed and knocked a nearby fire extinguisher from its bracket. As it clattered to the ground, the classroom door flew open and an outraged teacher appeared there.

"What the hell's going on?" Greaves was overweight, untidily bearded, and purple with indignance. He seemed to be concentrating on Andrew's interruption, rather than Jacob's relentless approach.

Andrew could barely speak for shortness of breath. Sweat beaded his face.

"Sir, please help…"

"Make sense, boy!"

The fire extinguisher connected with Greaves' skull with a gunshot crack. Andrew, startled, cried out on his behalf. The teacher staggered two steps backwards, his face suddenly vacant, before tumbling forwards into Andrew. The boy's knee injury flared as he struggled to prevent Greaves dropping like a dead weight, and clumsily he lowered him to the ground.

Andrew looked up and saw Jacob, expressionless once more, standing by the still open door of the classroom and swinging the fire extinguisher languidly back and forth. His legs and hands were now totally blood-stained. Only his eyes were alive.

Behind him, dozens of horrified faces pressed up against the glass.

Extinguisher in his left hand, Jacob reached calmly out with his right and slammed the classroom door shut, the sound echoing down the corridor. It made Andrew groan in desperation.

Stepping calmly over the prone Mr Greaves, Jacob Morgan began to advance on his petrified prey.

Suddenly, another voice rang out.

"Stop this!"

Kate Berridge now stood at the end of the corridor, her chest heaving, and mobile phone still in hand. Jacob saw her, and burst out laughing. After swinging the extinguisher around one last time, he flung it with all of his strength, directly at her head. Berridge shrieked and dived out of its way, but she found herself immediately intercepted. Jacob had dashed forward and collided with her, his arms clutching at her shoulders, dragging her screaming to the scuffed vinyl floor.

"Leave… us… alone!" spat Jacob, his breath like a serpent's hiss in her ear.

Berridge struggled to push him away, but his wiry arms carried incredible strength. Her every move was anticipated. Finally, by luck more than skill, she managed to push Jacob's chin backwards with the heel of her palm, and incapacitate him for the briefest of moments. Flicking her head around, Miss Berridge glared at Andrew, who was dithering wide-eyed next to the unconscious Greaves.

"Fire alarm!" she howled at him. "Go!"

Andrew's rubber soles squealed for traction and then he was running again, his gait a lopsided hobble. He could see the bright red alarm point about thirty feet ahead of him, beyond the next set of double doors, and he headed straight for it. His knee continued to burn.

Sneering at her, Jacob wrested his jaw away from Miss Berridge's grasp, rolled over, and then savagely kicked out with his right leg. It slammed hard into the centre of her face. Berridge's head sagged backwards and she rolled away onto her side, dazed, her nose already starting to swell in a scarlet bloom. Seemingly satisfied with his handiwork, Jacob leapt up and immediately continued his pursuit.

Jacob's footfalls spurred Andrew on, and he lunged forward with outstretched hands, desperately wrapping them around the fire-alarm box like a castaway clutching at driftwood. His momentum spun him around the box's axis and he only just steadied himself in time; his thumb stabbing at the plastic, pressing it inwards, and at last making contact with the alarm button.

Immediately, the harsh and metallic wail of the fire alarm began its assault on their senses.

Robert Brooks' composure suddenly dipped, replaced by embarrassment and horror. Something beyond his control was happening. Recovering quickly, he flashed an obsequious smile at the police officers.

"No need to be alarmed," he advised them, "if you pardon the expression. It's probably a drill. I mean, of course it's a drill. Yes." He looked theatrically at his watch. "Goodness, so it is. Bang on time, too. Clean forgot. If you'll just excuse me for one moment?" With that, Brooks gestured that the officers stay put, and he hastened back to Reception.

The thinner of the officers turned to the larger.

"Shame," he said, "I were hoping that were the lunch bell." His voice retained a tinge of the Yorkshire dales, and it emerged from beneath a full moustache.

"It's always lunchtime somewhere, Jed," replied the shabby, older man, before glancing mischievously at the retreating Brooks.

With a mutual nod of agreement, the two men ignored their instructions and followed Brooks regardless. At first, they set off at a curious saunter. When they saw the distress that the receptionist was in, however, they broke into a brisk stride.

And then, when the scream echoed around the main hall, loud enough to drown out the fire alarm, they began to run.

"Morgan! Stop this now!"

A radiant puce, Brooks was standing in the centre of the main hallway and shouting up at the grand staircase. Miss Biggs, the horn-rimmed receptionist, was sheltering behind him and echoing his outrage.

Above them on the balcony stood Jacob Morgan, steel-eyed and bloodied, his right arm clutching the sobbing Andrew Knight to his chest like a predator flaunting its kill. He was pushing a metal book-trolley back and forth distractedly with his left foot. "No, you stop this," Jacob countered. "Stop treating me like a child, and tell me where she is." His voice was unnervingly calm.

In contrast, the Headmaster's became more strident.

"Last warning, Morgan! This has gone on long enough! Let Knight go, and stop this!"

Jacob drew the trolley towards him, and then forced the captive Andrew face down onto its cold surface. Andrew shrieked in panic as his captor pushed the trolley onto the brink of the top step, with only Jacob's outstretched hand preventing it from falling. He held it there casually. "Okay, then. Shall I send him on down to you now?"

Warily, Brooks took a step forward. Andrew Knight's pale and trembling face was staring down at him, imploring him to intervene. Miss Biggs failed to stifle an anxious gasp. Even the janitor had stopped polishing the floor, and was looking on apprehensively.

Jacob Morgan's cold stare challenged them all.

Then, through the dissonance of the alarm, a new voice spoke clearly.

"Do as Brooks says."

Detective Inspector Fairfield stepped forward.

For the first time, doubt fluttered across Jacob's face.

Everyone turned to look at the incongruous and bedraggled figure that now stood among them. They tensed, for some reason naturally accepting Fairfield's authority, and awaited his next move.

The detective spoke again, and moved closer to the foot of the staircase. "You remember me, don't you Jacob? Duncan Fairfield? It's been a while. You've grown a bit since then, I see." He patted his own expanding girth mordantly, and added, "You and me both."

As Fairfield slowly stepped onto the first stair, his colleague, Detective Sergeant Caplain, quietly pushed past Brooks and Miss Biggs. He positioned himself, ready to follow Fairfield, but hung back.

Jacob's outstretched arms began to tremble, and his breath quickened. The boy's eyes narrowed as Fairfield grew closer. "Leave us alone," Jacob warned him, through gritted teeth. "You don't have the authority."

"Ah," said Fairfield calmly, "you wouldn't be saying that if you remembered me. Now, what can we do to jog your memory?"

Brooks, emboldened by this turn of events, spoke up.

"Don't be ridiculous, boy! Of course they have the authority, they're the police!"

"I don't think that's what he means, Mr Brooks," said a different voice. His waxing machine abandoned, the janitor was now approaching them. He was a bear of a man, tall and broad in his boiler suit. His long brown hair, thinned by middle age, was in a ponytail.

"Thank you for your input, Wilcox," said Brooks acerbically, "but wouldn't your talents be of better use to us in turning off that bloody alarm?"

"Oh — I'll go and do that for you, Mr Brooks," twittered Miss Biggs.

"Nobody move yet!" ordered Fairfield sternly from above, and again they all found themselves obeying him. Wilcox the janitor halted his approach, and looked on anxiously. Once Fairfield was certain that order had been restored, he turned back to Jacob and resumed their dialogue. "You want us to leave you alone, Jacob? Well, I'm sorry but that's not going to happen. Not while we still care about what happens to you. We can't leave you alone," he said, climbing yet another stair, "because that would mean you not getting the help you need. I've helped you before, Jacob. Do you remember? And that's why I'm here now," Finally Fairfield's scuffed shoes alighted on the step below the trolley, and he grasped its other handle. "To help."

Jacob's chest heaved, and he shook his head firmly.

"No," he countered, almost sobbing. "No, you're not! You're here to judge us. To punish us!"

"Well… that's one sort of help," Fairfield conceded.

Suddenly, there was a noise from the landing and Jacob shot a desperate look in its direction. Kate Berridge, unsteady on her feet and her nose swollen, emerged from the first floor doors but then hesitated at the scene before her. Clearly feeling cornered, Jacob's attention flicked back to Fairfield again.

"It was okay before," Fairfield could see the indecision in the boy's eyes and spoke steadily, "all those years ago, and it'll be okay now. I know you're scared, and I know you're confused. Just let this other lad go; then you and I can have a chat about this, and get you back to your parents."

For a long time Jacob held Fairfield's gaze, until at last resentment faded into resignation, and then finally into tears. Eventually Jacob sighed deeply, and released his hold on Andrew Knight.

"The right decision, lad," Fairfield told Jacob, and then took the weight of the trolley on his left shoulder. With his right arm he helped the distraught Andrew off the trolley, and into the custody of DS Caplain, who had promptly come running up the stairs to meet them.

It was then that the alarm bells abruptly ceased, courtesy of Miss Biggs.

A pregnant silence descended on the grand hallway.

Having rolled the empty trolley back across the balcony carpet, Fairfield led Jacob back down into reception. DS Caplain waited for Kate Berridge to join him at the top of the staircase, and then began escorting her down also.

"You all right, lass?" Caplain enquired.

"I've had worse days," she quipped despondently. "We'll need an ambulance, though. I think Morgan hurt Mr Greaves quite badly."

"Good as done," said Caplain, already dialling the number.

Upon reaching the marble floor of Reception, Fairfield and Jacob Morgan immediately found themselves surrounded: Brooks on one side, and Wilcox the janitor on the other.

"Why no handcuffs, Inspector?" fumed Brooks. "I demand this ... this... hooligan be restrained!"

"That shouldn't be necessary, sir. He and I have an understanding."

"Really?" Brooks was clearly not convinced. He wagged an officious finger at Jacob. "You're gone. Do you understand me? No inquiry. No appeal. Gone! I don't know why we gave you a chance in the first place; you've never been anything but trouble! The Governors fell for your little redemption act, but I always knew it was too good to be true. It's time you experienced some consequences to your actions, Mr Morgan! Perhaps it will help you grow up at last!"

Jacob studied him for a moment.

"Nobody ever grows up," he replied. "They just get better at hiding."

Fairfield glowered at Brooks and then, keen to avoid another flare up of hostility, he led Jacob away to some nearby reception chairs. Brooks, however, had no time to follow them because Miss Biggs immediately filled the space. She seemed calm and collected as she spoke, despite their ordeal. "Mr Brooks, I've just phoned the fire brigade, and told them not to come."

"What? Oh, yes. The alarm. Thank you, Patience."

"They weren't very pleased, though. I hope they still turn up on Sports Day."

Brooks winced in realisation. "Christ! It's Sports Day next week, isn't it! As if all this business wasn't enough…"

"Well, the police are here now," Biggs reassured him. "I'm sure they'll get to the bottom of things in no time."

"Thank you again, Patience," sighed Brooks. "I'd better get on and start dealing with this sorry mess then, I suppose. What an embarrassment. The Governors will all blame me, you know, even though they chose to let Morgan in here. I just hope we can keep it out of the papers."

Patience Biggs nodded sycophantically, and then smiled.

"It's not all bad news. There's one silver lining at least; everyone else thought the alarm was a drill, and we now have a playing field full of forty staff and hundreds of pupils. A record evacuation," she concluded with pride.

"Better ask chef to serve lunch then," said Brooks grimly.

For the next few minutes, Fairfield and Caplain stood sentinel over the silent Jacob while they phoned their colleagues at the station. The janitor, who up until that point had been loitering just out of earshot, waited until they had finished their calls and then approached them with an air of reverence.

"Excuse me officers," if the man had worn a cap, he would have been wringing it. His eye-line drifted to the seated Jacob Morgan, and then back again. "Samuel Wilcox, school caretaker."

"Yes, Mr Wilcox?" Fairfield greeted him distractedly.

"I was wondering if I might sit with Jacob for a while?"

Fairfield and Caplain exchanged glances.

"He and I are friends, you see," Wilcox explained, "and, although he doesn't show it, I'm sure he's probably just as frightened as we all are. Thought a friendly face might help."

Caplain glanced over at Jacob, who was still staring at the floor.

"Well, lad? Is that okay with you?"

Jacob shrugged.

"Okay then," said Caplain. "But we can't leave you alone, I'm afraid."

"That's fine, thank you." Wilcox lowered his bulky frame down onto a seat two chairs away from Jacob, and rested a hand on the boy's arm. "Don't worry son," Wilcox said softly, "we've talked about this before, haven't we? How to stay strong in times of trouble? We know that faith can get us through anything. Now, I realise that it might be difficult for you right now to see a way forward, but that's okay; I'll be praying for you, just like I always do."

Jacob slowly drew himself upright, the dried blood on his hands flaking away as he raked them across his lap, and looked the hopeful Wilcox square in the eye.

"I'm not your son," Jacob told him. "And it's not me you should be praying for."

3

Thirty miles away at RAF Greenwood, Greg Cole was waiting.

He stood at the edge of the visitors' parking area, a civilian fish out of water, uncertain what to do next. Although the July sunshine was doing its best to lift his spirits, he remained cold inside; a subconscious defence against what he knew was coming. As he waited, Greg couldn't help but think back to his previous, happier visit to this place. It had been the day after his fiftieth birthday, and expectations had been high. Back then, he had waited in the car park with a dozen other parents, all just as anxious and as excited as he had been. Today, all he could feel was his stomach tying itself into an empty knot.

Eventually, Greg heard the creak of a door. Two army officers appeared from the admin buildings and began walking briskly towards him, not marching, but falling into step with each other nonetheless. They were dressed impeccably in ceremonial uniforms and both wore stony, professional expressions. Greg walked slowly forward to meet them. Retaining their second-perfect timing, the officers saluted their guest.

"Good morning, sir," said the officer on the left. Greg was expecting his voice to match his demeanour, but instead of clipped, military tones he spoke softly and precisely. 'Sergeant Donovan, Major Foster," the officer continued, indicating first himself and then his companion. "Fourth Armoured."

Major Foster, the older of the two, extended his hand.

Greg nodded and placed his hand in the Major's, who shook it once, firmly. "Mr Cole," the Major said, "on behalf of Her Majesty's Armed Forces please may I offer you our sincerest condolences for your loss. When you're ready to do so, we'd like you to accompany us inside."

From the far side of the car park, unseen by either Greg Cole or his escort, another figure looked on as they made their way indoors. He was a man of sixty years or more, clad in corduroy and tweed, with a green bow tie at his throat. A battered black medical bag hung from one arm, and he carried the matching jacket to his waistcoat over the other.

The man dabbed perspiration away from his bloodshot cheeks, and waited patiently. Once the Cole party were far enough away, he hefted his bag and began to follow them.

Greg Cole remained numb, and his thoughts distracted, as his late son's commanding officers led him down bare, institutional corridors. After a while his senses shook him back to attention, suddenly aware that Major Foster had spoken to him.

"I'm sorry," Greg's voice was distant. He shook his head. "I didn't quite…"

"No, I'm sorry Mr Cole," interjected the Major politely. "I was just saying that your brother had already arrived, and should be waiting for us inside."

Greg frowned.

"My brother?"

Before Foster could explain further, the group halted at an innocuous set of double-doors that bore a white plastic sign. It read 'Chapel'. Sergeant Donovan held the doors open for Greg, and then looked back at him expectantly.

It was then that the emotional barriers fell, and the apprehension began to rise within Greg, ready to stifle him. His pulse quickened. Faced with the reality of what surely awaited him in the room beyond, he now hesitated at the threshold.

The Chapel was small and utilitarian, but had large windows and was warmly decorated. The plastic chairs that normally spanned the room had been stacked along the back walls, to clear the floor space for another purpose. At the centre of the Chapel, upon a trestle erected in front of the rudimentary altar, a closed coffin waited.

The military escorts hung back by the door, hands folded and heads bowed. Slowly, Greg approached his son's casket. It had a union flag neatly draped over the top. Greg laid a hand upon the crisp cloth, deeply touched by the care and dedication with which his son's comrades had brought Adam's body home from Germany. Again, Greg's mind travelled back to the same, persistent image: of saying goodbye to his son, so young, so indestructible, from this very airfield. Although uncontrollable at first, the rage and bitterness at Adam's demise had since passed. Now all that remained for Greg was an icy void, a hole created by the absence of both his anger and his only child.

Just then the stillness was broken, as the Chapel doors creaked slowly open again. An older man's head peered tentatively through the gap. He was practically bald, albeit with a thick, greying moustache, and wore a bow tie. He had a folded tweed jacket draped over one arm.

'Sorry," said the man, shuffling into the room fully, "I had to pop out for some fresh air."

"We'll leave you alone now, gentlemen," said Major Foster, after nodding in recognition to the new arrival, and then he walked out through the open door. "There's a telephone just outside in the corridor if you need anything. Just dial zero."

The bow tie wearing man, his back to Greg and yet to make eye contact with him, stood still and waited. He looked down at the wooden floor until the officers had departed, and the doors had drifted shut.

Only then did Kenneth Bulmer turn and look up.

"Hello, Old Boy," he said softly.

Greg Cole's face darkened.

"Am I to assume," he said flatly, "that you're my mysterious brother?"

"Yes, sorry about that. I needed to see you."

Greg gave a humourless snort."Perhaps grief has affected my memory, Bulmer," he said with sarcasm, "but you were told to never come near me, or my family, again. You need to leave. Before I do something you'll regret."

Bulmer almost smiled.

"Sorry to be blunt, Old Boy, but there aren't many of your family left to come near to."

Greg's arm dropped from his son's casket and he advanced on Bulmer, the anger plain on his face. A clear foot taller than the older man, he loomed over Bulmer and looked him square in the eye. Bulmer almost flinched, but stood his ground. "Haven't you caused enough damage?" spat Greg. "For Christ's sake, what on earth made you think you'd be welcome here? Today?" He shook his head in exasperation. "It's been almost twenty years, why couldn't you just stay away? We all hoped you were dead by now!"

Bulmer nodded, calmly. "Maybe that's something we can address in due course." Sidestepping Greg, he strolled over to Adam's coffin. 'So," he said, "did they tell you what happened?"

"What the hell is it to you?" Greg didn't turn to follow him.

"You misunderstand me," Bulmer ran his finger along the casket lid. "I already know what happened; I was just wondering what they'd told you."

In two strides Greg had crossed the space between them and grabbed Bulmer tightly by the arm, spinning him round. "I don't have time for this," he spat, "and I need it even less! The undertakers will be here within the hour and I would like to spend some time with my son. Go back to the past, Bulmer, where you belong! Do it now, or I'll bring those armed guards back in here. You know, the ones you just lied to."

Bulmer hesitated for a moment, apparently centring himself.

"Gladly," he said at length. "In fact soon I'll be leaving for good. Nevertheless, before I go I need to right a few wrongs, and attend to a few outstanding matters. One could even call it a spot of bookkeeping. What happened between us back in the day is only the start of it, I'm afraid." Carefully, Bulmer prised Greg's fingers from his arm. "This is why I need your help, Old Boy."

"You're senile if you think I'm helping you."

"I only ask that you put your prejudice aside for a moment."

"I'm not interested in talking to you."

"Then just listen. There are things you need to know."

"Leave. Now!"

Greg grabbed Bulmer's shoulders and shoved him away roughly. The older man staggered backwards and collided with the end of Adam Cole's coffin, which pivoted slightly beneath its flag, disrupting the neat folds. After taking a moment to regain his balance, a flushed Bulmer turned on his attacker and abruptly demanded:

"Tell me, Greg — when did you last speak to Susan?"

Greg scowled at him.

"We've not been together for years. You saw to that."

Bulmer's tone became urgent. "Well, in case you hadn't heard, she's gone, Greg, and this time she's not coming back. You need to understand that it's too late for her, just like it's too late for Adam. You need to listen to me, before it's too late for you! Don't just blindly accept what they're saying! We're running out of time. Please, let me put things right!"

Greg shook his head in despair, and then marched over to the Chapel doors. He held them open and waited there, barely containing his anger.

"Goodbye."

Kenneth Bulmer stared at the tense, trembling figure in the doorway for a moment, and then gathered himself. "I've nothing to lose, Old Boy," he told Greg, "and haven't done for years. But, despite how things might seem right now, you still do. I can stand against them alone if I must, but together we'll be stronger. So, take my advice and talk some more to your Action Man friends. Ask them. Ask them for the truth. Demand it."

From the pocket of his jacket, Bulmer produced two white business cards, which he placed on the surface of Adam's coffin. Then, taking great care, he straightened the skewed casket and brushed the flag back down into place. "Once you've done that," he concluded, "come and find me. I'll wait for you. But don't leave it too long, there's a good Chap."

Bulmer then walked obediently through the open door, and left the Chapel without another word.

Once Bulmer had gone, Greg Cole released his grip on the door handle and allowed it to swing shut. He let out a long, trembling sigh, before allowing the tension to dissipate from his shoulders and sagging back against the doorframe. Instinctively his fingers scrabbled for a cigarette, but then he remembered where he was and he stopped himself. Slowly, Greg went over to Adam's casket, muttering despondently as he did so. "Leave us alone. Just leave us alone..."

After a few moments, his eyes alighted on the two cards Bulmer had left behind. Something made Greg pick them up. One had Bulmer's contact details on and Greg huffed at it. But then he turned over the second card, and his gaze lingered there. It bore a striking logo against the pure white background: a stylised yellow crown, or perhaps a rising sun, atop a green horizon. It bore an address: an industrial estate on the outskirts of Harkham. And it bore a name.

Rowcroft Medical.

4

"Susan Cole," announced Mr Brooks. "One of my best teachers. At least she used to be. Which is why I felt you should know."

They had eventually made it to Brooks' scroll-panelled office, with Fairfield and Caplain sitting opposite the Headmaster's desk as though teacher had sent them there for the cane. The Jacob Morgan incident had delayed their agenda by several hours, but now that the wounded were in hospital, and now that Jacob was waiting for his parents in a police cell, they could finally discuss what had originally brought the detectives to Harkham Grammar.

"Well I have to admit, Mr Brooks," said Fairfield, "that when you first summoned us I was going to send a bobby down here. But then the Jacob Morgan connection piqued my curiosity. However, staging a practical demonstration for us might have been a step too far," he added ruefully.

At this, Brooks gave Fairfield a withering look.

Caplain picked up the conversation.

"So you're saying that Mrs Cole has gone missing?" he asked.

"I ... think so, yes," replied Brooks hesitantly.

"Well she either has, or she hasn't."

Brooks looked uneasy and leant back in his chair, a single finger tapping his lips. Eventually he said, "Before I relate this sorry tale to you gentlemen, you need to appreciate that Susan is invaluable to me. Not only is she the head of my English department, she's also a close confident, and a good friend to match. In light of this, as I'm sure you'll understand, one can overlook certain... proclivities, if it keeps things running smoothly."

"Indeed," remarked Fairfield, in a tone that urged Brooks to get to the point. Brooks smiled back thinly and continued.

"About two years ago, Susan began a covert relationship with another member of staff, if you can call him that. Samuel Wilcox, our resident caretaker. I believe you've met?"

The same vicarious look drifted across Fairfield and Caplain's faces as they mentally pictured what Brooks was describing. "Nothing wrong with that, though, is there sir?" Caplain observed.

"Not in essence, no, if it doesn't affect the school. To begin with they were quite discrete, and the situation was tolerable. But then, about six months ago, I'm sorry to say it became something of a ménage a trois," there was the slightest overtone of disgust in Brooks' voice.

Caplain's look of astonishment grew.

Fairfield, however, sighed with impatience. "That's all very titillating, Mr Brooks, but other than him attending her classes I don't see what his has to do with Jacob Mor... oh."

Fairfield stopped short as realisation dawned.

Brooks' taut smile said it all.

"Quite. Morgan gradually became obsessed. He started stalking Susan, turning up at her house, writing her strange little notes. I'm sure she wouldn't have encouraged him. However, if Susan has any flaws at all, it would be a reluctance to ask for help, and a tendency to fall for hard-luck stories. She set about trying to deal with Morgan by herself. At first, she spoke with his parents, but they lost control of him years ago, in my opinion. Unemployed, you see," this last addition was uttered with a knowing expression, as if it explained everything.

Fairfield frowned at this. 'Actually, Mr Brooks, I'll think you'll find that Ian and Barbara Morgan are as much victims as Andrew Knight was today. Jacob's a difficult lad to handle at the best of times, believe me."

"Oh, I do, Inspector," said Brooks stridently. "Don't forget, I read his psychiatric reports when he was first foisted upon me, so, yes indeed I do. Moreover, so do poor Mr Greaves and Miss Berridge. That poor girl, bless her, was only filling in at the last minute. Neither of them will be standing in front of a whiteboard for a while. You should be aware, by the way, that I will be recommending that they press charges."

"So, you think something untoward's happened to Susan Cole, then?" interjected Caplain. "Perhaps something Morgan's had a hand in?"

Brooks shifted uncomfortably, and then rose from his chair. He stood with his back to the room for a while, looking out of the window and across the quad, before continuing. "Last month was the final straw. Something must have cracked. The three of them had this blazing row on the school driveway, in full view of the pupils, and the staff... in fact anybody with eyes and ears. People noticed. People talked. Obviously, I asked Susan to come and see me, and demanded an explanation. She was distraught, but tight-lipped. Her fancy man was the same, and Jacob? Well, I gave up trying to get anything out of him long ago." Brooks paused, as though in reflection, and then added, "Susan got lucky, you see. It was the strangest thing."

"Lucky?" echoed Caplain.

"Yes," Brooks explained, "it was one of those mail-order competitions. Fifteen thousand pounds, and two weeks in Barbados.

But she had to go on a particular date, and fly from a particular airport, you know the sort of thing. The dates clashed with the last two weeks of term, but things are usually slow once the exams are over, so I let her take them." Brooks smiled magnanimously. "I'm a soft touch too, you see; I know you wouldn't think it."

The detectives just stared blankly at Brooks.

"Anyway," he rallied, "as it turns out, this wasn't such a good idea. From what I understand, it was this that caused all the trouble. Morgan became inconsolably upset at the thought of her going away, even threatening to stop her, but she put her foot down and off she went. She flew out a few days ago, on Saturday. Miss Berridge came in to cover for her.'

"So, what you're actually saying," said Fairfield patiently, "is that she's on holiday. With respect, Mr Brooks, calling the police because you haven't had a postcard yet is a little premature."

Brooks shook his head. "That's the thing. To make good use of her winnings, Susan had scheduled some home improvements for while she was away; replacement windows, better appliances, new this, new that. She left her next-door neighbour with a spare key, and asked her to deal with the window fitters when they arrived. Yesterday, when they'd finished the work, Mrs Shepperton — she's eighty-one, bless her — thought she'd call Susan's hotel in Barbados and give her the good news." Like a gunpowder plot conspirator, Brooks checked over both his shoulders before sitting back down in his leather chair. His voice grew hushed and urgent. "Except the hotel had no record of her booking! So this morning, an understandably concerned Mrs Shepperton called us here at the school, to see if we'd heard anything. But nobody has seen or heard from Susan Cole since Friday night!"

"Not even Wilcox?" Fairfield asked.

"Not that he's saying," answered Brooks with suspicion.

"Or Mrs Cole's family?" added Caplain.

Brooks tutted. "What family?" he quipped derisively. "She was married to her work. I wish my entire faculty was that loyal; nobody here will talk to me! That's why I called you, Inspector. We've had discipline problems before, but never on this scale. I was hoping that the law might have better luck where I did not, and restore some order."

Caplain smiled. "And you're worried about Mrs Cole, too."

"Of course!" snapped Brooks. "More than you could ever appreciate, Sergeant, and especially so if Morgan's at the bottom of it all. Now that you have him in custody, though, we can get him to talk; to tell us where she is!"

Fairfield rose as if to leave, and gathered his coat around him.

"I understand your anxiety," he said, "but it's a little early to be getting the thumbscrews out. Evidently, there's a lot to get our heads around here but first things first. Jacob needs to see his shrink before anything else. I've known the lad since he was twelve, and even back then there was always something gnawing away at his bright little bonce."

"I'm aware that he's still under psychiatric care, Inspector," Brooks told him tetchily. "In fact, in that respect he's the lucky one in all this! What help do the rest of us get? The people who have to deal with him, whether we like it or not? We've all gone out of our way to accommodate him, so what right does he have to bite our hands, eh? In what way could his life really be so terrible? He's got a place at Harkham Grammar School, for goodness sake!" Brooks became increasingly agitated as he spoke. The sepia eyes of his predecessors looked on disapprovingly from the walls.

"I wouldn't worry too much, sir," Fairfield advised him calmly, "Mrs Cole's probably changed hotels, or missed her connection or some such. You know what travelling's like this time of year. She's probably having having a whale of a time as we speak; sitting by a pool somewhere and sipping Pina Coladas."

"She doesn't drink," Brooks corrected him.

"Iced tea, then. She'll turn up back home on schedule, just you wait. However, in the interest of putting everyone's mind at rest Jeremy and I," Fairfield nodded towards Caplain, "will have a quick chat with your staff; get a description of Mrs Cole from your secretary; then maybe knock on a few doors; talk to the neighbours."

"Thank you, Inspector," said Brooks with an empty smile. "That's a great relief."

"Don't thank me yet, there's still Jacob to deal with. Just keep this favour fresh in your mind, in case I need you to repay me at short notice."

"Indeed. Please, let me know if there's anything else you need."

As the two detectives turned to leave, Brooks suddenly looked hopeful, as though remembering something important. "Oh, Inspector?" he called out. "If it does turn out to be, heaven forbid, a missing person case, will there be a media campaign? I'm at your disposal for television appeals, etcetera."

Fairfield and Caplain exchanged glances, but neither looked shocked by Brooks' immodesty. "It's early days," replied Fairfield. "Most cases like this get resolved within twenty-four hours, so I wouldn't get your hair done just yet."

"I only want to run a decent and reputable establishment, Inspector," appealed Brooks, in a complete non sequitur. "That's not too much to ask, is it?"

Caplain grinned at him. "Well you could always try Hendon, sir."

5

School closed early that day.

With the last of the emergency vehicles having departed, the drive and quad of Harkham Grammar was practically empty. All that remained were a smattering of faculty cars, a single motorcycle, and DI Caplain's saloon.

At the centre of it all, Duncan Fairfield stood on the yellowing grass, hands deep in his raincoat pockets and his mind deep in thought. To his back was the imposing main building, with its glass dome, louvered bell tower, and weather vane. To his left was the newer, and yet somehow shabbier, extension block of classrooms — or the 'Wendy House' as it was referred to by the pupils — and to his right the looming bulk of the red-brick gym building and then the playing fields beyond it. The fields were, of course, immaculate, even in the height of summer, all the way to the tree line where they met the edge of Harkham Common.

In his mind, Fairfield replayed an earlier scene from this same spot, when uniformed officers had led Jacob Morgan away. The bloodied teenager had been calm, and indifferent to the dozens of onlookers. Before he had been finally ushered into the back seat of a patrol car, Jacob had looked around just once, meekly, as if searching for a face in the crowd. Then the car door had slammed shut, and he had returned to simply staring ahead. At the time, Fairfield had searched the boy's vacant eyes for the passionate tearaway he had once known, but had found nothing.

He wondered whether anyone ever fulfilled their true potential.

This thought soon led Fairfield to ponder his own, less auspicious schooldays some forty-odd years ago, as well as the academic hills that his own son, David, was climbing in the here and now.

It was then that Jed Caplain appeared at Fairfield's side, with a mobile phone in his outstretched hand. "Sally's on the line, guv."

Fairfield took the phone, and held it awkwardly to his ear.

"Fairfield."

The characteristically eager voice of DC Sally Fisher greeted him. "Just checking in. How's it going your end?"

The summer breeze was rustling the phone speakers and Fairfield struggled to hear. He shielded the mouthpiece with his hand. Some time ago, his colleagues had told him that, when on a mobile, he had a tendency to shout. This was, of course, nonsense. "The plot thickens, Sally," he yelled into the handset. "The Headmaster has a possible misper for us. He's a pompous idiot, but he seems genuinely concerned, and there may even be a connection to our fractious pupil Mr Morgan. Any news from the hospital?"

"Morgan's out of A&E," reported Fisher. "He's had a once-over from the medical examiner and now he's cooling off in a cell. His parents are on their way, and we've been in touch with his psychiatrist's clinic."

"Good. I'm hoping the Morgans will be able to shed some light on this, and the sooner the shrink gets here the better. When's he due?"

"She, Sir. Dr Elspeth Hamilton MRCP, if you please," Fisher's voice had a tinge of mockery. "Dr Hamilton was speaking at a conference and regrettably unavailable, so she's driving up from Oxford tomorrow morning,"

Fairfield was quiet for a moment. He knew the Morgans of old; they were simple but proud, and had always wanted the best for Jacob despite his failings. They did not have, however, two brass farthings to rub together. Where were they getting the money for such top-flight medical treatment?

"That'll have to do," Fairfield replied eventually, with an air of resignation. "If the lad spends a night in the cells it's not the end of the world. In any case, keeping him close might benefit us if anyone decides to press charges. He's bright but misunderstood, and his list of enemies got longer today. The Jacob Morgan time bomb, Sally, is something I've been afraid would go off for a while now. "

"Well, it certainly went off with a bang," Fisher observed irreverently. "Those that were caught in the blast are being kept overnight at Harkham General. Greaves has a fractured skull, a dislocated jaw, and some blood loss. Kate Berridge's cut-price makeover consists of a broken nose, and a hairline fracture of the cheekbone. Andrew Knight came off worst, though; concussion, internal bleeding, and his left kneecap isn't where it used to be. His parents are whipping their lawyers into a feeding frenzy as we speak."

Fairfield winced. "Christ, what a mess. Hang on, Sally..."

Having felt a tap on his shoulder, Fairfield turned around so that Caplain could hand him two more items: a photocopy of some personnel records, and a photo of a middle-aged woman with an open, pleasant face and fading black curls. Fairfield resumed his conversation, reading the documents as he spoke. "Okay Sally, Jed's just managed to get a photo and address for our possible misper. It's probably nothing, but while we're waiting for Morgan's shrink to arrive it will give us something to do. We'll be back with you shortly. In the meantime, can you do me a favour and get hold of passenger lists for any flights from Heathrow to Barbados on Saturday? Also, find out if any local cab firms ran fares to the airport, and schedule a couple of uniforms to pop down to twenty-eight Waterleat Drive; see if anyone's home. No rush, though; tomorrow morning will do."

"Twenty-eight. Will do, Sir. See you soon."

The call ended.

Fairfield exhaled heavily and handed Jed Caplain his phone back. The two men exchanged a look that they both knew well.

"Pint?" said Caplain.

"Don't tempt me."

"We're all done here for now," Caplain reported. "Uniform are coming back in the morning to take more statements."

"Good. Did you get all you need from Brooks?"

"Eventually," Caplain tapped his notebook, "although that Biggs lass was a bit defensive over Cole's personnel records; thought I was going to have to fight her for them at one point."

They began to walk over to Caplain's car together, their shoes crunching a route across the gravel. Caplain let a few moments pass, a respectful pause, before speaking again. "So, how are you feeling about all this, Duncan? Morgan was under your wing for a while, wasn't he?"

Fairfield puffed out his cheeks and looked into the distance. "Sort of. He was only a lad back then, but folk were treating him like some sort of criminal mastermind. He had a little gang that would get up to mischief; vandalism, shoplifting, the usual teenage stuff, but under Morgan they were prolific. And then there was that temper. Jacob has a heart of gold in there somewhere, but once the red mist descends he's his own worst enemy. Aren't we all, though? Rightly or wrongly, I thought I could see through all that; thought I could turn him around, and put his skills to better use. To tell you the truth, Jed, I was a bit self-destructive and aimless at that age too, and it rather struck a chord with me. So, I contacted his victims and his parents, and pleaded Morgan's case."

"Which was?" Caplain's car chirped at them as he unlocked it.

"That he was a bright kid, acting up because he felt constrained; and that with the right help he might not re-offend. The authorities, not least of which this school, eventually gave him a chance; in many cases just to get me to shut up, I think. For the last couple of years things have been quiet. I'm happy to say I'd almost forgotten about him, Jed. I'd thought it was a done deal. That was until today, of course."

They each opened a car door. Caplain settled down behind the wheel, and Fairfield collapsed inelegantly into the passenger seat.

"So what about this Susan Cole thing?" Caplain asked. "Reckon there's a connection?"

"Kidnapping's a bit out of Morgan's league."

"That's not what it looked like at the top of the stairs, Duncan. He was throwing that Knight kid about like a bloody doll. I see what you're saying, but from what Brooks told us Susan Cole really seemed to push Morgan's buttons. Something sent him off the deep end today, that's for sure, so what if it was a guilty conscience?"

A sharp, metallic clatter caught their attention and they both looked up. A few yards away, they saw Samuel Wilcox preparing his motorcycle, a Harley Davison, for departure. He had replaced the boiler suit he had been wearing while waxing the floor with two-piece leathers. He was waggling a black and orange crash helmet down over his cheeks and tucking in his ponytail, seemingly oblivious to Fairfield and Caplain's presence. He wore a solemn expression.

"Now there's one statement I'm looking forward to reading," Caplain remarked. "The boyfriend. Wonder why he didn't go on holiday with her?"

"Well," suggested Fairfield, "perhaps the prize was for only one person. I doubt he could join in on a caretaker's salary, even from this place."

"Yeah, but… who ever heard of winning a holiday for one?" argued Caplain. "And Cole could easily have paid for Wilcox out of her fifteen grand."

"Perhaps she preferred the prospect of new double-glazing. Perhaps they chose to spend some time apart after their arguments."

Caplain considered this briefly.

"Then why was Wilcox so pally with Morgan just now?"

For a while they looked on in silence. Wilcox started his Harley, an imposing figure now in his biker's leathers, but then rode off down the drive at an incongruously conservative speed.

Shortly afterwards, Caplain started the ignition of his own car and put it into gear. "So, when you getting your car fixed, then?" he asked Fairfield playfully.

Fairfield reclined his seat, and leaned back into it.

"Just as soon as my mobile's fixed and I can call the garage."

"Use your landline."

"It's not reconnected yet. Tomorrow, they reckon."

"Phone from the nick, then."

"Improper use of funds, Jeremy. Tell you what; you drive, I'll think."

With that, Fairfield gathered his raincoat around him like a blanket and closed his eyes. Caplain studied him for a moment, released the handbrake, and then pulled away.

"Aye. The master at work," he mused.

6

Night was approaching.

As the summer sun finally sank behind the tree line, Dr Elspeth Hamilton flipped up the driver's sunshade, pleased that she no longer had to squint at the dual carriageway. At the same time, she treated herself to a glance in the mirror and smiled approvingly. Her chestnut hair remained tamed in its chignon twist but not too prim, and her glorious brown eyes — the only feature she really cared about — remained vibrant and clear.

Most acceptable.

Taking a deep breath, Elspeth adjusted her grip on the wheel, relaxed back into the red leather, and savoured the comforting rumble of her Bentley's engine. The twilight road flowed obediently by. It had been a long, tedious day. Tomorrow, however, was shaping up to be a most intriguing one.

It was then that her mobile phone lit up, and began its discordant wail.

Elspeth cursed under her breath, and pressed the answer button on her earpiece. "Hamilton." As the other voice talked, her face tightened in recognition. She listened patiently, adding to her side of the conversation every few seconds or so. With each sentence, she grew more apprehensive.

"Yes, they contacted me this afternoon," she said first, then:

"Nothing to be concerned about, I'm sure," followed by:

"I'm meeting the parents there first thing tomorrow. And a Detective Inspector Fairfield."

Elspeth's brow furrowed; at the sound of Fairfield's name her caller had become silent. At least fifteen seconds passed before she received a reply. Elspeth's next words after that were:

"Yes, Vanessa, I'm aware what's at stake."

It wasn't long before she followed this with a contrite:

"I'm sorry... yes, Miss Daniels," Elspeth's slender throat rose and fell at the rebuke. "I'll be in touch as soon as we have him."

The call ended.

Immediately Elspeth tore her earpiece out, and flung it onto the empty passenger seat. While keeping her eyes on the road, she reached out to switch off the phone in its cradle, glancing down briefly as her fingertips brushed the switch. It was then that she noticed the missed calls on its display. Intrigued, she plucked the phone from the dashboard and brought more detail up onto the screen. It was a number that she did not recognise, but it had called several times earlier that afternoon, when she had been in conference.

Two miles of road slipped past while she considered her next move.

With a huff of resignation, Elspeth selected 'Call', and scrabbled at the knot of cables into which her earpiece had fallen. By the time she was ready, the mysterious number had already rung several times but remained unanswered.

Elspeth Hamilton drove, and waited.

Miles away in Harkham General, Kate Berridge lay asleep in her hospital bed, whiling away her overnight observation as per doctors' orders. Locked away in the bedside cabinet, the ringing phone in her handbag went unheard.

Darkness fell outside her window.

Friday
19th July, 2002

1

By eight-thirty it was twenty-two degrees, and rising.

Because of Ramshill Street's layout, Harkham police station was always the last building to be touched by the morning sun; the taller buildings and dilapidated old clothing factory that surrounded it saw to that. The bus station at the far end of the road, however, was already basking in its rays.

Emerging from the mundane crowds of the depot, a young man marched purposefully into the sunlight. He appeared to be in his early thirties, slim and six feet tall, and radiated confidence. Light brown stubble dusted his closely shaved head, matching his ghost of a goatee beard in colour. He held a dark suit jacket over the shoulder of his crisp white shirt, and his other hand carried a duffel bag. His black leather shoes gleamed. As he passed the Sir Robert Peel public house, the young man bid good morning to the landlord, who was busy setting up al fresco tables to greet the sun.

Shortly afterwards, the young man noticed the signs announcing the police station, and picked up his pace. Leaving the warmth of the sunlight behind, and returning to shadow, Paul Black strode up to the front door as if today was the day he had been waiting for all his life.

The reception area was similar to that of most police stations, but with a dash of antique charm. Once upon a time, so the story went, it had been the town house of a Victorian gentleman and whoever had converted it to offices had obviously taken some pleasure in this conceit. Some of the original features still remained and sat incongruously next to more modern items; stained panels and moulded cornicing mixed with vinyl benches and plastic notice boards.

Maggie, a civilian worker, had been occupying the reception desk during daylight hours for as long as anyone could remember. As the street doors swung open she looked up, and saw that a handsome young man was now entering her domain.

"'Morning," she said, leaning on the counter as though she was the sole proprietor. Maggie looked as though she'd stepped out of a seaside postcard. Her colourful printed dresses and larger-than-life presence had earned her the station nickname of 'The Wench'.

"And a fine one it is too," enthused her visitor. "A fine day for my first day. Detective Sergeant Paul Black, transferring from Warwick CID." Taking Maggie completely by surprise, he proffered his right hand. After a small pause she shook it, but let go again as soon as it was polite to do so. "We're going to be working together," continued Black. "I'm supposed to report to a Detective Inspector Fairfield?"

Maggie's eyes narrowed.

"Really?" her tone was cautious, and returned none of Black's greeting. "First I've heard of such of thing; and believe me there's not a rat trips a trap round here without my knowing about it."

Black obligingly handed her some paperwork.

"I can promise you that everything's in order," he said. "I'm providing maternity cover, apparently?"

Maggie scrutinised each page of the document for a while, before acquiescing with a sniff. "I suppose that'll be covering for DS McElderry, then. You're a bit late, though; she had her little girl weeks ago. Talk about after the horse has bolted! What kept you?"

"You know the score; I go where they tell me to. I'm just glad of the promotion."

"Hmph," Maggie finally cracked a smile. "Do you know what? I bet Fairfield didn't organise a replacement in time! No wonder he didn't tell anyone else, he's probably only just got round to it. Honestly, that man needs a hat to find his head with sometimes."

Black laughed. "I'm sure that's not true."

After writing down a few details, Maggie returned Black's documents. "You're right, I'm being unfair. Fairfield's a fine copper; a chip off the old block." Maggie pressed a button, and the double doors at the far end of reception buzzed. The path deeper into the station was now open. "Up the stairs and first left. Ask for DS Caplain. You're lucky to be getting your feet under the table here, Mr Black; you might learn a thing or two."

Picking up his bag and jacket, Black smiled an acknowledgment and carried on through the doors. "That's the plan," he said.

Fairfield hurried down the station's top corridor, onto the stairs, and began to trot down them as quickly as his tender head would allow.

The previous night, Jed had coerced him into having dinner at the Caplain homestead. However, once they'd tucked the kids up in bed the wine had flowed, the clocks had slowed, and now the indulgence was taking its toll. Fairfield could feel his brain bouncing off the inside of his skull with every footfall, and it was taking all his concentration to stay focussed on the morning ahead.

Ian and Barbara Morgan were already waiting downstairs, and that stuck-up psychiatrist would be arriving at any second. Now all that stood between Fairfield and getting back to the case was a quick comfort break. He just about had time.

As he reached the first landing, Fairfield only just avoided a collision with a tall, skinny man who was bounding up the stairs. Deftly, the man stepped to one side and only just managed to hang on to his burden of cardboard folders. With a look of disdain he came to a halt, and indicated that Fairfield should do the same.

"Where's the fire, Duncan?"

The man was gaunt and middle aged, with thinning hair and a mighty, rudder-like nose. With his one free hand, Detective Chief Inspector Laurence Hill made a theatrical show of brushing down his woollen suit.

"Sorry, sir," said Fairfield, resigned to the lecture he knew was coming. "Urgent appointment."

DCI Hill's wrinkled brow collapsed into a frown.

"Well don't forget our little talk the other day, Duncan," he said condescendingly. "The one about delegation? I understand it's not always easy to let go, but you have an excellent team. What's more if you're ever feeling stretched — or perhaps a bit thin on the ground — my door is always open."

Fairfield's smile did not reach his eyes. "Of course, sir. But I'm sure we'll manage for the time being."

Hill changed tack, and adopted his business face.

"I understand you've launched a missing person enquiry?"

"That's right. Susan Cole, a local teacher. But it's early days."

"Really? From what I gathered, she's been AWOL for almost a week. Hardly early days, I would have said. Maybe it would be prudent to get some help from the media, and Joe Public?"

"Maybe we will, sir," Fairfield tried his best to sound tolerant. "But not just yet. We're giving it twenty-four hours of legwork first. Also there's the confidentiality issue; as yet we've been unable to contact Mrs Cole's next of kin."

"Very well. I'll trust your judgement, Duncan," with that, Hill straightened his armful of folders and continued up the stairs. "We're all one team, you know," he added, without looking back. Soon Hill had disappeared into the first floor, leaving Fairfield to stare up at the swinging doors.

He was never quite sure whether Hill expected too much of him, or too little, and Fairfield hadn't the energy to argue.

At least not today.

"Detective Inspector Fairfield, I presume?"

Paul Black was now standing on the stairs below Fairfield, and looking up at him eagerly. Fairfield's focus drifted around to this new arrival and, for a few awkward seconds, he simply stared at him.

"You're blocking the stairs," Fairfield eventually announced.

Black offered up his transfer documents.

"Paul Black. Your new DS."

Fairfield snatched the paperwork from him. "I'll be the judge of that," he said brusquely, and began skimming through the salient points. The pair of them stood in silence while Fairfield read. As they did so, other stair-users began inching slowly around them, like traffic around an accident. On each occasion Black smiled an apology, but Fairfield remained impassively unaware.

That was until Fairfield suddenly winced, and let out a small groan. He held a hand to his left temple.

"Everything all right, sir?" enquired Black.

"Just a headache," replied Fairfield dismissively, "and self-inflicted, I'm sorry to say. By the way, don't call me 'sir', I work for a living. 'Guv' or 'Inspector' is fine." He tilted his head, as though straining to hear something, and then added as an afterthought, "In return, I think we'll call you Blackie."

"Thank you. I'm really looking forward to..."

Black realised that nobody was listening, and his voice tailed off.

From outside the building he could now hear a car approaching, its sound amplified by the built-up street.

Fairfield had already crossed over to the landing window, and was staring out of it with a frown. Black joined him there, and saw a view of the road outside the station. It was mostly double-yellow lines, apart from a hashed area directly in front of the building, emblazoned with the words 'Police Vehicles Only'. It was into this box that a pale-blue Bentley had just driven. Fairfield and Black looked on as it was carefully parked, dead centre, and its engine fluttered into silence.

Soon afterwards, the driver's door swung open.

Long, tanned legs unfolded out of the open doorway. Slender hands followed, which then reached down to fit a high-heeled shoe, the same shade of blue as the Bentley, to each foot. The legs then straightened and their owner stood up and turned, exiting the car. She wore a dark skirt suit, and held a leather folder tightly to her chest while she closed and locked the door. A single, graceful movement had accomplished all of this.

"Oh for god's...," began Fairfield, before rounding on Black. "Okay Blackie: job number one. Get down there and tell that bloody woman to take her gaudy motor car around the back, where everyone else parks."

"Erm... yes sir. Sorry, I mean, Guv."

"And if she argues, clamp her. No. Better still, tow her."

Paul Black hesitated briefly and then, still clutching his duffel bag and jacket, turned round and hurried back down the stairs. Fairfield then took a moment to rub his aching temples, before finally continuing on his way. He made a mental note to ask Maggie for the largest pot of coffee she could find.

The flowers in the front garden of number twenty-eight Waterleat Drive were slowly dying in the heat.

DC Harvey Gossett lingered in the porch to appreciate the rhododendrons, carnations, and roses around him, and wondered if Susan Cole would ever return to tend them. Pessimistically, he considered watering them himself, and perhaps roping off the marigold borders before his heavy-booted colleagues trampled them.

Gossett's girlfriend and colleagues would often tease him about being a thirty-two year old teenager; something he didn't really mind. It wasn't because of his tendency to wear designer shirts and jeans that were at least a decade too young for him, though. Unlike most of his CID colleagues, Gossett prided himself on not letting the work take over, and on still taking time out to enjoy life and appreciate the little things. His analytical mind was perfect for detective work, but at times he felt that maybe he didn't quite fit in with the others on DI Fairfield's watch.

Gossett's companions, two uniformed constables, joined him on the porch and indicated that they were done for now. In silence, Gossett closed the brand-new front door and locked it with the key that Mrs Shepperton had given them; the same key that the double-glazing company had given to her. The front and back doors, the windows, and the conservatory were only two days old; some still had scraps of factory film clinging to their frames. As he tested the lock on the front door, Gossett wondered with regret what vital evidence the unsuspecting workers had destroyed.

As he and his colleagues returned to the street and to their vehicles, Gossett mentally prepared what he was going to say in his phone call back to the station. At Sally Fisher's request, Gossett and the others had scoured the house for Susan Cole's passport. If it was there, nobody had found it. What they had found, however, were the two extremes of a nested set of luggage: one very large suitcase and one very small. The whereabouts of the intermediate-sized ones was unknown.

They had interviewed Cole's immediate neighbours, but had received little more information than was already known, and there was no sign of Susan Cole having recently returned home. When he had opened Cole's front door, Gossett had found four days' worth of mail on the mat. It was unopened, and undisturbed from where it had fallen. The house was semi-detached, with an alleyway to its right hand side that led to the wide, open spaces of Harkham Common. From here someone could have easily entered the rear of the house unnoticed, but there were no signs of a break-in.

A finger tapped Gossett on his back.

"Are you police, then?" said a voice like sandpaper.

Gossett turned to see a man of advanced years standing behind him at a stoop. The man had a full head of white hair, and wore serge trousers with a high waist. A mustard-coloured shirt was tucked into them. Gossett marvelled at the man's question, surrounded as they were by uniformed officers and two squad cars. He resisted the urge for facetiousness.

"That's quite correct, sir. We're trying to find the lady who lives at this address. Do you know her? Or have you seen or heard anything suspicious in the last few days?"

"Hah!" scoffed the old man. "When don't we? Whole world's gone to pot!" he turned and pointed back down the road for Gossett's benefit. "I'm Tom Sullivan from number fifty, and I wish to make a complaint! Have you seen the state of my allotment? The little bastard!"

Gossett smiled at him benevolently.

"Well, Mr Sullivan, I could send an officer down to see you once we're done here, or perhaps you wouldn't mind popping into the station?"

Sullivan waved his hands at Gossett grumpily.

"Oh, don't bother!" he turned to leave. "If you're too busy."

"Mr Sullivan, I'm sure we can ..."

The old man muttered to himself as he shuffled back down the road.

"Always too busy... never bloody listen, anyway..."

When he was about ten yards away, Tom Sullivan turned back around and shouted at Gossett. "It's no wonder no-one's got any faith in the law these days! Instead of messing about with all that rubbish, you should be out catching real criminals! Like that thug, Jacob Morgan!"

Gossett was at the old man's side like a shot. "I'm sorry, Mr Sullivan – whom did you say?"

2

The offices of Harkham CID were on the first floor of the station building, directly above the archway and short tunnel that led to the car park at its centre. Before entering CID, Fairfield glanced out of the window and gave a nod of satisfaction; Dr Hamilton had finally moved her Bentley, after a little tongue-tied persuasion from DS Black.

"Good job, Blackie. Now that's done you, me, and that Hamilton woman all know where we stand. Let's start as we mean to go on, eh?"

Splaying the double doors before him, Fairfield strode into CID and threw his raincoat in the general direction of a wooden hat-stand. Paul Black followed him in, wide-eyed and taking in his new surroundings.

The office was long, thin and open plan. The street-facing side was a run of sash windows, with the opposite wall barely visible beneath densely populated notice boards and a large map of Harkham. Eventually the inner wall ended with a scrawled-on white board, and a small kitchen area. Beyond this, forming the rear wall of the gallery, was an office marked 'Detective Inspector'.

Five faces, all busy at their desks, looked up to greet the new arrivals. The murmur of conversation faded.

With Black loitering behind him, Fairfield stood at the centre of the dusty sunlight and dispensed orders. "Right, you lot. The bell's about to go for round two with Jacob Morgan, so I need everything you can give me. Oh, and by the way, this here's DS Black; he's joining us today." Fairfield gestured randomly behind him. "Sally, what's the latest?"

Sally Fisher was at the desk nearest to Fairfield, and swivelled her chair to face him. She was in her late twenties, freckled and slight, with sapphire eyes beneath a fringe of short, blonde hair. Before joining CID, during her short spell in uniform, Sally had gotten into trouble over her poisonously sharp wit, and her tendency not to suffer fools gladly. Nevertheless, Fairfield had snapped her up for his team precisely because of this; he liked how she kept folk on their toes. Fisher consulted a notepad as she spoke.

"Morgan's so-called victims have all survived the night in hospital, and should be ready for their statements now. Andrew Knight's parents are still keen to press charges, though; DS Caplain's on the phone to them as we speak, trying to pour oil on troubled waters. In other news, Susan Cole hasn't used her mobile phone since the early hours of Saturday morning, when she called a local cab firm. No credit-card transactions, either."

Like the second half of a double-act, the young man at the adjacent desk picked up the thread of Sally's contribution. As always, DC Potts was impeccably dressed and groomed to perfection. Fairfield had often mused as to how Des Potts must have originally ended up at Hendon by mistake, on his way to modelling school. "So listen to this," said Potts. "I spoke with Danny's Cabs and they confirm they picked up Susan Cole from her home at around four on Saturday morning. They drove to Heathrow, and the driver dropped her off at departures at around five thirty, suitcases, hand luggage, the lot."

"And what sort of mood was she in?" asked Fairfield. "Nervous, happy?"

"He said Cole was a Barbados bore during the journey, and was thrilled to be going."

Fairfield sighed, and frowned pensively.

"She obviously thought she was going somewhere."

"Harvey Gossett's just called in, too," chipped in Sally. "There's no sign of her passport at the house, but one, maybe two suitcases are unaccounted for. No paperwork on the holiday she won, either."

"What about the neighbour? The one that dealt with the tradesmen?"

"Alas the delightful Mrs Shepperton has, shall we say, a mind that wanders. Didn't like us waking her up either."

Fairfield smiled. "I thought they all got up at dawn at that age. How are getting on with Cole's next of kin?"

"The school records say that she's divorced. The ex-husband isn't answering his home or his office numbers. She has one son; he's in Germany with the army. We'll try him too."

Des Potts spoke next. "The travel company that supposedly arranged Cole's trip to paradise deny all knowledge of the booking. But we know that her flight took off on schedule, seven-thirty Saturday morning. Susan Cole checked in at six, and made it through the gate. No word yet on whether she went through Barbadian arrivals, though."

They waited for Fairfield to say something, but he was deep in thought. It was then that Paul Black, largely ignored by the others until now, broke the silence.

"Can I ask a question?"

"That's what you're here for, Blackie," murmured Fairfield.

"What does this all have to do with Jacob Morgan?"

Fairfield's mind drifted back to the previous evening, when they'd first interviewed Jacob Morgan. The boy's parents had endured the interview in an emotionally drained silence, their family solicitor at their side. Jacob Morgan himself had maintained the same fatalistic attitude, repeatedly intoning the same phrases, but never saying anything meaningful. His underlying theme, however, had remained constant: Susan Cole, and her much-anticipated return. After an hour they'd deemed the interview to be going nowhere and suspended it, pending the arrival of Elspeth Hamilton.

Fairfield straightened himself purposefully, and took a deep breath before answering Black's question.

"Let's go and find out."

3

Fairfield pressed record.

The two tapes began to turn, silent and incorruptible witnesses. Jed Caplain took this as his signal to begin.

"Interview with Jacob Morgan, 10:48 a.m., 19th July 2002," said Caplain. "Conducted by DI Fairfield and DS Caplain. Also present are Colin Burrows and Dr Elspeth Hamilton, in loco parentis."

The stone room was small and windowless. The two detectives, Jacob Morgan and his solicitor occupied its basic metal table, while Hamilton sat on a separate chair in the corner, behind Caplain. Her position gave her a clear view of Morgan's face, which was staring ahead blankly.

Earlier, before Jacob had joined them, Dr Hamilton had briefed the room on the boy's history. Her diagnosis was a bi-polar disorder, mild during childhood but becoming extreme over time, leading to possible schizophrenia. She had also defended her own position, telling them that over the last year or so she had made repeated requests to the Morgan family for Jacob to be isolated somewhere appropriate, under her exclusive care.

Somehow, though, Hamilton had avoided answering Fairfield's questions about how the Morgans could afford her rates, or why she was involved at all when her practice was some forty miles away. What had riled Fairfield the most, however, was that Hamilton had denied Ian and Barbara Morgan access to the interview, claiming that she needed to make an emotionally unbiased observation of her patient. Fairfield had reluctantly conceded, but insisted that the solicitor still attend. Subsequently the Morgans had retired to the canteen upstairs, where they were still waiting.

The psychiatrist had made it quite clear: she wanted Jacob all to herself.

Conscious of Hamilton's hawk-like presence, Fairfield began. "Right, Mr Morgan. Do you understand why you're here?"

Jacob nodded once.

"For the benefit of the tape, Mr Morgan nods. Jacob, right now we have a very long list of people that are annoyed with you. You could be facing some serious charges, so it's in your interest to co-operate. Your family and I need to know why you kicked off like that. Whatever it is, you can tell us. If you're in trouble, you need to tell us so that we can help you."

He paused to allow Jacob to speak, but the boy remained still and silent in his plastic chair. Jed Caplain spoke next, and posed the very same question that Jacob had been demanding an answer to all night.

"Where's Susan Cole?"

"She's not here," the boy replied immediately.

"I know that, lad. Where is she?"

"It's been three days."

That phrase again. Morgan had been repeating it constantly since his arrest, and had answered as though it was the most obvious thing in the world. Fairfield and Caplain exchanged glances.

"Surely it's been four days now, hasn't it?" said Fairfield.

"It's been three days. She promised me."

Burrows, the solicitor, interceded. "Inspector, I can't help but feel that you're wasting your time here. My client is clearly distressed at the predicament of someone he feels close to, nothing more, and this is exactly where we were yesterday. He should be released for now. Where's the value in just going round in circles? It's nonsensical."

"Fortunately, Mr Burrows," said Fairfield, "we have a secret weapon." He nodded in the direction of Hamilton, who was busily making notes in her leather folder. "Mrs Hamilton happens to be an expert in nonsense."

She spoke without looking up.

"Use the books."

Fairfield waited for her to continue, but then realised that was all they were going to get. "Well, thank you doctor. Glad you were here. Jed?"

Caplain produced two evidence bags, and placed them face up on the table. Each contained a thick, black book, visible through the clear plastic. Caplain narrated his actions for the tape. "I'm showing Mr Morgan exhibits thirteen and fourteen, books recovered from his room at his parents' house."

Fairfield slowly pushed the bags across the table and towards Jacob, noticing as he did so that the boy began to fidget at the sight of them.

"Recognise these?"

"Yes," Jacob's voice was quiet and distant.

"Quite a nice house your parents have, Jacob, despite their recent hard times. Lots of nice things. Your mum's porcelain collection especially. Sentimental photos going up the staircase. Until, that is, we get to your room Jacob. All my colleagues found were a mattress, a lamp, and these two books. What happened? Did your folks have to sell all your furniture so they could afford your shrink?"

Hamilton stopped writing for the first time and looked up with a start. Burrows looked equally indignant, but a glower from Fairfield prevented him from speaking up. Returning to the books, Fairfield pointed to each one in turn.

"What's that one, Jacob?"

"Bible."

"And this one?"

"Diary."

"Hmm. That's debatable."

By some breed of police telepathy, Jed Caplain was ready with the A4 photocopied sheets and handed them to Fairfield. He fanned a selection of the pages out on the table, upside down so that Jacob and Burrows could read them. They showed extracts from Jacob's diary. Caplain then handed additional copies to Hamilton. Fairfield leant forward, elbows on the table and hands clasped together.

"You see, diaries are usually daily records of the author's life. But these entries are about someone else's entirely."

Caplain took over, and pointed to the photocopies.

"We know this is your handwriting, Jacob. It's the same as in your schoolbooks. We've been through the whole diary, and you refer to no one apart from 'Her' and 'She'. Can we assume it's Mrs Cole you're talking about?"

Jacob glared at Caplain from beneath a sullen brow.

"You wouldn't understand. You're Imposters. You always doubt."

"Doubt what, son?"

"The truth"

Fairfield sat back and folded his arms.

"Well you haven't told us anything that we could doubt, yet!" he remarked, with a tinge of frustration. "And what on earth are you talking about with this 'imposters' thing? You keep saying it. Imposters for what? Anyone who's not in your little gang? Are we all imposters?"

"No," said Jacob.

"Come on Jacob," said Fairfield, "Give us the run-down. Who's in the club and who's not? Or is it a secret?"

Jacob sighed and looked straight past him, expressionless once more.

"For the benefit of the tape," said Fairfield, "Mr Morgan declines to answer."

Jacob's cold stare continued past Fairfield, past Caplain, and onward to the only other person left.

Elspeth Hamilton met and returned his gaze.

Just then there was a brief knock at the door of the interview room, and the elven features of Sally Fisher came into view.

"Sorry, Guv, a quick word?"

Fairfield nodded, spoke for the tape, and then paused it. "DC Fisher has entered the room. Interview suspended at 11:04." He pushed back his chair, and followed her into the bustle of the ground floor corridor. With its high, thin windows it was barely any brighter than the interview room.

"Yes, Sally?"

"Sorry to interrupt, but house-to-house has produced an unusual witness. One of the residents on Susan Cole's street, a Mr Sullivan, has an allotment nearby that was vandalised at the weekend. Totally trashed by all accounts, greenhouse, the lot. Seems Mr Sullivan didn't report it at the time as he has what Harvey called a 'chronic lack of confidence' in the modern police force."

Fairfield laughed humourlessly. "He's not alone."

"But here's the interesting bit," continued Fisher eagerly. "Sullivan was up with the lark that day, and saw the vandal running off. He swears blind that it was Jacob Morgan."

Fairfield perked up instantly. "When was this?"

"Saturday morning. About eight."

The cogs in Fairfield's mind creaked into motion. "Eight. Half an hour after Cole was supposedly safely on her plane. Is Sullivan going to make a formal statement?"

Fisher nodded. "Now that he has our ear, Mr Sullivan wants the full force of British Justice brought down on the lout who wrecked his cold-frame and mashed his marrows."

"And he's sure it was Morgan? I mean, he knows who Morgan is?"

"He used to deliver Sullivan's newspapers."

"Thanks, Sally. Good stuff. Can you ask Harvey to check if the neighbour's set of keys to Cole's house were newly cut, if possible. The original set, I mean. Chase up Blackie and Potts, too; we need those statements."

"Will do," Fisher began to walk off but then added, "Oh, and by the way, Morgan's parents are on their way down. They've taken about as much canteen tea as they can, and want to talk about taking Jacob home."

Fairfield acknowledged this with a slow sigh. Once Fisher had left him, he stood for a while in the half-light and considered what he had just learned.

Something wasn't right.

While they waited for Fairfield's return, Hamilton rose from her seat and began pacing around the room, ostensibly stretching her legs. Jacob's eyes remained locked upon her, and followed her as she walked. So did Caplain's, albeit in a more subtle manner, in appreciation of Hamilton's legs being just fine the length that they were.

Eventually Hamilton seemed to come to a decision, and sat down in Fairfield's vacant seat, directly opposite Jacob. "When you think about Susan, Jacob, how do you feel?" she asked, softly.

Jacob said nothing at first, and ground his bony jaw.

"Pity," was his eventual reply.

"Pity? For Susan, or for yourself?"

"For all of you."

The exchange was making Caplain uneasy. He decided to step in. "Erm, this should really all be going on the tape, love. Why don't we wait until the Inspector gets back? I'm sure he won't be long."

"I whole-heartedly agree," said Burrows.

However, Hamilton either didn't hear their opinions, or chose to ignore them. She went on with her questions. "We've all been asking where Susan is, but let me ask you something else." She leant closer across the table. "Who Susan is," she said. "Why do you care so much? Who is she to you, Jacob? In my book she's just a nobody; a frumpy, middle-aged schoolteacher with self-esteem issues. Let's be honest: would anybody else really care if she never came back?"

With a scream of rage, Jacob's arms shot out and grasped at Hamilton. Hamilton pushed her chair backwards just in time to elude his reach, but Jacob's sinewy arms flashed out again, creeping nearer. The table began tipping with the impact. Caplain was up in a second, as was Burrows.

"Mr Morgan!" the solicitor's voice was shaky. "I strongly advise that you…" Morgan leapt up and smacked his solicitor with the back of his hand. The man went down, dazed, and the table toppled over on top of him. Just as it did so the interview room door swung open and collided with it. The table was knocked free from Burrows and slid across the floor, coming to rest against the back wall with a metallic screech.

Fairfield was standing in the doorway, his face red.

"What the hell is going on here?!" he roared.

At Fairfield's appearance, Jacob backed away into the far corner of the room, his chest heaving, and sweat breaking on his brow. He pointed a trembling arm in the direction of Dr Hamilton, before gasping between laboured breaths, "Get... her...out... of here..."

Fairfield's initial anger began to subside and, after glancing suspiciously over at the psychiatrist, he stepped slowly into the room. "I think we can manage that. But first you'll have to promise to calm down, Jacob." He started to edge nearer.

"Get her out!" shrieked the boy, before crumpling slowly down into a ball, his arms covering his head, as if his cry had taken the last of his energy. He began to sob.

Fairfield frowned. He didn't consider the situation for very long.

"Right," he said, and grabbed Hamilton by the arm. He began frog marching her towards the door.

She instinctively tore herself from his grip.

"Get your hands off me, Inspector! Just who do you think you are?"

At this, Caplain found that he couldn't contain himself. "Someone who obviously cares a lot more about the lad's well-being than you, love!" he remarked angrily. "I saw her do it, Duncan! She was winding him up! Pushing his buttons!"

"I beg your pardon?" Hamilton exclaimed. "Are you telling me my business now? You're only one step up from a Traffic Warden!" She stabbed her finger at the sobbing youth in the corner. "In case you hadn't noticed, this boy is mentally ill. He needs specialist treatment! I can give that to him! If he continues unchecked, who knows what damage he'll cause? He needs isolating, for his own safety as much as everyone else's!" She threw up her arms in frustration. "You're just like his naïve, ignorant parents! If it wasn't for their stupid, objectionable attachment to this lunatic I'd have had him sectioned months ago!"

A pregnant hush descended upon the room.

Hamilton, her back to the door and breathing heavily following her outburst, suddenly became aware that everyone else was looking past her. She turned around.

Her laboured breaths died away.

There in the doorway, flanked by their uniformed escorts, stood Jacob's parents. How long they had been there Hamilton wasn't sure; but a single tear was rolling down Barbara Morgan's cheek.

Without missing a beat Hamilton rallied herself, brushed down her suit and zipped up her folder. Before leaving the room, she turned for one last comment. "If you need me, I shall be preparing my professional evaluation," she glanced at her watch. "As I understand it, you have ninety minutes before you have to either charge Jacob or let him go. Inspector, I expect you to do the honourable thing and release him into my care. I've left my number with your receptionist."

Hamilton marched out haughtily, and did not acknowledge the Morgans.

Ian Morgan watched her go. "Thanks for trying, Duncan," he said to Fairfield. The gratitude was sincere, but there was also despair in his voice.

Fairfield shook his head in disbelief. "Who the bloody hell does she think she is?"

"Shall I impound her Bentley?" Caplain was deadly serious.

"A nice thought, Jed, but no."

Fairfield stepped aside to allow the Morgans to enter and they did so, cautiously. Ian's arm was around his wife's shoulders, comforting her, and he acknowledged the recovering Burrows with a nod. Together they approached Jacob, who was still cowering in the corner, and looked down at him with a mixture of longing and apprehension. "Jacob love," said Barbara through her tears, "we're here for you. We're listening. Please talk to us, love. How can we help? Did you want to come home? Tell us what you want." She took a deep, faltering breath and then added, "What do you want?"

But Jacob's desperate eyes were looking through her, and fixing on only one person. They were staring at Duncan Fairfield, with the faintest glimmer of hope.

Fairfield's heart sank at the prospect of the decision before him.

4

Patience Biggs stood in the entrance hall of Harkham Grammar, directly underneath the apex of the glass dome, with her eyes firmly shut.

With her hair in its tight grey bun and her severe looks she resembled the cliché school secretary of old; and of course she lived up to the role. It was her primary duty to stay abreast of matters that concerned her school.

After all, so much depended on her.

She remained there, quite still, until the creaking of a door disturbed the tranquillity. Thirty yards away, Mr Brooks emerged from his office and reverently led the police officer called Potts down the back corridor, away from the main hall. At this point Miss Biggs cocked her head to one side, eyes still closed, as though listening hard for a sound that had long since faded.

So, she thought, they're going to search the lockers.

Paul Black paused before he left Andrew Knight's hospital room, to give the boy a smile of encouragement.

Recumbent in his bed, Andrew smiled weakly back. His forearm was in plaster, and his left leg lay under a gauze cage. The surgeons had done what they could to reconstruct his kneecap, but, assuming that it healed properly, it would still need some rigorous physiotherapy. Andrew's recollection of the previous day had only been partial, although the doctors had assured Black that it would probably improve as the boy's concussion subsided.

Earlier Mr Greaves, the geography teacher, had experienced no such problems with his memory. He had been furious at Jacob, and had launched into a tirade asking why Robert Brooks had not taken the boy in hand sooner. He had then gone on to criticise his colleagues' ability to cover his classes, and to proclaim that he couldn't wait to get out of the hospital. The doctors had ordered that he stay in over the weekend, however, much to the chagrin of the patient.

This just left Kate Berridge's statement for Black to collect.

Because she had received the lightest injuries, Berridge was going to be discharged at any moment now. Time was short. Black walked briskly down the corridors of Elleray Ward, smiling at a couple of nurses as they passed him, and soon arrived at Berridge's half-closed door. He knocked on it.

"C'm in," said a muffled voice.

He entered the room to find Kate sitting on her bed with half a beige cardigan in her mouth. Her nose was twice its normal size, even allowing for its hood of bandages and tape, and the skin around it looked purple and sore. Similar padding was taped to her left cheek. She was trying to dress herself, and failing.

Black promptly stepped forward and took one half of the cardigan. "Here, allow me," he said, and helped Berridge on with it.

She slid her arm into the sleeve, and breathed a deep sigh of relief.

"Thanks for the nick-of-time entrance," she said. "I am so sore, and so stiff, that I couldn't bend my shoulder enough to pull the bloody thing on!" Clearly in some discomfort, Kate rose from the bed. "Due to your gallant gesture, I shall recommend you to the staff nurse for a commendation." She then picked up her handbag, and started double-checking the contents without giving Black a further glance.

"Well, actually Miss Berridge," Black said, "I'd like to ask you a few questions before you go." Kate looked up to protest, but found herself face to face with his open warrant card. "DS Paul Black, Harkham CID."

"Oh," she smiled, as much as her injuries would allow. "I'll recommend you to the Chief Constable instead, then." She sagged despondently back down onto the bed. "I suppose there are no prizes on offer for guessing what your questions are about?"

Black walked over to the visitors' armchair in the corner of the room.

"Sorry to delay you. I know you must be anxious to get home."

Before he could take a seat, however, a nurse knocked on Kate's open door. "Excuse me," she said. "Is there a Detective Sergeant Black in here?"

Black took a step forward. "That's me."

"Phone call for you, Sergeant. Apparently it's urgent; you can take it out here." The nurse gestured behind her, to where a public phone hung on the wall.

Kate rose stiffly again and shouldered her bag. "Oh, well. It sounds like further damsels in distress need your help. Another time then, Detective Sergeant Paul Black?"

Her jovial familiarity made Black's cheeks blush. "Yes. Um... we'll need to speak with you later on. Today, preferably. Do we have your home address?"

"That you do. I'll put the kettle on."

Black smiled uncomfortably, and left the room.

The nurse, meanwhile, continued into the room and held a restraining hand up to Kate Berridge. "Not so fast, you. Stay there while I get you a wheel chair."

Kate scoffed. "Oh, don't talk rubbish!"

"You've had concussion. Even though you're leaving us, you're still not out of the woods yet. You could probably still use another night with your feet up."

Kate had already conceded defeat, but argued anyway. "Well what else did you think I was going to do when I got home? Get the ladders out and wash the windows?"

The nurse smiled at her in solidarity.

"Good. Wait here; I'll be back in a minute."

As the nurse returned to the corridor, Paul Black's telephone call was ending.

"Yes, Inspector. Right away," he concluded, and then hung up.

The nurse smiled politely at him as she passed, but instead of returning her smile Black gestured at her, indicating that she should stop. His manner was now intense and urgent.

"I need a psychiatric consultant," he told her.

The nurse cocked an eyebrow, apparently in agreement with him.

"The most senior one you have, please," continued Black, "and as soon as possible."

"You what?" Ian Morgan couldn't quite believe his ears.

They had left the cells behind, and were now talking in the privacy of Fairfield's office. Ian and Barbara Morgan sat in front of Fairfield's desk, while the Inspector was perched on the end of it. The Morgans were a reserved, middle-aged couple, and typical of Harkham's inhabitants. He was balding, with just a little extra weight, and she wore thick curls that required little maintenance. Their clothes were plain and functional.

"I'm going to have Jacob placed under full-time care," repeated Fairfield.

Barbara closed her eyes and slowly shook her head.

Ian made eye contact with Fairfield and said emphatically, "Not with her, though. Not with Hamilton."

"Give me a reason not to," Fairfield's reply came back instantly. He had no qualms about forcing the issue; the Morgans needed a way out, and Fairfield needed answers. "I've made some calls," he continued. "There's a psychiatric specialist up at Harkham General who comes highly recommended. However, you need to be straight with me. Over the years, you and I have kept Jacob away from real trouble, but it's getting tougher to do that. Now, more than ever, I need the truth."

"But," Ian looked desperate, as though swimming against the tide, "the people Jacob attacked? Won't they still want to press for assault charges?"

"At the moment they still could, yes, and especially if Andrew Knight's parents get their way. There's a criminal damage charge that's cropped up today, too. But if I put in a good word, and we make progress with Jacob's care, I'm sure that the prosecution service would look favourably on it." Seeing that his words were maybe getting through, Fairfield decided to take an educated gamble. "You've never even tried taking him somewhere else, have you?"

The Morgans were both holding back tears, looking at the floor, at each other, anywhere but at Fairfield, who took their silence as confirmation.

"Look," Fairfield continued, softening his tone. "Jacob may be over sixteen now, but he's clearly not of sound mind. So you still have a say in who treats him. With your permission, I can set it all up right now. But I'm going to have to know what I'm dealing with first; and that means I have to know about Hamilton. Why is she even involved? She seems to be distressing Jacob rather than helping him, and I'm struggling to make sense of it. You clearly can't stand her, and I think we know what Jacob's feelings on the matter are."

Ian Morgan sighed and looked across at his wife, who remained silent. He then nodded to Fairfield, a reluctant agreement.

Fairfield walked behind his desk and sat down. "In your own time," he said, softly.

After taking a moment to collect his words, Ian asked:

"You remember Rowcroft Medical?"

The question was academic. Everyone in Harkham knew the name, but Fairfield nodded anyway. "The drugs company that bought out your factory."

"Bought?" Ian shook his head. "It was a hostile take-over, nothing less. I was Financial Director at the factory when it happened. Jacob was thirteen; you'd arrested him for stealing clothes and selling them on?"

Fairfield could place the period easily. It had been about five years ago. He recalled how surprised he'd been when he'd first met Jacob's parents. He'd been expecting poorer, underprivileged people;

but instead he found a well kept, comfortable home and received a warm welcome that had almost made him feel guilty for arresting the boy.

"I remember."

"Well, what you wouldn't have known is that some colleagues and I were putting together a management buy-out. I was practically running the place anyway, and business would've improved no end if we could pull it off. Anyway, before we could get anywhere with it Rowcroft Medical steamed in and bought us out. Just like that. Not only us, either; all the business units on the estate."

Fairfield nodded to himself, recalling the outrage at the time. They'd made over six hundred people redundant. Rowcroft, a single pharmaceutical company, had forcibly secured an entire business park and then bulldozed it. In the present day, Rowcroft Medical's shiny white research campus dominated Harkham's eastern skyline, but the company was still not popular in the community. It had reneged on its promise to re-employ the job casualties it had created, choosing instead to bring in staff from other, smaller sites, and then to close those other sites down.

"So, there we were," Ian carried on. "I'd gambled all our free capital on the buy-out, and it was gone. So I threatened legal action. I knew it wouldn't even make a dent against their lawyers, but I was angry and I needed to be heard." To Fairfield's surprise, Ian then laughed. "You won't believe what happened next, though! Rowcroft only offered me a job! And of course, there I was, six months after the take-over, and unemployed for all of that. I'd applied for other things, but was never successful. The employers of Harkham had more than enough candidates to choose from at the time…"

"You should have taken it," interrupted Barbara. Clearly this matter was the cause of unresolved conflict between them.

Ian let it go.

"I turned it down. I stuck to our principles…"

"You mean you stuck to your principles!" snapped his wife again. "Stupid, stubborn man. We could have used the money for Jacob, instead of… all this!"

"Anyway," Ian spoke over her, "after Jacob got worse, we were contacted by Rowcroft again. Out of the blue. God knows how, but they seemed to know all about Jacob, and started warning us that his problems were more severe than we realised. They said that he might respond to new therapies that they'd developed, and asked if we'd like to trial them. They said they still felt bad over the factory, and my not taking the job, and offered to pay for Jacob's care."

"Generous," remarked Fairfield cynically, "but not without strings, surely? They can't go on paying for ever."

Ian Morgan shrugged. "Who knows? That was almost three years ago, and they still are…"

"For god's sake, you make it sound like we won the lottery, Ian," Barbara's tone was still bitter. "They're trying to buy us. Like they did the factory. Like they have the whole town. They have more money and power than they know what to do with. Why do you think all your attempts at finding work go wrong?"

Fairfield interceded. "So, it was Rowcroft that referred Jacob to Elspeth Hamilton?"

Barbara answered him. "It was. And the worst mistake we ever made was letting them. Now we can't get rid of her. No one else will take the case. Rowcroft's lawyers block any attempt at another referral. And, I'm sorry to say Mr Fairfield; they'll block this one too."

"We don't know that, sweetheart," argued Ian, ineffectually.

Fairfield checked his watch; there were only twelve minutes until Jacob's twenty-four hours were up. "Mr and Mrs Morgan. There are no easy options here, but from what I've heard today it seems obvious that unbiased care and a fresh start are Jacob's best chance. Please let me help. I can arrange something immediately, and I can do my best to protect him from criminal charges. Who knows, Jacob might even make it back to school for his final year as though nothing has happened, happier and healthier."

Barbara Morgan still looked uncertain.

"Hamilton won't like it," she told him. "She'll fight this tooth and nail."

"I don't like her, either," Fairfield replied. "So leave her to me."

The offer hung in the air between them. The noon heat was making the office uncomfortable. Fairfield thought of a cool beer in the Bobby. He thought of the eleven minutes that he had left with any control over Jacob Morgan's fate. He swallowed a pang of self-loathing and pressed the boy's parents once more. "Ian. Barbara. If we are going to do this, we need to do it now."

Ian Morgan looked at his wife. He nodded. It was a question.

Barbara nodded back. It was a confirmation. She faced Fairfield.

"Okay," she whispered.

Immediately Fairfield's hand grabbed the telephone.

5

They were holding the wake at the Village Hall.

It was a simple building, nothing more than a long wooden cabin with a stage at one end, but the setting was pleasant, and the interior agreeably decorated. There had certainly been enough room there; barely a dozen mourners had accompanied Greg Cole after the funeral. Even the Reverend Luce couldn't attend, as he needed to prepare for a Christening later that afternoon.

Greg's heart sank as, simply for something to do, he wandered over to the buffet and saw that the food had hardly diminished. The drinks table was his next stop, which had clearly received more visitors. It was then that Greg noticed Adam's army comrades, lined neatly up at the foot of the stage, resplendent in their formal uniforms and still with the sombre expressions they had worn earlier as Adam's pallbearers. Each was holding a half-finished pint of bitter, and looked about as likely to mingle as Greg himself was. Conversation among them was sparse.

One of the soldiers noticed him looking over, and solemnly raised his glass. Greg put down the paper plate he had taken from the buffet — he hadn't been hungry in any case — and took a dry white wine from the drinks table instead. He walked over to the soldiers, nodded in greeting, and raised his own drink in a toast, echoing the actions of the soldier he now remembered was called Private Penn.

"Afternoon, lads," said Greg. "I just wanted to say how much I appreciate your being here today, and what you did for Adam."

"Least we could do, Sir," replied Penn, lifting his beer again.

All six Privates then took a sip from their drinks, before lapsing back into an uneasy silence. As Greg had expected, the wine was thin and warm. "I, er," he began, awkwardly, after almost a full minute of silence. "Well... by all means, don't feel that you have to call me 'Sir'. I mean, if Adam hadn't joined up, you lot would've just been plain mates. So, you know...'Mr Cole' at the worst. Or even 'Greg', if you like." He concluded with a hopeful smile.

The Privates all smiled politely back, and everyone sipped their drinks.

Eventually, one of them spoke. It was the soldier next to Penn, whom earlier Greg had heard the others call 'Hoggsy' or something. The vicar had formally introduced them all at the church, but Greg's mind had been on other things at the time, not least of which the nagging doubt that Kenneth Bulmer might be lurking, uninvited, in the vestry.

"Upper Fording's certainly a nice village, Mr Cole," remarked Hoggsy. "Adam used to go on about it when he came back off leave, didn't he?" His fellow soldiers all nodded in agreement. "Always seemed to have a good time, you know, visiting his old dad and all that. Now, what was that pub he used to go on about?"

The soldiers, welcoming the diversion, all tried to recall the pub's name.

"Oh, the 'Black' something, wasn't it?"

"Yeah, Black Bull? Black Sheep?"

"No, no, no. It wasn't an animal name."

"Bloody was. Black something. Black Horse?"

Greg let them continue like this for a few moments, and then put them out of their misery. "The Black Bishop," he told them. They all groaned in realisation; so far this was the most life that the wake had seen.

"Of course!" cried Hoggsy in triumph. "Bloody Black Bishop!"

They all smiled again and shook their heads, Greg included, and took another sip. This time camaraderie had replaced the awkwardness.

"Yeah, Adam liked the Black Bishop all right," continued Hoggsy.

"Bit of an odd name, that," Private Penn observed. "I mean, they've only just started having black bishops, haven't they?"

"And gay ones," commented a third soldier, who may have been called Mac-something; a Scottish sounding name.

Again, glad of the digression, it was Greg who put their minds at rest. "Well actually," he explained, "back in the seventeen hundreds the village, and the surrounding land, was owned by a Lord Kettley. In the evenings, he'd leave his manor house and mingle with the villagers in the pub. He'd put on Chess tournaments there, and declared that anyone who could beat him would win some land and a stipend for life. He always, without fail, played black. So, there, you go. It's a chess reference. That's the story."

Greg saw six blank faces staring at him.

"So did anyone ever beat him?" asked Mac.

"No idea, I'm afraid."

"Well, Adam used to like it there," said Hoggsy, getting back on topic. "Said he liked the peace and quiet of the beer garden." He gave an ironic laugh. "Bit different from some of the places we'd visit in Dusseldorf, eh lads? Adam got into all kinds of ..."

Hoggsy suddenly became aware of what he was saying, and the congenial mood evaporated. Smiles faded, and eyes did their best to look elsewhere.

Greg took a sip of his wine, his expression giving nothing away, but with his gaze fixed upon Hoggsy. "So," Greg eventually said, quietly. "Were any of you there? Did any of you see it happen?"

At first, none of the men chose to answer. Mac pushed past and went to re-fill his pint at the drinks table. Private Penn downed what was left of his own drink, and shoved the empty glass into Mac's free hand as he passed. Clearing his throat, he looked up at Greg. "That's just it," he said. "If we had been with him, maybe he'd still..."

"Dave," interrupted Hoggsy, a note of caution in his voice.

"No, it's all right," Penn dismissed him. "I want to ask him."

Greg frowned. "Wait a minute," he said incredulously, "are you saying that when Adam got into that fight, he was out on his own?"

Penn nodded. "He was AWOL," the regret in his voice was obvious. "Kept talking about it, he did. For weeks. Then, one night, he just skipped base. He hadn't been himself for a while, mind. Not since they stopped his drugs."

"Stopped his drugs? You mean his Thyroxin?"

"That's what I wanted to ask you," continued Penn. "They told him that there was a delay on getting fresh stock from the UK, that they couldn't find the right brand in Germany. That's not right, though, is it? Was that right?"

Confusion swept over Greg like a fog, and he shook his head in bewilderment."I... I didn't know anything about this..."

"Well that's what I reckon did it," stated Penn. Next to him, Hoggsy nodded in agreement. "That's what sent him all strange. He went without it for weeks, and they still didn't give him any. We joked about it at first, reckoned they were cutting back on the prescription charges, but..."

"But this is outrageous!" said Greg, his voice rising in anger. "He needs... needed... that medicine every day of his life... why the hell were they relying on getting it from the UK in the first place? It's widely available!"

"Adam said it was some special variety," Hoggsy told him. "Normal Thyroxin didn't work on Adam's condition, or something, and he was testing some new one? Apparently the UK was the only place it came from."

It was then that Ken Bulmer's words returned to Greg's thoughts.

I was just wondering if they'd given you the truth, or the official story....

In their wake rode memories of Adam's medical treatment all those years ago, when his hypothyroidism had first been diagnosed, just as his mother's had been before him.

It's too late for them. Listen to me before it's too late for you.

"Are you all right, Mr Cole?"

Private Penn had asked the question.

"Yes... yes, I'm going out for some air," Greg muttered to no one in particular, and slammed his wine glass down on the edge of the stage. Lurching unsteadily through the other guests, he headed for the main doors. A middle-aged woman, dressed elegantly in black, stepped out into his path and smiled at him compassionately.

"Greg," she said. "I'm so sorry."

"Thanks." Greg answered her brusquely, and continued on to the exit without breaking his stride.

When he finally emerged into the afternoon sunlight, he collapsed against the wall and took a few moments to centre his thoughts. Hands on his knees, he steadied himself and stared down at the famished grass, his breathing uneven. He began trying to justify what he had just heard, to straighten it out in his mind. At first he dismissed it. What the hell did a bunch of foot-soldiers know, anyway? They were just cogs in a massive machine; they wouldn't be privy to medical decisions made above their heads. But they'd known Adam well enough to sense something was wrong, so why hadn't anyone in authority noticed it also? Or been told? Why on earth would anybody deliberately withdraw the use of a life-giving medicine from somebody?

From his son.

Greg's head began to spin. A wave of bile and grief welled up inside him. He needed to know more.

He couldn't ask Adam's superiors; they were already heading back to Germany. The Ministry of Defence, perhaps? What were the odds of getting a straight answer out of them? He sank back again dejectedly. If he wanted information he needed it from the horse's mouth, and that meant Ken Bulmer, the man who had started all this in the first place. The man that, years ago, had wrecked Greg's marriage and destroyed his life. Nevertheless, Bulmer's behaviour yesterday had seemed different. As unwelcome as his appearance had been, the man had seemed genuinely motivated to help, not to harm. Could Greg take the chance, after years of mistrust and hatred, that Bulmer was still playing some sort of game?

Greg reached round into the back pocket of his trousers — he had not changed them from yesterday, merely re-pressed them — and produced the crumpled business card that Bulmer had given him, the one for the company called Rowcroft Medical. He peered at it through foggy eyes. It had a name on the reverse that Greg had not previously noticed.

Miss Vanessa Daniels
Chief Executive, Special Projects

Pensively, Greg rolled the card between his fingers.

6

Kate Berridge blinked furiously as the nurse wheeled her into the sunlight. Typical, Kate thought; gorgeous sunny weather and the dressings on her face would already be giving her a Panda tan.

They left outpatients, and rolled down the path to the kerb of the pick-up area. "Here we are, then," breezed the nurse, "your taxi should be here shortly. Not that we mind a little wait in this lovely weather, eh?"

Kate smiled politely. The shame she felt at someone else carting her about like an invalid was almost intolerable, but it had been worth it. The conversation that she had overheard outside her room had been very interesting indeed. She looked over her shoulder and up at the nurse. "Is it OK if I use my mobile now?"

The nurse nodded. "Of course. It's just inside that we don't like it, because of all the delicate instruments"

Kate smiled again and thanked her, hoping that the nurse would register this dismissal and leave. Her companion, however, stayed annoyingly put, beaming up at the blue sky and clearly enjoying her spell outdoors. Kate rummaged in her handbag and retrieved her phone. After making the decision that a voice call wasn't the best plan, she angled the phone away from the nurse, switched to text messaging, and began to type.

Minimalism was a form of control for Vanessa Daniels.

Some said that her office at Rowcroft Medical lacked character. Daniels, however, saw it as a controlled environment, and the more that her business empire resembled it, the happier she was. The office was styled in white, chrome and glass, with the west wall consisting entirely of glass panels, floor to ceiling. Beyond them lay a panorama of the Harkham skyline, and the sprawling Rowcroft complex below. Daniels' desk bore only a white plastic telephone cradle, and a laptop computer. Behind it stretched two shelves of white box files; each was sealed and unlabelled.

The only splash of colour in the room was the modest bonsai garden that stood just inside the door. It served to remind Daniels that, eventually, even nature could be controlled.

Daniels was sitting behind her desk, focussed on her computer, when the door opened and her assistant showed Elspeth Hamilton into the office. Reverentially, Hamilton walked over to the solitary visitors' chair. It was a piece of white canvas stretched over a pyramid of chrome; a thin, silver priest kneeling for prayers. Daniels did not acknowledge her straight away. Eventually, Hamilton decided to speak first.

"Good afternoon, Miss Daniels."

Vanessa Daniels finally looked up at her for a moment, before gently closing her laptop screen and leaning back in her tall chair. She then crossed her legs, and smoothed out the creases in her pinstripe suit. Her pale features had a feline beauty that warranted little or no make-up, and her hair was a deep titian. Long and straight, it had been pulled back into a knot and ponytail that day. Her jade eyes, devoid of emotion, dared Hamilton to say something else.

Hamilton did so. "Thank you for seeing me without an appointment. As I was in Harkham, I thought we could discuss the current... situation."

"Is that all?" said Vanessa, with a disconcerting smile.

"I'm not sure what you mean, Miss Daniels."

"Then please allow me to explain. You see, I am a little confused. Your efforts have, to date, been worthy, but shown little in the way of evolution. You still lack experience, and you still lack knowledge. And yet, not six weeks ago, you insisted on independence from us. You demanded to be left alone, and to make your own decisions."

Hamilton shifted in her chair. "I think that standing on one's own two feet is the only true way to measure progress."

This amused Vanessa. "Laudable," she remarked. "But, if that's the case Miss Hamilton, what are you doing here? Why convene a meeting so soon? Surely even you can cope with a challenge this trivial?"

"With all due respect...," began Hamilton.

"Which, of course, means you intend to show none at all."

"Miss Daniels, I don't think what's happened is trivial. I've spoken with Morgan today and he's regressed massively. Even more worrying is that the secondary subject has rather publically failed to make an appearance. The police have become involved."

Vanessa Daniels stood and walked over to the wall of glass, ending up with her back to the room. As she spoke she addressed the sun-bathed horizon. "Well," she said, "that is their job, after all."

"But it means getting custody of Morgan from under their noses."

"That is yours."

Hamilton swallowed back her frustration.

"I understand that, Miss Daniels. But yesterday's events have made things twice as difficult."

"Then you'll receive twice as much credit for success. Achieving the next level should never be easy, Elspeth; that's why they're called challenges. We've already come to your aid once with this project. I wouldn't recommend relying on us to bail you out again," Vanessa turned around and held Hamilton with her green eyes. "What are your expectations for success?"

"High," proclaimed Hamilton, a little too quickly. "It's tricky, but we have the Morgans over a barrel, and the police really have no option but to follow my recommendations. I'm expecting a call any moment."

"Then we won't delay you much longer," Vanessa said, again with an unsettling smile. "And tell me; how have you found dealing with Duncan Fairfield?"

This non-sequitur made Hamilton hesitate. "The Inspector?" she replied eventually, and choosing her words with care. "He's boorish, opinionated, and slightly offensive if I'm honest."

Vanessa Daniels' next smile was warm and genuine.

"Perfect. Then it sounds like you have everything under control. I see no need for you to have any more contact with him."

"With Morgan?" queried Hamilton.

"With Fairfield," Vanessa's high-heels carried her to the end of the window and closer to the door, signalling that she now wished Hamilton to do the same. "Goodbye, Elspeth. It seems you were correct after all; giving you free reign was the right thing to do. I look forward to further good news."

A little uncertain of the dismissal, Hamilton nodded a farewell and departed.

Once Vanessa was alone again she crossed to her bonsai, examined it closely, and then frowned. Deftly, she produced a tiny pair of pruning shears and snipped away the part that no longer pleased her. Another victory over disorder.

"Perfect," she repeated.

"Good news, Dr Hamilton. I've decided to release Jacob for psychiatric treatment, pending his prosecution for assault."

Immediately the tension left her, and Elspeth Hamilton treated herself to a grin. Even the timing of Fairfield's call was impeccable; she had only just returned to the Rowcroft Medical car park after seeing Daniels. She slid back into the red leather chair of her Bentley and savoured the moment. "I knew you were an intelligent man, Inspector," she said, "I'd like to make the arrangements as quickly as possible. When can I collect Jacob?"

There was a small pause at the other end of the phone.

"I'm afraid it won't be today. We've had to transfer him to another facility for evaluation. We need to make an informed and independent bail decision, you understand."

Hamilton's grin turned downwards at the edges.

"Bail?" she said, incredulously. "But you already have my professional evaluation! I thought I'd made it quite clear what would be in my report. I can't believe you're considering letting him back out on the streets already! Nobody else is qualified to treat him, and certainly not without my consult! I demand to be involved!"

There was mischief in Fairfield's voice.

"Thank you for your kind offer, doctor, but I think they've got things covered for now. Jacob's parents are on hand to approve the arrangements, and everything is as they've requested. I'll call you as and when you're needed, I promise."

The line went dead.

Hamilton stared at the phone in disgust, unable to block the image of Fairfield's smug face from her mind. She tried hard not to panic, and to resist the urge to run straight back in to Rowcroft. After all, this was her challenge, and hers alone.

In the distance, the traffic from the bypass flyover rumbled past, oblivious and eternal.

Hamilton cursed under her breath. There was no way she could risk some naïve, so-called specialist inheriting Jacob's care. A normal, run of the mill psychologist wouldn't know what they were dealing with. Or, even worse, a more talented one might discover exactly what they were dealing with.

Either way, failure was not an option.

She turned the ignition on her Bentley and the gentle giant roared into life. Just as she was about to drive off, however, she noticed another text message symbol on her phone. Immediately her thumb was dancing over the keys, and she brought up the sender's number. It was the same one that had tried to get in touch with her last night.

She read the message.

Then the smile returned to her face.

"Got you."

7

Two vehicles pulled up outside Harkham police station, and parked directly over the police-only bay.

The silver BMW saloon opened its doors, and an expensively dressed couple in their forties stepped out. At the same time, the side door of the white transit van slid open and three men of far lesser elegance emerged; two were carrying cameras, and the third, the shabbiest of them all, wore an eager expression.

Without fail, the unexpected always put DCI Laurence Hill in a foul mood.

This was exactly what happened, therefore, when, hurrying out of the station to meet his driver and running late, Hill found his way blocked by a deputation from the local media. His mood worsened yet again when a sour-faced man in an Italian suit, of greater stock than Hill's own, approached and stood toe-to-toe with him on the steps of the station.

"Are you in authority here?" demanded the man.

"It appears that you're unaware sir," began Hill, with a practiced charm, "that we don't entertain the gentlemen of the press without prior appointment. And may I also ask that you move your vehicles to the visitors' car park?"

The man angrily turned his back on Hill, and addressed the journalists. "You see? They're fobbing us off already!"

The chatter of fast-shooting cameras began.

Hill ignored the man's outburst. "Quite. Now then, I am late for a meeting and my car is due here at any moment. This means that you will all have to depart or move your vehicles. Once you've accomplished this, you can then return, and make an official appointment for an interview."

The man squared up to Hill once more.

"We don't want a bloody interview!" the man bellowed. "We want justice! We want you to tell us you've thrown the book at that lunatic who tried to kill our son!"

Hill deflected the man's ire with a raised eyebrow. "I'm afraid, Mr —?"

"Knight. Philip Knight. That thug Morgan put our boy in hospital!"

"I'm afraid, Mr Knight, that I could not possibly discuss details of an on-going investigation with you at this time. As and when it is required, and I'm not for a moment saying that it will be, a press-conference shall be forthcoming."

As if on cue, the station doors opened. Hill glanced round and saw Fairfield, with Ian and Barbara Morgan behind him, halt dead in his tracks at the sight of the media circus. Fairfield quickly thrust out an arm out to shield the Morgans. Phillip Knight, however, spotted them immediately. The reporters crowded in. Knight advanced, trying to push past Hill, while gesturing and shouting at the Morgans. "Your boy's a nutter, Morgan! He should be put away for good!"

Then Knight's wife pushed past her husband, and joined in.

"My Andrew's traumatised for life! And it's your fault! He's an animal! You should have kept him caged or had him put down!"

Phillip Knight roared his agreement. "Do something about it, Morgan!" he yelled at Ian. "Before somebody else does!"

Still the cameras whirred.

Fairfield signalled back into reception that he needed reinforcements, before taking a deep breath and leading the Morgans outside. The brilliant sunshine dazzled them as they barged through the paparazzi, and headed towards the kerb. Just then, Jed Caplain's car came round the corner and squeezed up behind the journalists' van. Two uniformed Constables came hurrying down the station steps, and shielded Fairfield while he helped the Morgans into the back of Caplain's saloon. During all this, the Knights continued to hurl abuse in their direction, with the reporters recording every word for posterity.

Far to the right, and on the other side of the street, Fairfield could see DCI Hill calmly climbing into the back seat of his Daimler. Soon it was breezing past the fracas, untroubled.

At last the Morgans were in, they'd shut the doors, and Caplain had managed to reverse up to clear the van. As they pulled away, Philip Knight ran out into the road. The uniformed officers were after him in an instant, but Caplain had to swerve to avoid hitting the man. Knight stumbled, just managing to keep his balance, and shouted furiously after the receding vehicle.

"We know where you live, Morgan! I hope you can sleep at night!"

The constables led him back to the pavement. Fairfield was waiting for him there, an expression of contrived disappointment on his face.

"Oh dear, Mr Knight, that wasn't a threat we all just heard, was it?"

Despite the heat, Knight straightened his tie and fastened it even tighter. He brushed off his jacket with his hands. "Well it's a damn sight more than you've done, Inspector," he said indignantly. "From what we've heard that little shit is going off to get pampered, when he should be in jail! It's a bloody disgrace! We do pay your wages, you know!"

"Well, your cheque's late this month." Fairfield turned to Helen Knight. "Take my advice, dear, and get hubby home. Before he does anything else prosecutable on camera or, even worse, gets on my nerves."

Sensing that the main event had passed, the reporters looked over at Phillip Knight for guidance. Reluctantly, Knight nodded at them and they started drifting back to their van. Helen Knight fumed silently at Fairfield and unlocked their BMW. It beeped back at her curtly. Smiling, Fairfield held the passenger door open for Philip Knight in the manner of a chauffeur. Once Knight had climbed in, Fairfield made sure that the journalists were out of earshot, and leant into the car to address him.

"You may be surprised to hear this, sir, but we are taking yesterday's events very seriously, and the due process of the law is being done. Rest assured you're getting value for money. Now then, I hope that you are going home to calm down, as I will look very unfavourably upon any further freelance attempts to enforce justice the Philip Knight way. Understood?"

Knight scowled but said nothing, and then yanked the door from Fairfield's grasp. It slammed shut and the silver car wheelspan its way out of Ramshill Street.

"So," said a voice from behind Fairfield. "What about this press-conference, then?"

Fairfield turned to behold the familiar face of Terry Digger; the bedraggled and persistent reporter from the Harkham Herald. Experience had taught Fairfield that, if given half a chance, Digger would hang around like garlic and be just as difficult to get rid of. "If there is a conference, Terry, you'll be the first to know," Fairfield left it at that and began to climb the station steps.

"Right you are, Mr Fairfield! I'll be busy enough until then in any case, writing all this lot up!" Digger began climbing into the cab of his van.

In a shot, Fairfield was at his side again. "Oh no you do not, Terry! If we call a press conference, it will be so that the press can help us with the investigation. If you print any quotes or photos from this afternoon prior to that then trust me; it will be entirely unhelpful. You would definitely be taken off my Christmas card list."

Digger laughed. "Well, it's a good job I don't care whether I'm in your good books or not, then, isn't it Mr Fairfield? I'm just trying to live up to my name, you know." ·

Fairfield smiled to himself. "A burden I wouldn't wish on anyone. I mean it though, Terry. No story until I give the word. Whatever deal you've agreed with Knight, it certainly won't be worth getting on my bad side, I promise you."

With a conceited grin, Digger slammed the van door shut and waved at Fairfield through the open window. "See you at the conference!"

8

A blue haze had formed by the station's dustbins.

DI Fairfield was on his third roll-up, and his fiftieth theory. It was then that the echo of a car engine under the archway broke his concentration, and he looked over to see Jed Caplain returning from his journey. After parking and locking up, Caplain walked over to join him. He was taking the wrapper off a new packet of cigarettes as he approached.

Fairfield looked down at them. "Still smoking those pretend fags?"

"Aye," Jed perched on the low wall that kept the large, wheeled bins in check. "You get less baccy under your nails."

"So... how are they?" asked Fairfield.

"Well, my chest's actually felt worse since I went low-tar. How does that work?"

Fairfield scowled at Caplain's quip.

"I meant The Morgans."

"I know you did," said Caplain, becoming solemn again. "They're scared. The Knights going to the press shook them up a bit. As if they haven't got enough on their plates." He lit his own cigarette, and took a drag. "What's our next move, Duncan?"

"That's what I'm trying to decide. Everyone else seems to be lashing out without thinking, so I want to make sure that's not a mistake that we make too." Fairfield dropped his dwindling roll-up to the floor and rubbed it out with his shoe. Producing a tobacco pouch and paraphernalia from his pocket, he began constructing another. "Then there's Susan Cole. Are we dealing with two aspects of one crime here, or is the whole thing just one big bloody coincidence?"

Caplain laughed humourlessly. "What was it you told me your dad used to say? Assume a conspiracy, and then work backwards?"

"Don't know about a conspiracy," said Fairfield, "but we definitely couldn't do much better than assume the worst." He paused to seal his cigarette paper, and then said, "I'd like you to do me a favour."

"Fire away."

"I'm not sure the message got through to Phillip Knight. I don't trust that stuck-up prat not to try something when he thinks we're not looking. Can I leave you to arrange an obbo on the Morgan house tonight? Keep an eye out for trouble?"

"No probs," Caplain told him through a pall of smoke. "I'll take care of it myself."

"My other issue at the moment is Paul Black," Fairfield continued. "I don't have time to break in a new DS, but nor do I want to send him on milk-run errands at a time when we need everyone firing on all cylinders. I need to know the measure of the man. If you're going on that obbo tonight, why not take him with you? Sound him out, and let me know how he does?"

Caplain smiled; the realisation that he'd just been suckered. "Looking forward to it already. I haven't talked to him much, but he seems a bit wet behind the ears to me. Where on earth did we get him from?"

"Warwick, apparently. Got a glowing record, though, and a personal recommendation from DI Charwood. On the fast track, by all accounts. You should have a read of his file, Jed."

The rear door of the station opened and DC Gossett emerged, a brown padded envelope in his hand.

"Here you are! Been looking all over for you two."

Fairfield nodded in greeting. "Harvey! That's good timing, I was hoping to talk to you about that allotment chap. You've spoken to him; what chance is there that he could be persuaded against charges? That he'd let it drop?"

Gossett uttered a single laugh.

"I think you've got more chance of him forgiving Hitler."

"Thanks. I'm going to take that optimism and run with it."

"There is some good news, though," Gossett continued. "We've just spoken to a cabbie who swears blind that on Saturday morning he took a woman, answering Susan Cole's description, from Heathrow back to Harkham. Suitcases and all."

Fairfield paused, cigarette halfway to his mouth. "She doubled back…"

"About an hour ago the courier delivered the CCTV footage we requested from Heathrow," Gossett brandished the envelope he was holding. "Guv, you really need to see this."

Fairfield, Caplain and DC Potts sat in the station's Audio Visual room, a grandiose title for a small meeting room with a television in it. They waited patiently under the strip lights, while Gossett busied himself before a table of VCRs, DVD players, cassette decks, and anything else they might one day need to examine recorded media.

Fairfield leaned over to Des Potts.

"How goes it with Cole's next of kin?"

Potts nodded. "Still no sign of the ex-husband, but we spoke with her son's regiment in Dusseldorf. It's bad news I'm afraid. He went AWOL on Saturday."

"Bloody hell," remarked Caplain, "it runs in the family."

"Yeah, well let's hope not," continued Potts, "because this mystery has already been solved. They found Adam Cole's body on Monday morning, in a storm drain halfway between Dusseldorf and Köln."

"Köln?" Caplain frowned. "Where's that?"

Fairfield sighed. "It's near Cologne, Jed. Cause of death?"

"He was badly beaten," explained Potts. "German police say he was stabbed three times, but it was a blow to the head that did for him. He was dumped outside the city afterwards. Witness reports suggest he may have been in a bar fight in the small hours of Sunday morning, but nothing's been confirmed."

Gossett interrupted them by signalling that he was ready. They quietened down, and gave the television screen their full attention.

What they saw was the terminal's check-in concourse, from a high camera angle. The footage was from the small hours of the morning and the concourse was sparsely populated. In the foreground was a pillar, and the entrance to some lavatories. Gossett hit fast forward, and a handful of scratchy, monochrome figures went about their business, unaware of their starring roles. With no sound, the images took on a surreal quality.

"Here we are," Gossett let the recording play normally again. They saw a woman walk straight underneath the camera. She wore a loose, kaftan-like shirt, dark trousers, and slip-on shoes — colours were difficult to differentiate — and, in addition to the dark flight bag slung over her shoulder, she was dragging along a suitcase on its wheels. A medium sized suitcase. Her back was to the camera at first, but as she crossed to the right of the picture her face came into view.

For the first time, there she was.

Susan Cole.

Living, breathing, real.

After considering the queue at the Bureau de Change for a while, Susan turned and headed for the ladies' toilets.

"Keep your eye on the longhaired bloke," said Gossett, and pointed at the screen. A figure was leaning against one of the pillars by the toilets. It wore a long, dark duster coat and a baseball cap. From beneath the cap hung long, shoulder-length hair and his beard was almost as long again. As Susan passed this man, he deliberately looked down and away from her, with his face away from the camera, until she had gone inside the bathroom.

"Definitely a bit camera shy," remarked Fairfield.

They watched, entranced, as the longhaired figure gave one final glance around, and then disappeared into the ladies' after Susan.

"He's taking a risk, going in there," Potts muttered.

Gossett gave a quick shake of his head. "Not really. I checked, and this guy had been standing there for forty minutes so far, watching the comings and goings. He'd know whether or not anyone else would be in there." Gossett pressed fast-forward again. The time index in the top left of the screen advanced by four minutes, and a couple of passers-by sped comically across the frame.

When time then returned to normal, there was a collective murmur from the watching detectives as they saw Susan Cole's suitcase come tumbling out of the toilets, shortly followed by its owner. Susan quickly got to her feet, unsteady on the slippery floor, before grabbing her suitcase and breaking into a stumbling run. She headed back the way she had originally come, and under the camera. Their last image of Susan Cole was the look of anguish on her face.

Fairfield remained impassive. "Well, I think we may now have a clue as to why she came back home again. Where's Mr Greaseball?" he asked Gossett.

The recording jerked into fast forward again, until another three minutes had passed in the airport. The longhaired man finally emerged from the toilets. His duster and cap were now in his hand, and his hair was clinging to his face in long strips. It looked damp. They could now see that, under the duster, he had been wearing motorcycle leathers. After pausing briefly by the pillar to catch his breath, the man also ran off; but away from the camera and to the right.

A nearby sign read 'Short Term Parking'.

"Do we have any camera footage from the car park?" asked Fairfield.

Gossett paused the playback. "On its way. I rang Heathrow security as soon as I saw this. Should be here shortly."

Fairfield nodded and leant back into his chair again. If they had been riding a motorbike, he pondered, could Susan Cole's assailant have beaten her back to Harkham and been waiting for her? "Harvey, can you wind it back, and give us a good look at the attacker?" Gossett did so, and paused the image at a point where the waiting man was leaning in profile against his pillar. Fairfield stared hard at it. Everyone else stared hard at Fairfield. The image was grainy, pixelated and jittering, but a fraction of the man's face was visible beneath the peak of his cap.

Eventually Fairfield's eyes narrowed and he looked over at Caplain.

"Are you thinking what I'm thinking?" he said.

Miss Biggs strutted officiously out of the school's main entrance and into the front car park, just about keeping her balance over the gravel. She carried a brown envelope in her left hand.

"Mr Wilcox!" she called. "Don't go just yet!"

Samuel Wilcox turned at the sound of his name. He had been walking to the staff car park, across the lawn between the old and the new buildings. "Everything all right, Miss Biggs?"

The secretary finally caught up with him.

"Well, no, it's not, Mr Wilcox," she began.

A smile parted his thick beard. "I've told you before, call me Sam."

Miss Biggs was clearly awkward with this, but obliged anyway. "Well, Sam, you almost left for the holidays without your summer bonus!" she handed him the brown envelope.

"Thank you," he replied gratefully, and stuffed the envelope into a pocket at random. He began zipping up his leather jacket and boots. "My mind must have been on other things."

"Not at all. Thank you for all your hard work this year, keeping the place looking spick and span; not an easy job, I know. And try not to worry too much about everything that's gone on. It'll be sorted out before you know it, you'll see."

Wilcox didn't look convinced. He reached behind his head with both hands, and began putting his long hair into a ponytail. "Mr Brooks mentioned he might need me for sports day next week," Sam said.

Miss Biggs' cheek muscles were beginning to ache from her polite expression. "You deserve a break," she argued. "Especially with all that's going on. The rental company will be putting up all the marquees and the public address system; all you'd be doing is unlocking the gates! So thank you for the offer, Sam, but why don't you have an early break? Go home and spend some time with your fami… well, spend some time relaxing."

Wilcox looked at her with a mild suspicion, but then seemed to acquiesce. "Thank you, Miss Biggs," he said. "If you need me, though, just give me a shout." He walked round behind Brooks' car and began to wheel his Harley Davidson out into the open drive. Straddling it, he donned a black crash helmet.

"See you in September."

The bike growled into life, and then carried him away for the summer. Miss Biggs waved down the drive after him.

"Goodbye, Mr Wilcox" she said to herself.

9

It was half-five in the evening, the sun was low behind the woodlands of Harkham Common, and for the second time that day Harvey Gossett stood before Susan Cole's house. This time, however, there was no ambiguity about a police presence.

Patrol cars and marked vans dominated the road outside. The Forensic Team had spent the last few hours taking the house apart, and now it was swathed in incident tape. Moreover, DI Fairfield himself was in attendance.

Gossett and Fairfield had spent the last thirty minutes mulling over the possibilities. They know knew that Susan Cole had made it back to Harkham, but also that she'd insisted her taxi driver drop her off at the end of the road, and not at her front door. Fairfield could guess at her reasoning; she wanted to make sure first that no-one was watching. This implied that the incident at the airport wasn't just a mugger taking his chances. This implied that Susan Cole believed someone in particular was after her.

"Fingerprints?" Fairfield asked.

"Only Cole's and the window fitters'," replied Gossett.

Fairfield tutted and shook his head. Damn her home improvements. "So, when did they do their work?"

"Tuesday."

"And of course, if they'd noticed anything suspicious about the original windows, for instance signs of a break-in, they'd have let us know and not just trashed everything regardless," proposed Fairfield, with a touch of sarcasm. "Do we know what happened to the old windows and doors?"

"Scrapped, apparently," Gossett told him. "Bad timing."

"Or remarkably good timing," Fairfield ducked under the police tape and held it up for Gossett to follow him. They began to walk across the front garden. "And why aren't there anybody else's prints here? Even unidentified ones or partials? Postman even? Didn't the woman ever have any visitors?"

"Well, Jacob Morgan was stalking her, Guv. That could be considered a social life of sorts," quipped Gossett. A glower from Fairfield put him back on track. "There is something I noticed just now, though, in the garden. It looks like something heavy came over the wall from the alley, and then back over it onto the common."

"An intruder?" suggested Fairfield.

"Come and see for yourself."

Gossett led Fairfield over to the right, the side of the property that formed a boundary with the Common footpath. Fairfield tried the latch on the wooden gate that led to the back garden, and it opened for him. "So this was locked when you first came this morning?"

Gossett nodded. "From the other side. Cole must have locked it before she left for Barbados."

Fairfield nodded slowly, taking the evidence in.

"The keys. Any joy from Mrs Shepperton next door?"

"They were the originals, from the old front door, and the one and only. Old, copper-encrusted Yales."

"And tell me; when you popped round, did Mrs Shepperton answer the door straight away?"

"Guv?"

"How long did it take her? Roughly."

Gossett frowned. "I rang the bell a few times, but in the end I had to knock on the front window and wave at her."

Fairfield seemed satisfied with this answer. "Okay, how about this. Cole is assaulted at the airport. She high-tails it back here. The taxi drops her off down the road, what...seven a.m.? Seven-thirty? Plenty of daylight at this time of year; anyone watching the house would have easily spotted her." Fairfield began to gesticulate as he talked, wandering around the garden and waving his arms in the direction of the house. "Cole knows that Mrs Shepperton has the only set of keys, and that the poor old soul is as deaf as a post. She can't risk the noise necessary to wake her up. So she sneaks up the side path and decides to climb over. She throws her suitcase over the wall first, and then jumps down into the garden herself," Fairfield looked at Gossett expectantly. "And then breaks in to her own house, perhaps?"

Gossett raised his eyebrows. "Impossible to tell. And if she did, where did she go afterwards?"

Fairfield wagged a finger as he paced. "I think her pursuer was already here. Either waiting outside, or already in the house. Somehow."

"So do you think we're dealing with a kidnapping?" Gossett asked. "In broad daylight? Suitcases as well?"

Fairfield did not answer him. He crossed the bordered lawn of the back garden, past the virginal conservatory. Upon reaching the rear wall, Fairfield lifted himself up and peered over it, with one foot on a tree stump to steady his balance. The broad landscape of Harkham Common lay before him, with its central lake and rocky woodlands to the north. Fairfield tried to imagine the scene; at the time of day Susan Cole was last at home, there wouldn't have been that many people around, but there would definitely have been one or two. Some dog walkers, perhaps, or joggers.

After a few pensive moments, Fairfield hopped down from his perch and began striding back towards the street, with Gossett close at his heels. "OK, Harvey," Fairfield commanded, "as of now Harkham Common is closed. I want all entrances taped off and guards posted, starting with this one. First thing tomorrow, I want the whole place gone over with a fine toothed comb. We're looking for any sign of disruption, the suitcase, clothes from the suitcase, or god forbid a body. I'm going to speak to the DCI about a press conference. We're going public. If they ask, they ask. So we'll tell them." Fairfield gestured at their car. "Get on the radio and start making arrangements. I'll be back in a tick."

Gossett agreed, but hesitantly. "You're going somewhere?"

"I certainly am. Which number does the allotment bloke live at?"

As Fairfield approached number fifty, Tom Sullivan's residence, he saw something that he hadn't seen for many years, and it made him stop short.

Parked outside Sullivan's house was an old model, blood-red Jaguar, with a perfect wax finish on its long nose that gleamed in the setting sun. Fairfield took time out and stood next to it for a moment, to admire the sight. It was as he was bending down to peer in at the cream leather upholstery that he heard a shout, and turned round to see the front door of Sullivan's house swinging open.

Tom Sullivan was angrily herding somebody, a slender man in a pale linen suit, out of his house. "Get out of it! Bloody vulture! Take your fancy car and piss off in it!"

The expelled man straightened his clothes and hefted a black leather briefcase under his arm. He had tanned, weathered features that could have been young or old, and was remaining resolutely cheerful in the face of Sullivan's onslaught. "Mr Sullivan, please," protested the man complacently, "you could be throwing away your best chance at a secure future."

"I've told you once," yelled Sullivan, "I don't want your bloody money! I've no need of it at my age and I'm quite happy with my pension!" A hearty shove punctuated this reply, which made the man in the linen suit stumble backwards and drop his briefcase.

Sullivan leant out of his door and bellowed again.

"Now then, do I have to spell it out? F...u...c..."

It was at this point that Fairfield, who had begun to walk up Sullivan's pathway at the first signs of violence, interceded. "Mr Sullivan? Is everything all right here?" Fairfield showed his warrant card to both parties. Sullivan scoffed at it.

"Huh! Don't want you lot round here, neither!"

He slammed the door shut.

After a few seconds of shocked silence, the man who had been the target of Sullivan's anger exposed two rows of brilliant white teeth. "Well, thank you," he read Fairfield's still open warrant card, "Inspector."

"No problem," Fairfield answered him cautiously. "Any damage?"

"None at all. In my line of work, one gets used to a bit of rough and tumble. Goes with the territory."

"Really? And which territory would that be? Insurance?"

The man smiled again. "Something like that. Anyway, must dash. I'm on a schedule." Stopping briefly to scoop up his briefcase, the man in the linen suit strode back to his Jaguar. Dismissing the encounter for now, Fairfield returned to the matter at hand. He walked up to Tom Sullivan's front door and rang the bell.

"What?" The old man's muffled voice came from behind the door.

Fairfield could see a silhouette through the frosted glass. "It's DI Fairfield, Mr Sullivan, from Harkham CID. I'd just like a quick word, if I may."

Soon he heard rattling, and Fairfield recognised the sound of a security chain. A two-inch gap opened up, and Fairfield leant over to speak through it.

"Mr Sullivan, I need to talk to you about your allotment."

"It's all paid up."

"Can I come in, please?"

He could see the old man's head hovering behind the door.

"Identification?" it shouted.

Fairfield sighed. "Mr Sullivan, you saw it not two minutes ago."

"I saw a card, yes. Not necessarily you, though, is it?"

Fairfield took his warrant card from his pocket, and thin fingers snatched it from his grasp. Through the glass, Fairfield could see Sullivan waving the card about and trying to focus on it. Eventually the chain slid back, and the door opened. Sullivan slammed it shut again as soon as Fairfield was across the threshold, and handed the warrant card back to him.

"If you want any tea, you'll have to make it yourself."

Fairfield smiled in what he hoped was a reassuring manner.

"Thank you, Mr Sullivan; I'm hoping not to keep you for too long."

Sullivan stomped into his lounge, and indicated that Fairfield should follow. The house had a faded, mismatched décor that Fairfield guessed had not had any attention for decades. The walls were thick with photographs. Ornaments, newspapers or books cluttered every surface. Sullivan lowered himself into what was obviously his favourite chair. Fairfield had received no invitation to sit, and so gingerly perched on the nearby sofa. He was about to speak when the old man pre-empted him.

"Well?" Sullivan snapped.

Fairfield prepared his next sentence, trying to find the correct words to say to this old trooper, who already held a low opinion of the police. Fairfield had to find a way to convince him not to press charges, and that he should simply forgive the lad that had wrecked his allotment. Fairfield studied Sullivan's craggy, thunderous features for a moment and, with an involuntarily clearing of his throat, he began.

"Mr Sullivan. Your allotment."

Sullivan's eyes retained their steel.

"I appreciate how outraged you must be," continued Fairfield, "at the damage it has suffered. Now, I understand that you've identified Jacob Morgan in your statement…"

Suddenly, at the mention of Jacob's name, Sullivan's demeanour lightened. His body language became more convivial, and there was even the hint of a smile. "Jacob?" he said. "Oh, yes, good lad, that. Always says hello. Used to deliver my papers, you know."

There was a pause. Fairfield decided to proceed anyway, in case it had just been a senior moment. "You see, Mr Sullivan, we believe that Jacob is suffering from mental illness, and may not have been himself lately." Sullivan nodded sagely. Despite the sense that his elderly host was ridiculing him, Fairfield pressed on. "We feel that Jacob would be best helped by psychiatric care, rather than prosecution." Sullivan remained silent, so Fairfield went for the coup de grace. "So, I've come here today, Mr Sullivan, to appeal to your better nature, and to offer you a compromise. I fully understand that you have every right to refuse, and will bring no pressure to bear if that is your decision.

"If you were to decide to not pursue charges against Jacob Morgan, I will personally arrange for your allotment to be restored to its former glory as soon as possible, using local Community Service resources."

The old man nodded.

"Fine by me, Inspector."

"I could even see about Jacob taking part, once he's better of course."

"No, that's quite all right." Tom Sullivan's features, seasoned by years of outdoor work, creased up into one big smile.

Fairfield was stunned into silence. He had come here expecting to fight tooth and nail, to have to restore Sullivan's faith in the legal system, but, right before his eyes, the old man had seemingly reversed his opinion. In Fairfield's experience people with a grievance, or something to hide, rarely did this unless coerced to do so.

Just then, the throaty roar of a V6 engine took Fairfield's attention. Fairfield turned round in his seat in time to see a flash of red through Sullivan's net curtains. He recognised the Jaguar of the man who had been at the house earlier, and crossed over to the bay window of the lounge for a better look. As the car passed the house, the driver tooted his horn and waved, directly at Fairfield, who watched the car zoom up to the junction at the end of Waterleat Drive, and then disappear confidently into the traffic.

Bemused, Fairfield turned to face the room again. Sullivan had now risen from his chair and was looking toward him expectantly, with the same silly grin on his face. "Was that Eric White leaving?" he said. "Lovely man. Very helpful." He tottered off towards the hallway, but on the threshold stopped and turned back again, as though an idea had just occurred to him.

"Tea?"

10

It was going to be a long night. After taking a deep breath, and a last look at the setting sun, Jed Caplain opened the car door and sat in the passenger seat.

Surveillance duty was a no-win situation for him. Experience had taught him that, by the end of the night, both his brain and his buttocks would end up equally numb. Gallons of coffee were his usual defence, although at one point his wife had tried to get him to drink strange, herbal teas instead. These had failed to entice. Fortunately Claire, being the saint she was, hadn't taken it personally. The one thing that could stave off the boredom, however, was when you had a colleague for company; and sometimes the right colleague would even make the shift pass quite pleasantly, especially if it was overnight.

Tonight, however, Caplain was stuck with The New Boy: DS Paul Black, rounding off his first day with Harkham CID.

So far, mused Caplain, Black had come out even on merit points. During his day at the hospital, Black had failed to collect all three of the statements, but, on the other hand, had redeemed himself with his competent handling of Jacob Morgan's admission. The jury was definitely still out.

Caplain slammed the car door shut. From the driving seat, an eager face shone under the courtesy light.

"Evening, DS Caplain," Black enthused. "Or can I call you Jed?"

Caplain stared straight ahead. "Let's just get going, shall we?"

It was going to be a long night.

Nurse Tomkin hurtled down the corridor, through an avenue of fluorescent lights.

Jacob Morgan's screams urged her on.

She flipped her fob watch up from her blouse — nine forty-five — and muttered an expletive. The psychiatric wing at night, pitch black beyond the central corridor, was unsettling enough without having to listen to the boy's cries as well. Before long Tomkin had reached the solitary door at the end of the passage, and had begun fumbling with her key ring.

Finally the handle turned and she bustled through the door, reaching instinctively for the light-switch, but then remembering to switch on only the softer wall-lamps. Earlier that evening, the harsher ceiling lights had distressed Morgan intensely.

As her eyes became used to the light, Nurse Tomkin could see Jacob on his bed under the window, curled into a foetal ball amongst sweat-dampened linen, facing away from the door and towards the flickering lights of Harkham. His gown was undone at the back. He continued to scream, in the rhythm of a bawling infant, but with the sound of a tortured animal. His body flinched with each spasm of his lungs.

Tomkin approached him cautiously.

"Jacob," she gently reached out to him.

The moment her hand touched his shoulder, the screaming stopped.

Jacob visibly relaxed, causing Tomkin to do the same, if only slightly. Then the boy looked upwards and directly at her, the gentle light shading his eyes, and he uttered a single word.

"Mum?"

Tomkin smiled. "No, Jacob, your folks left a couple of hours ago. Were you having a bad dream?"

"I was calling for her," Jacob explained, in a simple tone, "trying to find her, to ask her to come back. It's been three days but she's still not back."

Tomkin began straightening the bed.

"Don't worry too much about it, sweetheart," she said maternally. "Handsome lad like you will have plenty more visitors tomorrow, I'm sure…"

Suddenly Jacob sat bolt upright, his eyes dilated with fear. He screamed again, this time a single cry of despair, and scrambled backwards, his feet trying to push against the tangled sheets. His back slammed hard against the windowsill.

For a second Tomkin's instinct was to back away, until she realised that Jacob was looking past her and out of the room. She turned to follow his gaze. A tall, well-dressed woman stood in the doorway, silhouetted by the stark light. The woman took two steps into the room, and smiled at them benevolently.

"Anything I can help with?" asked Elspeth Hamilton.

Taking his life in his hands, Fairfield gingerly descended the pitch-black steps. To date, he had managed to find at least one hundred things more interesting to do than to fix the light outside his basement flat.

Finally, he arrived at the bottom and chalked up another perilous journey survived. At least he was doing it sober; the previous night, after having drunk deeply from the Caplains' wine rack, had been a different story. Fairfield trudged three paces across his concrete estate, turned the key in his front door, and made good his escape from the world.

He stood for a moment, without switching on the light, before hanging his crumpled grey overcoat on its hook and continuing down the hallway. Bypassing the lounge and bedroom, he arrived at the kitchen and switched on the strip-lights underneath the wall units, avoiding the harsh main light. By the time they'd sputtered into life, the drinks cupboard was open. His fingers hesitated, however, as they touched the cold glass of the brandy bottle.

He wanted a drink, but he knew it never usually stopped at just the one. Not only did he need to be bright-eyed and bushy-tailed for the press conference tomorrow, but also he had to get up at five o'clock just to get there in time. He could imagine DCI Hill's reaction if Fairfield were to tackle the media smelling of booze, and looking like a used tissue.

Still, perhaps just the one.

He grabbed a tumbler, and filled it with brandy.

Suddenly the shriek of the ancient Trimphone in his lounge made Fairfield jump, as though he'd just been scolded for his lack of willpower. Fairfield hated the sound of his phone, and he'd hated having to borrow the petty cash from Maggie to get the blasted thing reconnected. Grudgingly he carried his drink to the lounge, switching on the hallway light and letting its glow creep through the door behind him. He reached for the bleating receiver.

And hesitated.

Immediately he felt ashamed, and balked at the guilt of what had just crossed his mind: that perhaps the call was news of Susan Cole, and that perhaps he wouldn't have to get up early for the press conference after all. Clearing his throat, and thinking professional thoughts, he answered the phone.

"Dad?"

Fairfield was uncertain whether the sound of his son's voice caused him relief, or anxiety. Eventually he said, "Davey... Hi, how are things going?"

As usual their conversation was stilted, with just enough pauses to betray their discomfort.

"I should be asking you that, really," remarked David. "I haven't heard from you since your good luck card, and that was in March!"

A sigh of disappointment escaped Fairfield's lips. He hoped David did not mistake it for one of impatience. Had it been four months already? "I'm sorry, Davey. It's been so busy here, I… I don't know where the time goes." Fairfield forced himself to change his tone. "So," he said, almost with enthusiasm, "what have you been up to since then? Lots of PT, I bet. Some self-defence, a bit of driver training?"

"It's not like that these days," David told his father patiently. "Sure, we've been doing those things on and off, but also stuff like online crime, you know, getting to grips with the latest gadgets, techno-scams, identity theft, so that we know at least as much as the villains do. That's the idea, anyway. And a lot of the training is more people-orientated; crisis management, that sort of thing. Yesterday we had a bloke from Centrex doing a careers seminar at the Peel Centre; Crime Scene Investigations, Forensics, Internet fraud…"

"Dog handling?" said Fairfield, hopefully.

David laughed.

"No, that's Internet pornography, not Internet Fraud, Dad…"

For the first time that day — that year? — Fairfield permitted himself a chuckle. It was incredible how much the place had changed since his day. Christ, what happened to just being a copper? "But you're enjoying it, though?"

There was another uncomfortable pause, until David said:

"Are you doing anything next week, Dad? I've got a couple of reading days and I thought I might come up. There's something I want to talk to you about."

Now Fairfield was astonished. In the last two years he had seen his son maybe three times, and always self-instigated. Never before had David offered to make the supreme effort of travelling the sixty-odd miles to visit his father. However, not wishing to be a twenty-four-seven policeman, and failing miserably, Fairfield found his suspicions twitching. "Is everything OK, Davey?"

Again, the silence was just too long.

"Davey boy?" persisted Fairfield.

"My name's David, Dad, I'm nineteen. Look, I'll call you next week, and then we can talk when I get there. Is it okay if I crash at yours?"

"Sure, I'll see you then," Fairfield had little choice.

"'Kay, bye."

"Have you spoken to your mother latel…"

There was a click. A couple of seconds later, Fairfield accepted that his son was no longer there and replaced the receiver. Deciding to view David's visit in a positive light, Fairfield swirled the brandy in its tumbler and steeled himself for a down-in-one; a toast to the little things.

It was then that his doorbell rang.

Fairfield froze, elbow still raised, and waited for confirmation.

The doorbell rang again, twice, and this time impatiently. Swearing under his breath, Fairfield trudged back up the hall to answer it, drink still in hand.

The man that Fairfield found standing outside his front door was a few years older than he was, and had thinning grey hair combed across a sunburned pate. Ruddy cheeks embraced a flourishing moustache, also grey, and the lips beneath them were framing a warm smile. Under a crumpled wax jacket, the visitor wore serge trousers, a plaid waistcoat, and a jade-green bow tie. One arm was laden with a box of four wine bottles, and the other with a carrier bag that smelled strongly of Chinese Food.

"Hello, Old Boy," said Kenneth Bulmer. "Remember me?"

11

They'd taken no chances. Two police constables and three hospital security guards had escorted their captive through Out Patients, abandoned her at the kerb, and marched back inside without another word.

Fuming, Elspeth Hamilton straightened her cashmere sweater and glowered up at the hospital, her eyes searching for Morgan's window on the fourth floor, as though she would still be able to spy on events there. How dare a state nurse and a back-street psychiatrist dictate what's best for her patient. Moreover, how dare some provincial detective stand in her way, especially when she was so close to her goal. No unauthorised visitors, by order of DI Fairfield. That's what they'd said, and her argument that Jacob was still her patient had fallen on deaf ears.

Suddenly self-conscious, Hamilton glanced around to check for witnesses, but it seemed that the lateness of the hour had saved her from any public embarrassment. Although she did not realise it, Hamilton had been dumped on almost the exact spot from which Kate Berridge had texted her only hours ago.

A stiff breeze was blowing from the hillside, and across the deserted car park.

From her handbag, Hamilton immediately produced a Cartier lighter and a matching case. She plucked the last remaining cigarette from its band, and sighed as she raised it to her lips. At first it would not light; the wind and some suicidal strands of chestnut hair were conspiring against her. The third attempt was successful. After holding the smoke deep in her lungs for a moment, she regained her composure and began the journey back to her Bentley.

The tap of her heels rolled along the high walls as Hamilton moved through pools of security light, scheming as she walked. Fairfield was simple-minded and stubborn. But, during her short time with Rowcroft, Hamilton had become aware of a few tricks to counter this; ways to guide the simple-minded onto a more agreeable path. Of course, she'd never tried any of these techniques herself, not at her low level, but the principle was sound and there was a first time for everything. It was risky, but the alternative didn't bear thinking about. Returning to Daniels empty handed was not an option.

Hamilton's focus gradually returned to her surroundings, and as she approached her Bentley she looked up. What she saw made her heart skip a beat. With the whole car park to choose from, somebody had parked another car next to hers.

A red Jaguar.

It was facing the opposite direction, so that their drivers' windows were side by side. As she grew closer, Hamilton saw the silhouette of a man sat behind the wheel, a silhouette given form by a pulsing cigarette ember of its own. She hesitated briefly, missing only one step, and then continued, making a point of not breaking her stride and of appearing unconcerned. She readied her keys.

Upon arrival at the cars Hamilton hung back, not really sure why she was nervous, and not wanting to risk confinement in the space between them. The man in the Jaguar saw her, and draped his cigarette-hand from his window. Loose ash fell to the tarmac. With his face partly in shadow, it was difficult to see how old he was. "Hello, Elspeth," the man said. "A little late for visiting hours, isn't it?"

"Please move your car," Hamilton tried her best to sound indifferent, but could hear the anxiety in her voice. "There's hardly any room for me to get in. Your paintwork probably didn't cost you much, but mine certainly did."

Eric White laughed, and took another drag of his cigarette.

"I can understand if you don't recognise me straight away. Don't worry, it'll sink in shortly." He leaned over to open his passenger door. "Why don't you get in? We can talk properly."

While White was away from the window, Hamilton dashed forward and clambered into the Bentley. In one, swift movement she flicked away her half-smoked cigarette, flung her handbag onto the passenger seat, and pinned the Jaguar's driver door shut with her own. She started the Bentley's engine and revved it repeatedly, as if desperate to create a barrier of sound.

Returning to his window, White looked on in amusement.

"I know you're scared," he told her at a shout, "but you really don't have to do that."

Immediately the noise from Hamilton's car subsided.

"You can't wait to get away, can you?" White continued, lowering his voice. "You're desperate to give in to your fear, and what's worse is you're probably not sure why. Well, let me enlighten you; it's because your subconscious knows who I am, but your surface thoughts haven't caught up yet. That's natural. Primal, even. Sensing when a predator is around is a vital skill that we would do well not to lose." White smiled. "Or, of course, it could just be that you're terrified of your little experiment falling apart, and having to admit to

Vanessa that you can't cope. I hear the Rowcroft board can be quite... punitive?"

For a while Hamilton just gripped her steering wheel, and stared resolutely ahead. Eventually, she wasn't sure why, she closed her door and wound down her window. "What do you want?" she asked tersely.

White's demeanour remained cheerful.

"Just wondered how our boy was getting on, that's all."

"He's not your boy."

"Nor yours, it would appear," White glanced pointedly back at the hospital building, and then leant further over towards Hamilton. His tone became conspiratorial. "Now, it's obvious that you're a woman of some potential, Dr Hamilton, and so I will tell you this in good faith. Vanessa Daniels' amateur outfit are in more trouble than they realise. Rowcroft has flourished so far purely by our good graces and occasional blind eyes, but now their star is well and truly in descent. Questions are being asked in high places. I know this, because high places are where I spend most of my time."

Hamilton's brow creased as realisation dawned.

"You're ... from Pelion?"

White nodded, and waited patiently for the next part.

"You're ... Eric White?"

"Bingo," declared White. "It seems you've heeded your subconscious at last." With a flourish, he produced an open packet of cigarettes; the same brand that Hamilton had just run out of. "Please, help yourself. I feel just terrible that you wasted your very last one."

Hamilton ignored the offer and stayed silent. White shrugged, and went on to light one from the dying embers of his own before tossing it to the ground. "There you go, Elspeth," he said. "A simple but telling demonstration. Pelion can anticipate your needs, even before you know them yourself. Rowcroft, on the other hand, force you to serve theirs. They don't, and will never, appreciate you. So why stay somewhere that, if you put a foot wrong, kicks you while you're down rather than helps you get back up again?"

Hamilton's jaw tightened. "Pelion's the past. Rowcroft is the future."

White nodded in mock appreciation. "Hmm. Yes, well recited. You can't really believe it though, surely? Pelion's global. Its methods have been tried and tested for... well, let's just say a very long time. Rowcroft is inconsequential in comparison. It has ideas above its station. Vanessa Daniels is blundering around in things she does not understand and, I'm sorry to say, making enemies of all the wrong people; the same people, might I add, that she upset when she left us, which is far from wise."

"She left for a reason. Pelion is bloated and old."

White ignored this and continued. "And now this Jacob Morgan thing has really topped it all. Do you realise how close the authorities are to blowing Rowcroft wide open? Perhaps I should let them; it would save me a job!" White chuckled for a moment, and then adopted a grave expression. "But I'm too soft, you see. Against my better judgment, I've already had to bail you out once today. That poor, deluded old fellow with the allotment..."

At this, Hamilton's expression finally broke and she turned to look at him, horrified. "Oh my god, you didn't..."

White frowned. "Dear oh dear, what a high opinion you have of me. No, just a simple configuration. He and Morgan will be best of friends for the foreseeable future, or until I decide otherwise."

Hamilton felt her pulse quicken. She knew that no configuration was ever simple. They could be dangerous and unpredictable, especially when the subject was as frail as Tom Sullivan. Configuration was an art still beyond Hamilton's reach, but she knew from reputation how Eric White had embraced it and made it his own. She couldn't help but wonder what unethical time bombs White might have left behind in Sullivan's psyche, just for kicks.

White sighed, clamped his cigarette between his teeth, and reached into his jacket pocket. "You're still a little on edge," he said, "so I'll tell you what. I realise you want to prove your worth — who doesn't — but don't go busting a gut for the likes of Vanessa Daniels. Or even me, for that matter. You need to prove it to yourself first. And that is something I completely understand." He produced a business card and a slim, chrome box from his pocket. He fed them through Hamilton's open window. "Take these," he suggested.

"I don't want anything from you," was her swift reply.

"Take these," he commanded, in exactly the same tone.

Hamilton found herself grabbing them immediately. The card had White's contact details on it. She placed it on her dashboard and then turned her attention to the box. After brushing open the tiny latch with her thumb, she opened it to reveal a glass phial. It contained an opaque liquid.

"Now then," White said eagerly, "as we all know, good things come in small packages. But bonus points are on offer if you can tell me what that is."

Hamilton considered the question, and then said:

"Your charisma?"

"Touché!" White laughed heartily. "There you go, Elspeth; that's your self-confidence returning; beating back your fear. Isn't it empowering when someone has real faith in you? Seriously, though; you've encountered what Daniels calls Compound Nine before, I trust?"

Hamilton's eyes narrowed, and she answered him cautiously. "It's a name I've heard mentioned at Rowcroft, but…"

"Well, it probably won't surprise you to learn that none of Vanessa's ideas are truly original. We at Pelion have our own version. It's based on my grandmother's recipe," he smiled playfully, "and it works along the same lines. It can give troublesome configurations a little… chemical kick." White paused, making sure his message was clear. "It can come in handy when confronted with, shall we say, a simple-minded or stubborn subject."

Hamilton's eyes grew wide, and she stared down at the Compound with renewed fascination. Eric White smiled at this.

"That's yours, by the way," he continued. "A little olive branch from myself, and from Pelion International; a token of our faith in your abilities. If anyone can stop this Morgan mess from escalating, and ensure the ending that we all want, then it's you, Elspeth. But I would recommend you take action sooner, rather than later. Take it from me; Rowcroft, and Vanessa Daniels, are unlikely to outlive your ambition."

White waited for Hamilton to respond, but she was transfixed by the Compound phial, holding it up to the street lamps and watching the light dance softly inside it. White nodded in satisfaction, and started the engine of his Jaguar.

"All I ask," he said in conclusion, "is that in a few days' time, when you find yourself beyond all of this and wondering why you were ever troubled by it, is that you make the right choice. Make this the last time you complete a task worthy of Rowcroft, and instead come and let Pelion provide challenges worthy of you." He slipped the gears into drive. "Best of British, my dear," he added. "See you on the other side."

The Jaguar's window sighed smoothly shut, and White drove away.

Alone in the night once more, Hamilton's paranoia suddenly returned and she slammed the phial back into its box. Hurriedly, she concealed the box in the glove compartment and flung that shut too. At first she looked nervously around her, wary of who might be watching, but soon found her eyes being drawn inevitably to the hospital building, and a dimly lit window on the fourth floor.

She considered it, briefly, but she knew it would be too dangerous.

Especially when there was a more deserving target.

12

The sun had finally settled below the horizon.

Patiently keeping watch on the dark street outside, Jed Caplain took a swig of spring water and zipped up his jacket.

They were parked on the opposite side of the road to the Morgans' house, and slightly up from it, giving them a decent view in each direction. The terraced houses lined only one side of the street, with the other consisting of dilapidated garage doors. It wasn't the most salubrious part of Harkham, but then, as Caplain thought of it, not the worst part either. With Rowcroft Medical having cost them their five bedrooms, less than a mile away, he knew that the Morgans lived in Welling Road by circumstance.

As he finished drinking the water, Caplain noticed that next to him Paul Black was trying hard not to smile. Caplain halted, with the bottle still half raised. "What?" he barked. When riled, Caplain's accent betrayed its Huddersfield roots, despite fifteen years of living down south.

"Nothing," Black found something to look at outside.

"Yes there is," Caplain persisted. "What's up with yer?"

"It's you, glugging down that water. I have to admit that I had this image of coppers your age being fried food and coffee junkies."

"I like to keep hydrated. So what's so bloody funny?"

"Well, for a start, all the other stuff you came out of the petrol station with." Black gestured at the passenger side foot-well, where a bag of pick-and-mix, some crisps and a king-size chocolate bar lay in waiting.

Caplain was incredulous. "You can laugh, pal, but you're going to want some calories when the temperature drops. Don't come crying to me at two in the morning, when you want some of me cheese and onion." With that, Caplain leaned back into his seat and drank some more water.

At this, Black turned round and unzipped a small backpack on the rear seat. When he reappeared he was holding two lunchboxes. One contained sandwiches, crusty, white, and plump, and the other held mixed green salad, with peppers and croutons, and two boiled eggs. A tartan flask followed, which Black placed between their two chairs, next to the handbrake. Finally a kiwi fruit appeared on the dashboard.

Black playfully offered his companion half a ham sandwich.

Caplain frowned at his companion's impromptu buffet.

"Bloody hell, Blackie, this isn't a flaming picnic!"

"Suit yourself," smiled Black, "but don't come crying to me at two in the morning, when your stomach's growling with acid indigestion." He took a hearty bite of the sandwich.

Caplain refused to let his indignance show, and silently amused himself by comparing the kiwi fruit to Black's stubbly head.

Ken Bulmer pushed straight past Fairfield and into the hall, his eyes coming to rest instantly on the brandy glass in the other man's hand. "Charming, you've started without me! Being the healthy chap that you are, I assume you've had nothing to eat in the meantime?" he held the takeaway bag aloft.

Fairfield's jaw flapped uselessly a few times before finally finding the words. "Ken...," he said. "Jesus! It's been years..."

Bulmer responded by dumping the wine-carrier in Fairfield's arms. "Don't worry about it. I'm just as guilty. I know how wrapped up you get, Old Boy. Probably got lots on your plate. Which reminds me..." he gestured at the wine. "Why don't you get those open, while I dish you up some tuck?"

Before Fairfield could protest, Bulmer had disappeared into the kitchen and begun to pile oriental delicacies onto his crockery. Suddenly feeling redundant in his own home, Fairfield took the wine into the lounge, placed it carefully on the writing desk, and felt for a corkscrew in the drawer. Grudgingly, he switched on the overhead lamp.

Deborah's picture appeared beneath it.

Fairfield hesitated. Her smiling, gentle features were daring him to be as happy as she was. He picked up the frame and dusted it with his thumb.

There was a clatter of plates and cutlery from the hall, followed by Bulmer's cultured tones. "You opened that plonk, yet Duncan? Don't know what it's like; it's from the supermarket, I'm afraid, but I've spent most of today sorting out digs and haven't had much time to... ah." Bulmer appeared at the lounge door with a precariously stacked tray, and then noticed what Fairfield was doing.

Fairfield put Deborah's picture back on the desk. He watched as Bulmer's features adopted their trademark confusion, and he smiled thinly for his benefit. Fairfield knew that Bulmer always found displays of emotion uncomfortable, and would project an air of affable bemusement instead. It had become a defence mechanism. In fact, in all the time that Fairfield had known him, Bulmer's tightly guarded walls had only ever allowed one person behind them.

And it hadn't been Fairfield.

A thought suddenly struck Jed Caplain, as he realised that he'd been the subject of a backward insult. "Hang on," he said, turning to face Black, "what do you mean, 'coppers my age'?"

"Oh. Sorry, no offence meant. I think it's good to have a variety of experience across the ranks. I mean, look at you and me. Both Detective Sergeants, but I'm in my thirties and you're in your...?" he looked at Caplain expectantly.

"Prime," stated Caplain.

"Of course," Black continued, with a grin, "and together we complement each other. All I was saying is that it's refreshing to meet someone of your era that doesn't conform to the stereotype."

Caplain couldn't believe his ears. "And that being?"

There was a moment of pregnant silence as Black thought of an example. "Well, it's like DI Fairfield," he finally observed.

"What about him?"

"Well, he's old school, really. Isn't he? I mean, don't get me wrong, but I don't think he's really right for today's Force."

"Your point?"

"OK, cards on the table Jed; you're what? Forty-five? Fifty?"

"Forty-six," snapped Caplain.

"And Fairfield's what, late fifties? He's done his thirty years in the job by now, surely. He can't be far off retirement. Wouldn't it be better for him to bow out gracefully and let people like you and me rise up a bit, you know, take a bit of the pressure off. Otherwise the future's going to pass us by just like it has him, and, well – let's face it – he's hardly had an illustrious career so far, has he?"

It was then that Caplain's hand slammed into the side of the driver's chair, inches away from Black's head. Black flinched, but with a gentle amusement that served to wind Caplain up even more.

"Listen, dickhead," Caplain's voice was low and threatening. "You'd best show some respect to us elderly coppers, especially when your gob's bigger than your brain and you've got no bloody experience; you'll need friends on the way up, 'cause you'll sure as hell have none on the way back down. The likes of you don't deserve to be in the same room, let alone serve, with a man like Duncan Fairfield..."

Black's laugh of derision caught Caplain by surprise.

"Come off it, Jed!" Black exclaimed. "Fairfield's done nothing but coast along on his father's reputation; and now that he's a couple of years from retirement he's got nothing to show for it."

Caplain dismissed this. "What the hell d'you know?"

"I don't need to know anything," argued Black. "The history books say it for me. Douglas Fairfield's on every syllabus in Hendon. He even died nicking villains! The man was a legend."

Caplain knew this wasn't true, but it should have been. These days a copper losing his life in the line of duty was commonplace, but back then it made the national papers. By the time he was killed, in the closing months of the sixties, Detective Superintendent Douglas Fairfield had achieved a certain notoriety in the media, and had been the copper that other coppers aspired to be. Even the Home Secretary had sent his condolences. Duncan, still a trainee at the time, had attended his father's memorial service and would often revisit it with Caplain, in the company of a brandy bottle. Law and order was in the Fairfield blood, he would proclaim; even his grandfather had been in The Job, but ended up as an Air Raid Warden instead. So proud of this was he, that sometimes Fairfield would search for his grandfather's face in the old sepia photographs that lined the corridors of Harkham nick.

Caplain could only imagine what the pressure must have been like on Fairfield to carve out a career under so huge a shadow, and to live up to that legacy.

Paul Black pressed home his point. "It's as clear as day, Jed. He's not a patch. Fairfield should admit defeat, and let someone else have a go."

"Oh aye?" Caplain asked suspiciously. "Someone like you, I suppose?"

Black's smile stopped just short of immodesty. "Me? With only a handful of years in the job? Don't be daft! I was thinking more along the lines of you, Jed. Give you a chance to stamp your own mark; before you turn round and find that it's you a couple of years from retirement, and wishing you'd done more."

The comment hung in the air for a while. Caplain sighed, annoyed at Black but conscious that the younger man had reached Sergeant in far less time than Caplain himself had. Maybe he had a point. Either way, Fairfield was being done an injustice. "Look, Fairfield's a fine officer. I've served with him for years, and very few of us can say we've had the career he's had. His record speaks for itself."

Black shook his head sceptically.

"Yeah, well it's what's not in the records that I'd be more worried about."

"Meaning?" Caplain became defensive again.

"Forget I said anything. I know he's a friend."

"Meaning?"

"Well," Black started to look uncomfortable. "You hear things, don't you? Chitchat, gossip. They say Fairfield's a few pips short of a lemon. Went off the rails a few years back."

"Oh they do, do they? And who are they particularly? Bone-idle officers like yourself, I suppose, hanging about the canteen with nothing better to do?"

"No. Well, maybe a few. But some of this I heard before I even came here."

At this Caplain looked puzzled; as far as he was aware, only a privileged few at Harkham knew the full details of Fairfield's past troubles. He frowned, folded his arms, and leant back against the passenger door.

"I think you'd better tell me what you've heard, lad."

Ken Bulmer had brought far too much food. They had eaten their meal sat on the carpet, at Fairfield's low coffee table, the surface of which was now awash with half-full containers, grease and bean sprouts. Seeing that Bulmer was topping up his wine glass again, Fairfield downed the contents of his own and proffered it across the table. "Don't be selfish," he mumbled.

The glass was promptly re-filled. Fairfield took it and leant back against the sofa, staring at Bulmer but saying nothing. This had been how the meal had progressed; neither man having much to say while they ate, and drinking that little bit faster to fill the silence.

"Cheers," said Fairfield eventually. "That was delicious."

"Actually it was salty and over-priced," countered Bulmer. "But you're very welcome, Old Boy."

"Less of the 'old' you bloody fossil," snarled Fairfield. "You'll always be six years my senior. And I'm sure you didn't turn up out of the blue like this just to feed me and insult me. I mean; god, how long's it been?"

Bulmer took a sip of his wine. "Since we laid eyes on each other? Eighteen years, give or take a lifetime or two. And four years since the last letter. You read it, I trust?"

Fairfield looked at the carpet. "Let's just say I did, and leave it at that."

They fell into silence and sat looking at each other again, drinks in hand; old acquaintances with everything and nothing to say. Bulmer took the first leap of faith, and raised his glass for a toast.

"Deborah."

Fairfield glared at Bulmer through narrow eyes. "I beg your pardon?"

"Well, you did ask why I was here, Old Boy. I'm staying in Harkham on business for a while, so it would have been churlish not to look you up," Bulmer's eyes flicked over to the photograph on Fairfield's desk, and then he added, "Today of all days."

There was a beat, and then Fairfield slowly closed his eyes in shame. July the Nineteenth. How could he have forgotten her birthday, for Christ's sake? And how had he let things slide so much that it had taken Bulmer, of all people, to remind him? Fairfield joined in Bulmer's toast, spoke his sister's name, and drank in silence

Shortly afterwards, Bulmer made another valiant attempt to break the ice. "So," he began, unbuttoning his waistcoat, "do I detect that you've had another wonderful day at the office?"

Fairfield stared into the depths of his wineglass. "You could say that. Twenty-four hours ago things were pottering along quite happily…"

"And now?"

"And now we've got emotionally disturbed teenagers attacking other emotionally disturbed teenagers, while their parents threaten to attack each other. Their teacher can't sort them out, because they've gone missing and I have a terrible feeling they're going to turn up dead before I can do anything about it. Then David's ringing me with cryptic reasons to come and sleep on the sofa, none of which he actually explained to me, which means there's every chance he's going to turn out to be another emotionally disturbed teenager. And, to cap it all, I've got to chair a bastard press-conference about it all first thing tomorrow." Fairfield punctuated his rant with a slug of wine.

Bulmer smiled mischievously. "You've giving a press-conference about David coming to stay?"

"You know what I mean."

"Sorry. Couldn't resist. So your missing person's a goner, then?"

"Not sure," Fairfield eased himself slowly up onto the sofa. "I can't discuss details, but let's just say I have my concerns."

Bulmer nodded gravely. "Sorry to hear that, Old Boy. I'm sure they'll turn up safely, though, with you on the case." He got to his feet and took a moment to steady himself. "Call of nature," he explained. "Back in a tick."

"Let's get one thing clear," said Caplain sternly. "I don't owe you any explanations."

Black nodded obediently.

"I'm going to put you right about Fairfield by telling you the truth," Caplain explained, "before some other bugger tells you something worse."

Again, Black nodded his consent to these conditions.

Caplain's eyes wandered away for a moment.

"Not that there is owt much worse," he said to himself.

Paul Black picked up on this. "It's okay, Jed," he said sympathetically, "if it really is that bad then you don't have to tell me if you you're not comfortable with it."

Caplain's laugh was brief, almost a snort.

"I may not have done psychology at Hendon, lad, but I know when it's being reversed."

"Of course you do. Sorry."

"Aye," Caplain took a deep, resigned breath, and began. "This all happened before I knew him, mind, so don't go asking for all the gory details and don't you dare breathe a bastard word of it outside of this car." Black indicated his compliance. "When he were a young man," continued Caplain, "Fairfield was best mates with another cadet called Bulmer. He was seeing Fairfield's sister, and that's how they met. Bulmer had already graduated, so he became a bit of a mentor. He didn't go far as a copper, though; eventually decided it weren't for him and retrained as a doctor."

Black frowned impatiently. "But this must have been decades ago. From what I've heard Fairfield's breakdown was quite recent."

"Hold your bloody horses," Caplain admonished him. "Do you want to hear this or don't you? A few years after Fairfield's father died, this chap Bulmer and Deborah Fairfield got hitched. They were all still close at that point. Actually, if I'm remembering it right, Bulmer and Fairfield even had joint weddings."

"Wait a minute," interrupted Black, "Fairfield's married?"

"Was. But that's what I'm coming to, isn't it?"

Black held up his hands in apology, and Caplain carried on.

"Duncan never really got over his father's death, and the job started to get to him. After a few rosy years everything fell apart. Fairfield hid in a bottle. Elaine left him, took the baby with her. That's when it started. It were shortly afterwards that he learned the news about his sister."

Black was transfixed. "Well? What happened?"

"Cancer," Caplain told him. "Terminal. Six months to live."

Black shook his head in empathy. "Poor girl. Especially back then, when it wasn't as treatable. And poor Fairfield; another loss can't have been easy."

Caplain nodded. "Aye. Except it weren't his sister that were diagnosed."

The colours in Deborah's photo had faded.

The desk on which it stood was one of the few areas in the basement flat that got natural light, and over time the sunshine had dulled her vibrant image. But her handwriting remained bold. Across the bottom right of the photo ran the words, in Deborah's beloved French, 'Ne beugle plus, mon gosse charmant... Tata.' It had then been signed with a single kiss.

Bulmer smiled warmly at the sight of her. Time may have eroded the picture but never the memory. That was something he was sure they all treasured. Sometimes Bulmer forgot that putting a brave face on things had become something of a habit for him, and that others weren't as well practised at it. As if on cue, he heard his one-time brother-in-law returning from the kitchen, and placed Deborah's photograph back on the desk just as Fairfield arrived. "That's the leftovers dealt with. I hope you're over there to open another bottle of wine," Fairfield growled, before collapsing back onto the sofa.

Bulmer picked up a bottle, and the corkscrew, and placed them on the table before Fairfield. "Quite right too. Let's have a little celebration."

Fairfield snorted derisively. "What've we got to celebrate?"

"Good grief, Old Boy, why not just the time we had with her? Why not the fact that you and I are still here, battling on? Why not anything at all?"

Fairfield's apathy was starting to feed on itself. "Oh, yes, I'll drink to that," he cried sarcastically, raising his still empty glass. "Here's to still having each other! Wonderful! Here's to you hanging around Harkham and reminding me, every day, of what I've been trying to forget."

Bulmer stabbed the corkscrew into the fresh Rioja cork. "Now now, Duncan; I didn't come out of things unscathed either, you know. If you wanted to forget so badly, why is Deborah's photo the only picture I see in this flat? I wouldn't presume to see a record of our unfashionable youth together, but where's Elaine, or David? Or your father? The photo's not even yours, Duncan."

"Deborah was all I had!" snapped Fairfield angrily.

Bulmer pulled the cork from the bottle, and deliberately kept his composure. "Well, it seems that she still is, doesn't it, Old Boy?" He stayed silent while the wine glugged into their glasses. Eventually he said, "Look, let's not do this, Old Chap. Let's look forward, not back. Maybe we've both had a bit too much of this," he turned the bottle and examined the label, "surprisingly palatable supermarket plonk. Seeing each other again like this is bound to wake a few ghosts."

"At least you remembered," mumbled Fairfield.

"Only because I spent yesterday filling in paperwork," replied Bulmer, "writing the date god knows how many times, and that's when it struck me. Last year I forgot, you know; same as you did today."

Fairfield shot him a look, as if Bulmer was taking him for a fool.

"Honestly, I clean forgot!" Bulmer insisted. "And what's worse, it wasn't until this year that I remembered I had!"

Fairfield twirled the wine around in his glass.

"If you hadn't turned up tonight I wouldn't have remembered, either. What does that say about me, Ken? Which of us is worse?"

Bulmer allowed himself a tiny smile.

"Don't know, Old Boy. Perhaps both of us. Or neither. What is it they say about time and healing?" Satisfied that the choppy waters had calmed again, Bulmer reclined deeply into the sofa cushions. "There's got to some closure eventually, so why not now? Can't have all this baggage hanging around if I'm going to retire, you know."

"You? Retire? You'll keep going until the day you drop."

"Again, quite so," Bulmer took a sip of his drink and mulled this over. When he spoke again he said, "However, sixty-two years is long enough in my opinion. I've one last project to finish, and then that'll be it. Time up. I'm just glad it's led me here, and to you. For the last few weeks, I've been making my peace wherever I can; trying hard to smooth over any cracks I may have left in the road behind me. So it would mean a lot to me if you and I could be friends again, Duncan."

"I'm not playing golf with you, if that's what you're getting at."

Bulmer chuckled. "That won't be a problem. You'll be spared the embarrassment of public ridicule, I assure you."

Fairfield grimaced. "Oh, you had to remind me, didn't you?" he looked at his watch. "Bloody press conference in six hours! Right. That's it." Fairfield swung his legs until he was sitting upright, slammed the Rioja cork purposefully back into the bottleneck and declared: "No more booze! I promised myself I wouldn't do this two nights running, and now I am definitely going to get some sleep." He rose uncertainly to his feet and trudged across the room. An arm flopped down onto Bulmer's shoulder. "I'm not trying to get rid of you, but…" Fairfield pointed vaguely in the direction of his avocado Trimphone. "I am currently enjoying a period of phone connection, so feel free to call a cab, or whatnot."

"Will do," Bulmer smiled hopefully at him. "No regrets, then?"

Fairfield paused for a moment. "We'll see. Maybe after a bit of time, like you say. I can't promise anything," Fairfield raised a hand to head off any protest. "You see, Ken, when all's said and done, I'm just a selfish, bitter old sod. It's true. Do you know what I thought to myself earlier on? Do you know what I found myself thinking?" He paused melodramatically, but Bulmer declined this rhetorical question and just shook his head. "The phone rang," explained Fairfield, "and I thought to myself: 'I hope they've found her. I hope the body's turned up. I hope Susan Cole's a goner, so I can have a lie-in tomorrow.' Now, how bloody selfish would you call that, eh?"

The colour drained from Bulmer's face, and he swallowed his mouthful of wine slowly. Fairfield waved an accusatory finger at him.

"There, you see? I'm right aren't I? Bloody…," he started to move again and staggered out of the lounge, "…selfish…old git." He paused at the door. "'Night, then. Don't be a stranger," he added sarcastically. Soon all that remained was his pendulous shadow, which wavered and then disappeared as Fairfield's bedroom door slammed shut.

Bulmer sat in silence, his face ashen with shock.

He repeated Susan Cole's name under his breath.

In Welling Road, the conversation inside the surveillance car was becoming heated.

"Oh, come off it," argued Black. "That all sounds a bit unlikely. Permanent remission? From bowel cancer?"

"All I know is what Fairfield told me," Caplain responded, "and that were in confidence, may I remind you. I'm telling you this for his sake, not yours. He's had a hard enough time putting it all behind him without folk stirring up gossip, so have a bit of respect and let that be an end to it."

Black frowned. "I'm just saying that it sounds a bit odd to me…"

"Who cares what it sounds like to you?" Caplain snapped. "Now shut up and give me one of your butties. Think of it as payment for information received."

"Okay, but you still haven't…"

"Not another word," warned Caplain. "And in case you'd forgotten, we're here because we've got a job to do."

The clock in the dashboard clicked onto two o'clock.

Suddenly there was a crash of breaking glass so loud, and so abrupt, that the two men jerked backwards in their seats.

Immediately Caplain was clambering out of the passenger door, knocking over his bottle of spring water and sending its contents pouring into the gutter.

"Come on, lad!" he shouted, already running across the road.

Slower to catch up, Black was now startled into life. He leapt from the car and was at the Morgan house in seconds. He saw that the downstairs window had been smashed clean in, and he saw Jed Caplain standing in front of it, his arms outstretched in appeasement. As Black drew nearer he recognised a second man, now trapped between Caplain and the house.

It was Philip Knight, father of Andrew.

Wild-eyed and damp with perspiration, Knight's head darted from one detective to the other, weighing his chances.

"Calm down, sir," said Caplain with authority. "No-one needs to get hurt."

Knight clearly disagreed. With a feral roar, he charged at them both with his cricket bat.

Saturday
20th July, 2002

1

Fairfield had risen late that morning and had grabbed the first available clothes. He had still found time, however, to make his usual detour via the newsagents in Millcroft Road. By eight o'clock he was in his office, consuming an on-the-move breakfast of an energy drink, two chocolate bars, and some extra-strong mints. His second hangover of as many days was showing no mercy.

He was reviewing his press conference notes one last time when DCI Hill entered the office, uninvited. "All set, then, Duncan? The wolves are already gathering downstairs, so you haven't much time to get changed."

"With you in a tick, sir," replied Fairfield tersely.

There was a beat, and then Hill spoke again. "You will be changing, I trust? I don't expect Sunday Best, Inspector, but if we're to be appearing before the media…"

"This is my Sunday Best, sir," said Fairfield without looking up.

Hill sighed. "Well at least smarten yourself up. Oh, and before I forget; do you know a Dr Hamilton?"

This was enough to get Fairfield's attention. He frowned and looked up from his paperwork. "I know of her, yes," he admitted with caution.

"Well kindly tell her I am not an answering service. She's telephoned me twice this morning already, to complain that she can't contact you. God knows how she got hold of my direct line, but please phone her back before she takes up any more of my time. See you in ten?" With that, Hill strutted out of Fairfield's office and CID.

"Will do, sir," sighed Fairfield to thin air, and shook his head in dismay. Maggie the receptionist had also given him two messages from Hamilton, as soon as he'd walked in. The woman certainly was persistent. Fairfield would let her sweat for a while longer, however.

Once he was convinced that his press conference material was as good as it would get, Fairfield eventually rose from his desk and into the bustle of CID. Harvey Gossett spotted him first. "Morning, guv. Listen, did Elspeth Hamilton get hold of you, she's been leaving mes…"

"No she has not, thank god," Fairfield cut him off. "And if she calls again tell her that I've taken Jacob to a correctional facility in the Algarve."

It was then that CID's double doors swung open to reveal what looked like two vagrants, fresh from a night on the streets. Gossett chuckled. "Christ, look what the cat dragged in!"

Sally Fisher joined in. "Must have been a big cat!"

Caplain smiled at them patiently. "Yeah, yeah. Well you should try spending the night in a car with this joker," he jerked an accusative thumb at Black as the two of them walked to their desks. "We're just here to file our flaming paperwork, and then we're off home to bed."

"What, together?" exclaimed Sally in mock horror. "I hope you both have a shower first."

"Hilarious," remarked Black. He was holding a brown padded bag that was straining at the seams with parcel tape, and he handed it over to Harvey Gossett. "Present for you. CCTV from the terminal car park; it was waiting at Reception."

Gossett beamed like an excited schoolboy. He tore open one end of the bag and tilted half a dozen DVDs into his hand. Two folded sheets of paper accompanied them. "Nice one," he said. "I'll start going through these straight away; hopefully we'll catch our biker friend arriving and leaving."

"Thanks, Harvey," said Fairfield. "Sally, any last minute good news before we face the masses? How are we getting on down at the common?"

Fisher shook her head. "Not very far. Night is definitely night in that place, but we've got some arc lamps coming over from Mareswood later today, so we can search well into the evening. We've sealed the common off to the public and set up a small incident room in the main car park. The search itself is being co-ordinated from another command point, up on the Coffee Table."

Fairfield smiled and nodded. That's what he'd have done.

"Coffee Table?" echoed Black.

Fairfield looked across at him. "Never underestimate local knowledge, lad. It's a big, flat crag of rock at the top of the common, overlooking the lake. Coffee Table's the local nickname for it. Excellent vantage point; good thinking, Sally. Once this bloody conference is out of the way you can drive me down there."

Caplain approached Fairfield, with bleary eyes and a smile.

"Glad we caught you before we knocked off," Caplain told him. "Just wanted to wish you luck."

Fairfield returned his tired smile. "Thanks, Jed, and thanks for last night. I hope Phillip Knight's seen the error of his ways after a few hours in the Harkham Hilton?"

"I'm saying yes," Black chipped in. "We gave him quite a dressing down before we handed him over for release. Also we've left a uniform at the house. I don't think the Morgans will get any more bother for a while."

"Would you believe Knight's defence was amnesia?" Caplain added scornfully. "Said he couldn't remember how he got there."

"Ah, I see," said Fairfield. "Another incident of sleep vandalism; there's a lot of it going about." He tutted ruefully. "I bloody knew he was going to try something, stupid sod. It concerns me what he'll do next. Knight's obviously in deep with Terry Digger, so now that the direct approach has failed, he might up his game with the press."

Caplain shook his head. "Same old problem. Them journos get ten per cent of a story, and then make up the other ninety."

With a sagely nod, Black also agreed. "That's the dilemma isn't it? It greases the wheels to have a little bit of coverage, but misreported cases cause even more damage. It can happen. Especially with a controversial one."

Fairfield's expression, and the temperature, dropped a degree.

"What's that supposed to mean?" he demanded.

Black smiled innocently, and started to backtrack. "Nothing, sir... guv. It's just I can see how people could easily misconstrue the approach taken with Jacob Morgan as leniency." By now Fairfield's stare was icy cold. "Those people not in full possession of the facts, obviously," concluded Black. Then, hurriedly, he added, "Which you are, of course, and are about to publicly announce them; so, that's good."

Fairfield held Black in his gaze for a moment, his expression dour and inscrutable. Eventually he spoke, calmly, but with an undercurrent of anger.

"Congratulations, Blackie."

This reaction was unexpected, and Black frowned.

"Thank you," he said hesitantly. "For what?"

"For making such excellent progress. You've only been here five minutes, and already you've acquired a death wish. Usually it takes a couple of years before my sergeants develop one of those."

Caplain winced and approached Fairfield again, attempting to pour oil on troubled waters. "I'm sure he didn't mean owt by it, guv..."

At this Fairfield's anger erupted.

"What do you think this is, Sergeant Caplain?" he snapped. "A democracy? Now, good work on nabbing Knight but may I suggest you both piss off home and get some kip before we fall out?" He then turned and brandished his briefing documents at DS Black. "Oh, and by the way, Blackie, I don't know how they did things in Warwick CID but what's also unacceptable is that my files are incomplete. On your way home, you can collect that statement from Kate Berridge that you still owe me. Then I want you back here for a two 'til ten. Bring it with you."

With that, Fairfield left them and marched angrily away to his press conference.

Black stared after him for a moment, and then looked pointedly across at Caplain. "Nothing like bowing out gracefully, eh, Jed?" he said, before going over to the kettle and filling it.

Shaking his head in disbelief, Caplain collapsed into his chair. He looked around at his colleagues, hoping to gauge their opinions, but by now their heads were all lowered again in industrious ignorance. Instead, Caplain nudged the picture frame on his desk around and smiled at the four faces that greeted him; his three daughters, and Claire, his wife. He then realised he had no idea whether Paul Black had a family, or was even single or not, despite having had the opportunity all last night to get to know their newest colleague a little better. And then a worse thought struck Caplain.

Perhaps he didn't know his oldest friends that well either.

2

The narrow road outside was blockaded by vehicles of the press, but Phillip Knight paid them no interest as he emerged from the station.

Still in the crumpled chinos and pink polo shirt they'd arrested him in, he sat on a low wall by the entrance and basked gratefully in the morning sun. It felt good after his night in the cells. Claustrophobia, however, was the least of his concerns. For all his bluster when dealing with those idiot policemen, the entire experience had left him bewildered and more than just a little afraid. This wasn't the first blackout he'd had, and not the first to get him into trouble, either.

He just wanted to go home.

Knight produced a phone and dialled his wife's number. He could tell from her tone that Helen was reluctant to collect him, especially after a curt reminder that he was next to the bus depot, but when the conversation turned to Andrew she mellowed. Knight swallowed hard as he listened to the overnight news from the hospital, and by the time the call ended, his lift secured, he wanted to return home more than ever.

Just then there was a commotion to his left. Knight looked over to see a horde of journalists scurrying down the station steps. They seemed to be in high spirits, chatting animatedly as they climbed into their cars, and loaded equipment into their vans. Eventually, one by one, the vehicles drove away.

A dignified silence returned to the street.

Only a battered white transit van remained, a vehicle that Knight recognised. Before long the echo of footsteps sounded from the car park archway, and a man appeared; a short, rodent faced man with tousled black curls and a brown leather jacket. He spotted Knight, and walked over to him, grinning. "Mr. Knight, good morning!" said Terry Digger. "Did they throw you out for bad behaviour too?"

"Nine o'clock, and already we've had bad days," remarked Knight.

"Par for the course!" Digger chuckled vacuously. He sat on the wall next to Knight, and asked, "How's Andrew getting on?"

Knight squinted up at the sun once more, and then replied without emotion. "Well, I'd know a lot more if they hadn't locked me up in this bloody place. But I just spoke to Helen. They took Andrew back into theatre in the small hours, to work on his knee some more. They think he might lose some mobility."

Digger winced. "Shit. I'm sorry, Phil. I really am."

Knight said nothing. He found himself wondering how much of Digger's sympathy was sincere, and how much stemmed from Knight's money. He decided not to volunteer any more detail about why he'd spent the night in the cells.

"So," said Digger, starting a new topic. "What's all this I hear about you breaking the Morgans' windows, then? I thought it was my job to spice up the story!"

Knight rolled his eyes. "Oh, for god's sake," he snapped, "I've just spent the last two hours telling those plods the same story; I have absolutely no recollection of even leaving my house last night, let alone walking miles to the arse end of town and smashing anybody's bloody window! And they won't return my bloody cricket bat!"

"So what do you remember?" asked Digger, clearly not convinced.

"It was late. I was sitting up, doing the crossword, with a glass of whisky. I must have nodded off, and the next thing I remember is arriving at this…" he gestured at the station walls, "fine establishment and being told that I'm appearing before the magistrate on the second of August!"

Digger took a sharp intake of breath. "Well, you were warned by the big cheese himself to stay away," he teased. "Bit obvious going straight for the mum and dad, won't buy you much sympathy. You should take a leaf out of my book, mate; work behind the scenes, take the system down from within."

Knight scoffed at this. "Says the man who was just kicked out of the side door."

"Ah, well, that's different," Digger adopted an air of fake humility. "All I did was point out a few simple facts — nothing that wouldn't stand up to scrutiny, mind — regarding the suspect that our constabulary had needlessly let off scot free, and asked them why they'd done so."

"Meaning Morgan, I suppose," said Knight. "And I assume you were as tactful as always?

"I may have been a little bit animated."

"You mean disruptive."

"I can't help feeling passionate about issues I care about," proclaimed Digger, "especially where our young people are involved. It felt good though. You should have seen Fairfield and Hill squirming on the hook in front of all those big hitters, too; BBC, ITN, Sky…the lot."

"How very noble of you," observed Knight dryly.

"Well like it or not, pal, we've kept the spotlight squarely on Morgan, just like we agreed."

Knight considered this for a moment, and then asked:

"So what about Susan Cole? Will they find her, do you think?"

"Probably. They're keen enough. Not our problem really, is it?" Digger slapped his thighs and then stood up. "Fancy a drink?"

Knight glanced over at the Sir Robert Peel public house, with its bolted doors, and then back again. "It's not even opening time yet, Terry. And besides, my wife will be here soon."

Digger grinned and produced a small hip flask. "Best get cracking, then."

Knight took it gratefully.

"Sally, whatever you're doing I suggest you stop," Gossett said earnestly, and beckoned Fisher over to his window desk. "It's the Heathrow car park footage. Think we've got him."

"That was quick work," Fisher pulled up her chair and sat next to him.

Gossett nodded. "Cross-referencing the time index from the lobby cameras made it easier. It was on the first file I checked," Gossett rewound the images on his computer screen, while keeping a close eye on the time counter. "Here we are. The timestamp's six minutes after our last sight of Susan Cole." Gossett pressed play.

In contrast to the recordings that they had viewed the previous day, which were of a brightly lit environment, the images from the car park were dim and sinister. Fisher watched with interest as the figure of a longhaired man ran towards a rank of parked motorcycles. It was the biker that had attacked Susan Cole. He tore off his bulky overcoat, and hurriedly stuffed it into the pannier of a bike that was obscured by its neighbours. Fisher took a stab anyway.

"Harley?" she suggested.

"Indeed," said Gossett. "A Springer Softail, if I'm not mistaken."

She raised an incredulous eyebrow. "And you can tell that from one wheel and an exhaust, can you?"

"There's a clearer shot further on," smiled Gossett, pressing fast-forward. Their subject performed a jerky dance, mounting and starting his bike in record time, but still with his back to the camera. By the time he'd turned to face it, he was wearing his helmet. Once the picture had returned to normal speed, the camera angle had changed and they were looking at the car park exit. The Harley roared up to the exit barriers in the nearest lane. "This gave us a good shot of the bike, and the registration," said Gossett, pausing it again.

Fisher nodded in recognition, and sighed.

"Alas," she remarked, "the burden of always being right…"

Just then, the doors to CID flew round on their hinges and smacked the adjoining walls on each side. The collision made everyone jump. DI Fairfield strode into the room under a seething black cloud.

Sally Fisher raised an eyebrow. "Good conference, then?"

Fairfield approached her at Gossett's desk.

"Well, now… let me see. Hill left the answers for all the 'controversial' questions to yours truly and took all the credit for the easy ones, and then that tosser Terry Digger launched a 'Hang Jacob Morgan' campaign."

Fisher tutted. "Digger again? What's his problem?"

"Apart from not showering? Well actually, he's outraged at the moral decline of society, and our part in hastening it by being lenient on Morgan. An uncharacteristically moral standpoint for our Mr Digger, admittedly, but no doubt prompted by a generous donation from the Knight family." Fairfield stomped into his office, flung his paperwork down, and stomped back out again. "Back in a minute. I need a fag."

Fisher intercepted him. "Actually, guv, you need to come over here."

Fairfield obliged and stood behind the two constables. Intrigued, he then leant in closer to the screen, peered at the bike, and scrutinised the rider. After a few seconds, Fairfield took a deep breath and asked Gossett to continue playback. The rider on the computer screen revved his bike impatiently, desperate for the barrier to lift.

"He was certainly in a hurry," observed Gossett.

Fairfield nodded. "Anxious to catch up with Cole's taxi, no doubt, and to stop his girlfriend from getting home and raising the alarm."

"Girlfriend?" queried Fisher.

"Girlfriend," Fairfield repeated. "Although I must say, I expected more from a religious man. The bike and the helmet match the one we saw Wilcox using at the school, too." He rubbed his chin thoughtfully, and then said, "Folks, I think that's our first question answered."

"Then how about another one, guv?" said Gossett ominously. He froze the image once more, and tapped the corner of the screen with his pen. "This line of cars in the background," he explained. "See this car here? I've seen this car today."

Fairfield and Fisher's eyes narrowed as they tried to focus. The picture was fuzzy, and the lighting diffuse, but the shape and registration number of the middle car in the row was unmistakeable.

Fairfield's expression turned to stone.

"Where?" he demanded.

"Here, now," answered Gossett. "In the station car park."

3

Fairfield burst from the station's back doors like a fighting bull from its pen. He saw it immediately, parked beneath the faded initials of 'CID' and in the space that his own car used to occupy; a familiar blue Bentley.

Elspeth Hamilton was leaning against the trunk, legs crossed and cigarette hand raised, waiting patiently for her quarry. A leather bag hung from her shoulder. "Mr Fairfield," she said calmly in greeting. "I was hoping to bump into you."

Fairfield centred himself and then approached her. "For a doctor you're rather dim, Miss Hamilton," he said brusquely. "You've already been informed today that I am not available for house calls."

Hamilton gave a wry smile. "So, you were at your desk after all. Typical."

Fairfield sighed in despair. "You came that close," he held up his right thumb and index finger, "to being arrested last night. You do realise that, don't you?"

"You said I could have access to my patient once you had your second opinion." Hamilton remained undaunted.

"Yes, but not in the middle of the night, and certainly not without police supervision."

"Is now a good time to mention the bruises that I received from my 'police supervision'?"

"Over-zealous hospital security, I'm afraid," Fairfield did not hide his insincerity. "Sorry about that. Jacob's evaluation is on-going; I'll let you know as soon as access is possible."

Hamilton was quiet for the next few seconds. "Mr Fairfield," she said at last, her voice softer, "you claim you have Jacob's best interests at heart. Can I ask why you won't let me near him, with the relationship that I've already built, but will let any old quack at Harkham General poke around in his head with no experience at all?"

Fairfield nodded. "Fair question. Off the record, doctor, I don't trust you. And neither, it would seem, does Jacob. His reaction to you in the interview room is evidence enough."

"Really? And when did you become the expert in mental health? Or his guardian angel, come to that?"

This made Fairfield think for a moment. In a way she was right; he couldn't really explain his deep-rooted feelings of benevolence for the boy. He just seemed to know, instinctively, that protecting him was the right thing to do; and that Hamilton was the enemy.

Hamilton reached into her bag, and produced a beige cardboard folder. "Look," she said, "animosity aside, one professional to another, there are things about Jacob that I think you should know." She walked over and handed him the open folder.

He took it without looking down. "What's this?"

"The current file on Jacob. It's one of many. The rest are back at Oxford, but this one contains the most relevant findings. You see, Jacob and I are currently involved in a crucial...," she searched for the word, "procedure. It has taken years to reach this point; every moment wasted could ruin the results, and with it his best chance yet of treatment. Please try to understand. Any delay could be crucial to Jacob's future."

"You didn't mention this before," Fairfield's tone was one of suspicion, not sympathy.

Hamilton nodded humbly. "I didn't think it best that too much went on public record. If you read the third page in, you'll see why"

For the first time Fairfield looked down at the folder.

It was open at the first page. It was a summary sheet, with a small photograph of Jacob and biographical details. Nothing new there. Impatiently, he turned the page and saw a simple table of appointments, ticked off and annotated.

He turned to the third page.

And frowned.

The block of text covered the entire surface, even up to the edge. Strange, angular symbols, interspersed with the more familiar alphabet, streamed down the page in alternating light and bold type. Puzzled, Fairfield looked up at Hamilton and tried to speak.

It was at that moment that the agony claimed him.

The first stab hit Fairfield at the base of the skull. Fireflies danced before his eyes. The pain then gripped the sides of his head like an eagle's talons. Instantly he let go of the folder and clasped both hands to his temples; his body doubling up and staggering backwards across the car park. The contents of the folder flew upwards and began to flutter down to the tarmac around him. Apart from the first three pages, they were all blank.

Fairfield lolled from side to side, his back now against the nearest car and his hands kneading his temples as if they were baker's dough. His features were puckered in torment but still he uttered no sound.

Hamilton stood by with calm detachment, all the time glancing back and forth and checking for witnesses. No smokers stood at the back door. No cars entering or leaving. No faces at the internal windows. Perhaps something was finally going her way. Deciding the coast was clear, Hamilton crouched down and busied herself gathering up the scattered paperwork. Once the crumpled pages were stowed safely back in the folder, she quickly brushed a stray hair away from her face and stood up again. She took a trembling, much-needed drag on her cigarette, stubbed it out with her toe, and looked on as Fairfield slowly sagged to the ground in a foetal ball.

Hamilton's head snapped round. For a moment she thought she heard movement from beyond the archway, and maybe a sound? Or was it the absence of sound; white noise she had not been aware of until it had stopped. A car engine, perhaps? Her pulse was racing; she hadn't expected Fairfield's reaction to be quite as dramatic.

The subject of her experiment remained in a twisted heap where he had fallen.

Allowing herself a brief smile, Hamilton reached into her bag and produced a syringe. The chamber already contained an opaque liquid. With a practised hand, she flicked free any air bubbles and crouched down to Fairfield's level. Manhandling his arm around to face her, she pushed up his sleeve and exposed his bare forearm.

"Okay, Mr Fairfield," she muttered, bringing the needle to bear on the veins in his elbow. "Time for a change of heart…"

4

Fairfield's skull exploded with pain for a second time.

His arms flailed as he twisted upright and the syringe, a heartbeat away from piercing the skin, was knocked from his attacker's hands. It skittered across the tarmac, coming to rest under the nearest of the wheeled bins by the back door.

Hamilton fell over and scrabbled backwards from Fairfield, propelled by her legs and losing her shoes as she did so. Fairfield lurched drunkenly upwards, and gripped a car bumper for leverage. Hamilton looked on in blind panic and bewilderment; this was not supposed to happen. Never, in the dozens of configurations she had seen Vanessa Daniels perform on training subjects, had one rejected the primary stage so aggressively. Her thoughts turned immediately to escape. Fairfield was between her and her vehicle. The keys were in her bag, and the bag lay only inches away from where Fairfield was shaking his bleary head back into consciousness. She had maybe ten seconds to save herself.

In every way, this was her last chance.

Just then, the back door of the police station opened. Two men and a woman emerged, cigarettes and lighters at the ready, laughing between themselves. They stopped short as they rounded the bins and spied the macabre tableau before them.

Hamilton, ungainly in her stocking feet, clambered upright and ran for her life. By the time the new arrivals had rushed over to the dazed Fairfield, she had disappeared through the archway into Ramshill Street, and was gone.

Maggie the receptionist laid a hand on Fairfield's arm in concern.

"Are you all right, Duncan? You're as white as a sheet!"

Fairfield nodded impatiently. "I'm fine, I'm fine," twinges of pain were making him wince and hold his forehead. "Will somebody please get after that bloody woman and arrest her?"

DC Des Potts, also one of Maggie's group, wasted no time.

"I'm on it, guv," he told him, and sprinted off in pursuit.

Harvey Gossett and Sally Fisher now emerged from the station, the latest in a gradual outpouring of staff as word got round. Fairfield, however, stubbornly brushed aside any aid. "For the last time, I'm all right!"

"Come on, guv," said Sally, "let's get you inside, and call the FME..."

"Don't bother, I'm fine! Circus over!" Fairfield flapped everyone away from him. "Let's get some work done."

Gradually the crowd drifted back into the station, until only Gossett, Fisher, and Maggie remained. As soon as the last well-wisher had disappeared indoors, Fairfield allowed himself a slow, unsteady breath and sagged back against the wall.

"How you doing, Duncan?" asked Maggie.

"Sore, confused and pissed off," Fairfield rubbed his head.

"So, it was Morgan's shrink!" declared Gossett. "What are the odds? The physician and the patient; they're as mad as each other."

Fairfield groaned, but not through discomfort this time. "Not really the issue now, Harvey, but yes, well done, you were right. Des nicked her yet?"

Fisher began to hurry back indoors. "I'll get control to liaise with traffic," she said, "get him some backup."

Maggie nodded reassuringly. "I don't know anyone that could outrun our Desmond."

"Don't worry, guv, we'll get her," added Gossett.

Fairfield held up a hand of warning, already tired of their platitudes.

"Yeah, well we don't have a choice, Harvey. If she's lost the plot enough to assault a police officer, there's no telling what else she'll pull to get at Morgan. Best warn our lot up at the hospital to be on their guard. God knows what she's hoping to achieve."

Gossett waved a finger at Hamilton's Bentley. "So, was it her at Heathrow with Wilcox?" he asked Fairfield.

"Didn't get a chance to enquire. One minute she's sweetness and light, trying to suck up to me, and the next minute she's...," Fairfield paused, as if struggling to remember. His hand curled round the back of his head, testing it for lumps. "Hitting me? She must have done, I suppose. Diverted my attention with her bloody files, and then she... well whatever she did she was fast, that's for certain." Fairfield gestured at Hamilton's car. "But it's given us one advantage at least; let's get forensics to look this rust-bucket over now that we have it."

Gossett, a fan of all things mechanical, grinned at this prospect.

"Oh well, if we must..."

At first, when he found himself in front of an off-licence, Paul Black thought that fatigue had brought him to the wrong address. Soon the penny dropped; a set of iron stairs rose up the side of the shop, and to the first-floor entrance porch of Kate Berridge's flat. He trudged laboriously up them to a hollow, metallic drumbeat and pushed the doorbell.

After a while Kate Berridge answered. Her nose was still swollen, and the normally classic sweep of her left cheekbone was an angry purple. Squinting in the sunlight, she looked Black up and down, noting in turn his own sunken eyes and crumpled clothes. "Ah, it's Detective Sergeant Paul Black, saviour of cardigan-wearing women everywhere. You look like I feel."

Black managed half a smile. "I hope you're feeling better, Miss Berridge. We didn't finish your statement yesterday."

Kate immediately recognised the 'I'm coming in anyway' subtext and held the door fully open for her visitor. "This means you'd like the kettle on, I suppose?" she said.

The entrance to the flat opened straight onto a large kitchen, and being a corner room it was spacious and light. A farmhouse dining table in oak dominated the room, surrounded by peripheral units of far lesser quality. At the far side a doorway, draped in a bead curtain, led to the rest of the flat.

Black waited a few paces inside as Kate busied herself at the sink, preparing tea. The water pressure was high and the tap roared inside the kettle. Unsure of what to do next, Black opted for small talk. "Nice size," he commented.

Kate's head turned round quickly, as if someone had called her name.

"I'm sorry?"

"The kitchen," repeated Black, "I said it's a nice size."

"Oh!" Kate laughed nervously. "I thought you said something else!"

Without explaining herself further, Kate plugged the kettle in and switched it on. She then folded her arms and leant back against the sink unit. "Yeah, it's not bad," she continued, looking around the room as though for the first time, "for a rental, that is. The oak table's mine, though; couldn't leave that one behind. This place is the best I could find at short notice, but you go where the work is, don't you."

"I know what you mean," Black nodded. "I've just transferred here from Warwick. Got myself a new place a few days ago but I'm still not sorted; too much baggage. I must have a clear-out one day." He smiled weakly, and Kate returned it.

After a few more awkward seconds had passed, the kettle boiled and Kate gestured at the table. "I don't mean to be rude, but it is Saturday and, you know, stuff to do… did you want to sit down? We'll get started."

"Thank you," Black pulled up a chair, and produced paperwork and a pen from his pocket.

Kate began to make the tea. "Sugar? You look like you need a boost."

"Yeah, sorry about the fancy dress," explained Black, "but I'm just finishing up a night shift, and you're my last call on the way home. I'm normally turned out better."

"Glad to hear it," smiled Kate. She sat down across from him and placed their mugs onto a straw mat. "I expect you're flat out at the moment, what with Susan's disappearance and everything. It's shaken us all up at the school, you know. Cast a bit of a shadow over the holidays. We're all terribly worried... and about poor Andrew too, and Jacob. I haven't known them as long as everyone else there, but... just so that you know, we're all really grateful for what you and your colleagues have done so far."

Black raised his mug in an imitation of a toast. "Well, they're a good team, from what I've seen so far. Here's to a happy and early outcome."

"If it's any consolation," said Kate, blowing on her tea. "You still don't look as dishevelled as that Inspector of yours, the one that that was at the school. I saw him just now, on the telly. He looked like a scarecrow's granddad."

"DI Fairfield?"

"The very same," Kate dabbed tenderly at her bandaged nose. "So, what do you think has happened to Susan?"

"We have some leads, but nothing concrete as yet." Black replied. "Going public this morning should pay dividends. Anyway, we're here to talk about you." He turned a fresh page on his notepad and looked up in anticipation.

Kate smiled at the rebuke. "'Need to know', eh?"

"Well we have to keep some details to ourselves," said Black. "Helps filter out the crank calls. I could tell you, but..."

"You'd have to kill me," she completed his sentence for him. "OK, point taken."

"Good. So, last Thursday. Jacob Morgan."

Kate studied Black for a moment. He wore an expectant look, pen poised. Was he keeping their conversation on track, or was he just in a hurry to leave? She moved her tea to one side and leant slightly further towards him, arms resting on the table in front of her. "I'll do you a deal, Detective Sergeant Paul Black; my statement in exchange for an evening of your time."

Black's face froze.

"Sorry?"

"Oh, go on!" Kate continued eagerly. "You're a stranger in this town, I'm a stranger in this town, and I haven't been out for a drink since I got here. We have lots in common; we've met some of the same police officers, for example. And you're not that much of a freak, despite your very trendy beard. Harkham's dull enough as it is, but without somebody to pal around with it's unbearable. So, how are you fixed for tonight?" She finished pleading her case and smiled mischievously.

Black was clearly struggling to keep up with this turn of events.

"Look," he said, "you're very kind to offer. However, not only am I knackered but also I'm working tonight. And besides all that, it would be..."

"Unprofessional?" Kate jumped in again. "Okay, Sunday then. What shift are you on tomorrow?"

"I finish at around four, but I can't see you, Miss Berridge," protested Black. "Not while I'm working this case..."

"So we'll talk about a different one. Good. That's settled." Kate sat back, arms folded. "Suppose you're ready for my statement, then?" Glad of the change of subject, Black smiled feebly and nodded. His pen began scribbling and Kate started to recount her tale. "Well, like a lot of things, it started with 'Great Expectations'..."

5

Cursing himself for sleeping in, Greg Cole trudged down the stairs.

At the bottom he paused and beheld the living room of his cottage in Upper Fording, his senses dulled and his eyes half-open. Two days away from home had not made it any tidier. After the revelations of Adam's wake, he'd spent the night with his mind ticking away, processing events, and channelling emotions. Sleep had eluded him. At one point, he had found himself sitting on his bed with a tumbler of scotch and two valium tablets; but in the end he had left each untouched.

No more drugs.

Lazily, he opened the curtains and then switched on the television for some company. It was the news. He let the waves of chatter and ident music wash over him and went on into the galley kitchen. Passing the answerphone, he saw that he had six messages waiting, but chose to ignore them for now. Instead he busied himself making coffee, while the television babbled on.

"Alan Roth, Sky News," it said, with the whirr of camera shutters audible in the background. "How is the investigation going so far, Inspector, and how can the public help?" A different voice answered this question. "Well, at the moment we are concentrating our efforts on two fronts. Firstly, we've begun a detailed search of Harkham Common; we have reason to believe that Susan Cole returned to this area shortly before her disappearance, exactly a week ago today."

At the sound of his ex-wife's name Greg Cole promptly returned to the lounge, alert and wide-eyed. He stood transfixed, an empty kettle in his hand, as the unkempt man on the press conference panel continued to speak: "I would like to appeal to anyone who may have been on Harkham Common, or in the area of Waterleat Drive, in the early hours of last Saturday morning, the thirteenth. Please come forward, even if you don't think you saw anything. The least little thing could be important."

Greg's blood ran cold.

The communications room of Harkham Station was cramped but industrious. At present it was alive with radio reports from officers in the field, and phone calls from the public. Paying this no heed, Fairfield marched through it and commandeered the radio headset of the nearest operator.

"Des? You there? It's DI Fairfield. Can you give me a sit rep? Over."

Affronted by this interruption, the Duty Sergeant came rushing over to protest. Before he could do so, the modulated voice of Des Potts broke through and diverted everyone's attention.

"I've just rendezvoused with traffic, guv. Hotel One Nine just reported what looked like our girl on the industrial estate."

"The Barton estate?"

"Yes guv. We're going over to check it out now. Over"

Fairfield nodded in recognition of the address. The pieces were falling into place.

Barton was Harkham's largest industrial estate; it sprawled beneath the ring-road flyover and contained nothing but offices, factories and car parks for a mile in each direction. Apart from the odd flamboyant logo, bus-stop advert, or graffiti, this area of Harkham was soulless and drab, even on a glorious day like today.

Des Potts greeted PCs Gavin Spence and Carl Hollander as they emerged from their traffic car and donned their caps. Having already briefed each other over the radio, they walked together in silence down the corrugated metal wall by which they'd stopped. Capped with razor wire, the wall eventually curved inwards to a flat-roofed building and three staggered road barriers. Their role was to block vehicle access, while a padlocked, chain-fenced corridor down one side of the building performed the same function for pedestrians. The only information offered to the outside world was a sign proclaiming: 'No Unauthorised Entry.'

This was the gateway to Rowcroft Medical.

There was no door, phone, or obvious way of getting anybody's attention when they arrived at the gatehouse, and so PC Spence knocked on the glass. Moments later an overweight man, wearing a vulgar green and yellow uniform, appeared at the mesh. He didn't unlock the door, and instead spoke through the fence with mild disinterest and a Welsh accent.

"Can I help you?"

"Police, Sir," said Spence needlessly. "We need to talk to the young lady you just admitted onto your premises. It's urgent."

"You must have the wrong address," replied the guard, "I haven't admitted anybody since the nine-thirty delivery."

Potts pushed past impatiently, holding out his CID credentials.

"Look, mate, we just saw her run in here. Open up, there's a good chap."

The guard's face underwent an expression, and then he glanced at the heavy padlock on the door. "Nobody comes in here without my knowledge; I got the key, see?"

"Admirable. So you'll be the man to let us in, then? So that we can look for ourselves?"

This prompted a sharp intake of breath from the guard. "Oh, couldn't do that, sir, not without prior appointment. Some very dangerous areas on this campus; chemicals, heavy machinery, all sorts. Not to mention delicate experiments that you could ruin soon as look at them. Even if you had a warrant, there are all sorts of safety protocols, and risk assessments to do before you even set foot beyond reception. We wouldn't want you to come to any harm, now, would we? Besides which, you're mistaken in the first place; there is no 'young lady' to find, sir."

Potts scowled at him. "She was here no more than three minutes ago, how can you not remember? There's such a thing as obstruction, you know."

"Yes, I remember, sir," the guard gave the faintest of smiles. "I used to be a police officer myself. However, in this case I really do think that you are mistaken. Good day." The guard turned his back and began to walk away.

Potts shouted after him: "Wait a minute! What about the cameras?" He cast an arm up at the CCTV points that surrounded the entrance.

The guard stopped and turned.

"I think you'll find that they've been on the blink recently, sir."

With that, the guard disappeared back into the gatehouse, leaving three of Harkham's finest seething with frustration.

As the squad car pulled into the lay-by in front of him, Sam Wilcox knew that this was it. The law had caught up with him at last. He turned off the engine of his Harley Davison, kicked down the stand, and sat back to await his fate.

He peered in at the silhouettes of the car's occupants, and studied their movements. Being stopped by the police was not something that happened to Wilcox very often, but this was now the second time in as many weeks, and he began to feel uneasy. Normally the officers would have been out of their vehicle by now, and getting down to some serious sarcasm. Instead they seemed to be taking their time, and having an intense conversation with their dashboard.

Wilcox heard the muffled twitter of their police radio. Were they reporting in already? No, they were getting instructions. He felt a twinge of panic. Were they psyching him out on purpose? Here on this slip road, out of sight of the dual carriageway, they could do anything they like and nobody would notice.

Then the other alternative occurred to Wilcox: had they found Susan? Had these coppers tracked him down deliberately? Was it bad news? His heart began to pound.

Eventually the passenger door of the patrol car opened and a WPC appeared. Then her colleague began to approach from the other side. They moved cautiously, as though assessing a wild animal. However, before either of them could speak, Wilcox removed his crash helmet and held it aloft in a gesture of surrender. His ragged beard parted in an awkward grin.

"Okay, Officers," he sighed, "you got me. It's a fair cop."

The WPC and her colleague exchanged glances. Kidnapping suspects, in their experience, did not normally say such things.

6

"Rowcroft Medical! I bloody knew it!"

Fairfield, fresh from hearing the latest updates from Des Potts, had returned to CID and was rallying his troops. He clamped a hand on Gossett's shoulder. "Harvey, I'm off down to the common to check on the search. While I'm gone, I want you to dig up all you can about Rowcroft, and our fugitive doctor. Find me the name of someone in charge so I can get some bodies in there and smoke Hamilton out. I'll check in with you later."

Fairfield nodded at Fisher, who was already waiting by the door with her car keys. "Let's get a shift on. DCI Hill's already down there, and we don't want him buggering everything up before we arrive."

Sally Fisher turned her car right into King's Willow Avenue, and straight into a war zone. The public entrance to Harkham Common, and the road leading up to it, was crammed so full of vehicles and journalists that it was impassable to everything except skinny pedestrians. Fisher slowed down and scanned ahead for a passing space.

In the passenger seat, Fairfield frowned with impatience. "Sound your horn!" he urged.

Fisher glanced worriedly at the bustle ahead of them.

"Guv, it's…"

"Come off it, Sally, most of them are bloody press, it's not as if they're real people."

Sally sighed and gave the horn the smallest of taps, lifting the clutch to inch forward as she did so, and trying to think happy thoughts. She attempted a change of subject.

"How's your head now, guv?"

"It hurts."

"You should still get it checked out you know. I think you've got concussion."

"I'm fine," Fairfield snapped.

"I don't think so," she teased. "You're not nearly as irritable or as grumpy as you normally are."

Fisher's words slowly sunk in and Fairfield sighed again, this time with remorse. "Sorry, Sally," he said at last. "Didn't mean to bite your head off. Just get us as close as you can to the incident room."

Sally grinned at the challenge. "I'll park you next to your desk. We can't have you actually walking anywhere, not in your condition."

They had travelled a further twenty yards but now found their way hindered by an Outside Broadcast trailer. A man was laying a thick electrical cable across the road from it like a speed bump. Fairfield dangled his warrant card from the window. "Can't you pin that to the skirting board or something?" he bellowed. "I'd like to get to my crime scene if you don't mind!" The man gave a humourless smile and lifted the cable. Fisher squeezed the car past him. Finally they arrived at the entrance to the common's car park, where three uniformed PCs ushered them through. Both Fairfield and Fisher breathed a sigh of relief as they left the media circus behind.

"Bloody press!" complained Fairfield.

"Don't be too hard on your public," Sally advised him playfully. "It's you they've come to see, you know."

They drove slowly between parched verges. Harkham Common was once the private gardens of Channing House, the building that now formed the older part of the Grammar School. For the last hundred years, however, it had been eight square miles of urban parkland, smack in the centre of town. Regarded as an oasis by the locals, sealing it off had caused uproar and dissent on a scale not witnessed for many years.

The common was long and narrow, with a kidney curve that followed the course of what used to be the river Cout. The lake at the common's centre was all that remained of this mighty waterway that, centuries ago, had given rise to Harkham in the first place. Above the northern shores of the lake rose a sickle-shaped crest of granite cliffs, capped by thick woodlands.

They arrived at the police incident room; a portacabin in the main car park, on the south side of the lake. Fisher parked opposite, and at the end of a row of other police vehicles. As he climbed out of the car, a reedy, electronic noise interrupted Fairfield from beneath his coat. He promptly began a search of his pockets.

Sally quickly recognised the tune. "Juliet Bravo, guv?" she grinned.

"Don't start," replied Fairfield, gruffly. "When the IT lot had it in for repair the other day, some sod set it as the ring tone and I can't work out how to change it back."

"Terrible," Sally chuckled. "I'd have a word with Harvey if I were you. Get it changed to something with a bit more class. Bergerac, perhaps?"

"Hah bloody hah," Fairfield finally found his mobile and held it up to his ear. "Fairfield." After a beat of silence, he studied the phone again, and this time pressed the 'answer' button. "Fairfield. Ah, Harvey," Fairfield impatiently put a finger in his ear and sat back in Fisher's car. As was his custom, he then raised his voice by ten decibels. "Good work. Let me know when he's there. We'll be at the common for now." Fairfield hung up the call. "That was Harvey," he told Fisher.

"Yes. That bit I caught."

"Uniform have picked up Samuel Wilcox," reported Fairfield, "heading down the A40 at full pelt. His plates definitely match those in the airport footage, but he's saying he has an alibi for Saturday morning. Should be at the nick in about half an hour; Harvey's going to go over his story."

They finally exited the car and began making their way over to the incident room. The area was bustling with uniformed activity. Fisher looked thoughtfully at Fairfield as they walked.

"You've met Wilcox. Do you reckon he's our man?"

"Difficult to tell. Gentle giant; bit of a bible-basher."

"And a biker?" added Fisher incredulously.

"Still waters, Sally," replied Fairfield enigmatically. "The evidence is stacked against him, and he's romantically involved with Susan Cole. And get this; he surrendered, apparently. All but held his hands out for the cuffs."

Fisher's sceptical eyes narrowed at this. "What, he confessed to attacking Cole?"

"Not exactly," began Fairfield. They climbed the iron steps of the portacabin, and he held the door open for Fisher. "Wilcox's guilty conscience was about something else entirely. Turns out Sussex cautioned him and a bunch of other bikers last weekend, for undertaking. He was told to produce his documents at Brighton nick within seven days and, guess what, he didn't. Says it slipped his mind."

Fisher nodded her thanks and entered the murk of the incident room, followed by Fairfield. "Understandable," Fisher said, "with everything that's been going on this week."

"Understandable," Fairfield agreed, "but unfortunate for us. They pulled Wilcox and his cronies over early last Saturday morning. The thirteenth."

"Oh," said Fisher.

"Oh indeed," Fairfield smiled wryly. "It would seem that we, Sally, are Wilcox's alibi."

A layer of onlookers had formed along the iron railings.

Frustrated dog-walkers and concerned citizens alike were keeping watch over the fringes of Harkham Common, hypnotised by the police presence and rooted to the spot by morbid curiosity. The Susan Cole story had dominated their televisions and newspapers all day, and now they wanted first hand news; they wanted to be the first to inform their less diligent acquaintances of every development.

But one pair of eyes among them, anonymous and steady, looked upon the events on Harkham Common with a growing dread, as if their owner already knew what was to come.

Ken Bulmer took an abrupt sip from his hip flask, and waited.

7

Vanessa Daniels stared dispassionately through the thick glass panels, at the patients in the ward beneath her. The observation corridor itself was dark, but the clinical glare from below was just enough to dilute the shadows through which she moved.

In the four chambers below, medical personnel were moving silently and efficiently through airlock doors, going about their business in white overalls and facemasks. They cast hardly any shadows in the bright and sterile environment. Each patient was separated from the other. Two young men occupied the beds on the left side, and two girls on the right. Each also wore a facemask, and to a normal observer would have appeared to be semi-conscious.

But Daniels knew better. She could feel the tortured writhing of their minds caressing the surface of her own, like flames. It was invigorating.

Then she felt something else. Others were approaching.

She raised her head and stared at the door. A split second later, it rolled open to reveal three figures. Two were Rowcroft security guards, bulky and impassive. Daniels' expression hardened as she strutted slowly over to the third.

"Extraordinary," she said at last, leaning in close and studying Elspeth Hamilton's bedraggled condition. "Do you want to know something odd? You remind me of someone that we used to have in this very ward."

Hamilton swallowed hard, but did not respond.

Daniels circled her. "I shalln't bore you with the whole story," she continued, "but suffice it to say we helped her. We trained her. We gave her every opportunity to excel. She never quite lived up to her potential, though. Disappointing, really."

Finally Hamilton found her voice, and with it more confidence than she had expected. "Vanessa, I'm sorry…"

"So are we all. Especially after she was given her very last chance only yesterday. It's a galling thing, you know, especially as so many others would have welcomed the chance to prove themselves. I blame myself partly. She was obviously poorly educated."

"I know more than you think."

Daniels paused, in mock admiration of this sudden bravado.

"Do you, now? And who's been whispering in your ear?" she asked playfully.

"Nobody," Hamilton lied. "You told me to resolve the Jacob Morgan situation on my own, and so I did my homework."

"If you'd done your homework, dear heart, then you wouldn't have tried to configure Duncan Fairfield, of all people, and not in broad daylight," Daniels' smile was predatory. "You really had no idea what you were doing, did you?"

"Nothing you haven't done dozens of times before!" snapped Hamilton. "Vanessa, you can't show me the path and then not expect me to follow it!"

Daniels' hand darted out like a snake and grasped Hamilton's chin, wrenching her head savagely around to face her. A small cry of shock passed Hamilton's lips. "Do you realise what you've done? Fairfield is off limits!" hissed Daniels angrily, her emerald eyes flaring. "Do you walk around with your eyes and ears shut?" She held Hamilton's gaze for a few seconds longer, but then released her grip and walked over to the observation windows. Clearly her outburst had embarrassed her.

Eventually, once she had regained control, Daniels spoke again.

"You're ambitious, Elspeth," she said softly, "but you are neither clever enough, nor stupid enough, to have done this of your own volition."

"Perhaps there are some things you can't see any longer," Hamilton tried to brazen it out. "Perhaps you're weakening. You're afraid I may outstrip you one day."

Daniels' smile was thin and joyless.

"Even when we're both cold in our graves, Elspeth, I'd still be more powerful than you. But common sense is the issue here, not augmentations. The Jacob Morgan incident has placed Rowcroft under an uncomfortable spotlight, and at precisely the worst time. With careful management, I was hoping to minimise any damage but your exploits have put paid to that. Not half an hour ago we had to turn the police away from our gates."

"I panicked," explained Hamilton. "I didn't know where else to go."

"Even more reason for me to think there's another party involved. If your plan had succeeded, then you would have trotted back to them instead and we would have been none the wiser. It occurs to me that, in coming here, it is not just the police from whom you seek sanctuary." Daniels turned to face Hamilton again. "You must tell me everything, Elspeth, and you must tell me now. Before it's too late."

"What about Jacob?" countered Hamilton.

"That is no longer your concern."

At this, Hamilton's barrier started to crumble. Tears began to streak the dirt on her face. "Please, Vanessa, let me finish this..."

"I can't, Elspeth. You know the rules. A challenge is a challenge, and you've failed yours. It is no longer within my power to augment you, so you have but one choice left to make. Darkness or oblivion. Tell me who it was that influenced you, and we shall simply return you to how you were. If you choose not to, well," Daniels' voice tailed off for a moment, and she glanced down at the comatose patients in their sterile beds. "Your fate will be beyond our control."

Hamilton sobbed and began to sag against the wall. The security guards immediately hoisted her up again. "Please..."

"Tell me," insisted Daniels, cold and clinical.

"Please, just one more chance. I've never failed you before..."

"Tell me who it was. Or I'll tear it out of you."

Daniels took a step forward.

"I can't...," moaned Hamilton.

"In ten seconds, Elspeth, I will know anyway. Open your mouth, or open your mind. It's your choice."

At a nod from Daniels, the guards clamped their hands around Hamilton's arms and held her bolt upright. She was now unable to defend herself, unable to wipe away her tears, unable to retreat as Daniels' mind locked onto her.

"Tell me."

Hamilton's eyes suddenly snapped shut. Her head twisted back and forth as she struggled to remember. "He was... his name was... he said that...," she frowned in frustration, and then she screamed in pain, struggling against the iron grip of the guards.

Daniels sighed and shook her head.

The guards released Hamilton. She tumbled to the metal floor, a quivering ruin.

"It would seem, my dear," Daniels told her, "that whoever it was they've taken no chances. Those are some quite impressive defences around your memories; a wise and reasonable precaution in this day and age. The regrettable flaw in their approach, however, is that the strength of ability such a thing would require narrows down the list of suspects considerably. To a very small number indeed."

At a signal from Daniels, the guards picked Hamilton up and started to lead her, stumbling and groaning, back out of the door. "Goodbye Elspeth," Daniels called after them, "you'll be pleased to know that you gave us what we needed, in spite of yourself. Now I must let my technicians have their sport with you. They may be lenient, and only strip you down to your bare essentials. Who knows? You might even remember who you once were."

With the last of her strength, Hamilton stared balefully at Daniels.

"I trusted you," murmured Hamilton.

"Good luck with that."

The door rolled shut again.

Daniels waited until she could no longer feel their minds, and then her complacent smile vanished. Alone once more in the half-light, she briefly lowered her mental barriers and took a long, tremulous breath. Then her balance wavered, and she had to steady herself on the railings.

Although Hamilton had not said his name aloud, his footprints in her mind had been unmistakable: Eric White was here.

Eric White had come for them all.

8

The sun was retreating from Harkham Common, as the summer day approached its end.

The crowds around the common walls had thinned out as night drew closer, but among them Ken Bulmer still moved, his tweed jacket now pulled around him and a takeaway coffee in his hand. Silently he watched every movement of the police officers that searched the common. Earlier they had erected arc lamps around the incident room and car park, enhancing the spectacle and making it even easier to discern what was happening. Beyond the car park, he could see yet more lights at the lake shore. The water shimmered beneath them.

Bulmer looked on as half a dozen dog-handlers returned to the main staging area from the direction of the cliff paths. Then he saw a familiar figure emerge from the incident room and lumber down the metal stairs to greet them.

Bulmer sipped his coffee, and watched.

Fairfield nodded in greeting at Inspector Menzies, his opposite number among Harkham's uniformed officers, who was leading the dog team.

"Anything, Brian?"

Menzies shook his leathery head. "Nothing substantial. Fag ends mostly. We've bagged a few items for forensics, but it's been over a week. Cole's garden may still be relatively untouched, but hundreds of people, animals and god-knows-what have traipsed through Harkham Common over the last seven days. We're lucky it hasn't rained." Menzies' voice sounded disillusioned and tired.

Fairfield reached down and ruffled the forehead of Menzies' German Shepherd. "I hope you behaved yourself and didn't leave anything behind," he told the dog. "It's the law. I read it on a bin over there." He looked up at Menzies and smiled, in an effort to raise morale.

Menzies just about managed to smile back. "Don't worry, Duncan. Uniform are good at clearing up everyone else's mess."

"Touché," said Fairfield. He scanned the crescent sweep of the cliff line, which was now a silhouette in the dusk. "Nothing from the woods?" he asked again.

Menzies sighed. "Like I said, nothing out of the ordinary. On either occasion." His addition referred to Fairfield's earlier insistence that they search the woods twice.

Fairfield began muttering, partly to himself. "But that's wrong. It doesn't figure. If I was fleeing over a busy common in daylight, and I wanted to go unseen, I would have turned left and headed up into those woods."

A new voice joined the conversation.

"How about down by Tom Sullivan's allotment?" Sally Fisher appeared at Fairfield's side. "Find anything there?" she asked Menzies. Fisher and Fairfield had discussed this earlier. The old man's allotment backed on to the north-westerly corner of the common, separated by a steep border of grass and overgrown brambles.

"One of the first places we did this morning," explained Menzies. "Bit of a jungle, but we got through it. Nothing remarkable."

Fairfield nodded, and then said, "What about the other side?"

"Other side?"

"The other side of the woods. By the school."

"The school?" Menzies shrugged. "What's to search? The woods stop dead at the top of the bank, and the bank goes down into a half-mile of open playing fields. Anyone crossing it would've been spotted."

"On a Saturday?" queried Fisher.

Fairfield gave her a half smile. "At my school we used to have rugby club on a Saturday. I wander if the caretaker saw anything?" he speculated.

"Good job we've got him in custody," said Fisher, continuing Fairfield's train of thought, "we can ask him."

As Ken Bulmer was admiring the fresh-faced young blonde who was talking to Fairfield, he saw another uniformed officer walk up to their group and demand the blonde's attention. The new arrival whispered something in her ear, and she reacted with astonishment. She in turn relayed something to Fairfield and they immediately abandoned their conversation with the dog unit, both following the messenger at a brisk pace to the car park and then down the main drive.

Intrigued, Bulmer traced their trajectory with his eyes and saw that their destination seemed to be the entrance gates. There was a commotion taking place there. Two constables appeared to be trying to calm down one individual in particular, and things were becoming animated. Almost at the end of his cold coffee, Bulmer glugged the last of it and looked on with curiosity. The gate officers were clearly having trouble controlling somebody. So much so, it would seem, that they'd had to send for an adult. Bulmer glanced to his right and saw that Fisher and Fairfield were only a minute or two away. This would be interesting.

As Bulmer's eyes returned to the gates, a gap formed in the crowd.

He saw another familiar face there.

In alarm, Bulmer dropped his coffee cup and broke into a run.

"Please be patient, sir," repeated the long-suffering constable, "someone in authority should be with you shortly."

"But I've shown you identification!" protested Greg Cole. "I've proved who I am, so let me in instead! Save them the trouble!"

"Yes Mr Cole, you may well have proved who you are," the officer cast a worried glance over the surrounding crowds, "but unless you want to be set upon by every journalist in a five mile radius I suggest you keep your voice down. DI Fairfield will be with you in just a second."

The officer glanced back over his shoulder to confirm this, and was reassured to see the two detectives approaching briskly, casting long shadows ahead of them. He turned back to address Greg Cole.

But Greg Cole had gone.

Stumbling free from the edge of the crowd, Greg prised the arm that had dragged him there away from his shoulder. He rounded on Ken Bulmer angrily, but kept his voice low.

"What the hell do you think you're doing?"

Bulmer's eyes narrowed. "Same question to you, Old Chap. I thought we already had this discussion."

"And you think I'm going to listen to you, of all people?" Greg scowled and waved an arm in the direction of the police-infested common. "Did you know about this?" he hissed. "When we saw each other at the airbase, did you know that my wife was missing? You told me she was gone; I thought you just meant from my life! I had to find out from the bloody news for god's sake!"

Dismissively, Greg turned as if to go back to the gates, but Bulmer caught his arm again.

"Ex-wife," corrected Bulmer, "and no, I only found out last night. I came down here to see what was happening, the same as you did. The difference being that, in your case, it was the wrong thing to do."

Greg pulled his arm free. He was larger and younger than Bulmer and did so easily. "Really?" he said, accusingly. "You show up after twenty years, twice in a week, and Susan's gone missing. And now you're telling me not to go to the police? I'm not an idiot, Bulmer."

"Then listen to me," Bulmer winced with irritation. "The police cannot help you. Their involvement will make things much worse and especially the police in this town. I've already told you, Greg: you need to visit the address I gave you. It's the only way." Greg looked at him with suspicion, but said nothing. Bulmer, growing increasingly agitated, risked a glance over Greg's shoulder and saw the luminous bulk of the gate officer making his way through the crowds, craning his neck and searching for a particular face. Frustrated, Bulmer quickly returned his attention to Greg. "Let me guess; you didn't keep the address."

"Of course I didn't keep the bloody address!" replied Greg. "For the same reason I haven't kept in touch with you, or sent you any Christmas cards! I don't want anything to do with you, Bulmer, or your so-called medicines, and I'm not getting involved in all that shit again just because you say so!"

"Then you are an idiot. Forget our history; this is about Susan. If you ever want to see her again, then you have to go there. Do you understand?"

Greg frowned. With cynicism souring his voice he said, "What do you mean by that? That she's at Rowcroft? They kill my son with their drugs, but they keep my wife as a souvenir, is that it?"

"Just go there, Greg!"

Suddenly Bulmer looked startled and backed away. Without another word, he pushed his way out of the crowds and hurried off into the side streets. Greg realised why as a hand landed on his shoulder. There was a police officer attached to it, and he was glaring at Greg disapprovingly.

"Don't go anywhere yet, Mr Cole," said the bobby, "it's time for your close up."

Greg found himself being swivelled around and marched back through the crowds. Soon they were at the gates again.

Duncan Fairfield was waiting impatiently for him there.

9

For the umpteenth time that evening, and mainly for something to do, the security guard glanced out of the gatehouse window.

There was now a figure waiting outside the barriers.

It had not been there the last time he'd looked.

The figure was a man, handsome in a weathered way, wearing a linen suit and an expression of calm patience. As he caught the security guard's eye, he smiled and gently raised a hand, as if to request entry. Despite this superficial politeness, the guard immediately felt uneasy.

His hand reached down for the alarm button.

But then it jerked to the left, seemingly of its own accord, and operated the barrier release lever instead. The guard stared at his disobedient limb in astonishment, his eyes wide, before reaching out with his other hand and opening the door of the security office. He found himself placing his head against the exposed jamb, and then slamming the door on it. As he slid to the floor, unconscious, the barriers tilted upwards.

Eric White nodded in satisfaction, and then entered Rowcroft Medical unchallenged.

Greg Cole's tea was becoming stale.

Susan Cole's ex-husband simply turning up at their incident room, unbidden, had caught Fairfield and his team off guard. They hadn't expected their first response to the public appeal to be so personal, and so direct. Having rushed Greg up to their portacabin office, away from prying eyes and cameras, they had supplied him with the customary cuppa and cobbled together an interview area of sorts. Fairfield had cleared all non-essential officers from the room, and had sat Greg at one of the three desks.

At first their conversation had been slow and cautious.

It was when Sally Fisher had offered her condolences on Adam Cole's untimely demise, however, that Greg had broken off eye contact and just stared down at the mud-streaked floor, his skin ashen under the strip lights. Fisher and Fairfield exchanged glances and waited for a moment, trying hard not only to maintain respect, but also to not pressure the man for answers.

"Mr Cole," asked Fairfield eventually, "did Susan ever mention a man called Samuel Wilcox?" The reply was a shake of Greg's head. "Or a Jacob Morgan?" added Fairfield.

"I told you," sighed Greg, clearly ill at ease. "I haven't spoken to Susan in ages. Not properly, not since the divorce. We take turns at putting Adam up when he comes back on leave, but that was all we would speak about. She never discussed her private life with me. Nor mine for that matter."

Sally's eyes narrowed.

"We didn't say that these men were part of Susan's private life."

"Stands to reason. All of her life was private to me, even when we were married."

"Don't forget your tea, Mr Cole," Fairfield said, and then continued: "Is this something she's done before? Disappeared, gone walkabout?" Another shake of the head. "Any history of mental instability?"

This prompted a mirthless chuckle from Greg. "Perhaps you could ask her shrink. That was the last time we spoke, you see; she called me, out of the blue, trying to get me and Adam to see some psychiatrist with her. I told her to get lost, and that there were no cracks in my head thank you very much."

Fairfield and Sally glanced at each other briefly.

"And what did she say to that?" prompted Fairfield.

"She said it wasn't about me, it was about our family," Greg scoffed. "What bloody family!"

"Mr Cole... how long ago was this?"

"A year or so. Eighteen months, perhaps."

"And did they proceed without you?"

"Probably. She said she was going to."

Fairfield looked up at Fisher, whose train of thought had arrived at exactly the same place as his. "We'll check," she said.

With this break in the conversation, Greg Cole finally took hold of his tea mug and raised it to his lips. He slurped some, and then put it straight back down on the desk. "It's cold," he remarked despondently.

Fairfield smiled in sympathy, leant forward and asked:

"Greg, do you know if Susan ever had any dealings with a company here in Harkham called Rowcroft Medical?"

Greg visibly tensed, and seemed to consider his next words.

"What... makes you ask?" he replied eventually.

"The way you just answered me," Fairfield told him. "So, while Sally makes you a nice, fresh cup of tea, why don't you help us find your wife, and tell us what you really know?"

Elspeth Hamilton reached out into the darkness, but there was nothing there. Her panicking heart beat faster.

They must have been in a corridor, or something like it; she was sure they had just come through a set of double doors, and the acoustics around them sounded close and dull. Then the two Rowcroft guards who were carrying her had stopped dead. The sudden change in momentum had shifted the pressure onto Hamilton's arms and now they were taking her full weight. The guard's fingers were digging into her. Hamilton had tried to probe her surroundings with her mind, to try to get some clue as to what the guards were waiting for, but she had soon realised that it was pointless. Her powers, as limited as they were, had been stripped away by Daniels' technicians.

At the same time as her sight.

From outside — outside the building? — came the sudden report of three loud bangs, startling and rapid, followed by the clattering of metal. A man's voice screamed, briefly, followed by a second. Then silence.

Hamilton felt the hands around her tense even more. Her pulse broke into a gallop, her breath quickening with it. Despite herself she twisted her head from side to side, searching for the source of the sounds with redundant eyes.

And then there was another crash: loud, immediate, and close. Its din filled the space around them and shook Hamilton's eardrums.

She heard one of her guards inhale sharply.

Her right arm was suddenly free.

From her left came a choking sound.

The support disappeared from her left arm now, and Hamilton felt herself slumping to one side, unbalanced, crying out as her head and shoulder struck a wall. Feeling naked, vulnerable, her breathing became ragged and deep.

Then something bizarre happened.

As she inhaled, as her heartbeat hammered on the inside of her chest, a dim and foggy light returned to her eyes. Its intensity rose and fell with her respiration, like theatre house lights before the next act. She saw shadows and outlines.

She saw two motionless shapes, crumpled on the floor.

She saw a figure approaching her.

It came nearer with each breath.

Eventually it leaned in close to her and Hamilton pointlessly shut her eyes in fear. She heard the voice of Eric White.

"I should be disappointed in you, my dear," it said. "We made such lovely plans together yesterday, and then you go and backslide like this. There's nothing more painful than the regret of a missed opportunity, don't you find? Nevertheless, try to look on the bright side, if you'll pardon the expression. I like you. You're going to live through today. So if I were you, Miss Hamilton, I'd run along now before you miss another opportunity. As you might have just heard, the door is now open."

Hamilton felt White's presence recede, and then the corridor was silent again. Once she was certain she was alone, she blinked her eyes experimentally and saw that total darkness had not returned; a soft half-light remained, with just enough form and detail to discern her surroundings.

A glimmer of hope.

Slowly, and keeping within touching distance of the wall, Hamilton began to stagger forwards.

Greg Cole sighed in resignation.

"Look, the reason I didn't go to see that shrink with Susan and Adam wasn't just because we didn't get on anymore, although that was part of it." He looked up at Fairfield for affirmation, who urged him on with a nod. "It was because it felt like history repeating itself," Greg continued. "We'd done it all before, almost twenty years ago now, and it was then that everything started falling apart."

Sally arrived with a fresh, steaming mug of tea. Greg accepted it gratefully.

"You'd seen a psychiatrist before, then?" said Fairfield.

"No, a doctor," Greg told him. "Down in the West Country. I'd been made redundant and was trying to find work at the time; things between us were already strained. Susan was expecting again, and we were worried because Adam had been born with thyroid problems. He was only four or five at the time, see. Our GP referred us to this... specialist."

"Specialist in what?" asked Sally, who had perched on the desk corner.

Greg clicked his tongue in contempt. "Wrecking your life, that's what. He gave Susan all these drugs. I found out later on that they weren't even legal. That's when she changed. Didn't recognise her anymore. Adam didn't really notice, but I did."

"But did the drugs work?" asked Fairfield. "Was the baby born healthy?"

Greg hesitated again and rubbed a hand over his eyes.

"No idea," he said in a small voice. "Susan lost it. And then I lost her. To him."

Fairfield shifted in his chair, and allowed a decent period of silence before continuing. "I'm sorry to hear that, Mr Cole," he said. "So, let me see if I'm understanding you here, because we're talking almost twenty years ago. Are you saying that this doctor that prescribed the drugs back then worked for Rowcroft?"

"No. I'm saying that I think he still does. I just saw him. Here, tonight. And he tried to gate-crash Adam's funeral the other day, too. He keeps telling me to visit Rowcroft; he says they have Susan."

At this revelation both detectives sat up straight, wide-eyed and astounded. "What?" exclaimed Fairfield. "And you're just telling us now? What about a name, Mr Cole? Does this doctor have a name?"

Greg opened his mouth to speak, but then the portacabin door swung open and interrupted him. Inspector Menzies was standing in the doorway, his face pale and drawn. He spoke breathlessly.

"Duncan, the scuba team's up from the lake. You need to come and see this."

Vanessa Daniels hurried deeper into the laboratory building and didn't look back.

The clamour of panicking security guards and scientists had faded away behind her some minutes ago, and she knew that time was short. At the far end of a dimly lit corridor she came to a smooth door with no handle, hardly perceptible in the gloom. After a final glance behind her, she faced it and spoke a single password.

"Symmetry."

The door slid quietly to one side, revealing a small, metal cubicle with a numeric keypad on its far wall. Daniels entered the elevator and began typing a code into the keypad, which lit up at her touch. Her finger hovered over the final digit of the eight number code, but did not press it. Daniels frowned in frustration and tried to force her finger forwards, but it was paralysed.

She looked up and saw Eric White leaning casually in the doorway.

"Before you scuttle off under your rock, Vanessa," he said, "we need to have a conversation."

Daniels glared at him defiantly.

"Who the hell do you think you are, forcing your way in like this? We agreed you'd stay away from us."

"We also agreed," smiled White, "that we would not tread on each other's toes. You've been keeping secrets from me, Vanessa. The fact that you've tried to keep me out of here by force would seem to confirm that."

"This is totally against the code, Eric!"

White tutted theatrically.

"Oh, please, those days are gone. Besides," he looked at Daniels pointedly, "there's no-one left to enforce it, is there? And so it's all down to who can shout the loudest."

Hands in his trouser pockets, White sauntered into the elevator and stood next to Daniels. "I'm not a monster, you know." When this remark failed to get a response, he continued, "I'll tell you what; give me the bumper tour and, if I'm impressed, I might even let you carry on your little schemes. Under Pelion's guidance, of course. Recent events have shown that you can't be trusted to manage things on your own."

"We don't need your permission," argued Hamilton, avoiding eye contact.

"True," White nodded convivially, "but then, neither do I need permission to drop a grenade down this lift shaft and leave you all for dead. If you co-operate, however, I shall try and refrain from doing so."

Daniels took a deep breath and stared straight ahead; her version of admitting defeat.

"There is," added White, "one condition."

"And that would be?"

"There are some associates of mine waiting at your front gate. Before we pop down and inspect your little underground sanctuary, I'd like you to arrange for Susan Cole to be taken to them. I've left a couple of your medics aware and functioning, so they should be up to the task."

Daniels' brow furrowed, and for the first time she looked White straight in the eye. "Susan Cole?" she queried.

"We know you have her."

"No, Eric. Not us. I thought Pelion did."

White's face twitched, and he studied Daniels through narrowed eyes for a moment. "And, for once, you're not lying." With amused curiosity, he added, "Well, well, I wonder where she is?"

Daniels' arm jerked suddenly, and she found she could move her finger again. Next to her, Eric White straightened himself, crossed his hands officiously over his linen jacket and nodded at the elevator controls. "It would appear that we really do need to have that conversation."

Daniels completed the code sequence, and the elevator began its descent.

Fairfield and Fisher had left Greg Cole in the custody of a uniformed officer, and then followed Menzies to the end of the lakeside path.

Other officers were clearing a line of three trestle tables there, and covering their surfaces with polythene sheets. In silence, they watched and waited as the silhouettes of the police divers approached. They were carrying something sodden and heavy.

Feeling a chill, Fisher folded her arms tight to her chest and then looked over at her colleagues. Menzies was standing with one foot up on the logs that flanked the path, arm resting on his leg, his jaw locked tight. Fairfield stood behind them all, hands thrust deep into his raincoat pockets, his expression grim.

A sergeant in a life jacket and waders approached them, leading the divers. The object they carried was large, and caked in mud. The assembled police officers parted to let them through, each face displaying the same mixture of trepidation and curiosity. Fairfield and his party followed the divers through the path they made, catching up with them just as they were carefully laying their find to rest on the polythene. The light from the arc lamps now made it clear what they had discovered.

Susan Cole's missing suitcase.

Fairfield realised that Menzies was looking at him expectantly, and that Sergeant Waders was waiting for Fairfield's next order as the senior officer present, a fresh pair of sterile gloves at the ready.

"Open it."

There was no enthusiasm in Fairfield's voice.

The Sergeant pulled on the gloves and Fairfield walked around to the side, preparing for his first glimpse. Fisher and Menzies took up position at the opposite end. The Sergeant was having trouble with the suitcase's two metal catches; the mud and grass was making them slippery. There was a pause as he turned and asked for some paper towels. This delay met with shuffling feet and the clearing of throats, each officer impatient to open the case, but also wise enough to fear what may be inside.

Soon a uniformed PC appeared with a handful of blue paper towels. The Sergeant methodically wiped the catches free of the dark mud, and then placed the towels into a forensics bag. After taking a deep breath, he placed his thumbs either side of the suitcase handle, and pushed. The catches sprung open. Water trickled from the locks as he lifted the lid, and the interior of the case remained in shadow until it was fully upright. Fairfield peered in. The shapes inside were crossed and tangled, and it took his eyes a few seconds to interpret them.

The suitcase was full of barbed wire. It curled around a long, pale object at its centre, trapping it like a fly in a web. Fairfield leaned closer. The shape in the middle wasn't just tangled in the wire, however. In places the wire had been deliberately wrapped around it, like a covering. And then Fairfield recognised what the central object actually was.

It was a weapon.

The hilt was a long, square piece of wood, painted white and splintered at the base as though broken from another, longer piece. The other end had been cut into a notch and a roughly triangular, foot-long shard of glass fixed into it; this was the blade. The whole apparatus was tied tightly to the hilt by multiple coils of barbed wire.

The tip of the glass was black with dried blood.

So focused were the officers on their discovery, that at first they didn't notice the other figure in their midst.

"That used to be mine," said a new voice.

Fairfield looked up to see Greg Cole standing at the back of the group, and staring at the suitcase with watery eyes.

"I'm sorry, sir," said the constable with him. "He was quite insistent."

"She never could look after things," added Greg wistfully.

Sally Fisher nodded to the constable in thanks, and then put an arm around Greg's shoulder. "Come with me," she said. "You really shouldn't be seeing all this…"

"Bulmer," said Greg immediately, concluding their earlier conversation. "That's his name. Kenneth Bulmer. He's staying here in town."

With a tense and stony expression, Fairfield watched Fisher lead Cole away, and made no comment on that which he already knew.

10

Their descent was swift, down through the ward building and beyond, and deep into the bowels of Rowcroft Medical where no light penetrated.

Eventually they glided to an unnervingly smooth halt, and the doors opened onto a corridor of brushed metal that was barely wider than the elevator itself. The corridor led to a single doorway, some three hundred yards away. Accompanied by the sinister spectre of Eric White, Vanessa Daniels stepped out of the lift and walked to the far door in silence.

As her palm hovered over the access scanner, an ironic smile drifted briefly across Daniels' lips. Where they had travelled to was the home of Rowcroft's real research; no tour ever came here, and none of their corporate sponsors or lawyers even knew it existed. For years they had hidden it from Pelion's prying eyes. And now, here she was, about to escort its Chief Executive right into the heart of it all.

The door slid open, and they entered The Chamber.

It was like walking outside into brilliant sunshine.

A warm breeze sighed through Daniels' hair and she stopped just inside the threshold, closing her eyes to savour the sensation. Eric White, hands clasped behind his back, stepped around her and gazed upward. As he strolled further into The Chamber, he became more intrigued. He knew, of course, that the unblemished white span of the dome that surrounded them wasn't a genuine sky; but its apex was so far up above that it might as well have been. Its base formed a perfectly circular, cavernous room. All surfaces were a sheer white; forming the illusion of an infinite space within its mathematically precise borders.

Around the edge of the dome sat a dozen huddled figures, clad in white robes, their knees and arms curled tightly into an upright foetal ball. None of their faces were visible and each was gently rocking, back and forth, back and forth. They moved at different rates for the most part, but every so often their swaying would slowly synchronise and they would rock in perfect unison for two or three seconds, before returning to their separate rhythms.

In the midst of the others stood a single, male figure, in a crisp clean suit of white that rendered him almost invisible. He stood in the exact centre of the dome's floor, and steadily turned by degrees to face each rocking figure in an anti-clockwise order. Upon arrival at each new target his head remained bowed, and his voice silent, for ten, maybe twenty seconds. Then it would slowly rise towards the heavens, and his jaw would drop downwards in a soundless scream. He would hold that position; and this was the point at which the movements of his mute audience would synchronise. Then the man would turn onwards to the next figure and the ritual would restart. They seemed oblivious to the presence of their new visitors.

White stood for a moment, admiring the precision and accuracy; numbers on a clock, ticking away the seconds of their own lives as they moved. He nodded approvingly at Daniels as she joined him.

— Not bad. Almost like the real thing. It's a lot smaller, of course, but not bad. You should be congratulated, Vanessa.

His mouth did not move. Neither did Daniels' during her reply.

— I've never seen the real thing.

— Well, then, that makes your achievement even more remarkable. You should be proud.

— We are. And we'll weather today just as we've always done. We don't need your help. So kindly leave.

White turned to face her fully.

— Hmm. Maybe not that proud. You should be mindful of your stubbornness.

— You've seen what you came here to see. You've slapped our wrists. Just go.

This remark prompted a gentle frown from White.

— Vanessa, your key field operative has gone off the rails, and your flagship experiment is hanging in tatters. I can smell your desperation. You think this noble enterprise is slipping through your fingers. And, if all that wasn't enough, there's the small matter of Kenneth Bulmer.

Daniels searched her memory for a second; the name was familiar. Then realisation struck her. — Bulmer? The pathologist?

White shook his head disapprovingly.

— What possessed you to bring him to Harkham, in the middle of all this? The man should be put out to pasture, not given a job in your centre of operations! Were you aware that the good Dr Bulmer is spilling his tawdry little secrets to all the wrong people? It seems his conscience has gotten the better of him.

The colour drained from Vanessa's face.

— What do you mean… all the wrong people?

This time the sadistic pleasure was clear in White's smile.

— Oh, no-one special. Susan Cole… Greg Cole…

"Duncan Fairfield," he whispered, in conclusion of his list.

It was the first time either of them had spoken aloud, and although little more than a sigh White's voice reverberated through The Chamber like the voice of God. The silence that followed it was palpable.

Slowly, Daniels looked round.

A chill ran down her spine.

The swaying had stopped; the human clock was suddenly still. Dozens of blank, robed faces were staring at them, and the gentleman at its centre was raising a cautionary finger to his lips.

White had beaten Daniels to the exit.

He blocked the lift corridor with his outstretched arms, and retreated before her as she strode out of The Chamber.

"What's the rush, Vanessa?" taunted White, with the gleeful smile of a bully in his element. "Surely you won't have me believe, with all the resources that I've just seen, that you haven't been keeping proper tabs on events up top? Surely you're aware of what Elspeth's little spat might mean for us? For all our kind?"

"Elspeth has paid the price," countered Daniels.

"Too little, too late; and not really the point."

"Get out of my way, Eric."

White continued to retreat from Daniels, walking backwards but with both hands still touching the walls. Daniels strode forward at the same pace, trying every few moments to duck around or pass him. He intercepted her at each turn.

"This is why we need to talk, Vanessa," persisted White, his voice thin and dull in the cramped metal corridor. "Things are worse than you think. Rowcroft can go unnoticed no longer; wheels are in motion, and far worse things than I are on their way to Harkham." He paused melodramatically, and then said, "My Employer will be here in only a few days."

"How nice for you, Eric," remarked Daniels with an acid tone. "Perhaps he's coming to check you're not fiddling your expenses."

"Nice," White said, "but we all answer to someone eventually. Before you go rushing back up to your office and barking orders at people, I would suggest you stop and think about the ramifications here, and the possible outcomes. My Employer doesn't know I've come to you like this, but I thought it unfair not to warn you. In fact, there's still time to resolve matters. We need to be very careful, and make sure that we end up with the outcome that's best for us."

"Don't you mean the outcome that's best for you?"

White looked theatrically pained.

"That's not very gracious of you, Vanessa. Rowcroft have messed up big time on this one and I'm here to help, not admonish you. We need to work closely on some damage limitations."

Daniels stopped suddenly, bringing them both to a halt. They were now only a few yards from the elevator door. After straightening the sides of her jacket and composing herself, Daniels glowered at White with indignance. "Damage limitations?" she repeated acerbically. "We've seen more than you realise, Eric. I know full well that you've been in the thick of things, stirring it up. I know you exerted your influence on Elspeth Hamilton, and soon so will everyone else. You're not very circumspect; one can hardly miss that vulgar red car of yours."

"Ah yes," said White whimsically, "I'm afraid I never could part with that old E-Type of mine. I'll probably be buried in it."

"Don't tempt me. It will look lovely in my parking spot, I'm sure."

"Whatever do you mean?"

"Don't come the innocent," Daniels sneered. "I'd be a fool not to see what was going on here. I can just picture the scene: your Employer arrives here in a few days' time, finding me suitably chastised and Eric White wagging his tail like an obedient dog, all problems solved?"

White chuckled to himself, but said nothing.

"Except, of course," Daniels continued, "what they won't realise is that the problem wouldn't have been half as bad if Eric White hadn't been here in the first place. Let me guess; you get a hearty slap on the back for sorting it all out, and I have to step down?"

White adopted a sombre expression.

"I think you're losing sight of the immediate danger, Vanessa. If Susan Cole is not found, and the Morgan boy not properly contained, we will have more than our career prospects to worry about. My Employer will see to that. Personally."

Daniels was quiet for a moment, and then said:

"And what do we do about Fairfield?"

White considered her question. "What we've always done. Keep our heads down, and our fingers crossed."

"What!" exclaimed Daniels. "You can't just expect ..."

"Trust me," White cut across her. "I can do this. Take advantage of that. Give me free rein, and forty-eight hours, and your troubles will be a distant memory. Morgan. Bulmer. Everything."

"Whether I trust you or not is academic. You're going to do what you're going to do whatever I say. You always did."

At this comment, White seemed genuinely touched.

"It made you no less the tutor," he smiled, and brushed Daniels' cheek with his fingers. "It's just that I found a better one."

Daniels' eyes narrowed and she pushed White's hand away.

"You're not taking Rowcroft," she told him.

"And, unless you accept my offer, you're not getting out of this alive," replied White. "Either way, Vanessa, your work here is done. What happens next is up to you though; live to fight another day or simply retire. Permanently."

White stepped aside and gestured at the elevator with a smile.

"Going up?" he said.

From his darkened hospital room, at the same spot by the window that he had occupied all day, Jacob watched as the last ray of sunlight flared briefly on the horizon and disappeared. As its warmth left his face, he closed his eyes and dreamed of salvation.

Sunday
21st July, 2002

1

Sunday had arrived slowly.

A sluggish mist had clung to the town since dawn, and was only now starting to lift. Restless, Fairfield had risen early and wandered through it to the Station, almost without noticing. His mind had been elsewhere, struggling to form a cohesive thought from the ideas that were swirling around it. Once he'd arrived at CID he found he was still too early, and, finding his offices empty, he had gone in search of a distraction.

He had decided to visit his grandfather.

So now Fairfield was standing alone in the corridor that bridged the station buildings, contemplating the many photographs that adorned its walls. He often did this; the photos provided him with context, and valuable perspective. They were a reminder of who he was. Or, at least, who he needed to be.

When he'd first come here to Harkham – how long ago had it been? — there had been an elder officer, probably younger than Fairfield was now, of course, who had told him that the photographs spanned two hundred years of Harkham history. Fairfield had taken that with a pinch of salt. Besides, they weren't just photos of the town, but of its people. The oldest image was from the 1860s, of labourers re-channelling the leat for irrigation. The men in the photo, sleeves rolled up, caps jammed down and framing their dour expressions, had stopped work to pose. Probably not yet used to cameras, they were leaning on their tool handles and looking impatient. Fairfield knew that DCI Hill had a fondness for that particular photo; something about teamwork, he'd said. It had been Hill who originally rescued the photos when the library was renovated, and that had hung them in the corridor as an inspiration to all. It had been one of his few popular ideas.

Fairfield had his own favourite picture, however.

It portrayed, in monochrome rather than sepia tones, a group of seven men in the serge uniforms and enamel helmets of Air Raid Wardens. They were assembled proudly around a portable water pump. In complete contrast to Hill's picture, the men in this one were smiling proudly, their teeth bright amid soot-smeared faces. A copperplate caption at the base of the frame proclaimed: 'Heroes of Harkham, 1940'. Beneath this, in smaller writing, were listed the names of the seven 'heroes' in alphabetical order. The middle name read 'Daniel Fairfield'.

Fairfield realised that his mind was becoming clearer, and he nodded a smile of appreciation towards his predecessor. It was then that he felt another presence behind him.

"Inspirational, aren't they?" said DCI Hill, hands clasped behind his back, and peering admiringly over Fairfield's shoulder. "Which one's yours, again?"

Fairfield frowned in annoyance; they'd covered this before. "The names are in alphabetical order, Sir, so I can't be sure, but I think it's this one," he pointed at the second man in from the left, "he bears the strongest resemblance to other family photos I've seen."

"Hmmm," Hill sniffed with uncertainty. "Difficult to tell, eh? Has a look of your father about him though; noble brow and all that," he looked Fairfield up and down with a mischievous grin. "Although these things skip a generation from time to time, so I'm told."

Fairfield ignored the barb and changed the subject. "How can I help, Sir?"

Hill turned away from the photos.

"Well actually, Duncan, I'd only just arrived and I thought I'd give you an update on the warrant you asked for last night."

Fairfield's expression lifted expectantly; following yesterday's developments he had phoned Hill and requested a warrant to search Rowcroft Medical's campus. He hadn't expected news so swiftly. And then the logical explanation occurred to him, and his face returned to its cynical default.

"Let me guess; it was dismissed out of hand."

"Now now," cajoled Hill, "let's not be too pessimistic. These things take time, especially with the amount of lawyers Rowcroft have at their disposal."

"Sir, with respect, time is something we don't have and neither does Susan Cole."

"I will try my best. But we don't know that there's a direct link."

Fairfield could feel the disquiet returning to his mind. "True, but there are about two dozen indirect ones," he said indignantly. "I don't know how much police-work you might have done in the past, Sir, but round here that's something we call reasonable suspicion."

"That's as maybe," replied Hill sharply, "but we're not talking about a dawn raid on a drug-dealer here. Assuming you would like a watertight prosecution from this, there are certain procedures and channels that we must follow, and follow correctly. This is my responsibility; continuing to pursue all other lines of investigation is yours." Hill tapped Fairfield's shoulder and turned to leave. "I'll let you know as soon as there's any news. Nil desparandum, Duncan."

Fairfield frowned as Hill walked away but then, after a few seconds had passed, he seemed to come a decision and called after him. "Sir?"

From the doors at the end of the corridor, Hill turned to reply.

"Yes, Duncan?"

"I don't suppose it would be…," Fairfield tailed off for a second, and then came back with a more confident tone. "Alexander Miller that's blocking this warrant, would it?"

Hill's gaunt features remained impassive, and gave nothing away. At length he said, "Mr Miller is one of Rowcroft's legal team, yes. I wouldn't know how much he's involved in this particular case, though."

Fairfield nodded, and then said, "Perhaps you can ask him later, Sir? At the nineteenth hole?"

Hill's smile was narrow, but he departed without answering.

Fairfield felt a small surge of achievement at having caught Hill on the back foot. He flashed a quick nod of solidarity at his grandfather. But Fairfield's mind was restless again, and this time with a new concern.

Until thirty seconds ago, he had never heard of Alexander Miller.

Fairfield tried to lock this thought away for now, and headed back to CID to see what other wonders the day would bring him.

2

For the third time in twenty-four hours, Harvey Gossett found himself face to face with Samuel Wilcox.

When arrested the previous day, Wilcox had been wearing only shorts and a t-shirt beneath his motorcycle leathers. Since then, he had changed into a grey, all-in-one paper suit; the sort normally reserved for soiled drunks in soiled cells. Coupled with Wilcox's full beard and long, shaggy mane, the effect was bordering on the comical.

However, none of this seemed to have dampened Sam Wilcox's mood. The man had remained resolute, and relatively cheerful. He also had a born-innocent attitude that almost had Gossett believing Wilcox's story, if it hadn't been for the weight of evidence against him. He certainly didn't come across as a hardened criminal capable of kidnap, assault, or possibly even murder. Not for the first time in his career, however, Gossett had to remind himself that sometimes even Nice Guys could still be guilty.

With them in the interview room was Wilcox's lawyer. Gossett wasn't sure about him yet; forties, Greek perhaps, and impeccably dressed. He had hardly spoken since his arrival, and had confined himself to furiously scribbling notes while the others conversed. The few words he had said had been brusque. He was hardly a stabilising presence.

"Mornin', Mr Gossett," said Wilcox, completely out of the blue.

Gossett was uncomfortable with this aspect of Wilcox's character; he was always so bloody polite. Had he not been handcuffed, he would have probably opened the interview room door for them all. Leaning hard on this guy was going to be like kicking a puppy. "And to you, Mr Wilcox," replied Gossett. "Now then. I'm afraid…"

"Sam," interjected Wilcox. "Call me Sam."

"Not sure about that," smiled Gossett awkwardly. "Because then you'd have to call me Harvey," he gestured over to another uniformed officer, standing guard by the door, "PC Tyrrell over there would have to be 'Andy', and I'd even have to call your brief by his first name, too." Gossett glanced over at Wilcox's lawyer. "Isn't that right, Chuckles?" he added. This resulted in broad grins from everyone in the room. Except for, of course, Chuckles himself.

"Now, let's back to this," continued Gossett. "We've had approval to keep you here another twenty-four hours, so we're stuck with each other for a bit longer yet."

"But why?" asked Wilcox softly. "I ain't done nothin' except leave my driving licence at home."

"It's a bit more complicated than that…"

"Can't my family come see me?" Wilcox pleaded. "And what's happening about my bike?"

"Your wife is being kept up to date with developments, Mr Wilcox, and no-one's going to steal your bike from a bunch of coppers, now, are they?"

This witticism did little to allay Wilcox's concern. Gossett smiled as he pictured the Harley next to Hamilton's Bentley in their car park. If this trend continued, then he could do a roaring trade in classic vehicles. Changing tack, he leaned forward and spoke sympathetically. "The quicker we sort all this out, the easier it's going to be on everyone. Now, we've been talking to your friend Neville Baker. He continues to corroborate your story about a bike rally to Brighton…"

"It's not a story."

"But the rally didn't leave Brighton sea-front until 12.30pm. You say you were on the road by six. Why leave so early?"

"To beat the traffic."

"On a motorcycle? Surely holiday tailbacks on the M25 are nothing to the calibre of machines you and Neville ride?"

Wilcox shook his head.

"Look, Mr Gossett," still the same calm, unflappable voice. "We left early 'cos that's when we like to leave. Every year the same. 'Specially on a beautiful morning like that one. Takes our time, we does, stops off for a bit of brekkie, admire the countryside, and still get there in plenty of time."

Gossett sat back, linking his hands behind his head.

"So, did that include a visit to Heathrow?"

"No. I already said that."

"But Sam, we've got you on camera!"

For the first time he seemed to have said something that Wilcox didn't care for much. "So you says," the big man countered coldly, "but I ain't stupid, and I know where I was and where I wasn't."

"You've seen the stills. In more than one of them your registration is clearly legible."

Wilcox fidgeted. His paper suit rustled. "Don't care; it can't have been me. I was with Neville, on the motorway." He leaned forward to address Gossett square in the eye. "And you ain't got Neville's bike on camera, have you? You ain't seen him anywhere round the airport that morning, have you? No. 'Cause we weren't there! And if that ain't enough, ask the bobbies down in Sussex what pulled us over!"

Wilcox sat back in his chair, arms defiantly folded. Beside him, Chuckles turned over his pad and commenced his sixth page of notes.

Gossett took a deep breath, deciding to pursue another angle.

"Is he a good mate, this Neville?"

"He's not a liar, if that's what you mean."

"Well no, probably not," admitted Gossett, with his customary sarcasm. "In fact, contrary to popular belief, Sam, you'd be surprised at how few actual liars we get in here. Nearly everybody turns out to be innocent. But try and see it from our perspective. This straight up, honest citizen mate of yours also happens to be a Window Fitter for Nu-Glaze, who had access to Susan Cole's house, and went in there three days later with the perfect excuse to knock it about, renovate and sterilise it without arousing suspicion."

Wilcox frowned. "Neville's as honest as the day is long, and I trusts him. You lot ain't doin' right by either of us. There's more than just two 'Arleys in England, you know."

Gossett waited for Chuckles' biro to catch up with Wilcox's words. The lawyer's pen stopped moving, and its owner looked up again, expectantly.

"So if you trust Neville so much, Sam," Gossett continued, "did you ever confide in him about your relationship with Susan Cole?"

Gossett was pleased to see Wilcox's guard drop a little, the muscles tensing in his face, and doubt playing momentarily across his eyes. For the first time in an hour, Chuckles had something to say, and leant over to whisper in his client's ear. After he had finished, Wilcox gave an indignant sniff. "I'm a married man, Mr Gossett."

"Very laudable," said Gossett, "but not entirely relevant. Sources at the school tell us that you and Mrs Cole had a very close relationship, and one that was beyond the professional."

Wilcox uttered a sour laugh. "Sources? Patience bloody Biggs, I'll bet. Nosey old trout."

"Not something I'd expect from you, though, Sam," pressed Gossett. "A solid, god-fearing chap like yourself, committing adultery?"

Sam Wilcox sat back and gathered his thoughts for a moment before continuing. "Wouldn't call it a relationship, Mr Gossett. We'd just spend time together, 'ave a laugh, you know. Me and Cheryl were 'aving a bad time of things and there were Susan, you know...on 'er own, widowed..."

"Divorced, actually," interrupted Gossett.

"Whatever," mumbled Wilcox, glancing up at him briefly. "Wouldn't surprise me. She's got more skeletons in 'er cupboard than Sweeny Todd, that one."

Gossett leaned forward with renewed interest. "Like what, Sam? Did something come between you two last week? Is that why you argued?"

"'S private," snapped Wilcox.

"Well, of course that's up to you."

Chuckles muttered fresh instructions to Wilcox, who shifted uncomfortably in his seat. "I want it on record," he said eventually, "that this all started ages ago, and well before you say Susan went missing."

Gossett nodded at the tape machine at the end of their table. "It's all on the record, Sam. So, what can you tell us?"

At first, Sam Wilcox stroked his beard nervously, raking his work-hardened fingers through the dense hair. Despite their being in a sealed room, he still checked around him before speaking.

"It were the Morgan lad."

"Jacob Morgan?"

"I had to help, see? She could never have coped on 'er own. I had to save 'em both, I did. He was relentless, like a demon. But I had the strength of the Lord on my side... trouble was, I wasn't expecting the lad to take the Good Book to heart quite so much..."

In fascination, Gossett sat back and let Sam Wilcox tell his tale.

Even Chuckles stopped to listen.

3

Fairfield took a deep breath, not sure where to start.

CID were assembled before him, a record turnout for a summer Sunday. This included Jed Caplain and Paul Black, their clothes freshly ironed and their demeanour greatly improved by a good night's sleep. Gradually the room turned to face him, and the conversation simmered down.

"Okay, lads and lasses," he began. "It's day eight. And, as you all know by now, we found Susan's suitcase last night, and what appears to be a hand-made weapon. It had blood on it. Forensics are fast-tracking it as we speak. Our working theory is that it was constructed from parts of Tom Sullivan's greenhouse. As the vandalism complaint against Jacob Morgan was never pursued, this has obvious implications. SOCO are heading down to the allotments this morning." Fairfield, folder in hand, gestured across the room. "Blackie, that's your job for today. Get down there, oversee the operation, and let me know the instant they find anything."

"Guv," acknowledged Black, satisfied with this responsibility on only his third day.

"Now," continued Fairfield. "The suitcase was found under the cliffs, at the back end of the lake. Divers will be resuming their search of that area today. Sally, Des, I'd like you to man the incident room down there. Blackie will just be the other side of the hill if you need him, too. We're getting close to the truth now, folks, so let's keep this moving forward." Their tasks assigned, the assembled detectives started to clear up their desks, rise from their chairs and prepare to leave. Fairfield held up his hands for one last address, "Oh, and it goes without saying that the first person to arrest the woman who attacked me yesterday gets a bottle of malt for their troubles."

The detectives muttered busily between themselves as they began to file out of the room, leaving a handful of officers behind to man the phones. Fairfield gestured to Jed Caplain that he should hang back.

"You shouldn't build their hopes up, you know," Caplain said, once the office had emptied.

Fairfield was immediately on the defensive.

"What do you mean?"

Caplain grinned. "You couldn't afford a bottle of malt if you tried."

Fairfield relaxed again, but only slightly. "Yeah, well, after yesterday I deserved that I suppose." He herded Caplain towards his office. "Come on. There's stuff you need to know."

It took an hour and four cups of black coffee, but eventually Fairfield had brought Caplain up to speed with the rest of his suspicions.

"Blimey," said Caplain at last. "That'll teach me to take a day out. You didn't mention anything about the Rowcroft connection in your briefing, though?"

"No, not yet," Fairfield admitted. "I've got a feeling that there are two sides to this case, and Susan Cole is what links them. If we focus our manpower on finding her, then everything else should fall into place."

"But you're going to look into Rowcroft yourself? On the quiet, like?"

"Ourselves, Jed," Fairfield tossed back the last of his coffee. "Rowcroft seems to have a larger influence in this town than I realised, and I need someone I can trust. If you're up for it, that is. I wouldn't think any less of you if you weren't."

This prompted a furrowing of Caplain's brow.

"Why me over anyone else? Why not the DCI?"

"You don't really need me to answer that, do you Jed? After all these years? We're a team. And something tells me that we'll be pulling Christmas crackers before the DCI secures a warrant. In the meantime you and I can ostensibly be investigating the Cole case; one or two Rowcroft-related questions may pop up from time to time, though, don't you think?"

Caplain smiled, but it didn't last too long. After a few moments of silence between them, he eventually said, "Duncan, have you spoken to Harvey yet this morning?"

Fairfield nodded gravely.

"And he told you what Wilcox said?" added Caplain.

"He did," said Fairfield at last. "But I'm not sure about it."

"Why?"

"Because it doesn't fit with my experience, for one thing."

Caplain's scornful laugh was out there before he could stop it.

"Well don't you think we should ask Ian and Barbara Morgan first? It could be relevant, especially in light of what you've just told me."

"Yes, and it could also be a pile of crap," argued Fairfield. "It could be our suspect trying to muddy the waters."

"Well, that's just it, Duncan," said Caplain, turning the empty coffee-mug in his hand. "Maybe Wilcox isn't our only suspect. Maybe we should prepare ourselves for the possibility that there are at least two suspects in the frame here; after all it's what Robert Brooks has been saying from day one."

"You mean Jacob," remarked Fairfield flatly.

"Well don't you think so too? I'm starting to think that Morgan knows a lot more about what happened that Saturday morning than he's letting on."

Fairfield folded his arms. "Yes, and who's to say Wilcox doesn't either? We've seen the movie of practically the whole kidnap attempt and Wilcox has the starring role! Of course he's going to try and blame Morgan, it's the easy option!"

"Even if he was at Heathrow," argued Caplain, "Wilcox has an alibi for the time Cole was last seen at her house. Morgan doesn't. They could even have been in it together, like some sort of tag team."

"I don't buy that," Fairfield told him. "Remember how worried Morgan was, panicking even, over Susan Cole's whereabouts? Yes, I understand he was obsessed with her, but that could just as easily explain his reaction; like an addict going into withdrawal."

Caplain shook his head judgementally.

"Well either way he needs sorting out, if you ask me. No offence, Duncan, I know you're friendly with his family and that, but the lad's a nutter."

Fairfield was quiet for a moment, and then stood.

"The quacks tell me that he's a lot calmer now, and responding to treatment," he said, reaching for his overcoat. "I think we should go and see him, ask him a few more questions in light of Wilcox's testimony. Put the record straight."

Caplain also stood. "As long as you're happy to abide by what he says."

Fairfield ignored this, and opened the office door as if to leave. He looked back to see if Caplain was following, but Caplain was still where he'd left him, an accusatory expression on his face.

"What?" asked Fairfield.

"The Morgans would probably like to see their son, too."

"Fine," tutted Fairfield. "We'll pick them up on the way."

Caplain's eyes narrowed. "You know full well what I'm getting at, Duncan."

There was a beat, an unspoken exchange between the two men. Eventually Fairfield conceded. He sighed and walked back into the office. After dumping his coat, he picked up the phone and said,

"Have it your way. We're not going in there without some cold, hard facts though. I'll phone Family Records now. See you at the car in five."

Caplain went to the door, but then stopped.

"Okay," he said. "Maybe we can talk about Ken Bulmer on the way. Or were you not going to bring me in on that part?"

Halfway through dialling, Fairfield sighed again.

"Bloody hell, Jed, I thought you already had a wife?"

"Come off it, Duncan, half the station heard Cole say his name. I know you two have history. If he's back on the scene, I'd like to help if I can."

"Don't worry about it, Jed," Fairfield told him abruptly. "I can handle it myself."

At this, Caplain simply nodded and put on his jacket. "Yeah, well. I wouldn't want it interfering in all our other secret missions, would I? Thanks for the update, Duncan," he said bitterly. "I'll share it with the rest of our team, shall I?"

Caplain slammed the door and left Fairfield alone in his office.

For the next few minutes Fairfield closed his eyes, and waited for his mind to calm itself again. He then took a deep breath, finished dialling the number, and as the phone rang he prepared what he was going to say.

A voicemail message eventually answered his call, spoken in its owner's clipped and aristocratic tones: "This is Ken. Thank you very much for calling, but just because I managed to record this message, please don't assume I will have the technical wherewithal to retrieve yours. You can speak after the beep, though, just in case."

Fairfield said nothing and hung up.

4

Knee deep in weeds and grass, and with one foot in a ditch, Paul Black shook his mobile phone and glowered at it. Where the allotments met the common, they formed a valley that was certain death for a phone signal.

Finally he saw one bar creep onto the display.

Black glanced round at his colleagues. They were engrossed in Tom Sullivan's ruined plot. Ensuring they were out of earshot, Black sifted through the contacts on his phone and pressed 'dial'. He checked his watch as it rang. Nine forty-five, not too early for a Sunday.

"Hello?" Kate Berridge's voice was thin and weary.

"Morning," Black started, conversationally, but then he remembered he was addressing a woman he had only just met. "Miss Berridge, it's DS Black. Sorry to wake you."

"It's Kate," she insisted, as though it was the thousandth time she had said it. "And don't worry; I had to get up to answer the phone anyway. How are things, Paul? We still on for later?"

"Listen, Kate," Black said, awkwardly. "That's kind of why I'm ringing. You see, we've had a breakthrough this end, and it looks like I'll be tied up for the rest of the day."

There was a small pause at the other end of the line.

"Oh," said Kate, sounding genuinely disappointed. "Well, okay then, how about later in the week? There's only two days of term left, so I probably won't be making it back to work anytime soon. At least I'll miss Sports Day, though, that's something."

"Actually, Kate," Black interrupted, tripping over his words. "I think it's probably better that we wait until after this business has all died down."

"That again. I should admire your honesty and steadfast professionalism, I suppose. What's a girl alone in a strange town to do?"

Black seemed at a loss when presented with this rhetorical question. Eventually Kate spoke again, to fill the silence.

"Hello? You still there?"

"Yeah, look, Kate, I need to go…"

"Hello?" she repeated. "I can only just… where are you?"

"Back of Waterleat Drive. Reception's pretty bad here."

"Yeah, I saw all the police there yesterday. Is it Susan?"

"I can't say," Black replied, and changed the subject. "Look, I hope you're feeling better soon. How about I call you in a couple of weeks?"

"Oh, I get it," good-natured irritation was creeping into Kate's voice. "You just don't want to be seen out on a date with an ambulance case, her nose in a sling!"

"I really have to go now. I'm sorry," Black ended the call, and began wading back through the foliage to his colleagues

In her bedroom, Kate Berridge stared in disbelief at her silent telephone. She was fully dressed, her hair brushed perfectly into place, and her face bore no bandages or dressings. Little sign of her injuries remained.

After three seconds, she angrily tossed the phone across the bed. "Shit."

"Time for a cuppa, Duncan?"

As always, Barbara Morgan was being the perfect host under difficult circumstances; but then Fairfield had never visited the Morgan household under anything else.

They were in the threadbare lounge. A ragged block of chipboard was covering the window following Philip Knight's attack, the glass having not yet been replaced. They had switched on the lamps next to Fairfield and Caplain's sofa, in response to the lack of natural light. Ian Morgan was sitting on his own beneath the serving hatch, hunched and despondent, his face as grey and as thin as their second hand carpet. From the doorway, his wife waited patiently for their guests to reply.

"Sounds lovely, Barbara, ta," replied Fairfield, smiling kindly.

"Still two sugars?"

"Spot on. Jed'll have the same."

Barbara returned Fairfield's smile, a mixture of hospitality and the relief of having something normal to do. After she had departed for the kitchen, Ian Morgan began fidgeting, and scratched the back of his head. "So," he said. It was an empty comment, some small talk to fill the silence.

Fairfield smiled again, and leaned forward to address his host. "Ian," he said softly, "while we're having our tea, there's a couple of things we'd like to confirm with you. Before we set off for the Hospital."

There was a pause, during which Ian didn't reply. Fairfield took this as an agreement and looked back at Caplain, a reluctant signal to proceed.

"Mr Morgan," asked Caplain, "could you confirm Jacob's date of birth for us?"

Ian's hand now reached around the back of his neck, which he began to rub vigorously. He frowned. "Date of birth?" his voice was cracked and distant. "Well, that's easy, it's… January. The Eighth. Nineteen… Nineteen Eighty Six."

"Thanks," Caplain said. "That's the date we have. So, may we ask, how long was it before you adopted him?"

Ian's restlessness stopped dead in its tracks.

"S-sorry?" he stammered.

Fairfield shut his eyes, and he took a long breath.

Ian stared at the two officers in disbelief. Barbara's tuneless humming serenaded them from behind the closed doors of the serving hatch, as she busied herself making tea. The rumble of the boiling kettle grew gradually louder.

Eventually Ian spoke. "I… we… how did you know? You couldn't…"

"Have found out through normal channels?" Caplain concluded Ian's sentence for him. "You're right. And if it hadn't been for a witness coming forward, we wouldn't have double-checked with Family Records. There's no adoption certificate on file, and the parental details on Jacob's birth certificate are fake. So, we're assuming that Jacob came to you by other means. By other channels."

Between them, Fairfield remained quiet.

Ian Morgan sighed, momentarily closing his eyes in thought before answering. "It was complicated," he began. "I'm… well, I can't father children, you see, and when…" In mid-sentence, he stopped talking and looked up sharply. Barbara Morgan had popped her head around the lounge door. She smiled nervously, with a hint of embarrassment.

"Sorry, boys, but we seem to be out of sugar. Is sweetener okay?"

"That's fine, Mrs Morgan. No problem at all," beamed Caplain, perhaps a little too enthusiastically. Barbara hovered uncomfortably at the door for a moment, as though aware she was missing something, before heading back into the kitchen.

Fairfield looked over at Ian, in time to catch a fleeting expression of guilt. "She doesn't know, does she?" declared Fairfield, breaking his silence. "She thinks it was all above board. You've probably got a fake adoption certificate of your own somewhere, haven't you?"

Nervously, Ian glanced sideways at the door.

"Like I said. It was complicated."

From beyond the serving hatch they heard the kettle clicking off, its din soon replaced by the clattering of cupboard doors and crockery.

"Well, if you're going to enlighten us," pressed Fairfield angrily, "you don't have long. Shall I save us all some time and say Rowcroft Medical?"

Ian nodded grimly, and lowered his voice. "Jacob was about four years old. Barbara still thinks that an agency introduced him, but it was a friend of a friend, if you get my drift, pretending to be an Adoption Agent. No questions asked, and all that." He closed his eyes once more, and slowly shook his head. "If I'd known then it was Rowcroft behind it all, I'd have shown them the door." He gestured around them at his tattered home. "And look at the results," he continued. "I wish I'd just walked away."

"Why didn't you?" asked Caplain. "You could have adopted the traditional way."

"We tried," Ian's reply was desperate and ashamed. "And every time we were rejected... we thought we'd never have a child of our own."

"That's right!" said a brighter voice to his left. Barbara came in, carrying four mugs of tea on a plastic tray. A plate of digestive biscuits accompanied them. She carefully walked between the two sofas, and over to the small coffee table in the centre of the room. "We were starting to lose hope, weren't we? But luckily that last agency we tried came up trumps for us."

She placed the tray on the table and handed out the mugs. Caplain and Fairfield accepted theirs with a nod of thanks. Ian took his without a word. Barbara carried her mug to the far sofa, and lowered herself down next to her husband. "Yes, that was a stroke of luck," she said, her voice coloured by sadness. "I don't know what we'd have done without our Jacob. Our poor Jacob. I sometimes wonder whether we did the right thing, telling him."

"He knows he's adopted?" asked Caplain, and exchanged a glance with Fairfield. This fitted with Jacob having confided in Sam Wilcox.

Barbara nodded. "We told him a while back. It was after that he started to... go off the rails a bit, and come to the notice of the authorities." She glanced at Fairfield. "Luckily, kind people like Duncan were around to help."

Fairfield attempted to strike the right balance between confidence and sympathy. "Jacob should be fine, Barbara," he said. "Dr Montgomery up at the Hospital is a first class physician, and we're on top of the assault charge for now. Rest assured that, whatever happens, we'll ensure it's the best outcome for Jacob."

Barbara Morgan smiled, and sipped her tea. It was either that, or break into tears.

5

They were already waiting with Nurse Tomkin, outside Jacob's room, when Doctor Montgomery appeared. The uniformed officers on duty at the corridor entrance knew him by sight, and let him straight past. He was a broad and imposing man, at least six and a half feet tall, with a thick tangle of curls that had become greyer as he had neared fifty. In archetypal fashion he was carrying a clipboard, and a stethoscope was curled around his collar. As he approached he beamed at them, and thrust out a massive right hand in greeting.

"How do you do, we meet at last," he boomed, his voice deep and authoritative. "Dr Clifford Montgomery, consultant psychologist." He shook the Morgans' hands enthusiastically, and then nodded a cursory acquaintance to Fairfield and Caplain. "I'm glad I caught you all, actually," continued Montgomery. "I was hoping we could have a little chat before we went in to see Jacob."

"Is he all right?" Barbara asked him anxiously.

"Please, don't be alarmed." Montgomery held up an apologetic hand and rallied before continuing, as if in satisfaction with what he was about to say. "I've spent some very productive sessions with Jacob. I think that maybe his recent troubles were a blessing in disguise; if his condition had gone unchecked for very much longer, he may well have suffered some permanent damage." Noticing the Morgans' concerned reaction, he quickly moved on. "So it's good that he's here with us. Sadly, however, he needs more than we can offer him. Our psychiatric facilities are basic, and the help we can provide is limited. So I'm going to recommend that Jacob is moved somewhere more beneficial. I've been in touch with a colleague of mine at Gardner Heritage; it's a specialist facility…"

"We know what it is," interrupted Ian, sharply. He drew his wife closer.

"Indeed," Montgomery paused to inject just the right amount of empathy. Glancing quickly through the window in Jacob's door, he then turned and beamed at the Nurse, who had been waiting patiently since his arrival. "Nurse Tomkin will take you in to see Jacob now. I'll join you in there shortly, and we can discuss it further." He held the door open while Tomkin and the Morgans filed through, smiling in reassurance. Once it had closed again his manner became business-like, and he addressed Fairfield.

"Inspector," Montgomery said, "assuming you're okay with the move, my chap at Gardner Heritage says he has a space opening up on Tuesday evening."

Fairfield held up a prohibitive hand. "We appreciate all you've done, Clifford, but before you get too excited can I just point out that Jacob is still on bail, and his movements should be checked out with us first? Not to mention just springing it on his parents like that!"

"My apologies, gentlemen. I am aware of the procedure. Nevertheless, this is a General Hospital in every sense of the word and I'm afraid we only have so many doses of Lithium and Respiridone to offer. It's like cultivating the desert with a watering can. The faster we medicate him, the faster it wears off. My responsibility is Jacob's well-being, and if an opportunity to get him a better standard of care has arisen then I think we should grab it with both hands. Take whatever precautions you wish, it's not my concern. At the end of the day, though, our boy's only up for assault, isn't he?"

"For now," remarked Caplain.

Fairfield shot Caplain a look and then turned back to Montgomery. "Tuesday, you say?"

"We're hoping Tuesday afternoon. It's only an hour's drive away, and at that time of day his medication should make him easier to cope with."

"Okay," said Fairfield. "But I want at least two officers in the ambulance with him, and an unmarked car as escort."

Montgomery scoffed dismissively.

"Really, I don't think that will be necessary…"

Fairfield moved on without missing a beat.

"My responsibility is Jacob's well-being too, doctor. We'll need at least twenty-four hours to plan a secure route, so you'll need to confirm the schedule with us by midday tomorrow at the latest."

At this, Montgomery sniffed in annoyance. Without further comment he opened Jacob's door again, and went in to join the Morgans.

Fairfield and Caplain were now alone in the corridor.

"Are we not going in?" asked Caplain.

Fairfield shook his head, and produced tobacco and papers out of his overcoat pocket. "Not just yet," he said, engrossed in rolling a cigarette. "Let them have some time with him, before we go wading in with our insensitive size twelves."

Caplain studied Fairfield for a moment, and then asked, "Did you see the Morgans' faces when Gardner was mentioned? They're scared of getting another Elspeth Hamilton."

"It's still the best move. Gardner Heritage is in the countryside and has a dirty great wall around it. It's miles from anywhere, and defendable."

Caplain stopped short and frowned.

"Defendable?" he repeated. "And this place isn't? If I didn't know you better, Duncan, I'd say you were more bothered about locking Morgan away than curing him. How's about we add a couple more armoured cars to his convoy?" he added sarcastically.

"Hamilton wanted him," Fairfield explained, licking his cigarette paper closed, "which means Rowcroft wanted him. Which means we don't trust anyone, and we make our own luck. Sure I'd like Jacob to get better, but why treat him in the open when you can treat him behind a locked door?"

"And why be logical when you can be paranoid?" scoffed Caplain. "Look, Duncan, just because they got to your friend Bulmer, it doesn't mean they got to Montgomery."

Fairfield stopped what he was doing and glowered at him.

A thin, electronic fanfare broke the moment. In annoyance, Fairfield retrieved his mobile from his coat and took a few steps away from Jacob's room. The call didn't last long. Caplain monitored Fairfield's face for clues, but it was still tense from their previous exchange and quite inscrutable.

Eventually Fairfield walked back to him, phone still in his hand. "Forensics are back," he told Caplain dejectedly. "The blood on the glass is a match for the DNA we took from Susan Cole's house. The hilt is from Sullivan's cold frame. Morgan's prints are all over it."

Caplain smiled ruefully. "I take it all back," he said. "Let's lock him up now and have done with it."

Jacob's door swung open and Nurse Tomkin emerged. "Gentlemen," she said reproachfully, "did I just hear a mobile phone?" Her eyes came to rest on the offending article in Fairfield's grasp. She pointed up at the wall, to the silhouette of a mobile phone with a thick red line struck through it. Fairfield theatrically turned his phone off. It bleeped pathetically in protest before dimming its lights. "Thank you," said the Nurse, whereupon she snatched the unlit cigarette from Fairfield's lips. She tucked it into her pocket, and disappeared behind the closing door.

With a look of resignation, Fairfield approached the door and peered through the circular window. Jacob was laying quietly in his bed, on top of the covers and barely conscious, while his parents sat huddled next to him. They held his hand as they spoke softly.

Montgomery stood benevolently by them, keeping a respectful distance, and clutching his clipboard to his broad chest.

Caplain joined him at the door.

"Look, mate," he began, his tone conciliatory. "We can agree to disagree about Jacob, but before we put that family through any more heartache shouldn't we get some answers of our own?"

Fairfield steeled himself. Caplain was right. They could plan defensively for ever and a day, but then they would only ever be playing on Rowcroft's terms. It was time to go on the offensive themselves. It was time to play Rowcroft at their own game.

And it was then that Fairfield realised.

For the first time in decades, he needed Ken Bulmer.

6

The terraced bed and breakfast on Weir Road was a perfect fit for Kenneth Bulmer's requirements.

In return for a three month stay, the cantankerous landlady had eventually agreed to his conditions; first floor, front of house, and with all his domestic arrangements catered for. The décor was dated and overly floral, but this was irrelevant. Its strategic position at the junction of two long, open roads, and the commanding view of all their approaches, more than made up for it.

With care Bulmer hung his newly delivered dry cleaning in the wardrobe, and returned to his seat in the bay window. On his first night there, Bulmer had moved the room's single chair into the centre of the window and sat vigil until dawn, so certain had he been that the wolves of Rowcroft would sense his true intentions and hunt him down.

But no one had come.

And now, after just a few days, things had totally changed. Greg Cole had not reacted as planned, and Bulmer had failed to deliver him to Rowcroft. He had also been weak, and given in to his desire to see Fairfield far too soon. Now it was just as likely to be the police that came for him. His only chance was to build the smallest of bridges with Fairfield. But how could Bulmer explain things without saying too much?

Suddenly there was a knock on his door.

Startled, Bulmer frowned and checked out of the window again. He hadn't seen anyone approach along the path; he hadn't heard the screech of the front gate. Cautiously, he approached the locked and bolted door to his room, and peered through the spy-hole.

Astonished at what he saw, he hurriedly opened it.

Elspeth Hamilton staggered past him into the room. Like a time-lapse recording of decay, she seemed to grow increasingly dishevelled and unsteady on her feet with each step. A coating of cobwebs and dust dulled her knotted hair. What remained of her grey suit was torn and stained. Her flesh-tone stockings were now no more than a broad mesh, curled at the seams, with her grubby, bleeding feet protruding from their gaping ends. She crumpled against Bulmer's single bed, and then slid to the bare boards of the floor, her feet pushing the central rug into a crest. Then she was still. Her head lolled backwards, and she closed her eyes.

"Good lord!" exclaimed Bulmer under his breath, before shutting the door and fumbling the locks closed again. He then scurried the few paces to the fallen Hamilton and crouched over her. "Are you all right, my dear?"

At the sound of Bulmer's voice Hamilton's head wavered, scanning from side to side as if searching for the source of it. Her pallid eyes soon swung in his direction, and it was then that her hands shot upwards and gripped his head.

Bulmer winced. "I say, steady on..."

Hamilton glared at him and then finally spoke, her voice a hoarse, desperate whisper.

"Help me."

After thanking her for her hard work during the day, Paul Black helped the WPC load the container into the van and slid the side-door shut.

He walked down the narrow alleyway and back to the allotments, where the last of the SOCO team were just packing up. Ducking under the perimeter tape, Black joined DCs Des Potts and Sally Fisher, who had recently clambered down from the common's edge to join him. "Sorry about that," he said to them, a little breathless, "had to bag everything up for forensics."

"Well at least you had something to bag," remarked Potts. "The divers were down for hours and all they found was shopping trollies and rocks."

"So, it's definite, then?" Fisher asked Black. "The spear thing was made from bits of this place?"

"It's looking that way," Black replied. "But," he glanced at his watch, "as its gone five, I'm knocking off now. I wouldn't want you to feel like you've wasted the day, so I'm going to let you have the honour of accompanying this lot back to the nick, and typing up the reports for me." He gestured over at the nearby SOCO officers. "Sergeant Reed over there will fill in any blanks." As Potts and Fisher looked on in astonishment, Black picked up his jacket, slung it over his shoulder, and turned to go. "You know I'd do the same for you." He strode off up the alleyway, and back to Waterleat Drive.

After a few moments, Potts spoke up.

"This is war," he said, watching Black disappear down the side street. "He's only been here three days, who does he think he is?"

"Our superior officer, Des," said Fisher in exasperation. "So put your male pride away and think nice thoughts. If he pushes it too far,

I'm sure the DI would love nothing more than to take him down a peg or two."

"Hmmph!" snorted Potts. "Knowing our luck, Black'll probably solve the Susan Cole case single-handed and get a medal!"

Fisher lowered the corners of her mouth in mock sadness.

"Aw, never mind, Des, you're much better looking and nobody can take that away from you."

Suddenly Des Potts' brow furrowed. "Hold up," he said, staring intently down the alleyway again, "who's that with Black?"

Fisher walked over and took the same line of sight. At the far end of the alley, Black was talking to a young woman. A young woman with a bandaged face.

Kate Berridge had appeared at the end of the alleyway, blocking Black's route, and delaying his master-plan of a hot shower and a cold beer.

She was dressed for the summer, with a lemon shirt draped loosely over a white vest-top. The vest showed off her trim figure, which flowed into khaki shorts and long, brown legs. They ended in a pair of white trainers.

"Surprise?" she said, feebly, holding up a thermos flask in one hand, and the largest Tupperware container Black had ever seen in the other. "Thought you might need freshening up. Apple juice, and a few bits to eat. Sandwiches, that sort of thing. We could have a picnic, if you like?"

Black noticed that some flexibility had returned to her facial expressions, and that the bulky dressings that had covered her injuries the previous day had been swapped for fresh, smaller ones. From her smile she seemed genuinely pleased to see him, and it occurred to Black that he was starting to see what she really looked like.

"Thanks, you shouldn't have," he replied, slowly. "I hope you didn't go to too much trouble, we're all done here now. Besides which, the common's still closed to the public. No picnics."

Nothing could dent Kate Berridge's optimism. Her tone remained just as cheerful. "I totally understand," she said. "When I first came here, all I wanted to do was to get through the working day, and then hide in my flat."

"Well, it's not quite like…"

"Oh, it's okay," she assured him. "My flat has a tiny balcony with a pot plant on it. Bit of a suntrap this time of day. And being a shut-in has given me time to practice my cooking; we can abandon the picnic for something more substantial if you like?" Black looked uncertain. "Oh come on, Detective Sergeant Paul Black," she teased. "Come out of your comfort zone a little. I did. Just imagine how much bottle it took to venture out and find you, looking like this!" She peered cross-eyed at her injured nose, and then smiled in anticipation.

Black cleared his throat melodramatically. "We went over this... while you and I are involved in the same case..."

"We don't have to talk about the case."

"But... it's not just the investigation. When we make an arrest, and it goes to trial... it could be months, years... just talking socially with you now, like this, can prejudice all sorts of things."

Kate tapped the side of her bandage.

"I won't tell if you won't. And don't tell me you're not flattered."

Black sighed in resignation. "Okay, but I'll have to go back to mine first; have a shower and grab some fresh clothes..."

"No problem," beamed Kate, "that'll bring us nicely up to dinner time."

It was then that Sally Fisher appeared beside Black, with a mischievous expression on her face. "Thought you were dashing off, Sir?" she said to Black, before smiling at Kate Berridge with an expectant look.

"I am," Black told her, a little too quickly. "Um, this is Kate Berridge, the teacher that Jacob Morgan attacked last week; I'd forgotten that I'd arranged to interview her this afternoon but luckily Miss Berridge has reminded me."

Fisher nodded, and then glanced at Kate's flask.

"I see. Planning a long interview, were we?"

Kate smiled at this, but Black's sense of humour had evaporated. "I'll see you tomorrow, Constable," he told Fisher, and then escorted Kate down the street to his car.

As Fisher watched them drive away, Des Potts arrived at her side.

"Well," said Fisher, "at least he's taking an interest in the wider case. We should feel encouraged, I suppose."

Potts shook his head slowly, partly in admiration and partly in disapproval. "As long as that's all he's taking an interest in," he said.

7

To Kate's great surprise not only did Paul Black's apartment turn out to be a maisonette — he had corrected her terminology upon their arrival — but it also turned out to be in the up-market Barton Pines. Even after her short time here, Kate knew that this part of Harkham was considered to be of the more desirable ones.

She had been even more pleased, however, when Black hadn't insisted that she wait in the car. This would give her a chance to have a nose around his lodgings, while he showered and got dressed.

"I think I'm in the wrong job," Kate had quipped, as they had strolled up the short gravel drive to the entrance stairs at the side of the house.

"I was very lucky to get it," agreed Black. "The guy was dropping off his keys at the agents just as I was walking in the door."

The semi-detached property was sprawling, as were its grounds, rising to five stories including the basement and loft conversion. Black's apartments comprised the top three floors. Eventually they had arrived in a small hallway, dominated by the stairs to the maisonette's upper levels. Beyond them an archway marked the threshold of the main living area; a lounge and dining room knocked into one. Soft evening light illuminated its antique furniture, and over-stocked bookshelves, which Kate thought to be quite grand and bohemian.

Black had asked her to make herself at home, claimed that he wouldn't be five minutes, and then bounded upstairs two at a time.

Kate smiled; she could tell that he was nervous.

After sauntering into the lounge, Kate briefly considered what looked to be a very comfortable leather armchair, but then decided that sitting around would be a wasted opportunity. She stood still for a moment and listened, waiting for the tell-tale sound of the shower from upstairs. It soon arrived. Satisfied that she now had a few minutes of uninterrupted time to kill, she began to investigate her surroundings more closely.

Firstly, Kate crossed to the coffee table where Black had dumped the contents of his pockets: a mobile phone, a small wallet containing only credit cards and receipts, loose change, and car keys.

She quickly leafed through the contents of the wallet, pausing briefly to study Black's driving licence. She noted his date of birth, and although a little surprised, she nodded approvingly. Not in bad shape for his age. She had assumed he was younger. She replaced the wallet exactly where she had found it, and moved on to his mobile phone.

With calm efficiency, she displayed the contact numbers in its memory, and began to page down through them one by one.

This took her less time than expected. Apart from those of his new colleagues, there were only two other numbers: 'Train Times', and 'Home'. Christ, she thought, this man really was a loner. Frowning, she returned the phone to its previous key-locked state and placed it down on the table. Feeling slightly frustrated, she turned her attention to the back of the room.

Overlooking the dining table was a large mahogany dresser, possibly antique, on the counter of which stood a line of framed photographs.

She inspected each picture. None carried any annotation, so Kate could only guess as to the identities of their subjects. Eventually she came to a picture that clearly held pride of place. It was a group pose, containing the heads and shoulders of a dozen men. They were wearing climbing gear. Two rows of smiling faces beamed back at her, with the familiar, but obviously younger, features of Paul Black buried at the heart of the assembly. He had no goatee, and his hair was longer than the close-shaved velvet of his current style.

The image was bigger, and had a better quality frame. It also looked comparatively recent, unlike its neighbours which seemed to be from distant eras. Torn, black and white photos mingled with the faded colours of old Kodak snapshots. Kate imagined them to be scenes from Black's childhood.

Only the group photo was recent, taken within the last five years, Kate guessed, and for some reason it puzzled her. She picked it up and carried it with her to the bottom of the stairs. "Paul?" she called out experimentally. There was no answer.

She called again, this time louder, but heard only the gentle song of the shower. After placing a tentative foot on the lowest step, she slowly ascended with Black's photograph still in her hand. The stairs were wooden, stripped and varnished, adorned only by a simple burgundy carpet down the centre.

Eventually Kate arrived at the first floor landing. The L-shape of the downstairs hallway was repeated up here and she now had a choice of three doors before her. From behind the nearest one came the sounds of water and ablution. She walked to the door that was furthest away, noticing as she approached that the door wasn't closed but merely ajar. After a precautionary glance back at the bathroom, she reached out with her right leg and gently kicked it. It swung open, and thankfully her brand new trainers left no marks on its paintwork. Kate peered through to see a light, airy room with a double bed dominating its centre. Black's dirt stained clothes lay slung across its surface.

She was about to set foot in the bedroom when the noise of the shower sputtered and stopped.

Kate's mind shifted up a gear.

She had maybe two minutes before Black left the bathroom, and that was if he stayed by the shower and didn't dry off elsewhere. It would take her at least that long to search his bedroom properly.

Moreover, there was still one more door behind which to check.

With the same foot she had used to open it, she hooked the bedroom door and moved it back to its original position. Softly but quickly, she made her way to the final door, which was an only inch away from the bathroom. Now that the shower had stopped, Kate became acutely aware of every sound she made. The door in front of her looked to be a Victorian original; thick, solid and bearing a sturdy iron lock. She curled her fingers around the handle and gave it an experimental turn.

It was locked.

She winced as the mortise, worn lose from a century of service, rattled in its housing. It was the loudest noise she had ever heard. Kate closed her eyes, and waited for the inevitable.

"Hello?" the bathroom door inched open and Black's voice drifted out on a cloud of steam. Kate decided that honesty was the best policy; she gripped the side of the photo frame she was holding and quickly snapped the metal stand free of the backing plate. By the time Black's head peered out of the bathroom door and caught sight of her, she was standing there with a piece of the frame in each hand, looking suitably helpless.

"Oh, hi... I'm sorry," she said nervously, "I was trying to find you. I didn't know which door was the bathroom, and... ," she gestured with the broken photo. "I had a little accident... sorry."

Black smiled back at her, apparently as embarrassed as she was.

"Don't worry about it. I have some super-glue. I think. I haven't unpacked everything yet; it's probably in the kitchen somewhere."

Kate sidestepped this clear hint for her to return downstairs, and nodded at the locked door behind her. "This 'maisonette' of yours just keeps on going, doesn't it?"

There was a beat as Black considered her curiosity. The embarrassment briefly left his voice. "Stairs to the attic. It's a loft conversion, but I don't use it. At least not yet," he said, evenly. "It's only storage at the moment."

"I see," laughed Kate nervously. "That's where the bodies are kept, eh?"

"Something like that. Look, sorry to be a pain but I'd like to get dressed?" He nodded over at his bedroom.

Kate mouthed the word 'sorry' at him, tip-toeing past and then back down the stairs; lingering long enough to ensure that he noticed her flirtatious glance through the door.

Black watched her go, unsure of what had just happened, and reached out for his towel.

8

"So," said Jed Caplain as they climbed the narrow stairs, "we're a team of three now, are we? Thought you said we couldn't trust anyone."

Beside him, a breathless Fairfield nodded. "But if we had to, who else would you say is the least likely to be in bed with Rowcroft right now?"

"I'm not happy with it," Caplain shook his head doubtfully. "Phoning Greg Cole out of the blue like that. Dumping all this on his shoulders. It's against regs, Duncan. And not only is he a witness, but he could also be a suspect."

Mindful of the buxom lady ascending the stairs in front of them, Fairfield lowered his voice and indicated that Caplain should do the same. "If our business here doesn't go according to plan, Jed, then we'll need a Plan B."

"What, to combat Rowcroft's Plans C through Z?" countered Caplain sullenly. "All I'm saying about Cole is that he may not be reliable, let alone trustworthy. He's in shock. The man's just lost his wife and kid."

They finally reached a dimly lit landing, and the first floor of the guesthouse. "It never did me any harm," replied Fairfield.

Ken Bulmer's landlady, still fuming at the interruption to her dinner, pointed a pudgy finger at room four. Caplain reached the door first, and was about to knock on it when Fairfield restrained him. "Wait."

Caplain looked at him enquiringly.

"Second thoughts?"

"No, it's just…," Fairfield frowned and then turned to address the landlady, who was supervising proceedings with reproachful scowl. "Mrs Bayliss, thank you for showing us up; I think we can take things from here." With a parting look of disparagement, the over made-up landlady disappeared down the stairs again, puffing and mumbling as she went. Once she had gone, Fairfield turned back to Caplain.

"I think there's someone in there," said Fairfield, softly.

Caplain smiled mockingly. "Well I should hope so; otherwise we've had a wasted trip."

"I mean other than Bulmer."

"Really?" Caplain tilted his head. "Can't hear a thing through this old door. Did you hear something?"

Fairfield's jaw tensed, and he pinched his brow. "No. At least I don't think so. I'm just saying: be on your guard."

Fairfield rapped twice upon the door. They heard the clatter of disengaging chains, and shortly they were face to face with Kenneth Bulmer. He was pale, and his collar was uncharacteristically unbuttoned.

"What kept you, Old Boy?" he said.

The door closed behind them.

After locking it again Bulmer lingered at the threshold, as though guarding the exit, a point that was not lost on Fairfield. Before them the ragged figure of Elspeth Hamilton lay supine on the bed, moaning and muttering. Fairfield and Caplain stared at her incredulously, and hesitated from going nearer.

"I believe you know each other," remarked Bulmer from the door.

"Aye," Caplain said, with a tinge of regret.

Fairfield looked Hamilton up and down.

"What the hell happened to her?"

At the sound of Fairfield's voice, Hamilton's muttering stopped and she sat upright against the pillows, one hand supporting her weight and the other tentatively exploring the air around her. "Inspector? Where are you? Please come closer…" She was slurring through her smile, as if intoxicated. "I promise no concealed weapons; no clipboards or deadly files this time. I'm not going to accost you."

Fairfield's eyebrows lifted. "After our last little encounter? If it's all the same to you, I'll wait here out of arm's reach."

"She's telling the truth, Old Boy," Bulmer told him. "I've popped one or two drugs into her system but that's only delaying the inevitable. She's fading fast."

Caplain scoffed at this. "It's tempting to leave her to it, after all the stuff she's pulled over the last couple of days."

"You'd leave her to suffer and die, Sergeant?" Bulmer frowned.

"I'd think about it; she's on Rowcroft's payroll, after all."

"So am I," said Bulmer, "would you leave me to it too?"

Caplain didn't answer.

Fairfield walked away from Hamilton's bed, leaving her probing the space where he had been standing. With a sombre expression, he turned the window chair around to face the room, gathered his raincoat, and sat down. "Well, this is cosy. What have we stumbled upon here, then? Class reunion? Comparing notes, are we?" He searched for a reaction in Bulmer and Hamilton's faces, but saw none. "Two physicians with one patient in common, perhaps?"

"Duncan, I haven't seen Susan Cole for over ten years," Bulmer protested.

"I know," Fairfield told him, "we've spoken to her husband, something I've heard you weren't keen for us to do? And from what he told us, I'm not surprised she wanted no more to do with you. Strange you didn't say anything the other night, though. When you were at mine, when I told you she was missing." Fairfield looked over at Hamilton. "And you, Miss Hamilton, failed to mention that Susan Cole was also a patient of yours. You've been treating her and Jacob Morgan simultaneously."

The unsteady Elspeth Hamilton smiled.

"Confidentiality, Inspector," she argued.

Fairfield's eyes narrowed. "Really, well not within these four walls. Let's get straight to the point, shall we? A woman's life is at stake here." He looked back at Bulmer. "Ken... no more bullshit, where's Susan?"

Bulmer's reply was calm and deliberate. "I don't know."

"That's not what you told Greg Cole," said Caplain.

"That's right, Sergeant," Bulmer snapped at him. "But tell me; how many white lies do you tell your children, eh? To motivate them? Or keep them safe?"

"So Rowcroft don't have her?" cried Fairfield in frustration.

"I told you," answered Bulmer, "I don't know. They might. They might not. All I know is that the bond is especially strong between family members. All I know is what they wanted to have."

From the bed, Hamilton began to giggle childishly.

"Which was?" urged Caplain, impatient for Bulmer to continue.

Bulmer took a deep breath and leaned back against the door. "Why the full set, Old Boy, what else?" he said, unthreading his bow tie from his collar and slouching in defeat. "The full set."

Terry Digger wasn't surprised to see the same old faces as he walked into the Falcon Arms. After twelve years of breaking headlines at the Harkham Herald, he had come to know the regulars at this, the nearest hostelry to the paper, very well indeed. What had surprised him, however, was the telephone call that had led him here; and the promise of an exclusive interview with the missing teacher's husband.

The pub was long and narrow, with the public bar at the back. Digger spotted Greg Cole at once; he was sitting in the far corner, his back to the wall and staring out into the bar. Digger could also see that another man was sitting across the table from Cole, directly opposite and with his back to the room. The journalist weaved his way through the hubbub, approaching slowly in an effort to identify the second man before they saw him.

But then Terry Digger was surprised for the second time.

As Greg Cole spotted Digger, and nodded a greeting, the second man also turned in his chair. "Evening, Terry," said Philip Knight. "Twice in as many days; people will talk."

Digger hesitated for a second, taking in the situation, before offering a twisted grin of bonhomie and throwing his tattered jacket over the back of a free chair. "I should hope so," he said back to Knight, "because when people talk, I write it down and then people read it."

The man who had called the meeting stood up and offered his hand to Digger. "Greg Cole. Thank you for coming at such short notice."

"Well," said Digger magnanimously, "I was supposed to be going to my Auntie's funeral but as you asked me so nicely..." Greg was stymied by this and clearly unsure how to react, so Digger put him out of his misery. "Only joking, Mr Cole, only joking; I wouldn't have turned you down for all the chips in China. Normally I have to go looking for the scoops; it's not often they come and find me."

This seemed to satisfy Greg, and he wandered over to the bar.

Digger sat in his chair, in anticipation of his pint.

Philip Knight looked at him but said nothing. Around them the clamour of a Sunday evening in Harkham continued regardless. Eventually Digger said to Knight, "Young Andrew still on the mend, I trust?"

"Physically," Knight took a sip of his bitter. "But psychologically, who knows. Perhaps he'll take after his father in that regard."

"Fingers crossed," remarked Digger gravely. He left a respectful gap, and then leant forward. "What's all this about, anyway?" he whispered, tilting his head in the general direction of the bar, and Greg Cole.

Knight shook his head.

"Search me. I certainly have better things to do, believe me, but he told me it was about Morgan. That's all I know. He won't say anymore until we're all here."

"All? There's more to come?"

"One more, apparently."

From behind them came an austere, clipped voice. "I can't for a moment think that I am late, so you all must have been early."

They looked round and saw a middle-aged woman, grey-haired and willowy, wrapped neatly in a prim blue coat. She seemed to have arrived just in time for Greg Cole's return from the bar, and he handed her a gin and bitter lemon without being asked.

Patience Biggs, school secretary of Harkham Grammar, sat down opposite the bewildered Digger and Knight, her back straight, and laid her hands flat on the table. "Good evening, gentlemen. As you are all so prompt, I can only assume that what Mr Cole has gathered us here for is urgent. So, shall we begin?"

9

"Do you remember the years after Deborah's death?"

Bulmer's question caught Fairfield unprepared. He tried to appear unaffected, to treat it like just another witness interview, but he couldn't hide the emotion in his reply. "What the hell does that have to do with anything?" he snapped.

Caplain looked nervously from one man to the other. The tension in the room was palpable.

"Even though we hadn't spoken for all that time," explained Bulmer, "when we resumed contact I wasn't entirely honest with you."

"Thanks for the newsflash," Fairfield said bitterly. "Greg Cole told me what you did down in Cornwall, or wherever it was. He blames your treatment for his wife's depression."

Bulmer swallowed hard, and cast his eyes to the ceiling. "Treatment," he repeated, softly. "Such a reassuring word. It makes people better. After all, isn't that what a physician is supposed to do?" Then his voice hardened again. "I didn't make people better, though, Old Boy. I just made them... different."

"What the hell's that supposed to mean?"

"It was good money. I didn't realise what I was getting into until it was too late, or who I was really working for. I shouldn't even be talking about it."

"Hah!" Suddenly Elspeth Hamilton cried out in contempt, making everyone in the room jump. She swung her legs round and sat upright on the edge of the bed. "That's right," she said, "no-one ever realises until it's too late. Except the ones they hand pick of course. But I don't envy them; they probably realise more than they can cope with."

Caplain was starting to get bored of the riddles. "Look, lass, who are you talking about?" he demanded. "Rowcroft again?"

"Pelion," replied Bulmer. "That's where the real power lies. Rowcroft are just happy amateurs compared to them. There's not a butterfly flaps its wings on this Earth without Pelion's permission."

"Don't talk soft," said Caplain disdainfully. "No-one's got that much power, and especially not a bunch of chemists!"

"He's here, you know," Hamilton cut across them with simple, child-like tone. "He's settling all his accounts, and he'll be taking Rowcroft with him. He very nearly took me with him."

"For crying out loud!" roared Fairfield. "I've heard nothing since I walked in this room that'll help me find Susan Cole. None of this changes anything!"

"But that's where you're wrong, Old Boy," Bulmer said. He walked across the room, past Fairfield, and took one last look at the darkening street. He pulled the curtains closed, and then continued, "It affects everything. To say that Susan's disappearance is but the tip of the iceberg is the understatement of our age."

"So tell me!" urged Fairfield. "Give me something to work with!"

"Help you to help me?" scoffed Bulmer. "Doesn't work like that, Old Boy. Like it or not, you're already involved. I've taken complete leave of my senses saying this much."

Fairfield sighed in frustration.

"So, Cole was your patient twenty years ago. Big deal. Why maintain all the cloak and dagger now? After so long?"

"Because what started back then is still happening," stated Bulmer.

"That's not an answer."

"It'll have to do."

"Then why tell me at all?" cried Fairfield. "Apart from you airing your conscience and giving it a good scrub, how does this help me?"

Bulmer said nothing, hesitant to proceed.

"Well?" pressed Fairfield.

"Duncan," said Bulmer cautiously. "Please know… that I am truly sorry."

"Christ, Ken, I thought we'd had this conversation the other night?"

"No, not that. It's just… if I go on, if I tell you the rest… you'll probably never speak to me again."

"Now you're being ridiculous," smiled Fairfield dismissively.

"Only now?" remarked Caplain.

"I'm serious, Old Boy," Bulmer spoke across them, his voice descending into self-pity. "During those lost years I was a different man. I parted company with my ethics. I made rash allegiances, from which I can never escape."

"We all fall in with the wrong crowd from time to time," said Caplain, not quite sure why he was attempting to boost morale. "Just look who I ended up with," he added, tilting his head towards Fairfield.

Bulmer ignored him, and it took a few seconds before he spoke again.

"They made me tell her it was dead."

Fairfield and Caplain exchanged glances.

"Dead?" Fairfield repeated.

"The baby. Susan's other child."

Fairfield processed this for a moment. "So," he said carefully, "you're saying it... she gave birth after all?"

Bulmer didn't answer his question directly.

"It was taken away. I lied to her and she went back to her life, believing that Adam was her only child." Bulmer took a deep breath. "I made a cowardly choice all those years ago," he continued. "About the cancer, I mean, and what came afterwards."

Fairfield was becoming increasingly uncomfortable with this.

"Ken...," he began.

"But, as the saying goes," Bulmer persisted, talking over him, "the true test of any choice is not whether you made the right decision, but whether you'd make the same decision again. So that's what I've done. That's why I'm here. A contract of employment with Pelion is as good as selling them your soul. So if I can't ever be free of that particular burden, I can at least try to satisfy my own conscience; before my deeds catch up with me."

"What about me!" cried Hamilton pathetically. "You need to fix me first!"

"Miss Hamilton," sighed Bulmer, "that's no longer who I am."

"But you just said a Pelion contract was for life," Caplain argued.

"That's right, dear chap," smiled Bulmer thinly, "but they can't get at what's in here." He clutched his chest. "If I can end my days as Kenneth Bulmer, and true to my principals, then perhaps someone up there will smile kindly on me."

"It... won't... happen," teased Hamilton, in a sing-song voice, and much to Bulmer's annoyance. "Look at me," she mewed. "Do you think someone smiled kindly on me?"

"Well, I have to admit you've looked... cleaner," remarked Fairfield.

Hamilton's head turned slowly, and locked onto Fairfield's voice. "How long until you retire, Inspector?" she asked. Fairfield frowned at this non sequitur and didn't answer, so Hamilton hazarded a guess. "Two, three years? My point is; if you've no idea how long you've got, you relax too much in the here and now."

Fairfield gave a single, contemptuous laugh. "You make it sound like retirement and death go hand in hand," he said. "There's more to life than work, you know."

"Very philosophical. Where did you hear that?" Hamilton leant forward to address him, almost slipping onto the floor. "Imagine if it truly was the end of your life, though," she said, earnestly. "Imagine if you knew exactly when you were going to die, and your only entertainment was the fun of counting down the seconds. And then, when you reach the big day, God says, 'Actually, have another twenty four hours. On me.' And then another. And another. Until each day you find yourself waking up knowing that your death is long overdue, and that today could be the day, and that if you make just one tiny mistake, it could be? What if your work was your life? What if it was your only reason?"

"Reason for what?"

"Everything."

Fairfield laughed derisively again, and crossed his arms.

"So, what are you telling me? That you've got something terminal?"

"What if," persisted Hamilton, "what if, when you did well at your job, each and every time, you were rewarded beyond your wildest dreams, and when you failed, the punishments were just as cruel?"

Fairfield's eyes narrowed.

"You're telling me that's how it is at Rowcroft?"

Hamilton nodded.

"So, let me guess," ventured Fairfield, "you've messed up, and you've come running to Ken before they do something 'just as cruel' to you?"

"It's a bit late for that," Hamilton told him. "Sometimes, just taking those rewards back again is punishment enough." Her voice softened, and her sightless eyes began to drift. "Glaucoma," she said eventually. "It started in my last year of university. I was nearly blind by the time I graduated, but soon afterwards there was almost nothing left. Nobody would employ me. I was left to rot on an NHS waiting list. But then Rowcroft rode to my rescue," she said acerbically. "They said they needed my psychiatric skills, and that I didn't need eyes to listen, and would I mind helping them out on a special project? They were so pleased with my work, they fixed my sight. And over the years that's not all they've fixed, or improved upon. They have tremendous abilities, Inspector. And horrible power."

"And now?" Fairfield was still sceptical.

"And now," Hamilton stared down at the floor, "all my augmentations are gone. I can already feel my body sliding back to how it was, destroying itself from within... If they find me again, they'll finish me. I need help. I need protection."

At this Fairfield rose from his seat, and began to drag it closer to Hamilton. Caplain stepped forward to protest, but Fairfield glanced up at him, telling him it was okay. With a handkerchief, Bulmer mopped his brow anxiously. Fairfield turned the chair so that the back was between him and Hamilton, and then straddled it. He looked down at her dejected features and said, "If this lot are as well-connected and as powerful as you make out, what makes you think that I can protect you?"

"They only pick fights they think they can win," replied Hamilton, instantly. "They wouldn't tangle with you."

"Why?"

"Trust me. They just wouldn't."

Fairfield snorted.

"Didn't stop you attacking me yesterday, did it?"

"It stopped me today, though. I know better now."

"And you're half-blind and knackered, don't forget."

"I've been worse, and done worse."

Fairfield considered this for a moment.

"Well, then, you don't need my help, do you? You need to explain yourself before I so much as hold open a door for you. For a start, what happened in the station car park yesterday? When you got me to read that file? Before I agree to anything at all, I need to know what you did to me."

There was a pause. Hamilton slowly raised her head.

She was about to speak.

Suddenly, Bulmer barged his way between them. "That's enough!" he exclaimed. With the palm of his open hand, Bulmer pushed Hamilton's head brutally down onto the pillow. Fairfield leapt to his feet, but before either he or Caplain could protest, Bulmer had injected a syringe into Hamilton's neck.

"Ken! What the hell?!" cried Fairfield.

"Sorry Old Boy," said Bulmer, a little breathless, "didn't mean to startle you. I suddenly remembered there was a wee something in my bag of goodies that might ease this young lady's pain after all."

Fairfield scowled at him. "I was just starting to get somewhere."

"Those were questions you don't need the answers to, Duncan."

"I beg to differ."

Bulmer sighed in exasperation. "Look, let's just say that with Rowcroft and Pelion around you should always be careful what you read. The eyes are the windows to the soul, Old Boy; sometimes things can wander in and take hold without anyone noticing. Sometimes by accident, and sometimes on purpose."

"That's not an explanation," Fairfield told him.

"No," Bulmer was emphatic, "it's a warning. Instruction can be concealed in anything; junk mail, bus stops; even the labels on your clothes. Some of us are more susceptible than others, but the bottom line is if you've not written it yourself, don't trust it! And even then, don't let it out of your sight."

There was a beat as the detectives processed this.

"I've had enough of this, guv," said Caplain eventually, and he turned to Fairfield. "I'm late for my tea. Are we helping him, or arresting him?"

"Oh please do, Sergeant," Bulmer said flippantly, before Fairfield could answer. "Lock me away; God knows I deserve it. But what are you going to charge me with, hmm? There's only one way justice can be served here, and that's by my making reparations to those whose lives I've harmed."

"So help us find Susan, Ken!" pleaded Fairfield. "Stop holding back!"

"I have to, Duncan, don't you see? You have to trust me, Old Boy! Leave me to finish this one last experiment; I can't tell you any more without it costing lives!"

"And what about your life, Ken?"

Bulmer took a deep breath, and sat down on the bed. Gently, he stroked the matted hair of the now sleeping Hamilton as he spoke. "You don't understand what you're dealing with. Six years ago — after I'd finally come to my senses — I tracked Susan Cole down. Not in person, you understand. Just her address, and her phone number. I called her anonymously, giving her just enough information to convince her I was genuine... and I told her that her son was still alive."

"Smooth," Caplain observed. "Did you tell her where he was?"

"No, because I didn't know myself," said Bulmer blankly. "They never told me. I didn't even know whether he really was alive by that time. I just told her the basic facts, and that it had all been a horrendous mistake. She went insane. She screamed down the phone at me and I hung up. That was the last time I ever spoke to her."

"So far," added Fairfield.

Bulmer shook his head. "From then on she devoted every second to tracking down her son. It brought her to Harkham, and so I had to follow." Bulmer looked up at Fairfield once again, with pleading in his eyes. "You have to understand, Old Boy; I never really thought she would find him, because Pelion always cover their tracks. They've been getting away with it for years, Duncan, and they're the very best at it. They're as corrupt as sin and probably just as old. It didn't make sense that Susan could overcome their security measures so easily. I began to worry, and made some enquiries.

"A few months ago I found out that Pelion had allowed just the right amount of information to reach Susan, so as to lead her here. They wanted it to happen. And then I realised; the experiment I started for Pelion all those years ago hasn't ended. You see, Old Boy, it's still my responsibility. It's still my problem, and one that I created…"

Bulmer looked up at them, with regret darkening his eyes.

"When I created Jacob Morgan."

10

Paul Black returned from the bathroom to find his wine glass full to the brim, yet again.

As they'd driven back to Kate's small apartment, she had insisted on popping into the off-licence below her, where she was already on first name terms with the proprietor. All great meals needed the correct accompaniment, she had argued. At this point Black had declared his intention to drive home once dinner was over, and so a game of cat and mouse had ensued, with Kate attempting to share out as much wine as possible and Black trotting out every excuse in the book. His resolve had stood fast at a single glass, but then he'd made the fatal mistake of leaving the room.

He now took his seat opposite Kate, a look of mild annoyance and resignation on his face. Kate grinned at this eagerly. "Well, go on then, Mr Connoisseur," she said, her face flushed from the bottle and a half she had already consumed. "It's a fresh one. A Merlot. Tell me what you think!"

Black held the glass up to the light by its stem. The lighting in the kitchen was warm and delivered by a low hanging lamp above the dining table. He turned the glass slowly between his fingers, watching the soft light sparkle and play at its heart. "Nice colour," he said, without sounding pretentious. He replaced the glass on the table, untasted.

"Oh, go on! Just a sip!" protested Kate.

Resting his elbows on the table's edge, Black linked his fingers together and rested his head on them. His smile alone was enough to reiterate every excuse he had made in the last two hours.

Kate couldn't stand the silence, and spoke up again.

"You haven't even told me whether you liked dinner or not."

"It was frozen pizza."

"Which I lovingly prepared; and not even a courtesy belch."

"I think you've more than made up for that on your own."

"Charming. What about some dessert, then?"

"What is it?"

"Lemon Meringue."

"Home-made?"

"Frozen."

"No thanks. Not a big meringue fan."

"Would it have made a difference if it had been home-made?"

"No."

"So what desserts do you like?"

"Cherry pie and ice cream."

"Ah!" Kate's sudden cry almost made Black's eardrums pop. She slapped the table in triumph. "A personal fact! At last! And after only three days! Give me another week and I might even get your favourite movie out of you!"

"The Usual Suspects. And I should be going; thanks for dinner."

Pushing his untouched wine-glass across to her, Black stood up and reached out for his jacket, which was hanging behind the front door.

"Wait," Kate also rose from her seat, and hurried around the table to join him, wine still in hand. "I'm sorry."

"I told you this was a bad idea," there was no malice in Black's voice.

"I know. It's just that... well," began Kate, awkwardly. She sighed. "Look, cards on the table..."

Black took an exaggerated glance over her shoulder.

"I can't see any."

"Funny," she responded without missing a beat, and took his hand. "Look; you're a nice bloke, and yes, perhaps I fancy you a little bit... but... I'd just like to get to know you a bit. That's all for now. I promise."

"I'm a very private person. There wouldn't be anything for you to find out, even if we did become closer."

Kate shook her head. "I don't believe that for a moment. That photo of yours, the one that I... accidentally re-arranged this evening. You seemed to be in the thick of it there, having a whale of a time with all your mates."

"That was taken a good few years ago," said Black. "Those 'mates' were just my colleagues. We went on a team-building course."

"Listen to you," Kate scoffed. "'Just my colleagues', indeed. If you weren't close, then why have the picture on your sideboard?"

"I can see this is turning nasty," Black half-joked. "Thanks for the pizza, and enjoy the rest of the wine." Turning his back on her, Black grabbed his jacket from its hook. Kate let out a small groan of frustration, and collapsed back in her chair.

"Wait," she said, and downed her wine in one gulp. "Don't go."

After a moment of indecision, Black turned back round to face her.

"Thanks," she continued. "I know you're probably just being polite, but then you're a decent bloke, so I shouldn't be surprised. I'm not very good at this. I must be coming across like a right sad old cow, eh?"

Black resumed his seat. "You don't have to apologise," he told her, placing his folded jacket on the table top. "You've been through a lot. I should have listened to my own judgement on this one, but I didn't. So, my mistake."

Kate gestured up at her bandaged nose, and the surgical tape on her left cheek. "Couldn't resist my makeover, eh?"

"Now you're just fishing for compliments," answered Black, kindly.

"That's me all over."

Kate reached behind her and tore a paper towel from its dispenser. She dabbed at her eyes, and sniffed. "Delayed reaction, I suppose," she said. "Thursday shook me up badly, and you were a friendly face. You hear about it, don't you? Strangers bonding in times of trauma. To tell you the truth, I'm scared of what's going to happen next." She looked up and met Black's gaze. "It shakes your confidence, something like that. It really does. The same questions keep popping up in your head, all the time, like bile. Was it something I said, or didn't say, that set it all off? Did I make a mistake as a teacher? I only took the class for a few days; who the hell's going to employ me after this?"

It was now Black's turn to extend an arm across the table top, gripping Kate's left hand tightly. She frowned at him, a mixture of appreciation and puzzlement.

"You don't have to worry," said Black, encouragingly. "None of Thursday afternoon was your fault. It's on record now that Morgan's mentally unstable."

"Poor Jacob. That wasn't him, you know, it really wasn't. How's he doing? He's up at the hospital, isn't he?" asked Kate, sniffing again.

Black's tone became sombre. "Not too well, I'm afraid," he replied. "By all accounts it seems he's in the middle of some kind of breakdown. You weren't to know."

"Oh my god…," Kate held her crumpled tissue to her mouth. "I know I should be angry at him, but… I wouldn't wish that on anyone. Do they think he'll recover?"

Black nodded. "They're hopeful. He's going to a different unit in a couple of days, for some specialist help."

Suddenly, Kate's mood brightened.

"I knew it!" she said.

Confusion clouded Black's features.

"Knew what?"

"I knew I could get you talking about the case!" she giggled.

Black's embarrassment at this revelation was obvious. Kate's gentle laughter continued as she topped up her wine glass, and casually threw the empty bottle at the green plastic dustbin in the corner. The bottle ricocheted off one side and went in, more by luck than by judgement. "I'm sorry," she grinned. "That was a bit cruel but I couldn't resist it." She raised her glass in a toast. "Truce?"

Black grudgingly picked up his wine, and chinked it against hers. Keeping eye contact, he threw half the contents down his neck before she could blink.

"Do you know what?" she rested her chin on her arm, and smiled philosophically. "I reckon I'd have made a good copper."

Black smiled back, humouring her, as he sipped the rest of his wine. He chastised himself for giving out confidential details, and for not realising he'd done so until it was too late. Had he been sloppy, or had Kate just been very good?

Under the table, Black's free hand slipped Kate's spare front door key, which he had palmed from its hook when retrieving his jacket, into his trouser pocket.

11

There was a deputation waiting for them when they arrived back at the hospital. Dr Montgomery and Nurse Tomkin were already standing outside Jacob Morgan's room, and glowered at the approaching detectives like night-club bouncers.

As they drew near, Montgomery said to Fairfield, "You should not be doing this, Duncan; it's long after visiting hours and Jacob is a minor. His parents should be contacted."

"That might be a tall order, doctor," replied Fairfield, after exchanging the briefest of glances with Caplain. "And besides; I won't do anything without your blessing. This is important police business, however, so your co-operation would be most helpful."

Montgomery frowned. "And would you let me do something against your better judgement?" he argued.

"Probably," Fairfield smiled. "But then I can always arrest you afterwards."

Montgomery sighed and looked firstly at his watch, and then at Nurse Tomkin who shrugged a reluctant agreement. "Very well," said Montgomery, "I suppose he would have been disturbed shortly for his medication in any case. Five minutes, gentlemen, and no more."

While Montgomery and Tomkin monitored proceedings from the doorway, Fairfield and Caplain took up positions next to Jacob's bed, in the very chairs that Ian and Barbara Morgan had occupied only hours ago. The police guards had remained outside in the corridor, ever vigilant.

Jacob was lying curled up on the bed, facing them, with his covers thrown back. His aversion to bright lights persisted, and so only a single lamp illuminated him from his nightstand.

From his overcoat pocket Fairfield produced a clear plastic bag. It contained a pile of photocopied sheets and a large, brown envelope. Caplain produced a Dictaphone and softly recorded an introduction, stating where they were and who was present, before leaving it on the bedside cabinet, record button still running.

Fairfield appraised the figure on the bed in front of him, and tried to look past it to find the young man he had once known. The boy's limbs were emaciated and limp within his baggy pyjamas. Jacob's already gaunt features were hollow and grey, his skin drawn tight and his half-open eyelids shot with prominent veins. His insipid gaze, at one time shining with intelligence, slowly floated down to meet Fairfield's like a compass finding north. There was no sign of the energetic, bright teenager of a week ago. He was a completely different person.

Different.

The word echoed around Fairfield's head.

I didn't make them better again; I made them different.

Had Jacob's soul been doomed from the very start?

Fairfield opened with a smile, even though Jacob didn't respond. "Hello, Jacob, it's Duncan Fairfield. Do you remember DS Caplain, from the other day?" He gestured to Caplain, but Jacob's eyes did not register it.

"We need to ask you some difficult questions," continued Fairfield, "but we'd like you to really concentrate on your answers, and try not to get too upset." Fairfield slid the wad of paper and the envelope from the plastic bag. He held up the photocopies first. "You remember these, Jacob? They're from the diary we found in your room. You write about your teacher a lot in it, Mrs Cole." Fairfield fanned out the pages of the facsimile dairy, leafed through to a particular entry, and angled it towards the dim light source. "January 3rd," he read aloud, in a grand voice, "Six days in the wilderness have ended. I return to my sanctuary, I return to my saviour." Then his voice descended to normal again as he added: "Dad made ham, egg and chips for tea, and was sad."

Fairfield looked up from the pages and addressed Jacob directly. "January 3rd, Jacob; the day you all went back to school. Now, I know that sometimes, once all the mince pies and presents are gone, it can be a bit of a downer being stuck at home, but... sanctuary and saviour? What did you mean by that, Jacob?"

Silently, Nurse Tomkin walked into Fairfield's eye-line and held up two fingers, indicating how many minutes they had left. Fairfield smiled humourlessly back at her.

"Mum," said Jacob eventually.

Intrigued by this response, Caplain reached over to Jacob's nightstand and picked up the picture of the Morgan family that he found there. He handed it to Fairfield. Jacob seemed to be staring past them now, and so Fairfield held the picture up directly in his line of sight. He rested his finger against the image of Barbara Morgan. "Who is this, Jacob?"

After a few seconds, Jacob responded.

"Mum."

"For the tape," said Fairfield, "Jacob has correctly identified a photograph of Barbara Morgan. And who's this?"

After handing the family portrait back to Caplain, Fairfield rummaged inside the brown envelope he had brought with him and held up another photo, this time a little lower. Jacob's eyes readjusted to look at it properly. For a moment he seemed transfixed by it, before eventually answering:

"Mum."

Fairfield placed the photograph of Susan Cole, a still image culled from the Heathrow footage, back in the envelope and again described his actions aloud for the tape. He and Caplain both shifted uneasily in their chairs.

Fairfield produced one, final picture.

"And this one? Who is this, Jacob?"

They looked on anxiously as Jacob's breathing quickened and his heavy eyelids drew back. His head pressed back hard against the pillow, as if he was trying to shy away. When he eventually answered, his voice was low and thin.

"Devil."

As if choreographed, the eyebrows of both detectives rose in surprise. The photograph was a grainy enlargement of the Heathrow Biker, posing for the CCTV at the airport.

"Thank you, Jacob," Fairfield put the envelope and the photocopies back into their bag. "We just need to ask one more question." He could hear Nurse Tomkin's teeth grinding with impatience. "Do you remember what happened last Saturday morning? Do you remember why you broke Mr Sullivan's greenhouse?"

"Devil!" screamed Jacob, and suddenly he leapt from his bed, his features naked with terror. He kicked out at the nightstand and it flew across the room, spewing its contents across the floor. The lamp rolled along on its side, casting nightmarish shadows across the walls and ceiling as Jacob thrashed about in panic. With a petrifying cry, his thin, powerful arms grabbed the metal base of his bed and flipped it up into the ceiling, tearing cables and fixtures from the wall behind it. Fairfield and Caplain stumbled backwards to avoid the inevitable impact, and Nurse Tomkin's hand flew out to the silent alarm. The bed only just missed the detectives as it crashed down again onto its side, but the impact knocked Fairfield's evidence bag flying from his hands, the photocopied pages of Jacob's diary fluttering across the room like feathers in a pillow fight. Now standing in the small space between the upturned bed and the outer wall, Jacob wrapped his arms around his torso, as if freezing cold, hugging himself as he whirled round and around, muttering constantly, his eyes wide with anxiety.

"Devil. Devil. Devil. Devil. Devil…"

Shakily Nurse Tomkin began to prepare a syringe for Jacob's medication. Montgomery stepped forward to intervene, but Fairfield restrained him with an outstretched arm.

"Devil. Devil. Devil," Jacob continued to wander this way and that, his hold on his own body growing tighter, as if protecting himself, his restless murmuring increasing in pace. He seemed oblivious to the people in the room with him. "Devil. Devil. Stop the Devil. Stop the Devil. Stopthedevil. Stopthedevil. Stopthedevilstopthedevil…"

The police officers from outside the room, alerted by the commotion, barged in through the door but Caplain held them back, partly so that events would not escalate, and partly so they could block a potential escape route.

Gradually Fairfield eased himself closer to the agitated boy.

Nurse Tomkin gesticulated at Fairfield urgently, syringe in hand. Jacob somehow sensed her intentions and backed away closer to the wall, without looking up at them. Fairfield scowled at Tomkin and then glanced round quickly at the five people behind him. "Please. Stay where you are," he said. "Trust me."

"Trust you?!" hissed Tomkin under her breath. "You're the one that set him off!"

A moment of doubt flickered through Fairfield's mind, but then he recalled the stand-off at Harkham Grammar three days ago; of how Jacob had been unreachable in his fortress at the top of the stairs, and of how he seemed to suddenly mellow at Fairfield's behest. Did the boy have a genuine respect for Fairfield, or had it been a fluke?

"Stopthedevilstopthedevilstopthedevil…"

Fairfield inched closer, and spoke softly.

"Jacob, it's okay. The devil is gone. We're here to protect you."

Jacob ignored him, and so Fairfield took a step nearer. Nurse Tomkin took a step forward with him. He turned and glared at her. "What did I just say?!"

"If we all just grab hold of him, I can sedate him!" The frustration was clear in Tomkin's voice.

"No! I said stop!"

Suddenly Jacob's whispering babble ceased.

His eyes screwed up in misery, his adrenaline-locked jaw relaxed, and he began to cry, silently, pathetically. Still holding himself, Jacob fell back against the wall and slid slowly down to a crouch. Fairfield stepped forward to him, and crouched down to the same level. He reached out with a comforting arm.

"Careful, Duncan," Caplain warned.

"It's okay," Fairfield quietly reassured them both. He placed a hand on each of Jacob's shoulders, and Jacob's sodden features rose to meet his gaze. The boy's eyes were red-raw and bloodshot, his pale cheeks flushed. Then, as though reacting to the turn of a hidden valve, he sagged forward into Fairfield's waiting arms. Fairfield held him tightly.

Caplain and the hospital staff looked on in disbelief as Jacob Morgan sobbed uncontrollably into Fairfield's shoulder.

Keeping his sights firmly on the tragic scene in front of him, Caplain slowly walked over to the one surviving nightstand, where the Dictaphone was still loyally recording. He picked it up and spoke into the microphone. "Um," he cleared his throat with a light cough, "for the benefit of the tape, Mr Morgan has reacted to the photograph of Samuel Wilcox with some… distress." He clicked the stop button.

"She's gone," moaned Jacob, his voice stifled. "She's really gone…"

Fairfield gently ruffled the boy's hair.

"I know, lad. I know," he said. "And I'm sorry. So very sorry. If there's anyone who would love to see your mother alive and well again, it's me."

Fairfield became aware of a slight movement to his right, and looked down to see Nurse Tomkin quietly removing the syringe from Jacob's exposed arm, plunger depressed. It reminded Fairfield of Hamilton's attack on him yesterday, and then of Hamilton's own treatment at the hands of Ken Bulmer only a short while ago. He tightened his hold on Jacob.

"It's me," Fairfield repeated, under his breath.

Slowly the tension began to dispel from the room.

"Keep crying, lad," advised Caplain. "That coat could do with a wash."

Jacob had not spoken again that evening.

They were now sitting outside the hospital, in Caplain's car, smoking endless cigarettes and trying to process the events of the last few hours.

One thing they had agreed on was not to tell the Morgans about Jacob's outburst. Not just yet. Now, more than ever, Fairfield was certain that Jacob's move to Gardner Heritage was justified. To be on the safe side he'd ordered the police guard on Jacob's room, and his convoy on Tuesday, doubled.

"It's decision time, Jed," said Fairfield at last.

Caplain frowned.

"About what part exactly? I keep hoping I'm going to wake up. Do you think, right, if I were to click me heels together..."

"We're going to have to bring the DCI in on Hamilton," Fairfield continued. "That part we can't do on our own. But how much do we tell everyone else at the nick about today? For example we can't break cover on Ken; not yet."

"We don't need to," stated Caplain. "We've enough evidence behind our version of events, without having to bring Bulmer into it."

"But can we trust Hamilton not to say anything?" replied Fairfield, dejectedly. "Especially if Hill doesn't go for it, and leaves her out in the cold? She's unpredictable. If it comes down to it, besides Wilcox's statement and the forensics, what do we really have?"

Caplain turned in his seat, better to face his colleague.

"Look," he said, earnestly. "I know you're a bit shaken by Jacob and all that, but what other explanation do the facts fit?" As he spoke, he began counting off each event on his fingers. "It starts with Jacob's dodgy adoption. Ten years later, his adopted parents tell him the truth, and he takes it badly; ends up in juvenile court and starts an unhealthy obsession with meeting his real parents.

"Enter Susan Cole, searching for her long lost son. She ends up teaching Jacob's class. They latch on to each other. Jacob's obsession sends him even further round the twist. Wilcox, Cole's lover, gets over-protective. Tries to stop her going away, Jacob tries to protect her. Some sort of scuffle at Cole's house, perhaps? Susan realises it's gone too far, flees the scene, leaves Jacob behind, but tells him she'll be back for him. Wilcox's window fitter mate goes in to her house to clean up the evidence."

Fairfield shook his head. "So where is she, then? She must have seen herself on the TV, and in the papers. Why dump the suitcase? And what about her blood on the broken glass? We know Jacob was at the scene, too, we've got his prints. If Jacob went up against Wilcox, then why not just smack him straight down? Why take the time to construct a weapon? You saw the raw power in the lad just now, same as I did. The strength of him. Harvey says Wilcox doesn't have a mark on him."

Caplain sighed, and shook his head.

"And then there's Rowcroft Medical and Pelion," Fairfield continued, grimly. "We should think bigger, look further; smoke the real culprits out into the open."

A look of disdain coloured Caplain's face.

"All the same, I think we should just go ahead and stick to what we actually know for sure. Don't forget we've got to make this all hold up in court at some point, if we get a result."

"Oh, we'll get a result," Fairfield's eyes were cold, and his expression tense. "One way or the other, I'm going to see that justice is done." Fairfield clamped his half-smoked roll-up between his teeth, and produced his mobile phone. With both hands he then worked the keyboard slowly and deliberately, before finally pressing the send button.

Having silently observed all this, Caplain smiled with curiosity and said, "I didn't think you liked making calls on that, let alone sending text messages?"

"Normally I don't. Folks' spelling's bad enough without removing all the vowels. But we need to get under Rowcroft's skin, Jed. It's down to us. And legal channels, for now, don't seem to be open."

Caplain frowned, still not cottoning on.

"So what were that, then?" he asked, nodding at Fairfield's phone.

Fairfield gave him a self-satisfied smile.

"Plan B."

In the public bar of the Falcon Arms, Greg Cole's mobile lit up and announced an incoming message. Picking up his phone, he read it to himself while the faces of Philip Knight, Patience Biggs, and Terry Digger looked on expectantly.

After only a couple of seconds, Cole closed the message and said: "We're on."

Terry Digger bared his nicotine-stained teeth in an eager grin, drained the dregs of his pint, and rose from his chair. "I'll see you all on the other side, then," he said. "I've got a deadline to catch."

Monday
22nd July, 2002

1

Paul Black was wearing yesterday's clothes.

His eyes drifted open and caught sight of the time. Immediately a surge of panic jump-started his system and he was looking for his shoes. Three seconds later, he remembered that he wasn't at home.

Black's bare foot kicked over a wine glass on the floor. Images of empty green bottles drifted across his conscience, and he silently gave thanks that he no longer suffered from hangovers like the ones he'd had as a teenager. Right now his priority was getting home, changed, and then straight to work. He wanted to get there early, just in case Fisher and Potts had let him down with the paperwork last night. Suddenly he remembered Kate, and that she was conspicuous by her absence.

His left hand shot down to his trouser pocket, and with relief he found that the purloined key was still there. It would come in handy if his suspicions were true. Part of him hoped that they weren't.

From down the hallway came the throaty gurgle of a flushing toilet.

So, she was still home. Not much time. He had to find his shoes. As he dashed across the hallway, and towards the kitchen's string door, his big toe found them by accident. Black suppressed the pain and made no sound. Grabbing his scattered belongings, he resumed his hurried, hopping course for the kitchen.

"I'm going to give you the benefit of the doubt, and assume you're eager to make me breakfast."

Kate's voice skewered Black where he stood, and he turned to smile at her, a shoe in each hand. She was standing outside the open door of the bathroom, fresh plasters and bandages on her face, and clad in a towelling bathrobe that was too large for her. Black pictured her having stolen it from a swanky hotel. Kate pulled the bathroom light cord sharply, punctuating her appearance with a metaphorical exclamation mark.

"Morning," Black said, nervously.

Kate's bare feet padded down the carpet towards him. "Is that what it is?" she raised a hand to her temple. "From the lack of moisture inside my head, and the raging pain, I'd assumed we'd gone to Hell and the light of the flames was what woke me."

Black humoured her and shook his head.

"Hell wouldn't have carpet."

Yawning, Kate brushed past him and through the string doors, which clattered like hailstones. Black followed her into the kitchen. The table still bore the scars of the previous evening's excesses; empty wine bottles and stained red rings now sullied the noble oak.

"Tea?" she asked, hand reaching for the kettle.

"Actually, Kate..."

She turned slowly.

"You're not serious," she half-frowned, half-smiled.

Black was already reaching for his jacket. "I'm really sorry, but I've got to freshen up before work, and..."

"Oh, I see," Kate began to walk slowly towards him, hands on her hips. Behind her, the kettle rumbled to boiling point. "That old chestnut, eh? You invite your way into my flat..."

"Actually, it was your..."

"And then you drink all my wine, make me cook for you..."

"You... we got the wine especially; we went halves..."

"Get me drunk, manoeuvre yourself into my bed..."

"Yes, but... that's not strictly true, is it?"

"Just wait until I contact your superiors about this."

By now Kate was confronting her startled house-guest toe to toe. She kept a straight face for at least five seconds, until Black's worried expression made her relent. She slapped his chest with the flapping cuff of her robe.

"You big Muppet!" she laughed. "Blimey, if you're this easy to wind up it's no wonder you get stick at work!"

Black became indignant.

"Who says I get stick?"

"You talk in your sleep," she teased. "And who exactly is this 'Mr Tickles'?" Concern soon returned to Black's face, but again Kate's love of dumb animals prevailed and she relented. "Don't worry, Paul," she said, with a tinge of disappointment. "You were a perfect gentleman, despite all that wine. How was the sofa, anyway?"

The tension fell from Black's shoulders and he smiled, finally relieved to understand something she said. "Oh, the sofa was fine," he said convivially. "Slept like a baby. By the way, I've folded up the duvet and stuff and put them on the armchair."

"Lovely, thanks," she kept eye contact, returning the smile. "I told you that you're a gentleman."

Black took his jacket from behind the front door, this time without comment. He slung the jacket over his arm, and turned to say goodbye. "Sorry," he said. "But I really must dash."

"I know," she sighed, and rested her arm on his. "Best of luck with the case. I really mean that. If anyone can find Susan, it'll be you. And maybe then, once this has all died down, we can pick up where we left off? Let me give you my number..." She wandered towards the string door.

"I already took it from your file," Black called after her. "I called you yesterday, remember?"

Kate turned and stood framed in the doorway, holding the beads apart either side of her. "Well, you'd better give me yours, then." Black obediently began patting his pockets, searching for a business card. Kate rolled her eyes to the heavens. "It's all right, Paul," she interjected patiently, "you called me yesterday, remember? And the station's in the Yellow Pages. And, if all else fails, it's three nines isn't it?"

Black gave her a weak smile as he opened the door to freedom.

"Well... bye, then," he said.

The door had slammed shut again before Kate could respond. She closed her eyes and muttered: "Give me strength." She then produced a phone from the voluminous pocket of her bathrobe, and dialled.

At the summit of Harkham Police Station sat the office of DCI Laurence Hill.

Converted from the original attic, the office nestled between the roof beams and evoked the mood of a country cottage. Hill's desk was beneath the only window. With the morning sun at his back, he was now sitting at this desk and ploughing through the weekly chore that was the overtime budgets. The peace and quiet of coming in early to clear one's in-tray was an acceptable trade-off, he believed, for the five flights of stairs that he had to tackle every day.

A knock at the door broke Hill's concentration. Almost straight away it swung open and DI Fairfield peered round it, before Hill could admit him. "Room service, sir?" Fairfield quipped.

Hill humoured this with a lacklustre smile and gestured at Fairfield's badly pressed shirt. "I would have expected, as head waiter, a little more starch in your collar."

"My apologies; the Silver Service staff are serving breakfast in the cells."

Hill indicated that Fairfield should enter fully and he did so, closing the door behind him. Without being asked, he sat in one of the chairs next to Hill's desk. Hill replaced the cap on his fountain pen and rested it gently on his desk, before leaning casually back in his own chair.

"On the subject of cells," began Hill, "I understand that you made an arrest last night? The Morgan boy's psychiatrist, the one that assaulted you?"

"That's right," Fairfield answered with satisfaction, "she's downstairs as we speak."

Hill nodded, and then slid a piece of paper from his in-tray. He dangled it gingerly. "And this morning, Duncan, I find a request on my desk for her admission into a Witness Protection Programme?" Hill's tone was incredulous, as though asked to spend the day as a pantomime dame.

"Correct," Fairfield cleared his throat, and then took his gamble. "New facts have come to light that lead me to believe Miss Hamilton can assist us in our enquiries, but will be persecuted if she does so."

"Really? Persecution by whom?"

Fairfield's jaw tightened and he said, "Rowcroft Medical, sir."

"I see," said Hill, without reaction. He then picked up his briefcase and pulled out a folded newspaper. He laid it out flat on the desk, upside down, so that Fairfield could read the front page. "So this is merely a coincidence, I take it?"

Fairfield glanced casually down at the headline, it read:

ROWCROFT RIOT: TEENAGE DRUGS BLUNDER

Fairfield raised an eyebrow in mock surprise. "Well I can't say I'm particularly shocked, sir; I've suspected a link between teenagers and drugs for a while now…"

"Don't waste my time!" snapped Hill. "This has your mark all over it! I told you to be patient. I told you I would negotiate a warrant, so that we could do this in a circumspect manner."

"We don't have time for that, sir."

"You have as much time as I damn well say you do!" Hill exclaimed. "And what's more you have an open-and-shut case downstairs with Samuel Wilcox. All this flummery with Rowcroft is pointless. I don't know how you got the Herald to go along with it, Fairfield, but if Rowcroft track this back to you it puts the department in a very awkward position indeed. I might have trouble defending you."

"I expect you would."

"I beg your pardon?"

"What I meant," rallied Fairfield, "is that such a thing would indeed be indefensible, sir. But if Rowcroft make the connection then that's also a good thing; they can consider it a shot across the bows; let them know we're watching them, and make them tell us where Susan Cole is."

Hill threw up his hands in exasperation.

"This isn't a war, Duncan!"

Fairfield was quiet for a moment. Eventually he leaned forward to rest on his knees, and looked Hill straight in the eye. "Okay, so I'll tell you what I know," he said. "But hear me out, Laurence. Hear me out, and then tell me if you think it's a war or not."

2

For the first time in years, Ken Bulmer was facing the day with resolve rather than regret.

Confession was good for the soul, they said; well perhaps that all depended on to whom one confessed. Keeping secrets from Duncan Fairfield all these years had weighed heavy on Bulmer's heart. He still knew that his actions would have consequences, and for none more so than himself; but now he was ready to accept them. He secretly hoped that the end would come soon, while his resolve still held.

Before any more regret crept in.

Regret for not telling Fairfield the rest, for not telling him the whole truth. But that could never happen. Regret that he had lost Deborah to make it this far, and that he would probably never know whether his final experiment had succeeded. Regret that without Susan Cole his list of intended confessors would never be complete.

There was still, however, one more person that he had to see.

Bulmer ambled down the pale corridors of Harkham General, nodding and smiling a warm greeting to those that he passed. Had he been wearing his hat he would have tipped it, but it would have clashed with the long, white doctor's coat he was wearing to aid his bluff. The coat had not been difficult to come by; he had amassed several of his own across the years. Remembering to keep his wrinkled, ruddy features smiling Bulmer passed the reception desk of the Psychiatric Ward, waved jovially to the girls behind it, and entered the corridor to Jacob Morgan's room.

He briefly interrupted his stride when he saw the police officers standing guard outside the door, but pressed on regardless. The officers were talking to another man, someone Bulmer didn't think he knew, who was wearing a linen suit. Bulmer had not expected such a heavy guard; but then he considered the level of concern Fairfield had for the boy, and decided that it pleased him. He walked on.

As he got nearer, he saw the man in the linen suit give something to one of the officers. It was a yellow envelope. Mr Linen Suit thanked the officer, and walked away. He caught Bulmer's eye as they passed each other, and smiled politely in greeting. His ageless features radiated honesty. Bulmer was about to smile back, to maintain his happy-go-lucky cover, but something about this man in particular set his nerves on edge, as though a signal had waned in an out again as the man had passed him. Bulmer frowned, involuntarily, managing only a blank nod of his head. Once Linen Suit had walked more than five or six feet away, the strange effect subsided.

Bulmer came to the end of the corridor and drew level with the officers outside Jacob's door. Glancing back at Mr Linen Suit one last time, he addressed the officer who had taken the envelope.

"I say, who was that fellow?" Bulmer asked, conversationally.

"Unscheduled visitor," replied the Constable, in a tone that implied total disinterest. "Had to turn him away. Not on our list, see."

"Quite," beamed Bulmer. He nodded at the yellow envelope in the Constable's hand. "Get Well Soon card?"

"Couldn't say, Sir."

"Did he leave a name?"

The Constable raised his brow incredulously at Bulmer.

"Right, you can't say," Bulmer spoke for him. "Quite understand." He stepped forward to grip the door handle, but found his way blocked.

"I'm sorry, Sir," said another Constable. "We can't admit anyone who's not on the list."

Bulmer chuckled in camaraderie. "Now, come along, lads," he said, hooking a thumb under the lapel of his doctor's coat and pushing out his forged identity badge. "I'm late for an important consult," he continued persuasively, "and on top of that I'm the boy's... well, I'm a friend of the family, you see. What do you say, Old Chap?"

He smiled hopefully at the Constables.

"I'm sorry, Sir," intoned the first Constable. "But you're not on the list."

Bulmer began to lose his earlier buoyancy. "I'm also a friend of Detective Inspector Fairfield," he said, with an air of insinuation. "I can always make a quick call; get him to order you to let me in..."

"It was Fairfield that wrote the list in the first place, sir. You're not on it."

"How do you know I'm not on it? Let me see a copy."

"We don't have a copy with us, sir."

"Oh, so you're doing this from memory, are you?" scoffed Bulmer.

"It's a very short list," commented Constable Two.

Bulmer sighed. Had he mistaken a thawing of relations with Fairfield for trust?

Suddenly, he felt the phone in his pocket vibrate. After noting the number he silenced it impatiently, without answering the call. "Right then," admonished Bulmer, waving a finger at the officers like a deadly weapon, "I've got to go. I'll be back, and I'll be on your blessed list before you can say 'jobsworth'. Mark my words."

Bulmer turned to go.

"Don't you have a bleeper, then?" asked Constable Envelope, out of the blue and in a manner approaching suspicion.

After taking a moment to let the whiplash of this non sequitur subside, Bulmer turned back and smiled benevolently at them both. "I'm a pathologist, gentlemen," he said, mordantly. "Nothing much ever bleeps in the vicinity of my patients. And in the rare event that I am needed for a clinical emergency, time is rarely of the essence."

DCI Hill pulled the door of Elspeth Hamilton's cell shut with a clash of steel, and glared suspiciously at Fairfield.

"It's bizarre, isn't it," prompted Fairfield. "In just twenty-four hours she's gone from vixen to vegetable. The FME reckons he's never seen anything like it; says he's not ruling out hospitalisation. That would be fun, wouldn't it? She can have the room next to Morgan's. Shame about all her designer gear, although I think she's carrying off the paper suit nicely."

They began to walk back to the booking area.

Hill's eyes narrowed. "I must admit, Inspector, to feeling a tad disappointed. She didn't try and re-write my brain, despite my having a dry-cleaning ticket on me," he said, sarcastically, "and I was expecting her to have a ray gun, at least."

Fairfield ignored the barb in his superior's comment. "As I explained, Sir, any augmentations she may once have had were removed by Rowcroft, as a punishment. I don't think we've anything untoward to fear from her now."

"Assuming she's telling the truth, and assuming you've not gone completely insane, of course," Hill came back at him disdainfully. "I'm finding it quite hard to take all this seriously, Duncan. You're asking me to believe that these people can just switch prodigious abilities on and off like Christmas lights, and without the rest of the scientific community getting a whiff of it?"

"Yes, Sir. Pelion probably sabotaged their sense of smell, sir."

"Are you trying to get yourself deliberately pensioned off?" frustration entered Hill's voice.

"Her story seems to tie together certain facts…"

"But why on earth believe her in the first place?" Hill took a deep breath and pushed his spectacles back up onto his promontory nose. When he spoke again his voice was more rational. "Now listen.

We've already discussed this. Every Sunday for the last four-and-a-half years I have played golf with Alexander Miller; he works very closely with Rowcroft as their solicitor and advisor on corporate law. I'm sure he would have mentioned it by now if anything illicit or immoral were going on there."

They had reached the booking area door, and Fairfield pressed the buzzer to alert the Duty Sergeant to their presence. "Don't suppose he's got a thousand yard swing and never misses a putt, does he sir?" Fairfield said in mock conspiracy. "If so then we might be on to something."

Hill sighed deeply.

"If you must know, his round is usually inferior to my own."

"Ah," Fairfield nodded knowingly, "that's probably deliberate. It's the old sycophancy ploy. He's more than likely keeping tabs on you and hoping you'll let slip some top-secret police titbits."

"Don't be ridiculous," protested Hill. "If I was being secretly surveilled I'd be the first to know about it, wouldn't I!" He briskly brought the conversation back onto topic. "Remind me again why we're requesting that Witness Protection look after this Hamilton woman?"

Fairfield adopted Hill's own terminology. "In case some other nutty scientists try and zap her brain again, sir," he replied. "Or worse, just plain kill her."

"And we've assessed the risks of this actually happening, have we?"

The door to the Booking Area buzzed and then swung open. Fairfield and Hill walked through it. "I'm sufficiently convinced of the risk," continued Fairfield earnestly. "Des Potts has our Witness Protection contact standing by; all we need is your go-ahead."

"And all I need is evidence, Duncan."

"If I could actually get in to Rowcroft with a search warrant I could get all the bloody evidence you want!"

"Ah, yes, well that's the good news," said Hill. "Mr Miller called me earlier today; we should have a warrant in our hands first thing tomorrow."

"Tomorrow?" exclaimed Fairfield. "That's too late, sir. If they don't know about Hamilton's defection yet, they soon will. We need to get in there now, especially if they have Susan Cole."

Hill held up a defensive hand. "I'm sorry, Duncan, but tomorrow morning is the best you're going to get. In the meantime, may I suggest you hurry up and do something with Samuel Wilcox? That's if you have time, of course, after preparing your full-scale assault on

Rowcroft." Walking away, Hill then turned back and added dryly, "Of course, you may want to set your phasers to stun."

Fairfield watched him go and silently fumed. Another day's delay would give Rowcroft all the time they needed to squirrel away any evidence; and they might still change their minds at the last minute if they caught wind that Hamilton was in custody. Digger's newspaper article would divert their attention for the moment, but not for long.

He needed more time, and he needed more information

Fairfield walked into a nearby office, pulled the door shut, and dialled Ken Bulmer's number.

3

Ken Bulmer chose to trust the calling number this time, and cautiously hit the answer button. The other passengers in the hospital bus stop queue glared at the interruption, and so Bulmer walked a few paces out of earshot. When he heard Duncan Fairfield's voice, he relaxed slightly.

"Glad it's you, Old Boy," Bulmer said, checking the car park in each direction as he spoke. "Rowcroft have been trying to call me all morning; I get the impression they're not best pleased about something."

"Well I'm hoping it's not because of our girl," Fairfield told him, "from what she says they think she's out of the picture. I think it's more likely to be about a certain public outcry; did you see this morning's Herald?"

"I did, but I couldn't believe what I was seeing," Bulmer glanced over at the bus queue; one man was sitting on the bench reading the newspaper. A further copy was protruding from the back of a young mother's buggy. "They normally keep such a tight control on the media. They fear the power in the message because they're so happy to wield it themselves."

"Perhaps they didn't have time to stop it."

"Well I pity the poor blighter who put their neck on the line to write the article," remarked Bulmer gravely, "they'll be lucky to have a neck left before the day's out."

There was a moment of pregnant silence.

"Listen Ken," Fairfield eventually resumed, "I need more. Can we meet?"

"Any news on Susan?" was Bulmer's instant response.

"Not since last night."

"Then I can't tell you any more, Old Boy. I need her. I'm sorry, truly I am, but the clock is ticking and there are still things I must do."

"Don't do this, Ken," cautioned Fairfield, "don't tie my hands. I need to act and I need to act soon."

Bulmer took a deep breath, and considered his encounter with the constables. "Then I need you to do something for me first. Jacob. You need to let me in to see him."

"That depends. Meet me and we'll talk about it."

The growl of a diesel engine distracted Bulmer momentarily, and he turned to see that the bus was pulling into the lay-by. The man on the bench had closed his newspaper, and the queue was shuffling forward. "Very well," agreed Bulmer reluctantly. "I'm heading into town now. But I'm warning you, Duncan; information comes with a price. Has it not occurred to you that maybe I'm trying to protect you from what else might be out there? You need to collect your wounded as soon as possible, and then leave the battlefield."

"Let me worry about that," said Fairfield.

Bulmer hesitated, rubbing his eyes in frustration. Shielding Fairfield from the truth was becoming unbearably difficult. "You're a manipulative old sod sometimes, Duncan Fairfield," he said, without emotion, "and too curious by far. It'll be the death of you."

"Maybe that's why I'm a copper. Shall we say St Andrew's, in forty minutes?"

Fairfield hung up.

Bulmer joined the trudge of the bus queue and filed on board. Preoccupied with Fairfield's demands, he waved his senior citizen's pass at the driver without speaking and sat on a side bench halfway down the cabin. He placed his battered leather medicine bag, swollen by his doctor disguise, on one of the spare seats next to him.

The bus grumbled into life and pulled away.

A moment later, as they were leaving the hospital grounds, Bulmer heard a voice say to him, "Shall we try this again?"

A man lowered himself into the remaining spare seat, a man in a linen suit. Immediately Bulmer recognised him from outside Jacob's room; as the man he had seen giving a greetings card to the police officer. The same, curious sensation of unease began to return.

Eric White nestled into the cramped space and then turned to smile at Bulmer, their noses inches away from each other. "It was most rude of me to ignore you back there, Kenneth," said White, extending his right hand from a crooked elbow. "Please forgive me."

Bulmer took the proffered hand and shook it. A sudden familiarity floated up from the depths of his memory. "Do I know you, young man?"

"It's possible. We used to work together. I certainly know you, however, by reputation at least. And we have a mutual acquaintance, as I understand."

Bulmer's familiarity passed into recognition, and then into confusion; surely the man before him would be too young? "We do?" he frowned.

White nodded. "Yes indeed," he replied eagerly. "Miss Vanessa Daniels. She and I are business partners."

Bulmer's blood ran cold. White's broad smile wasn't fooling him for a second. It had to be the same man. God knows how, after all this time, but it had to be. "So," said Bulmer, flatly, "the head boy is taking over the class at last, is he?"

White waved a dismissive hand.

"I dislike such terms. We're all one team," he said. "We all work for Pelion in the end." He picked idly at a thread on his trouser leg. "Which brings me to why I'm here; a spot of damage limitation." White looked up and held Bulmer's gaze. "At present I have only one function in life, Doctor Bulmer; to represent my Employer's interests to the best of my abilities. Just like you had only the one function. One task to perform. It wasn't hard. Technicians just need to administer the drugs, follow their instructions, and stay in the background. That's the way it works." White wagged a recriminatory finger in the Doctor's face. Bulmer's eyes were wide and he swallowed hard in discomfort. "But no," continued White. "You set up experiments of your own, and had a sordid fling with one of your patients, didn't you? So here we are today, in a right old mess. And what doesn't help is your recent... laxity with confidential facts? We need to work on tightening those loose lips of yours, my friend."

"I'm human," replied Bulmer, coldly, "which is more than you and your kind will ever be. Unlike you, I have a conscience."

"True, however your memory seems to be failing at the expense of it. It wasn't that long ago that you were more than happy to do business with us; at the time you snapped our offer off at the wrist, if I remember rightly."

"Well you wouldn't remember rightly," countered Bulmer, trying for a reaction from White, "because you'd have been at school. Unless, of course, Pelion have pressed your pause button. Risky business, lad. Genetic augmentations are treacherous. Take it from an ex-technician."

"An ex-technician with a limited talent," replied White smoothly. "I'm superior to you in ways you've never even heard of, so mind your tongue."

"Is that so? And here's me thinking we were all one team. What's next on your wish-list of skills, I wonder?" Bulmer glanced pointedly at White's crumpled jacket. "Ironing lessons?"

"People often underestimate me, Kenneth," White said. "They don't do it twice."

Bulmer snorted derisively. "You don't understand, do you, dear chap? I don't care any longer. I've made my peace, cleaned my slate. I'm not afraid of you or your bloody Company."

White gave an appreciative nod

"Fair enough," he said. "I respect that. Of course, when I mentioned damage limitation earlier, I should have been more specific. My job is to limit the damage done to us, The Company. The damage done to you, on the other hand, well... the world's our oyster, really, isn't it?"

White lifted his left hand, and extended the first three fingers.

Bulmer doubled over in pain, clutching his stomach with both arms, his face turning red and his eyes bulging. The bus seat lurched back against its fixings. The other passengers did not react to this, and were seemingly content to gaze out of the window instead.

White stood, and took a position directly in front of Bulmer. The older man let out another excruciating groan, and slid onto his knees. He swayed for a moment, as if engaged in a bizarre prayer, before the momentum of the bus rolled him over onto his side. He lay still where he fell, his breathing irregular and shallow. White crouched down so that his mouth was just level with Bulmer's ear.

"Should I loosen that silly bow tie of yours?" asked White, conversationally. "Is that what I should do? I'm sorry, but First Aid's a bit of a mystery to me, and unfortunately nobody else on this bus can perceive us, or will ever remember you and I being here."

White extended a fourth finger.

Bulmer's groans became a childlike shriek. He tensed into an even tighter ball. White moved his face closer still.

"Do you know what you're feeling, old man?" he whispered. "Twenty years of delayed suffering. The opening of the floodgates. You see, it turns out that genetic augmentations can be treacherous. We've kept those tumours safe and sound for you, Kenneth; you can have them back whenever you're ready.

"Wait a minute, though! I forgot! You're at peace, aren't you; you're ready to die. In light of our deal this presents us with something of a dilemma, and I for one always prefer to honour a deal. Nature has to have a balance."

Bulmer's face twisted as a fresh wave of pain shot through his system. Tears were streaming down his cheeks.

"So, I guess we'll just have to pass your ailments on to everyone you ever cared about," continued White, casually, as if deciding when to do his shopping. "Nothing else for it. Tell you what, I'll even torture and kill that bastard child of yours, how about that? End your experiments for good. And don't think I can't get to him. Even now he's got a nice Get Well Soon card from his Uncle Eric, while your so-called friends won't even let you near him."

"Leave him," gasped Bulmer. "Leave... him alone. He's suffered... he's suffered..."

"Enough?" White completed Bulmer's sentence. "Oh, he's suffered all right, but enough? Debatable."

"Take me instead," Bulmer could hardly talk between the spasms of pain.

"Too easy. If you're not bothered if you die or not, it's no fun."

A bell sounded on the bus.

White looked round to see that an elderly woman had pressed the 'Next Stop' button and was manoeuvring herself towards the doors. He curled his extended fingers back into a fist. Immediately the burning ceased in Bulmer's gut, and the pain subsided.

Gasping with relief, Bulmer stretched himself out and turned onto his left side, leaving a patch of sweat behind him on the dusty floor. As the bus began to crawl down through its gears, Eric White spoke one last message into Bulmer's ear.

"I think this is where you get off," White said, before slamming Bulmer's medicine bag down next to the old man's head. "Your onward journey is straightforward. Stop working against us. Honour our previous arrangement. Or they will all suffer. And, if we ever have to speak on this again, Doctor Bulmer, I hope you understand me when I say it will be for the final time."

The bus pulled into its next stop, the doors hissed open, but neither the passenger nor the driver moved. It was as if they were awaiting permission. The seated passengers remained docile and silent.

White stared down at Bulmer expectantly.

With a look of shame and contrition on his face, Bulmer hoisted himself to his feet, dusted down his tweeds, and collected his bag. Staggering, he lumbered to the front of the bus, at times knocking into the oblivious passengers, before finally stepping down into the street and collapsing dejectedly against the wall there.

White nodded in satisfaction, and returned to his seat.

The elderly woman thanked the driver, and then disembarked.

As the bus continued on its journey, White quickly waved at the receding Ken Bulmer. It was after this that he spotted a copy of the Harkham Herald protruding from a nearby baby-buggy. Intrigued, White plucked the newspaper from its elastic bonds, to no protest from the owner, and began reading. After a few moments, he laughed out loud.

"Utter rubbish," he remarked disappointedly. "Why do they never ask someone who was there?"

4

Caplain caught up with Fairfield on his way to the station car park. They spoke as they hurried down the corridor.

"Duncan," he muttered surreptitiously, "we have a problem."

"That's an understatement," replied Fairfield. "What's up?"

"Our hand's being forced with Wilcox."

Fairfield rolled his eyes. "Don't tell me, the DCI's been on at you for a result. He was pressuring me this morning, too."

"Not the DCI," said Caplain ominously. "A line up."

Fairfield slowed and frowned at him. "What bloody line-up?"

"It's the public appeal. Two witnesses have come forward this morning, saying they saw a man resembling Wilcox's picture near Susan Cole's house on Saturday. Blackie's already over in the north wing, sorting some volunteers into an in identity parade."

"And he's found five other blokes as big as Wilcox?"

Caplain nodded. "Fair play to him. Blackie's a soft sod, but I reckon he'll turn out all right, you know."

Fairfield shook his head and resumed his brisk pace.

"Let's just take each day as it comes, shall we? Doesn't sound like anything you and DS Black can't handle, just be careful. It might even work in our favour. If you secure an ID then we can spin it out for at least another day with the paperwork. But for Christ's sake don't make any decisions on charging Wilcox until I get back."

Pushing open the double doors, they emerged into sunlight just in time to see two cars arriving in the car park. They recognised the first as being that of Sally Fisher; the second was unknown to them, a dark green Saab. Caplain opened his cigarettes and passed one to Fairfield.

"I'll try and delay the inevitable as much as I can," Caplain warned him. "But Hill's keen to wrap this up today."

"Hopefully we will, one way or another. Just keep your powder dry for a few more hours, that's all I ask." Fairfield patted his pockets for a moment, and then drew out his lighter. "I'm just popping out for one last stab at our friend in the bow tie."

"Not literally, I hope?"

Fairfield nodded across the courtyard, to where a battered blue Vauxhall was lurking. "Plus my car's finally back. I want to make sure those herberts down at Larry's have fixed my brakes properly, so, if anyone asks, that's where I've gone. I'll be back in a couple of hours."

"That's optimistic."

"It won't take long," declared Fairfield grimly. "I'm going to get to the bottom of this; to hell with Ken Bulmer's professional ethics."

Caplain smiled wryly. "Says the man who covertly libelled a multi-million pound company in the local newspaper. What about your professional ethics?"

Fairfield lit his cigarette.

"Until I see justice served, Jeremy, I don't have any."

For lunchtime at the Falcon Arms, trade was unusually quiet.

Greg Cole glanced casually across the public bar at its latest arrival, a man with a briefcase. Despite having had several available to him, the man had sat at the table adjacent to Greg's, in violation of the unwritten law of personal space.

Immediately Greg was suspicious.

The man was in a dark brown suit and wore a pin across his shirt collar; a practice Greg hadn't seen for at least a decade. He appeared to be in his fifties, and had shoulder-length grey hair. Efficient and organised, the newcomer had arranged a variety of items on the table before him like a surgeon's instruments; a newspaper, a fountain pen, a phone, and a tall glass of what appeared to be lemonade. Without acknowledging anyone else around him, the man settled back and started his crossword.

Greg parked his suspicions, but lowered his voice all the same. "Digger's late," he said to Philip Knight and Patience Biggs, who were sitting opposite him, "I'm beginning to think he's only in it for his by-lines."

Knight shook his head. "He stood up for us the other day, and for Andrew," he argued. "His heart's in the right place and he's got the common touch. I think he aspires to be a Fleet Street crusader."

"Even so," offered Miss Biggs, "I think we should be wary. Last night's article was quite strong. I'd thought he'd at least edit it down..."

"It was all anonymous," Knight reminded her.

"So you say. But really, 'Sources behind the scenes at Harkham Grammar' indeed? Mr Brooks will know that was me in an instant! And it's Sports Day tomorrow!"

"We did the right thing," insisted Greg. "None of it was made-up; we just told it like it is. And if it embarrasses them into helping the police find Susan, well, so much the better."

Miss Biggs' mouth curled with distaste. "Yes, but.... did Digger really have to make it so... sensational?"

"That's what sells papers, love," said the voice of Terry Digger. He was now standing next to their table. "Writing the words is the easy bit," he added, "it's getting folk to read them that brings the money in." He took a seat, between Miss Biggs and Greg. "Sorry I'm late; I was talking about the follow-up piece with the editor and lost track of time," he turned to Miss Biggs and said, "Everyone's got a fatal flaw, darling, and do you know what yours is? You worry too much about what the rest of the world thinks of you."

"Oh really?" responded Miss Biggs sourly. "And what's yours?"

Digger beamed smugly.

"That's very kind of you, Patience, I'll have a pint of best please." His joke was not met with good humour.

"For god's sake," admonished Greg, "let's just get on with it shall we?"

"Couldn't agree more," said the man at the next table, suddenly.

The four conspirators fell silent and stared over at their neighbour, who looked up from his crossword to greet them with a dull smile. "Thirteen down," he proceeded to read aloud, "'Scapegoats try arms misguidedly'; seven letters. Any ideas?"

His request was met with blank stares.

With a much warmer smile, the man put down his crossword and shuffled along the leather bench. "No? Oh well, that can wait I suppose. Alexander Miller," he informed them, before opening his briefcase and taking out a thick, beige folder. "I'm a lawyer, I'm afraid, but please don't hold it against me. I'm glad everyone's here; it saves me tracking you all down."

Miller leaned over and began handing out the contents of the folder. "This is yours, Mr Cole," he handed a pile of stapled white cartridge paper to Greg, and then the same to Knight and Biggs in turn, addressing them formally with their surnames as he did so. They each accepted the documents in mute bewilderment.

Eventually Greg said, "What the hell is this?"

"Just a little something for your signatures," replied Miller casually. "I would heartily recommend that you read them first, however." He chuckled. "Wouldn't want to sign your lives away, now, would you?"

Terry Digger, the only person to whom Miller had not served papers, leapt up from his seat like a startled animal. "Right, well, I'll be off then; you lot obviously have a lot to discuss... you won't want me hanging round like yesterday's dinner."

"On the contrary, Mr Digger," Miller intercepted him with an outstretched hand, "I need your undivided attention more than anyone's. You're going to deliver a message for me."

During this exchange, Philip Knight had been busily leafing through his document. "So, this a retraction, then?" he asked Miller.

"Not quite," Miller told him, "more of a declaration of intent for the future." He fixed his gaze on Greg Cole. "My Clients are willing to let your little rant in today's paper pass uncontested, but by signing this document you undertake to cease and desist from any further libellous activities concerning Rowcroft Medical."

Cole, undaunted, stared straight back at him.

"It's only libel if it's not true."

"That's one view," remarked Miller graciously, "another being, of course, that it's only murder if one meant to do it. Whatever the legal angle, the victim in question remains just as dead; and believe me, Mr Cole, there's no legal angle you could come up with that I'm not already intimately familiar with."

"Well you've got me there," Cole admitted sarcastically, "your making threats in front of witnesses is a really cunning move."

"No threat implied," smiled Miller.

"No threat required," added Knight from across the table, his eyes still scanning the small print, "with these Terms and Conditions. They've got us whether we sign it or not."

"Indeed," Miller confirmed, "I'm glad you brought up the issue of witnesses, Mr Cole, because Mr Digger here has just witnessed you all reading the document. You will see that, under clause three, the correctly signed document forms a cease and desist order. If it is read but remains unsigned, however, it still constitutes an official warning. Whatever the outcome, you shall all receive your own copies once they've been counter-signed by a Rowcroft official. That way there's no confusion."

Digger snorted derisively. "Yeah, but I've not signed anything! You think I'm just going to roll over and be your witness?" He waved a cautionary finger at his compatriots. "I don't trust this bloke as far as I could throw him, and none of you should either; he's just trying to intimidate us. Tear it all up! Sign nothing! If they really thought they were blameless in all this they'd have already thrown the book at us!"

Miss Biggs and Philip Knight looked across at Greg for guidance. Greg longed to name-drop, to warn Miller off by mentioning Fairfield's involvement, but he wasn't sure whether his co-conspirators would also run a mile. For his anti-Rowcroft band to do its job, and distract them while Fairfield found Susan, he had to remain resolute.

After a few moments consideration, he spoke to Alexander Miller again.

"Mr Miller," Greg said, with a stony expression. "You might well have read the newspaper article, but you don't seem to have understood it. You've come here to threaten us with your contracts, but I don't think you appreciate that the damage is already done; the trauma already inflicted. Miss Biggs here saw first hand the outcome of Rowcroft's infamous ethics, and Philip's son paid the price for it. As for myself, my entire family has been torn apart and I'm only able to sit with you here today by the miracle of prescription drugs. They might even be Rowcroft products, who knows? And do you know the worst thing? The worst thing is that it's only now that Rowcroft have sat up and taken notice. If we hadn't made a noise, if we hadn't stood up for ourselves, you'd have ruined my family's life and not even been aware you'd done it. And that, Mr Miller, is why you and your Rowcroft Official can take your documents and file them down the nearest u-bend, pre-digested or otherwise; I'll leave that to you."

Empowered by Cole's speech, Knight and Biggs looked smugly back at Miller and awaited his response. Terry Digger, on the other hand, glanced nervously at Miller from the corner of his eye, and awaited a hail of bullets.

But Miller seemed unperturbed by what he'd heard.

"I admire your conviction, Mr Cole," he said eventually, "and I appreciate that, in your particular case, you're conveying that you've got nothing to lose and so I should back off. But I'm obliged to point out that I did indeed read and understand your article, and what it taught me was this: that you have absolutely no concept of with whom you are fucking." A self-righteous smile punctuated this statement, and then Miller continued. "For an article that was supposed to be a damning exposé, my dear friends, it didn't even scratch the surface. But trust me; if you do not sign and comply with these documents, you will receive first hand a full and unexpurgated exclusive on just how unethical my Clients can be. The only downside will be that none of you, or your families, will live long enough to read it. I take it you are familiar with the phrase 'publish and be damned'?"

The table fell silent as Miller's words registered.

After a beat, it was Digger who spoke first.

"Now," he said, "just so we're clear; that was a threat, right?"

Miller rounded on him. "Just so we're clear, Mr Digger, you do not have the luxury of complacency either. Your editor and I are old acquaintances, and we will shortly be coming to an understanding. Your paper, if needs be, can print exactly what we want it to, and you yourself will have witnessed whatever I say you've witnessed. We would prefer, however, to let nature take its course, and leave people to make up their own minds."

Digger swallowed hard. "As long as they come to the same conclusions?" he ventured.

Miller smiled and patted Digger convivially on the shoulder.

"I think," he said, "that we are now on the same page."

"You're forgetting something," piped up Knight, "there are already thousands of copies of the article in circulation. We can't do anything about that."

"And you," countered Miller, "are forgetting where your allegiances lie. Have you forgotten who sponsored your accountancy firm, and helped you get established, Mr Knight? Do the right thing today and, as a reward for your endeavours over the years, my Clients may even take in interest in your son's recuperation."

Knight cast his eyes downwards. The unsigned document stared back at him.

"Don't, Phil," muttered Greg, sensing the other's intention.

Miller turned to face Miss Biggs.

"And you, my dear," he said, "don't really want to be back on the job-market shelf at your time of life, do you? With no husband to support you? I would bear in mind, if I were you, who calls the tunes to which Headmaster Brooks yearns to dance. Your board of governors is comprised of a majority who are, shall we say, sympathetic to Rowcroft's pivotal role in the community."

Patience Biggs sighed and stared up at the nicotine-streaked ceiling.

Miller said nothing further, choosing instead to sit back and resume the study of his crossword. Although superficially engrossed, it was clear that he was merely awaiting the inevitable.

It did not take long to arrive.

Miss Biggs was the first to sign. She threw the biro back into her handbag as though it were scalding her, and walked away without a word. Greg Cole watched her go with dismay. Then he heard Philip Knight saying:

"I'm sorry, Greg," Knight produced a pen from the inside pocket of his suit jacket. "It was great. We had our say. But now I've got to think about Andrew."

Greg didn't hide his frustration at this. "You mean your son that's about to be cured by the same people that maimed him in the first place?" he snapped.

"Sorry," repeated Knight. He scribbled a signature on Miller's document and pushed it over to the lawyer in a heap, before picking up his half-empty pint and busying himself with staring into it.

Miller slipped the signed papers into his briefcase. "Thank you," he said perfunctorily, and looked expectantly at Greg.

Suddenly, Greg got to his feet. He loomed over the seated Miller.

Digger's muscles immediately tensed, in case he needed to flee. He and Knight looked on in apprehension as Greg reached out his hand.

Miller stared up at him impassively.

Greg's fingers plucked Miller's pen and newspaper from his grasp. He wrote something in the crossword grid with the fountain pen, drained the last of his own drink, and then tossed everything down onto the table together. "That's all you're getting from me," he said coldly, before striding out of the pub.

Silence filled the space that Greg left behind.

Digger and Knight exchanged a nervous glance.

Eventually Miller retrieved his folded newspaper from where it lay, next to Greg Cole's unsigned document. After reading the new addition to the crossword, conspicuous in its alternative script, Miller looked up and smiled.

It read; 'MARTYRS'

Thirteen down was now complete.

5

As Fairfield slowly climbed the stairs to St. Andrew's church, he wondered if he would find Ken Bulmer already occupying a confessional booth.

At the top of the tarnished steps he paused briefly to catch his breath. St. Andrews was like many town-centre churches; built apart from secular land originally but, over the decades, encroached upon until it had become just another building in a long line. Fairfield pushed open one side of the heavy oak doors and entered, grateful for the cool interior and a break from the arid July air.

Inside the church was high and open. The Victorian designers had eschewed pillars and vaulting in preference of carved iron struts and wooden panelling, modestly painted in beige and green. The seating was on two levels, with a balcony of tiered benches above the ground-level pews. Natural light was in short supply due to the conurbation outside, but a single stained-glass window remained unaffected at the far end. Through it, the summer sun was casting a kaleidoscope of colour.

Fairfield took a seat in the pews, near to the entrance but far enough to the side to not be immediately noticed by newcomers. He stretched an arm out across the back of his seat and waited. After recent events, the church was an oasis of calm.

He looked at his watch.

Bulmer was overdue. Growing impatient, he began rummaging around for his mobile phone. Just as his fingers found it, however, there was a creak from behind him, and slow footsteps echoed on the tiled floor. Fairfield turned in his seat, ready to lambaste the doctor for his late arrival.

However, it was not Bulmer.

Fairfield's eyes fell upon an entirely different figure.

Paul Black waited patiently for the last of the line-up volunteers to leave the room.

As each filed past, he politely thanked them and directed them to the administration offices to be paid. Once the final volunteer was out of the door, Black pulled it shut and breathed a sigh of relief. He and Caplain were now alone in the line-up room, which was a storage area with height guides painted on the back wall. Further down the corridor, Wilcox and his lawyer awaited them under guard.

Black looked at Caplain, Caplain looked at Black.

"Well," said Black, eventually. "I don't think you can get more definite than that." His statement was enthusiastic, and uttered with finality.

"Aye," nodded Caplain, but in a manner more reserved than that of his colleague. Black noticed this reticence and frowned.

"You're not convinced? By a double-whammy ID parade?"

"I know," Caplain sighed. "It's perfect. Open and shut. All wrapped up."

"And?"

"And that's what I don't like about it. Every time we have any doubts about Wilcox — any doubts at all — up pops another bit of damning evidence."

Black smiled incredulously.

"I think you'll find that's a common symptom among the guilty. He wasn't even very careful to cover his tracks."

"What about the ticket he got on the way to Brighton?"

"That could have been anybody," Black argued.

Caplain scowled at the empty wall where the line-up had just stood. "No," he said eventually. "I'm going to wait until Fairfield gets back. Run it past him."

"He'll say the same as me."

Caplain's expression grew colder.

"We wait, Blackie."

Black shook his head in disbelief.

"You need to remember our chat in the car, Jed; this is just the sort of thing I'm talking about. Look at us: we rank the same, but the difference between us is I'm still willing to take risks to get ahead. I've still got my ambition."

"We wait," repeated Caplain.

"No," said Black, seemingly coming to a decision. He began walking over to the door. "I'm going to call Fairfield. And if he's not answering I shall get Hill to authorise a charge."

At the same second as Black's fingers grasped the handle, he suddenly found his way blocked by Caplain's outstretched arm; it slammed into the door with a crash like storm clouds, and made Black flinch.

Caplain looked him straight in the eye, and said:

"We... wait."

It was impossible to tell how old the man was, especially with the sun behind him.

Then the newcomer removed his broad-brimmed Fedora.

As the church door drifted shut, Fairfield's eyes readjusted and saw more detail in the elderly gentleman's features. The texture of his skin, combined with the posture of his limbs and shoulders, suggested a man of extremely advanced years, but the neatly trimmed beard and crest of shoulder-length white hair framed a face that shone with vigour and curiosity. Unblemished eyes burned under a solid brow.

He was of slim build and dressed in a tailored, double-breasted suit. It was a deep mahogany colour to match the hat, which he now held loosely by its brim in his left hand. Fairfield could also see something else in this hand, behind the hat; a plain black cane. Not a walking stick, but a cane. Ridiculously, images of Hercules Poirot, strutting along the promenade at Monte Carlo with his own ubiquitous cane, danced across Fairfield's thoughts.

The Elderly Gentleman paused just beyond the doors, showing no sign of having noticed Fairfield. He seemed to be absorbing the ambience of the church. Eventually he smiled a craggy smile and walked slowly forwards, down the central aisle, with the echoing footfalls of his leather shoes syncopated by the tap of his cane. He moved not with the hobbling gait of the infirm but rather the slow, elegant stride of nobility taking the air.

Fairfield's gaze followed him.

Step. Step. Tap. Step. Step. Tap.

Finally, the old man drew level with Fairfield's pew.

And stopped.

His wizened face turned towards Fairfield. His teeth were clearly not his own any more, but were immaculately finished like everything else.

"Is anyone sitting here?" The consonants were defined and cultured, and rich in tone, although Fairfield wasn't sure how much of that was due to the acoustics. The occasional rasp in the breath was the only thing that betrayed the man's physical age.

Fairfield realised his own throat was dry, and had to swallow hard before replying. "Er... no..."

"Would you mind?"

"Be my guest," answered Fairfield, instinctively moving further up a pew that could have comfortably accommodated thirty people. The Elderly Gentleman smiled again in gratitude, sat a respectful distance away from Fairfield, and leant his cane against the pew in front of them. He crossed his legs, and then crossed his hands over his knees.

Silence returned to the church.

The two men sat there for a while without speaking, during which time Fairfield looked at his watch a dozen times. The Elderly Gentleman simply sat in contemplation, nodding to himself occasionally, the same half-smile of satisfaction on his uneven lips. So when he eventually spoke again, Fairfield almost jumped out of his skin.

"They say he moves in mysterious ways, Inspector."

Fairfield hesitated, but soon found himself saying, "I presume you mean the Man Upstairs?"

The Elderly Gentleman continued to stare straight ahead; to the altar at the far end of the church and the rainbow that was dancing across it. "I suppose I do, yes. Interestingly enough, that was the very question I was just considering."

Fairfield studied the old man's features.

"Have we met before?" he enquired tentatively.

"No," said The Elderly Gentleman airily, and then he sniffed.

Fairfield frowned.

"It's just that you called me 'Inspector'..."

"Oh!" The Elderly Gentleman's crossed hands flapped in embarrassment. "I'm sorry, how rude of me. Of course, you've probably been promoted by now."

Fairfield couldn't believe what he was hearing.

"Well, actually, no; I probably won't go any further, either; I'm retiring in just under three years, you see..."

"Three years is a long time," said The Elderly Gentleman, with a sagely nod.

Despite not being sure why he was having this conversation, Fairfield laughed it off anyway. "I doubt even twenty years would be long enough for me. I've been stuck at DI for twelve years now, and the villains haven't exactly been dropping at my feet..."

For the first time, The Elderly Gentleman's eyes turned in Fairfield's direction. The whimsical smile evaporated. "You should have faith in yourself," he advised.

Another snort of derision from Fairfield.

"That's academic if nobody else has faith in me."

"Are you a religious man, Inspector?"

"Look around you; this isn't exactly the library."

At this the Elderly Gentleman looked amused, as though by the endearing misbehaviour of a child. "One should never confuse Faith with Religion," he said.

"Really?" Fairfield could not have sounded less interested.

"Indeed," continued The Elderly Gentleman. "Religion is literal, and is imposed on the individual by others. Faith is abstract, and can arrive in the heart unbidden. If strong enough, it can feed the soul when all other nourishment has passed away into dust."

Fairfield had heard enough. He moved forward onto the edge of his seat, as if to stand. "Look, thanks for the chat but I'm supposed to be meeting someone. I'll go and wait outside if it's all the same to you; give you and your theologies some quality time together."

"Once the soul is alone then follows madness," The Elderly Gentleman stated, continuing his train of thought and seemingly ignoring Fairfield's attempt to leave. "Such a fate has befallen the boy. The object of his Faith has become the object of his Religion. Any force for good it may once have had has been corrupted."

"The boy?" Fairfield repeated suspiciously. "And who would that be?"

"Those that are empowered by their Faith control their own journey," continued The Elderly Gentleman, undaunted. "But those that depend on Religion are like passengers in a speeding car. They trust in God to steer them on their way, but will never take the wheel themselves. And if the car should leave the road, then they are the first to place blame at God's door."

"And what about those that depend on neither?" queried Fairfield.

"They are lost," replied The Elderly Gentleman, with sadness touching his voice. "But perhaps fortunate to have never known what they have lost." He turned away again to look at the window.

Fairfield redoubled his efforts to depart.

"Nice talking to you," he said, "but I'm off. Police business."

Abruptly, and before Fairfield could move, The Elderly Gentleman gathered his cane and hat and rose from the pew. Once more Fairfield noticed the man's smoothness of movement; he had to be at least thirty years older than him, if not more. "Please, forgive my curiosity," the Gentleman said as he straightened his jacket. "I came only out of curiosity. Perhaps that was selfish of me. It's been quite a while, you see."

Fairfield politely shrugged his shoulders. "I'm sorry," he said softly. "I don't know what you're talking about."

The Elderly Gentleman gave a wry smile.

"You don't need to. You only need to understand."

"Understand what?"

The Elderly Gentleman spread his arms wide and looked around him, deliberately mocking Fairfield's earlier gesture of sarcasm. "This church is only a century old, and already it is irrelevant. Modern religions have replaced it: money, politics, and science. The names of Religion change. And with each evolution it erodes the foundations of simple, human Faith." He raised his cane and slammed it back down on Fairfield's pew, point first. Fairfield flinched. "People have stopped trusting God," the old man whispered, the echo of his cane's impact still fluttering around the high ceilings, "and started playing God." He turned to leave. The slow tapping of his cane filled the church.

"Wait!" Fairfield called after him. "Why do you talk like you know me?"

The Elderly Gentleman replied to him without looking back, and without breaking his stride. "Why do you talk like you don't? You should leave now, Duncan; your friend will not be coming." He opened the door, and passed into daylight.

Fairfield leapt to his feet and began weaving his way hurriedly out of the pews. "Wait! Who are you?" He stumbled into the aisle, the soles of his shoes skidding on the tiles, and sprinted up to the door.

He flung it open.

By rights, the Elderly Gentleman should still have been in sight, but there was no sign of him. Even Fairfield, a sprightly fifty-six years of age, would have taken at least five seconds to run down the steps, even at full speed. He jogged down to his parked car as quickly as he could, looking frantically up and down the street, but the Elderly Gentleman had vanished as suddenly and as mysteriously as he had first appeared.

Panic gripped Fairfield as his parting words came back to him.

Your friend will not be coming.

Quickly he grabbed his mobile, but then remembered that he'd switched it off before entering the church. He held the power button down with his thumb and waited, muttering impatiently. Sluggishly the screen came to life. Fairfield cursed his inexperience with such things as his fingers fumbled through the unfamiliar menus. But then his mind caught up with him, and his eyes actually read the words on the screen.

3 Missed Calls.

He manipulated the keys until the wretched device displayed the call details. All of them had occurred within a five-minute period, and the most recent was just fifteen minutes old. Each had come from Ken Bulmer's mobile. Finally, Fairfield noticed the a closed envelope in the top left corner of the screen. A text message, time-stamped a mere six minutes ago. He opened the message; it was just two words long.

ERIC WHITE.

Fairfield knew instinctively that it was a warning.

He struggled to recall the name, and then it struck him. The man in the red Jaguar. The man who had visited Tom Sullivan just before the old timer's change of heart. Now Bulmer had changed his mind, and not shown up to an appointment made less than an hour ago. Fairfield's skin went cold as he recalled Hamilton's tales of configurations, and the power Rowcroft had to bend a person's will.

It was as if the Elderly Gentleman had kept Fairfield talking just long enough to take Bulmer out of the game.

Fairfield's eyes wandered upwards, and to the two cameras above the entrance of St. Andrew's church.

He wouldn't get far.

6

Harvey Gossett hung up the telephone and crossed over to Sally Fisher's desk, a puzzled look on his face. "That was Fairfield," he told her. "He sounded like he was about to have a heart attack; thought it was a dodgy phone call for a moment."

"What did he need?" asked Sally, not looking up from her screen.

"Camera footage for Laurel Road. Outside the church."

"That's the other side of town," reasoned Sally. "Cole couldn't have made it that far without being seen, surely?"

"No, not from Saturday," Gossett explained, "from fifteen minutes ago. And he wanted uniforms sent round to a B&B in Weir Road; don't ask me what that's all about." He waited for Fisher to comment, but now she was preoccupied with her computer.

Fisher leant in closer to her screen. "Harvey... I need your geek powers. What's up with this e-mail?"

Gossett walked round and looked over her shoulder. The message that she was reading had strange blocks and lines at the beginning and end. "Oh, don't worry about that," he said, after giving it an official once-over, "it's the encoding. Some of it's been tagged with the wrong font along the way; Wingdings from China probably. It's a classic junk mail symptom."

Fisher frowned. "Yeah, but this isn't junk mail. It's from Nu-Glaze. All their previous ones have been fine."

"See if the attachments are okay," prompted Gossett.

One by one, Fisher double-clicked the attached documents and brought all seven images up on the screen. "Looks like what I asked for," she reported. "Scans of job sheets."

Gossett patted the back of Fisher's chair convivially.

"There you go then; no harm done."

The documents seemed to hold Fisher's gaze for a moment. Eventually she clicked 'Print'.

In the line-up room, the tension was escalating.

"Charge him!" protested Black.

"With what?" cried Caplain. "We still don't know there's been a crime here."

"Attempted murder, for starters."

"No evidence to support that."

"What about Cole's blood?" said Black earnestly.

"Not in enough quantity."

"Okay then, how about a broken alibi; video footage; clean-up operation by an accomplice; placed at the scene; and he was having it away with her! What more do you want, Jed?"

"Well, Susan Cole herself would be nice."

Black smiled warily, as though humouring him. "Come off it," he said, "you can't really believe that's going to happen? None of us are saying it, but we're all thinking it, Jed; if she was still alive then why hasn't she gotten in touch?"

"Alive or dead, she's the only one can tell us the whole story."

"Wilcox will tell us!" Black exclaimed. "We just need to lean on him! We've only got him for another five hours and he walks!"

"Without a crime, what else can we do?" argued Caplain. "We can always pull him in later, as and when evidence presents itself."

"Or, we can grab him now and upgrade the charge when her body turns up!" Black turned Caplain's argument back on him. "Look, the DCI said he wanted a result today."

"Well he can't have one."

"Fairfield must have thought there was a case to answer, otherwise he wouldn't have asked for one."

A sharp knock at the door interrupted their dialogue, and they fell silent. Sally Fisher peered in, and looked over at Caplain. "Sarge, there's an impatient lawyer and a large man in handcuffs next door, that have been waiting for the last quarter of an hour with nothing to do; shall we tell them what's going on, or shall we start serving the hors d'oeuvres?"

Caplain's shoulders sagged, and the tension left him. "Thanks Sally. Sorry for the delay, we're just having a bit of a debate."

Black was more blunt.

"Sally," he said urgently, "what's your take on Wilcox?"

Caplain rolled his eyes. Fisher came all the way into the room, and pushed the door to. "Well," she reflected calmly, "if you asked me, which you just have, I'd say he was in it up to his neck. Which is quite a way up."

"Thank you!" said Black triumphantly.

"But," Fisher added quickly, "whether we can do anything about it is another matter," She handed over a thin bundle of paperwork. "Maybe these will help; documents from Nu-Glaze. Not only was Neville Baker in charge of the job at Cole's house last Tuesday, but their records also show that he took the original order as well; over the phone, with no preliminary viewing of the site."

Caplain frowned. "Just like that?" he asked rhetorically. "You don't just ring them up and say 'five windows, please, in white', surely?"

"Well that's just it," a trace of a smile appeared on Sally's face. "The job sheet says the order was placed last month; the nineteenth, supposedly the day Cole won her money, but Harvey cross-referenced Cole's phone records and the call never happened. In fact, the only call from Cole's landline was last Saturday morning, at ten thirty-three."

"So," said Caplain, putting the pieces together, "if Baker was there to answer the call and take the order, then he couldn't have been halfway to Brighton with Wilcox..."

"Which means somebody is lying, and they've tampered with the records to do it," concluded Fisher.

"I told you!" exclaimed Black eagerly.

"And what did I tell you?" parried Caplain sternly. "Here we are again, arguing the toss over Wilcox's guilt, and 'abracadabra'; the perfect evidence falls into our laps."

"Steady on, Sarge," Fisher interjected, in mock offence, "that's three days' legwork behind that result."

"Exactly," said Black, waving a finger at Sally in thanks. "They tried to cover it up but we found them out, plain and simple. Wilcox made the call to Baker from the scene, using Cole's phone. They probably got two other mates to get themselves pulled over in Sussex, and just say they were Wilcox and Baker. Admit it, Jed, we've got him."

Caplain held up a warning hand. "But that doesn't tally with everyone else's story," he stated, albeit with doubt in his voice. "Robert Brooks told us about the fitters coming in, so he must have known prior to that weekend, and old Mrs Shepperton next door was downright expecting them; she had the bloody keys, for goodness sake."

Black sighed impatiently. "We need to talk to Fairfield."

"Agreed," said Caplain. "So, like I said at the outset, we wait until he comes back."

Black tutted. "It's the twenty-first century now, you know," he waved his mobile phone at Caplain. "Where is he, anyway?"

Caplain was about to answer and then stopped. In the heat of his and Black's debate, he had started to forget himself. Moreover, in light of the huge trust that Fairfield had placed in him, he now started to regret opening up to Black that night in the car. It was not a mistake he would be making again.

"Fairfield?" Caplain answered eventually, "He's... organising a warrant for Rowcroft."

Fisher looked puzzled. "Well, if he was I don't think he is any longer," she remarked. "Harvey spoke to him a moment ago; he sounded like he was in trouble. Something about a Bed and Breakfast in Weir Road?"

At this Caplain's blood slowed to ice.

"Phone him," he instructed Black. "Phone him now."

7

It might have been dark in her cell, it might not.

The mist that now gathered before Elspeth Hamilton's failing sight could be concealing anything. She hadn't expected it to deteriorate so quickly. With each passing second the world grew dimmer, and her panic increased.

She could feel the scraping of the paper clothing on her skin. She could hear the creaking of the plastic-coated mattress on which she sat, with her back wedged into the corner of her cell and her knees drawn up to her chin like a nervous child. She could smell the upturned food tray on the floor. But these were all physical things; none of these was what scared her.

What scared her were the places to which her waking mind had begun to wander. Robbed of its anchor in the visual world, her subconscious had begun seeking new entertainment.

What she had just experienced had caught her completely unprepared. Her captors had provided dinner, for which she had stubbornly refused assistance. The mashed potatoes had been lukewarm and difficult to eat. She was still not used to seeing with her fingers, or to getting starchy mash under her nails. Frustration had gotten the better of her, and, in a rage, she had flung the plastic tray to the floor. At least she wouldn't have to look at the mess.

It was then that it had happened.

At the same time that her anger had flared, her eyesight had returned.

It had been brief, and had lasted no longer than her outburst of rage, but for a split second she had seen four grey walls, and a stained vinyl floor.

But not the ones of her cell.

She had seen no upturned dinner lying at her feet, and the door had been open. The entire layout of the room had been wrong, and she had seen new things. There were bookshelves, boxes and other people in there with her. She had looked down at her own, paper-suited form only to see that it contained different legs, a broad, muscular thorax, and a beard that was definitely not hers.

She was seeing through another's eyes.

Then, just as suddenly, the darkness had returned.

Like an after-image in her mind, however, strange thoughts and emotions had lingered. Then it had come to her: she had momentarily touched the thoughts of another soul nearby. This revelation shocked and terrified her. It made no sense. Such abilities were the privilege of only the most highly trained, and the most highly augmented. Even then, it required rare mental discipline to use such powers safely, and without sending one or both parties insane. This was impossible.

Unless it had been a fluke, a one-off, a result of the jumbled genes and chemicals coursing through her mind. She had to know one way or the other. It was either that, or give in to the fear for good.

Hamilton began to concentrate.

She searched the darkness once again for the other soul. She could sense it, just out of her reach. But then it drew nearer, and Hamilton recognised its shape. It was the man who had fought her for control of Jacob's heart and spirit.

It was her enemy.

Paul Black caught up with them as they were escorting the handcuffed Sam Wilcox across the station car park. Caplain looked at him expectantly.

"Well?"

"Engaged," Black told him, "I tried him five times."

Caplain cursed under his breath.

Reginald Beavis, Wilcox's solicitor, was walking alongside Caplain. He waved a hand to get his attention. "Do you mind, Sergeant? I believe we were talking? My client generously agreed to your identity parade, and if the results were inconclusive then you should release him from custody at once," insisted Beavis.

"They weren't inconclusive, Mr Beavis, far from it," said Caplain, wearily.

"Then will you be charging Mr Wilcox with anything? Or are we to simply sit around contemplating our navels until the ridiculously long custody period expires, and ends this litany of harassment?"

"DI Fairfield will make that determination."

"Ridiculous!" Beavis proclaimed. "Are you expecting me to believe that the entire station revolves around one man?"

Caplain closed his eyes, and sighed. "Hold up," he ordered.

Wilcox and his escorts, a constable at each elbow, came to a halt in the middle of the car park. Behind them, Caplain exchanged a look with Paul Black and then turned to face Beavis directly, his tone becoming firmer.

"Mr Beavis," he said, "rest assured we love proper procedure just as much as you do. Proper procedures, Mr. Beavis, such as waiting for the Investigating Officer to make the necessary decisions, and, oh, while we're at it," he added, his irritation escalating, "how about having the decency to not argue the toss about your Client's fate when we're stood in a bloody car park, when none of it's on the record, and when your Client is standing right in front of you?"

"This is preposterous!" exclaimed Beavis. "I refuse to participate in such a farce."

"Fine!" shouted Caplain, stepping closer to the lawyer. "I'll just charge him right here and now, then, shall I?"

It was then that Wilcox whirled round to face them so sharply, and so suddenly, that it almost spun the officers on his arms around like a waltzer ride. They stumbled, and then reinforced their grip. Up until now, he had trudged along with them like a beast of burden, his head lowered. Now he was standing tall, his face clear and confident.

It was as if someone had flicked a switch.

"Please don't," Wilcox said, his voice small and simple.

They all stared at him in shock.

"As the Good Lord is my witness, I didn't do nothin'. Please… all I did was try and help the lad… teach 'im about our Saviour… This ain't right. None of this is right. I never saw Susan after she left, and that's the truth. I love her. Why would I harm her?"

Black's face hardened and he glanced scornfully over at Caplain. He was surprised to see, however, that Caplain had been moved by Wilcox's appeal.

"Sam," began Caplain, taking a couple of steps forward, "there's nothing to worry about. In a couple of hours this will all be over, one way or another. And, if what you're telling is the truth, then you'll be fine."

"Yeah," scoffed Black under his breath. "'Cause that worked out great in the Bible, didn't it."

Beavis' jaw fell in silent outrage.

Caplain glared at his colleague. "Blackie. It's long past the time where you shut up."

Wilcox, however, nodded solemnly.

"He's right Mr Caplain. Truth was on the Lord's side at Gethsemane. But he still suffered and died, right enough."

"For a good cause, though," argued Black derisively. "Wasn't that the point?"

Once again Caplain winced, and he rounded on Black.

"That's quite enough for now," he told him. "Don't mock his beliefs."

Wilcox turned to his solicitor.

"Mr Beavis. I'd like to pray, if I might."

Beavis, from the summit of his moral high ground, looked across at Caplain for confirmation.

"I... don't see why not," said Caplain steadily.

"But not in my cell again," added Wilcox.

"Well, I don't know..."

Wilcox smiled serenely. "With respect, Mr Caplain, I'm never sure whether anyone's listenin'. You can't help but feel alone." He glanced up at the clear summer sky. "More chance of the Main Man hearin' us out here. Better acoustics."

At this Beavis remained impassive, and Black just turned away, shaking his head in disbelief. Caplain took a deep breath and then, eventually, nodded his assent to Wilcox's guards.

They released their prisoner.

The wheelie bins were dirty, and they stank, but the low wall around them made a serviceable place to kneel for prayers.

While his guards waited at a respectful distance, Sam Wilcox lowered himself into a kneeling position and leant against it, as gracefully as his handcuffed arms would allow. His shoulders ached, and the sinews in his arms were taut and uncomfortable. He centred himself, disconnecting the distractions of the senses and focusing on what he was down there to do. The sound of his lawyer's voice, still remonstrating with Black and Caplain, melted away.

Then, when he was fully prepared, he reached down behind the wall.

His outstretched fingers touched something small, delicate, and plastic.

Hooking at it with his fingertips he drew it nearer, until he could grasp it entirely. Then, taking care not to harm himself, and with as much haste as he could without arousing suspicion, he slid the syringe under the elasticated cuff of his suit.

A smile slowly spread across Sam Wilcox's face.

But it was not his.

Hamilton's consciousness snapped back into place with an agonising whiplash. She uttered a single cry. Her sightless eyes flew open and she sucked at the precious air like a surfacing diver. Eventually she managed to stabilise her ragged breathing, and sat back against the cold tiles, exhausted.

With the same smile of accomplishment.

And waited.

8

Fairfield was so shocked when Bulmer finally answered his phone, that for a moment he forgot what he was going to say. "Yes, hello? Ken?" he said, anxiously.

"Hello, Dear Chap. Something the matter?"

Bulmer's voice sounded matter-of-fact and sociable.

Fairfield frowned and shook his head. "That's what I should be asking you! What happened today? Are you all right?"

"I'm sorry, Old Boy. Really I am. I'd love to help you, but on reflection it may not be the best thing for everybody in the long run."

From outside the boarding house, Fairfield took a step back and looked up at the bay windows of Bulmer's room. The curtains were drawn. The three bobbies that Gossett had sent to meet him were waiting patiently at the gate for instruction.

"They've got to you, haven't they?" Fairfield asked his phone, angrily. "They bloody well got to you. Christ, they must have been listening in on our calls; I was out the door and at the church within half an hour…"

He could hear Bulmer's infuriating smile as he spoke.

"Nobody 'got to me', Duncan," chuckled Bulmer. "I told you; my slate is clean. Whatever's round the corner I shall face it proudly, and on my own two feet."

"You're lying, Ken," Fairfield felt the pit of his stomach plummet. "Tell me what happened."

There was a pause from the phone, and then finally Bulmer said:

"When a secret will cause more damage spoken than kept, it's not a lie. Tell me you understand that much, at least."

"You're not convincing me. Listen, I'm just outside; your landlady's not answering the door so stop being cryptic and come down and let us in. I've got some officers with me. They can look after you until all this is over."

"Oh, please!" scoffed Bulmer. "I've told you, everything's all right."

"As far as you're concerned it is, but that doesn't mean you're not in danger. You're scaring me, Ken."

"Thanks for the offer, but I'm not home at the moment anyway." There was another beat as Bulmer contemplated his next words. "Tell you what, Old Boy," he said, like a patient parent bribing their child. "Why don't we meet up tomorrow evening? I'll explain it all to you then."

"How about this evening?" countered Fairfield immediately.

"Not possible, I'm afraid," sighed Bulmer. "Besides, it's your turn to bring wine and takeaway. Chinese again, perhaps? Or did you fancy something else?"

A cold, black space suddenly opened up in Fairfield's heart, as he finally understood what Bulmer already knew. So, like his old friend before him, he forced himself to smile through the intolerable pain. "I can stop by the supermarket and get something from the salad bar," Fairfield joked, stifling his emotions. "How about some tofu, washed down with some carrot juice?"

Bulmer's laughter shook the speaker, but both men knew that it was a hollow joy. "Sounds wonderful, Old Chap," said Bulmer, and then, after a pause: "You'll see me tomorrow."

Fairfield noted the phrasing. He also noted that nobody had mentioned a time for their appointment. He forced himself to speak. "I'll look forward to it," he said, after a long, unsteady breath. "Take care of yourself, Ken. We've had our ups and downs, but…"

"Oh, don't be so wet," interrupted Bulmer. "Nothing needs to be said that we don't both know already. Just do one thing for me, though, will you?"

"Absolutely."

"Keep Jacob safe for me; it's him they want. Chin up, Old Chap."

The call clicked to an end.

Turning his back to the waiting constables, Fairfield sniffed back the moisture in his eyes and took three long breaths.

Whether he would grow to forgive Bulmer, he didn't know. Nevertheless, the stubborn old sod was his last link to Deborah, and the life Fairfield once had. As much as he had hated him back then, once Bulmer was gone then Fairfield would truly be alone. Soon his job wouldn't need him. His son was an independent young man now, and his wife was a distant memory. All he had now was photographs and an empty heart. The only thing he could look forward to with any certainty was his eternally faultless ancestors, staring smugly down at him from history.

Then he remembered the Elderly Gentleman's warning, and realised that there was still one last person depending on him.

It wasn't too late.

Bulmer had been right — they would try again for Jacob.

Maybe there was still time to save them both.

By this time tomorrow, he would know.

9

Eric White sealed the final envelope and tossed it onto Vanessa Daniels' desk. It spun across the smooth glass surface, and slid to a halt next to four others.

"There you are," he said, in triumph. "Post those, and we're done. Or, better still, save the stamps and configure a postman to deliver them for free. Look after the pennies, I always say."

Vanessa picked the letter up and studied it. In the top left corner of the envelope was her company's logo; a small, yellow sunburst atop three green lines. She clucked in contempt. "So, that's it, is it?" she sneered. "Send these contracts back and all our problems are over?"

White threw himself down into the canvas chair by her desk, his home from home over the last couple of days. It bounced gently under his weight. "Your Mr Miller and his team have done quite a tidy job on them. Credit where it's due, those documents are really quite impressive. It must be the imminent change of leadership galvanising their efforts, what do you think?"

"What do I think?" repeated Daniels coldly. "I think that if they're ever tracked back to this office by the authorities, they've got my signature all over them."

White beamed, as if all the cares of the world had left him for good. "My dear Vanessa, you of all people should appreciate that the pen is mightier than the sword; not to mention the power that lies within a well-crafted piece of prose. And I'm quietly confident about my little delivery to Jacob. Not wanting to brag, of course, but that one should have the most stirring impact."

Daniels tossed the letter back onto her desk.

"I lack your faith, Eric."

White laughed. "That's because you're judging things by your previous efforts. Configuration documents work best when they're subtle." Shaking his head, he scolded her playfully. "Holiday in the Bahamas, indeed…"

The couple lapsed into silence. Daniels walked over to her panoramic glass wall and watched the sunset. After a while she lit a cigarette, which flared against the fiery orange of the horizon, insignificant in comparison.

White appraised her from his seat, hands clasped behind his head. "Thinking about the morning?" he asked.

Keeping her back to him, Daniels took a drag before answering. "I'm sure everyone's looking forward to it just as much as you are, Eric," she said, sarcastically.

White winced.

"I hope that isn't sour grapes I'm hearing," he teased. "It really is the best solution for everyone, you know. My Employer will have arrived by this time tomorrow, and I don't think that you'd want him walking in on things as they are, would you?"

Daniels blew a soft cloud of smoke into the amber light. "You know my opinion on that," she stated. "We may yet live to fight another day, but don't expect me to like it. I'm under no illusions. I know that my chances, in particular, remain slim."

White rose from his chair, smiling, and sauntered over to the window to join her. After walking right up to her back, he pressed his own body against hers and slid his arms around the waist of her tailored shirt, beneath her jacket. He rested his chin on her shoulder. Daniels' eyes screwed up tight in disgust.

"Your chances, my sweet," White whispered softly into her ear, "are as slim or as good as you want them to be. And your continuing co-operation will definitely stand you in good favour…"

"Get away from me," she said, softly but with menace.

"And, technically, I will be your boss soon…"

White's hand began to slide downwards.

Daniels took a long, hard draw of her cigarette, until the tip was fierce and red. She then stabbed it down hard onto White's wandering hand, twisting it sharply in a cascade of sparks.

White pulled away from her violently, at first clutching at his hand like a wounded animal but then slapping down the tiny fires in his suit. His deep-set eyes blazed at her instead. Daniels remained standing at the window, and fished into her jacket pocket for another cigarette. She lit it, and then said. "Please don't make me waste any more of these, Eric. They don't come cheap, and I'm going to be out of a job soon."

White's lips parted in a grimace.

"Oh, you can count on that," he sneered.

"There's one thing you haven't counted on, though," continued Daniels. "You can take over this facility and its assets; its network of contacts, its projects … but you'll never have the loyalty of its staff." She turned to address him directly. "And you'll never have me," she added. "Even if you have to configure me to do it. I will never have said yes to you."

The phone on her desk buzzed; a page from the intercom rather than an incoming call. Leaving White nursing his hand, Daniels sat back at her desk. She pressed the intercom button.

"What?"

"Sorry for the interruption, Miss Daniels," the voice was tinny and distorted. "But the young lady you were expecting has arrived."

White couldn't resist the opportunity.

"How touching," he remarked mockingly. "Somebody wants to come and wish you good luck on your last night in charge."

Ignoring him, Daniels replied to the intercom.

"Let her in," she ordered, and then switched it off. "Kate Berridge," she told White. "I believe you wanted to meet her?"

White nodded in satisfaction. "Ah, yes; Jacob's watcher at the school. I understand it is she we have to thank for the information on Jacob's little journey tomorrow?"

"Indeed. She shows great promise, this one. She's already got one of the local detectives wrapped around her finger. It's a good resource to have, Eric, so go gently with her. Despite our reputation, we never punish those who exceed our expectations; you'd do well to put your paranoia aside and remember that."

White didn't answer. Instead he gave his hand one last rub and displayed it proudly to Daniels. The burn had all but healed; only a red blemish remained. He walked slowly and purposefully around her desk, and then grabbed the back of her chair.

"My dear Vanessa. Be thankful that I am blessed with an agreeable disposition. My Employer," he said, softly and calmly, "does not share it and believe me; if you try stubbing your fag out on his hand, he'll break you in half without a second thought."

Daniels' eyes narrowed, and she glared back at him. If she was perturbed by his threat, she wasn't showing it. "You're just as fragile as I am, Eric," she said. "Let's hope this plan of yours works tomorrow, or we'll be dying together."

White smiled down at her, his full confidence returning.

"I think you're in my chair," he said.

She could hear the twilight as it fell; the change in the ambience, the different sounds. The chatter of voices became sparser, and the rumble of traffic thinner. Distant noises were now clear, and carried further.

Through the insubstantial wall between them, she could feel her Enemy's heartbeat. The time was now right.

In the growing darkness, Elspeth Hamilton reached beyond the confines of her cell once again. Her mind swept through it like a beacon, luring stricken craft to their doom, or like a hawk surveilling the countryside from on high.

There.

Her sightless eyes found him, and her talons dug deep.

A muffled call, echoing in the dark.

She had heard Sam Wilcox's cry of alarm, despite the tiles and the concrete that separated them, at the same time as she had felt it. Was he reacting to her presence in his mind? Could he sense her intrusion? Or had she made him cry out without realising? Hamilton's fear melted away, replaced by scientific curiosity. After all, she had nowhere special to be for the next few hours, and nothing at hand to keep her occupied.

Perhaps she would have some fun with her new toy.

It was going to be a long night, after all.

In the soft light of his room, Jacob Morgan smiled excitedly.

Yet again, he plucked the card from the nightstand. Holding it at arm's length, with the card still closed, he beheld the design on its front and admired it. As majestic as the dusky sunlight that now shone through his window, so the dawn depicted on the card rose proudly into the limitless sky. Rays of stylised sunbeams stabbed the heavens like points on a crown. The words 'Get Well Soon' ran in golden script through the verdant grass below it.

After a few moments, Jacob opened the card and read the hand-written inscription to himself. He had already done so countless times that afternoon.

To my darling boy,

The worst is over now.
See you tomorrow.

All my love,

Mum xx

Jacob clutched the card lovingly to his chest. As he caressed the crucifix suspended around his neck, his now permanent smile became an insane rictus, distorting his face.

"You betcha," he whispered.

Tuesday
23rd July, 2002

1

Their car needed a wash.

Helen Knight ignored it as she trotted past, cursing the driveway gravel as it seeped into her sandals. She carried the newspaper, and the morning post from their roadside letterbox, tucked under her arm. Eventually she reached their side porch, and knocked the stones free from her heels against the doorway.

"Postman's early today," she mused aloud, as she drifted into the open-plan kitchen beyond. She tossed the newspaper onto the kitchen's central island.

Philip Knight picked it up and nervously scanned the headlines. "Anything for me?" he asked warily.

After sorting through the rest of her haul, Helen handed him three envelopes. The uppermost carried the portcullis emblem of Parliament House. "Looks important," she observed.

Knight grabbed it. "I can't believe we've got a reply so quickly," he said, as he turned the letter over and slid his little finger under the flap. "Let's hope its good news…"

Helen nodded hesitantly, not sharing her husband's optimism. Their letter of complaint to their MP had only been posted on Saturday morning. This meant a turnaround of a single day, maximum, assuming it had arrived first-thing Monday, and she knew that good news took longer to organise than bad.

After drawing a folded sheet of cartridge paper from the envelope, Philip opened it out and read quietly to himself.

Helen could tell what it said from his expression alone, and she decided to press on with the day's events. "Could you give me a lift to the hospital on your way in today?"

But Philip could not change the subject so easily.

"Load of rubbish," he said, ramming the paper back into its envelope. "There's nothing they can do until the case is brought to the attention of the Crown Prosecution Service." He threw the letter aside in frustration. "Ridiculous! The whole point's that Morgan probably won't be prosecuted! And here am I, with a bloody criminal damage charge hanging over me! Where's the justice in it?"

"I thought you said you had contacts, dear?" teased his wife, trying to keep the morning light hearted. Philip just glowered at her. "Why don't you open one of the others?" she continued, and then made a half-hearted joke; "It says you've won twenty thousand pounds on one of them. We could do with that."

Philip huffed and turned his attention to the second letter. The narrative on the envelope did indeed promise great prizes within. "It's junk mail," he said. "A scam. You probably have to buy half the contents of their catalogue."

"Just open it and shred the addressey parts, then," suggested Helen, walking round to the other side of the island and grabbing a saucepan from the overhead rack. "Scrambled eggs okay?"

Philip ripped open the envelope. The text of the letter began: 'Dear Lucky Winner,' and he almost stopped there at the cheesiness of it all.

But something made him read on.

Each passing line drew him deeper into the words, while the surrounding world faded until all he could see, touch or feel was the letter. Helen was speaking but her voice became distant and then finally silent. As his eyes reached the last paragraph, in the section marked 'Your Winning Number', a row of seemingly random characters met them there.

From that moment on, he knew precisely what had to be done.

Suddenly the world returned. His senses snapped back into focus, as though he had woken sharply from a daydream. There was no disorientation, and his earlier feelings of disappointment had been replaced by determination, and a sense of purpose.

"So," asked his wife from across the kitchen, "are all our troubles over, then?"

Philip Knight smiled.

And left the final letter, a legal envelope sporting a yellow sunburst logo in its corner, unopened on the counter.

Fearful of what the day might bring, but impatient for it to begin, Duncan Fairfield had stayed awake in case he missed it.

When the brandy had run out in the small hours of the morning, he had switched to water and coffee. He yearned to be already standing at the heart of Rowcroft, beating the truth out of them, before they had the chance to destroy anyone else's life.

And so, after four hours of staring into the void, Fairfield had driven to the Barton Estate, parked opposite Rowcroft's gates, and waited.

It was seven o'clock when the troops began to gather. The Rowcroft campus was huge, and Fairfield had requested at least thirty men, not counting himself and the other detectives, with which to search it. Two dog teams would also be there. Inspector Menzies had pledged some of the reinforcements from Harkham Common, so hopefully their numbers would swell to forty, maybe forty-five. Police vans lined the street, ferrying load after load of uniformed Constables to their rendezvous.

Fairfield checked his watch: seven fifty-eight. Wearing a determined expression, he climbed out of the car.

The road by the entrance barriers was bustling with activity. Fairfield marched through the assembled officers and along Rowcroft's iron perimeter to Sally Fisher's car, which had just pulled up on the opposite side of the road.

Fisher, Potts and Gossett got out and met Fairfield half way. Together they continued on to the front of the raid team. Caplain and Black were already there, with Inspector Menzies, who held up his hand for silence. Gradually the urgent murmuring subsided, and all eyes turned to the front.

After checking his watch again, Fairfield removed the warrant from his coat pocket and tapped it twice on his open palm, as if ensuring it was real.

"Okay," he said. "Let's go."

He strode purposefully towards the Rowcroft gates.

Fifty officers followed him.

2

Patience Biggs knew that she was in serious trouble.

While struggling to pin her coarse hair into its bun she hurried down the stairs of her apartment block, handbag dangling from her elbow, and her high heels threatening to snap on each concrete step.

To be late, today of all days, would be unthinkable. It was the last day of Summer Term. Headmaster would be expecting her to oversee the final arrangements for Sports Day. The construction of the large grandstand — from which the parents and governors could proudly watch their young sporting heroes — had already begun the previous evening, and this morning Miss Biggs was supposed to oversee its completion and safety checks. The event itself would start at ten o'clock, and Biggs needed to be completely in control by the time Mr Brooks turned up at nine.

But her alarm had not gone off, and now she was hideously, unbelievably late.

She made it down the final flight and into the communal hallway. As she scurried to the exit, she glanced at the pigeonholes on the wall. There was nothing in the hole with her flat number on it; the Postman couldn't have been yet. Or so it appeared. The next thing she noticed was the huge pile of mail underneath the front-door letterbox. The Postman had been after all, but had performed his usual trick of shoving everything through in one haphazard lump. Lucky her; she was the first one down.

She crouched next to the pile of post and made the mental calculations; it would take at least five minutes that she didn't have to sort it all out properly. Ignoring her conscience, she rifled through the pile to find her own letters. There were only two; a daunting, legal looking one with a sunburst logo, and a brightly decorated one promising her exciting gifts.

Not stopping to open either, she stuffed them in her bag for later. The bus was due any minute; she'd read them once she was safely on board and underway. Springing back up to her feet, she hoisted her bag onto her shoulder and hurried out of the front door.

Greg Cole had not intended to get out of bed, but his aching brain and arid mouth had persuaded him otherwise.

Upon his return home last night, the bottle of scotch that he had spurned on Saturday evening had proved hard to ignore, and the two of them had become reacquainted. Together they had toasted the bizarre and tragic events of the last seven days. Eventually, when glimpses of sunlight had disturbed him, Greg had plodded downstairs to get some water.

From the bottom of his stairs, he was now peering through the gloom of his curtained lounge at something unusual. A fan of white paper was protruding from his cottage's letterbox. Swaying slightly, Cole squinted at his wristwatch. The village postie had certainly outdone himself today, as had the paperboy.

He plucked the new arrivals from the iron jaws and studied them. After placing the newspaper to one side, he carried the junk mail and the envelope from Rowcroft over to a roll-top bureau. A personal shredder sat expectantly beneath it. With a glow of satisfaction, Greg fed the unopened envelope into the shredder and watched its sunburst logo thrash against the onslaught of metal teeth. Within seconds, it was gone.

He nodded to himself in approval.

Then, after pouring a pint of water from the kitchen tap, Cole returned to the lounge and collapsed in his favourite chair. He held up his brand new Harkham Herald and scanned the headlines. When he read the words 'Rowcroft Retraction: An Apology', and the by-line of 'Terrance Digger', Cole couldn't help but utter a single, rueful laugh. The front page bore instructions to turn to page five for more details, which he did.

Cole hesitated for a moment, confused by what he saw. It must have been a printing error, he reasoned; why else would an entire page of the paper be full of gibberish and mathematical symbols?

It was then that the pain exploded inside his skull.

The water tumbled from his hand, its glass shattering on the unyielding floorboards. He swiftly followed it, rolling in the shards, his hands clutching temples that felt they too could splinter at any moment.

Then, as the newly configured Greg Cole writhed in agony, there was a fresh clatter from the direction of his front door, and another concertina of newsprint pushed its way through the letterbox.

And if he could have heard anything through his torment, Greg Cole would have heard the whistling of his regular paperboy as he rode away up the lane.

"Detective Inspector Fairfield, Harkham CID. We have a warrant to search these premises."

Fairfield held the warrant up to the fence.

The Security Guard peered down at it. Instead of the hideous uniform he had been in on Saturday, the Guard was now wearing plain black trousers, and a white open-necked shirt. Only a clip-on ID badge denoted his role as an official. After completing his inspection, he looked back up at Fairfield and said, "I'm sorry, Sir, but I can't let you in. I've no orders to do so, see."

Fairfield adopted a theatrical air of confusion.

"Sorry, perhaps you missed the part where I said 'warrant'? You don't have much say in the matter, sunshine, so get those barriers up."

"That's not my decision to make, I'm afraid, Sir."

"Right," Fairfield turned round to Inspector Menzies. "Brian, don't suppose you've got a screwdriver to hand, have you? For those barriers? Or a saw perhaps?"

A new voice joined the conversation.

"That won't be necessary, Inspector."

A man with collar-length grey hair, and wearing a pressed brown suit, had joined the Guard. Fairfield turned his attention to the newcomer.

"Are you in charge here?"

"In a manner of speaking. My name is Alexander Miller. How can I help you, gentlemen?"

Fairfield recognised the name at once, but kept it to himself. "Stop pissing about," he said. "You know why we're here. Let us in."

Miller took a moment to survey the host of police uniforms behind Fairfield, and then extended an open hand. "May I examine your warrant, please? Before I let your band of merry men loose on these premises, I would like to check all is in order."

Fairfield exchanged a look of uncertainty with Caplain, before rolling the warrant up and poking it through the wire links of the fence. Miller took the warrant and began to read.

Meanwhile, the morning sun was taking its toll on the raiding party. An impatient Fairfield drummed his fingers on the wall of the gatehouse.

Eventually a broad smile appeared on Miller's face. He rolled the warrant back up, and returned it to Fairfield through the fence. "I'm sorry, Inspector, but I must deny you access. I think there's been some mistake."

"This warrant has passed through the hands of the best," Fairfield argued, his temper rising, "and it's watertight."

"I know," said Miller convivially, "it was I who negotiated it. However, I'm afraid it doesn't allow you entry to these premises today. You're just too late, Inspector."

Miller's conceited attitude began to concern Fairfield. A knot developed in his stomach. "What's that supposed to mean?" he asked, suspiciously.

Miller pointed at the warrant. "That document gives you full and free access to the commercial premises of Rowcroft Medical Ltd. But I'm afraid that company no longer exists."

It took a second for Fairfield to register the words.

"Since when?" he said flatly, in disbelief.

"Sadly they went into liquidation at midnight, Inspector. As a corporate entity, there is no such thing as Rowcroft Medical any longer. So, even if you were to find whatever it is that you're looking for, there's nobody left to prosecute. Sorry."

Fairfield did not reply. His grip slowly tightened on the warrant and it began to crumple. Jed Caplain pushed past him and spoke to Miller. "So who's is all this now?" he demanded, gesturing at the industrial complex beyond.

"An associated company has acquired the site," Miller told him.

Fairfield looked up at the lawyer.

"Pelion?" he asked with disgust.

Again the self-satisfied smile from Miller.

"At present that is commercially sensitive information," he explained. "However there will be a press-conference here tomorrow morning; all will be revealed then. Eleven o'clock sharp. Hopefully we'll see you there."

Miller waved cheerfully at the group, and then returned to the campus. The Guard, silent throughout this exchange, leant forward and spoke to Fairfield through the fence. "Told you," he said, and then went back inside the gatehouse.

Fairfield didn't say a word.

Soon he turned round and began barging his way back through the raiding party, the creased warrant still in his hand. Caplain broke off from the group to follow him. Inspector Menzies, meanwhile, turned to address the rest of the team. "Okay, you lot. Rain stops play. Let's start getting back in those vans now..."

Fairfield was striding quickly and Caplain had to run to catch up.

"Duncan, wait," he said as he eventually matched Fairfield's pace. "All's not lost; we'll get another warrant."

"No, we won't," snapped Fairfield. "Nor did we ever get one. They were just stringing it all out while they took Rowcroft apart and tucked it out of harm's way."

"Nobody's immune from the law. We'll get them in the end."

Fairfield laughed disparagingly.

"You'd like to think so, wouldn't you?" he said, his voice hollow. "I'm about to test that theory. I'll let you know how I get on."

"What do you mean?" asked Caplain cautiously.

They reached Fairfield's car. "He knew," stated Fairfield, throwing open the driver's door. "That bastard knew. He must have done."

Moments later Jed Caplain, and the rest of his colleagues, looked on in astonishment as Fairfield's saloon revved angrily and then roared away. It left the discarded search warrant fluttering in its slipstream.

3

"How's your handicap?" demanded Fairfield, as he burst into DCI Hill's office without warning.

Hill looked up from his paperwork and smiled, unsure whether his visitor's face was red with rage, or from the climb to the attic.

"Good morning, Duncan," he said sarcastically. "Please do come in."

Fairfield marched angrily over to Hill's desk and confronted him. "If anything was wrong with Rowcroft, you said, then your mate Miller would be the first to know about it, you said."

"Ah," said Hill, closing the folder that he was working on, and leaning casually back in his chair, "the raid. Bit of a wasted journey, I hear."

"You could say that. And you knew that it would be," accused Fairfield.

"My dear Duncan," Hill chuckled, "if I'd known that Pelion was going to absorb Rowcroft back into the fold, don't you think I'd have sold my shares first?"

Fairfield's brow darkened even further. "I beg your pardon?"

"Oh do relax, man. I'm joking, of course."

Hill gestured at a nearby chair. Fairfield collapsed into it.

"I'm not laughing," he muttered, petulantly.

Hill leant forward onto his desk, and clasped his hands together. His expression became grim. "Neither am I, Inspector. You're spending twenty-four hours a day grumbling about conspiracy theories, while precious little police-work is being done. What's going on, Duncan? My patience has its limits."

"Wilcox has been charged, Sir," Fairfield told him, like a boy making excuses for his late homework.

"So I understand, but on a traffic offence? We need to keep up the momentum, Duncan. This has become a high-profile case."

"You're the one who made promises to the media."

"And you're the one not delivering on them," came Hill's retort. "Despite that, however, I gave you the benefit of the doubt over that damned newspaper article. Despite that, however, I went out on a limb to approve Hamilton's admission into Witness Protection for you — trust your instincts, you said — and to what end? It is I who will have to explain to Division where all that money went, and why. We need results, Duncan, not a crusade."

"If Rowcroft had panned out…"

"Forget Rowcroft!" bellowed Hill, before returning to his normal, supercilious tones. "Forget wild theories and suspicions, what about the mountain of evidence you already have?"

Fairfield ground his jaw in silence. He wanted to vent the anger and embarrassment he felt after Rowcroft had made a fool of him. He wanted to ask Hill there and then whether he could be trusted. Nevertheless, for now, Fairfield kept the turbulence within him suppressed. It was a lifelong skill.

"I'm sorry, Sir," he insisted at last, "but Rowcroft are at the heart of this all. I'm more certain now than ever. This takeover by Pelion is just a tactic. It gives them a clean slate in the eyes of the law. They knew we were onto them, and they panicked. I bet you'll find the same people are still in charge."

Hill took a deep breath. "Okay, Duncan. Now look, I'm sensing that you are distrustful of my connections, which are purely social I might add. Would it help assuage some of your doubts if I used them to our advantage? I'm prepared to talk to Alex Miller, if you like, and see what I can find out."

This offer pleasantly surprised Fairfield, but did nothing to diminish his suspicion. "Thank you," he said warily.

"In return, however," warned Hill, "I want this case resolved quickly and professionally, and I want an end to these conspiracy theories of yours. Stick to the case you have. That's the deal. Understand?"

Fairfield nodded reluctantly.

"Good. So, with Jacob Morgan being sectioned today, I'm hoping we can draw a line under that particular element. Which leaves us with but one conundrum to resolve: is Wilcox our man or not?"

Immediately Fairfield recognised the sub-text to Hill's question. He wouldn't put it past Hill to use whatever Fairfield said next to distance himself from the case, and from any executive decisions that came back to haunt them. "The evidence certainly seems comprehensive," replied Fairfield, "if not a little circumstantial, and more than a little convenient."

Hill smiled.

"So is that a 'yes' or a 'no', Inspector?"

Fairfield was saved by the bell.

Hill waited for his telephone to ring twice more before he picked it up, and spoke his name.

Fairfield let his eyes wander around the office while he waited for the call to end. Strangely, he found himself reminded of Robert Brooks' office at Harkham Grammar; display cabinets, photographs and certificates were the order of the day. Hill on the golf course seemed to be a popular theme. Eventually Fairfield heard Hill say thank you to his caller, and he turned back to him just as the DCI was replacing the receiver.

Laurence Hill left his hand resting on top of the phone, and looked up at Fairfield with a dour expression.

"Everything all right, Sir?" asked Fairfield, although it was clear from Hill's eyes that it was not.

"We're needed downstairs. Samuel Wilcox is dead."

Fairfield was speechless. His bravado evaporated.

Hill continued to glare at him.

"And now a death in custody, Inspector. Just not your day, is it?"

Reginald Beavis scowled across the desk at the two senior detectives and, not for the first time since they had entered Interview Room One, smacked the wall beside him with his fist.

"I have never, in all my years of practicing law, experienced such atrocious and unprofessional conduct! I am assuming, of course, that the constabulary will be conducting an investigation, and taking full responsibility for Mr Wilcox's death? His family will require an official explanation, and doubtlessly considerable compensation, for their loss."

Hill did his best to remain diplomatic and calm. Beside him, Fairfield simply sat in silence, his arms folded.

"Mr Beavis," said Hill, "if any investigation into this tragic matter points to negligence on our behalf, then of course we will respond accordingly. However, the initial findings would seem to indicate otherwise."

"He topped himself," added Fairfield, his first words since the meeting began.

Hill winced. "The evidence would seem to point to Mr Wilcox's suicide…"

"Ah, yes," scoffed Beavis, "the syringe. And how the hell does a man in police custody suddenly acquire a needle full of lethal drugs? Aren't your prisoners monitored?"

"We are still determining the origins of the syringe and its contents. I'm sure you'll appreciate that it's still very early, and we know nothing definitively. Rest assured we will update you with any and all information as it comes in."

"Edited for public consumption, of course," sneered Beavis.

"You'll have full access to the same data as we do," Hill assured him.

"Forgive me if my confidence is not overwhelming," Beavis rose from his chair, prompting the two officers to stand with him. "This isn't over, gentlemen," continued Beavis, "not by a long chalk. I have to leave now. I'm meeting Mr Wilcox's widow at the coroner's office. I shall return this afternoon, however, and I expect something a little more substantial from you."

As Beavis walked past their side of the desk, Hill stepped forward to him. "Please could you convey our sincerest condolences to Mrs Wilcox?"

Beavis gave a snort of derision.

"Chief Inspector; with the greatest of respect I think that neither Mrs Wilcox, nor her father-less children, will want to hear anything from you. Good day." Beavis marched up to the Interview Room door, and the Constable standing guard there escorted him through it.

Fairfield and Hill were left alone in the room.

Hill dismissed the guard and closed the door, ensuring that the red occupancy light stayed on. He walked back to Fairfield, his features tense, and pinioned him with his gaze.

"Where the hell did that syringe come from, Duncan?"

"I'm not sure, Sir, but I have my suspicions."

There was a moment of uncomfortable silence.

"Well?" snapped the DCI eventually. "Are they a secret?"

"No, Sir," ventured Fairfield, "but I'm not certain. I think Dr. Hamilton had a syringe in her hand when she attacked me but it's vague; I was delirious for a while, with the pain in my head, and…"

"So what are you saying? That Hamilton passed Wilcox the syringe while they were on the same cell block? Are we looking at two security violations instead of one here?"

Fairfield frowned as he struggled to remember. "Hamilton and I tussled for a few seconds; she probably dropped it then."

"Oh, fabulous!" cried Hill. "So it was just lying around in our car park for a few days?"

"Wilcox was out of his cell for quite a long time yesterday; it's possible that he somehow got hold of it then."

The disbelief in Hill's features intensified.

"Wasn't the man searched?" he exclaimed.

"I couldn't say, Sir."

"Why not? You were the officer in charge!"

Fairfield swallowed hard.

"Because I wasn't here, Sir."

Hill threw his arms up in despair, and collapsed back into his seat. He leant on the scuffed desk and looked up at Fairfield incredulously. "Is that supposed to be an excuse? A man died on your watch, Inspector!"

"I'm aware of that, Sir…"

"So where were you?"

"Meeting an informant."

Hill considered this for a few moments. "Who?" he asked eventually. "I didn't think you had any active informants at present."

"It was a spur of the moment thing."

"And was this mysterious informant of any use to us?"

"Well, actually Sir, he didn't show. But he would have provided a vital back door into Rowcroft…"

Hill raised a dismissive hand at the sound of the word. "Enough!" he snapped, stopping Fairfield in mid-sentence, his head bowed low and staring at the desk top. When he finally spoke he did so with a sigh, and without looking back up.

"Duncan, I'd completely understand if, with everything that's been going on, you wanted take a temporary leave of absence," Hill said calmly. "Shall we say for a minimum of two weeks, effective immediately?" It was a dictat delivered in a velvet glove, not a suggestion. "Don't worry, I'll clear it with Division."

For Fairfield, it took a moment for the reality of the words to sink in. "Sir?"

"You heard me."

Fairfield became indignant.

"Don't do this, sir. Not now, not today. You're making a big mistake."

"And don't make me suspend you, Duncan. Go. Now."

"But… the Cole case…"

Hill stood and walked over to the door. After flicking the occupancy light back to green, he waited there with his hand on the door handle. "There is no Cole case," he said sadly. "Not any more. Let's face it, Duncan; we've pulled at the only threads we could find and it's unravelled before our eyes. Morgan will never be declared medically fit to testify, and our main suspect is dead."

"And Rowcroft are conveniently off the hook," added Fairfield, bitterly. "Sending this case to the archives is a far easier decision for you to make this morning than it was twenty-four hours ago, isn't it, Sir?"

Fairfield let the inference hang in the air.

Hill looked at him benevolently, but his stare remained cold.

"I'll pretend I didn't hear that." He pushed down on the handle and opened the door. "Go home."

4

"We are currently closed for business. Thank you for calling."

Kate Berridge hung up the call and took a nervous swig of coffee. The same recorded message had confronted her when she'd called Rowcroft's general office number, and now here it was on Vanessa Daniels' direct line. Kate's anxious fingers began drumming on her kitchen table. She had only been able to reach Paul Black's voice mail the previous evening, and now her handlers at Rowcroft were ignoring her. It was as if the world had gone away and not left her a note.

She tried dialling Rowcroft's main switchboard again.

"We are currently closed for business. Thank you for calling."

Despondently, Kate cradled her head in her hands. Fear began to gnaw at her. She could not understand it. She'd even been there last night, in person, to receive her reward. She'd stood in Daniels' office. Everything had seemed normal; even that strange colleague of Vanessa's, the one Kate had never met before, had seemed pleased with her.

Kate ran her fingers along her now unblemished cheekbones, where only twenty-four hours ago there had been scars. It had taken a matter of moments for Miss Daniels to supercharge Kate's healing abilities, and there was promise of yet more abilities to come. In her heart, Kate knew that she could complete any challenge they threw at her, and she was impatient to continue her journey.

But now, after enough of a taste to intoxicate her, the opportunity seemed to have vanished into thin air.

Nervousness became panic.

Kate took a deep breath, and tapped another number into her phone. There was still a job to do, and no time to lose.

"Hello?" Paul Black's voice sounded apprehensive.

"Hey Paul," Kate tried her best to appear casual. "Guess who."

"Kate," Black stated, an answer rather than a greeting. "Sorry I didn't reply to your messages yesterday. To say it was an eventful day is putting it mildly; I meant to get back to you, but in the end I just crashed out."

Kate forced a laugh. "Ah, that must be my fault," she remarked sagely. "Obviously we kept you up too late on a school night."

"Listen, Kate," Black ignored her quip, "I can't talk right now. We've got a big mobilisation underway, and I need to get up to the hospital."

"Well, that's kind of why I'm calling; to wish you luck for today."

There was a pause, after which Black replied:

"Thanks."

"Let me know how you get on. Maybe we can meet up afterwards?"

"Perhaps. I'll call you later if I get a chance. Bye."

The sudden ending to their conversation did nothing for Kate's paranoia. She tossed her phone onto the table, and glowered at it.

She hated waiting.

Fairfield's pounding at the front door had already put Betty Bayliss in a bad mood; she was in the middle of serving the last of her breakfast guests, and it was clear nobody else was going to answer the knocking. After apologising to table four, she shuffled down the hallway, muttering, and wiping her hands.

With an artificial smile, she swung open the door.

"I need to speak to Mr Bulmer," Fairfield told her impatiently, and without preamble.

Mrs Bayliss' smile dropped away. "Well I'm afraid he's not here. Came back late, and then left again early."

Fairfield quietly uttered a terrible curse. His face was flushed, and he was short of breath as he spoke. "Did he say when he'd be back?"

"No," answered Mrs Bayliss, pursing her heavily made-up lips, "but then he didn't have to; paid up in full, he did. Checked out. Opened his post, ran upstairs, and packed his bags."

Fairfield steadied himself for a moment.

"Mrs Bayliss," he said after a while, "can you…"

"I mean, I wouldn't have minded but we were just starting to serve breakfast and he comes running back down to reception…"

"Right. Did you catch…"

"Demanding his bill, ringing the bell," Mrs Bayliss continued, "incessantly," she added pointedly, with a glance at Fairfield, "didn't give a jot as to how busy Graeme and I were…"

"Did he say anything specific…"

"'Cause we don't have much time in the mornings, see, not since our Laura got married, she always used to help out, but now there's just the two of us everything needs to go like clockwork but, oh no, he didn't care about that just threw a cheque at us and ran out of the door. See, if Laura were still living here she would have been manning the reception, dealing with the early leavers, she was always better with the computer anyway, but she got married end of last year and left us…"

"Mrs Bayliss!" Fairfield interrupted her sharply. "Do you have a forwarding address, or anything at all?"

"Well of course we do," she said with a frown, "she's our daughter after all, even if she has gotten wed to a useless layabout. They got a place in Ashby in the end. Don't like it much to tell the truth. You've got to go downstairs into the basement to use the facilities and they didn't bother decorating…"

Fairfield smacked the door frame in exasperation. Without another word, he marched angrily away down Weir Road. Mrs Bayliss watched him yank open the door of a battered old Vauxhall, and drive away in a manner that matched his disposition.

"Well now," she remarked piously, "he won't win many friends with that attitude."

To keep Jacob Morgan's convoy separated from the visiting public, they had used barriers and cones to create a staging area at the far end of the hospital grounds. At its centre stood an ambulance that had seen better days, and had long ago been refitted for prisoner transport. Two squad cars and two unmarked ones flanked the ambulance, ready for escort duty.

The newly arrived Jed Caplain emerged from one of the unmarked cars, noting with satisfaction that DS Black had already assembled their team for a briefing. Black jogged over to meet him half way, and raised a hand in greeting. "Good afternoon," he said with mock humility, "Acting-Inspector Caplain!"

Caplain winced and glanced around uncomfortably. "Steady on, Blackie," he said quietly as they drew level, "I were a Detective Sergeant when I woke up this morning, and I still am."

"Whatever you say, Guv," grinned Black.

"And don't call me that, either," frowned Caplain.

"Well, what else should I call you if I can't call you by your rank, or call you 'Guv', Guv?"

"That's enough."

"Sorry," Black adopted a more formal tone. "Congratulations, you deserve it."

"Yeah, well… Thanks, but shame about the circumstances. It should have been us that were hauled over the coals about Wilcox, not Fairfield."

"The situation was of Fairfield's making, Jed. We just did the best we could with it. And we'll continue to do our best now that he's gone."

Caplain cast Black a sideways glance, clearly not convinced. He let the matter drop for now. Soon they joined the main group, where Harvey Gossett was going over a road map with one of the Area Car drivers.

"So, how is Fairfield?" enquired Black. "Word on the grapevine is that he's had a health scare or something?"

"I wouldn't know," Caplain deliberately evaded the question. "Hill gave me the news and then I was bundled off here."

"Got any plans for the department, then?" asked Black casually.

"No, I don't," Caplain's voice was firm, to warn Black that he was in danger of crossing the line. "I'm only a caretaker. Fairfield'll be sat back in his chair in no time, you'll see."

Black humoured him and nodded politely. "Of course," he said. "And it's about time you had your shot at the wheel. It's somewhat ironic, really. There we were, chatting about Fairfield being a few strawberries short of a trifle, and all of a sudden…"

"You can pack that talk in, an' all!" snapped Caplain.

"Yes, Guv," Black smiled at him obediently.

Caplain rolled his eyes to the heavens before addressing the rest of the team, who had congregated at the back of the ambulance to discuss the task ahead. As well as DCs Gossett, Potts and Fisher, four traffic officers were present, including PCs Spence and Hollander. Hollander dropped his half-finished cigarette as Black and Caplain approached, and extinguished it under his boot.

"Right, everyone," Caplain raised his voice slightly to be heard over the bypass traffic behind them. "I appreciate that today's been a difficult one already, but we need to put this morning's events out of our minds and focus on our job here. We've got a couple of hours until our guest of honour is ready for his day-trip so let's use them wisely. I'm not expecting any trouble, but we need to double-check for changes with control and traffic right up until we leave, go over the route, and make sure everybody knows which contingency plan is which."

Caplain paused for a moment, to keep his emotions in check. Then he realised; the eight faces in front of him were doing the same, and needed reassuring just as much as he did.

"It's Fairfield's plan," he added proudly. "Let's not let him down."

5

Nurse Tomkin zipped up the toiletries holder and tucked it into the front pocket of Jacob's travel bag. "There we are, all packed," she said confidently, for Jacob's benefit more than her own.

Jacob was sitting in one of the visitors' chairs — the first time he had left his bed since his outburst of Sunday night — and was dressed in the brand-new jeans and navy t-shirt that his parents had brought him earlier that morning. They had already gone on ahead to Gardner Heritage, so that he would be greeted by familiar faces.

Jacob's leg was jiggling up and down anxiously, and he beamed at Nurse Tomkin. "Going to see my mum," he announced.

"That's right," she replied, a little puzzled, "and that's not all you've got to look forward to, Jacob. Once you've been for an ambulance ride, you'll find a lot of things will be better."

Jacob rocked back and forth in his chair, excitement brightening his pale features. "Going to see her…"

There was a perfunctory tap on the open door and Jed Caplain walked through, wearing a speculative expression. Nurse Tomkin beckoned him in, but the preoccupied Jacob paid him little heed.

"Morning, lass," Caplain said to the nurse. "I hope you've recovered from the other night?"

"Oh I've taken some worse knocks in my time, don't you worry," smiled Tomkin. "I'm just glad that the end is in sight; it's a much better fit for his needs at Gardner."

Caplain nodded. "Well our lot are just putting the finishing touches to things outside, so I thought I'd pop up and see how everything was going." He walked slowly towards Jacob's chair — but not too far — and spoke to the boy from a wary distance. "Hello, Jacob," said Caplain convivially, "you're looking in much better fettle today. How are you feeling?"

Jacob's eyes narrowed at the sound of Caplain's voice, and initially he didn't respond. Eventually the boy's head drifted round, and reacted to Caplain as though this was the first time he'd ever seen him.

"It's good," said Jacob flatly. "Today's the day. You betcha."

"Aye," Caplain confirmed, albeit a little bemused. "So you don't need to worry. It's just a nice drive in the sunshine, and Dr. Montgomery will make sure you're comfortable. You'll be with friends all the way. Not an Imposter for miles." As he said it, Caplain instantly regretted his use of the term, and tried not to wince too obviously.

But this new, calmer Jacob seemed unperturbed. Instead he said: "Is Mr Fairfield coming?"

Caplain hesitated, before eventually deciding to reveal the truth. "No lad, he's not. He wishes you well, though."

Jacob's brow creased in disapproval. "Need to say goodbye," he said.

"I'm sure he'll come and visit you at your new place."

"He'll need to," declared Jacob firmly. "It's been three days."

The unexpected repetition of this favourite phrase made Caplain stop short, and he exchanged a glance with Nurse Tomkin, who was busy folding away Jacob's bedclothes.

It was then that they heard a new voice.

"Like I told you years ago, lad; I might not always be punctual, but I'll always be there when you need me."

Caplain looked round.

Fairfield was standing in the open doorway. He was lingering on the threshold, and waiting for permission to enter. Caplain nodded to the uniformed officers that were standing guard, and they let Fairfield through. "Sorry, Duncan," explained Caplain, "they're just obeying orders. Hill's turned everything upside down."

Fairfield nodded stoically, and cast a sideways glance at Tomkin.

Catching the hint, Caplain asked Nurse Tomkin politely if she wouldn't mind just leaving them alone for a couple of minutes. With her standard grizzle of protest, Tomkin reluctantly agreed and left the room.

Fairfield strolled over to Jacob and stood right next to him. A warm and satisfied smile from the boy greeted him, and Fairfield patted the back of his head paternally. "Didn't think I'd let you run off without a farewell, now, did you?" Fairfield looked back at Caplain. "I see the escort's coming together nicely out there, Jed. You'll be off soon, I reckon."

Caplain checked over his shoulder and then made sure the door was pushed to. "What the hell's going on, Duncan?" he asked, lowering his voice. "What's all this about sick leave? And do we really need this escort if Rowcroft are out of the picture now?"

"The sick leave story is just what Hill's putting out," explained Fairfield, "probably to save his face as much as mine. As for Rowcroft, don't let your guard down; go ahead with it like we planned because I don't think anything's changed. If anything, it's gotten worse. Hill can't be trusted, Ken Bulmer's dropped off the face of the earth, and I'm starting to think that Elspeth Hamilton played us, just to get an escape route out of this unholy mess. Rowcroft was just a name. Just do as we planned, and it should be fine."

Jacob, whom they had both assumed was away in his own world, smiled at this and began to rock back and forth in his chair again. "It should be fine," he repeated Fairfield's words. "Just do as we planned, and it should be fine." The two detectives turned to look at him, and then Jacob added, "We did as we planned. It's been three days, and now everything's fine."

Fairfield perched on the edge of the bed so that he was at Jacob's level. "Better late than never, eh, Jacob?"

Astonishingly, Jacob laughed out loud at this.

"It doesn't matter. Mr Wilcox taught me to be patient, and he was right. Good things happen for those who wait. Good Mr Wilcox."

Jacob continued to rock contentedly.

Caplain shifted uncomfortably at the mention of Wilcox's name. He was sure nobody would have shared that morning's tragic discovery with Jacob yet. Fairfield, in contrast, seemed to have his interest piqued and leaned forward to keep Jacob's attention. "Mr Wilcox?" Fairfield quoted back at the boy, a puzzled look on his face. "But... isn't he The Devil?"

Jacob's rocking abruptly ceased.

The boy suddenly became anxious, and his brow knotted in confusion. "I thought... that you'd read my diary."

"I did read it, Jacob," insisted Fairfield. "We all did. We read from it together the other night, don't you remember? I brought copies of the pages here to your room."

Jacob's breathing quickened, and he started to become agitated.

"Not copies," he admonished, "never copies. How can you deliver a message with copies? Don't be daft, Mr Wilcox says. Don't be daft."

Caplain took a step forward. "We're not sure what you're saying, lad. What message?"

But Jacob ignored him. He'd fixed Fairfield with his glacial stare and wasn't letting go. "You said you'd read it. You have to read it to the very end, or the message is lost. You're the only one who will understand. You're the only one I trust. Just do what we planned, and everything will be fine!"

Fairfield's eyes narrowed. "Understand what?"

"The message!" exclaimed the boy. "It's for you!"

It was then that the door flew open and Dr. Montgomery strode in. Nurse Tomkin and the two guards were flanking him. From his expression, it was clear that he was not amused. "Now, now, gentlemen," he began reprovingly, "mustn't have our boy getting distressed on his big day. Inspector Fairfield, I'm going to have ask you to leave, dear fellow." Montgomery gestured at the uniformed officers beside him in turn. "Sorry, orders from on high. Not a lot I could do."

In panic, Jacob looked at Montgomery, to Fairfield, and then back again. He shook his head in denial. "No… this is wrong…"

Caplain took a deep breath, uncomfortable that he was powerless to intervene. Fairfield, however, crouched down next to Jacob's chair and, after resting a hand on the boy's arm, smiled benevolently. "Don't be concerned," he told Jacob, "Neither I, nor Mr Caplain here, will let anything happen that's not in the plan."

This seemed to pacify Jacob. His head became still.

"You'll stick to the plan?"

"I'll try," replied Fairfield, uncertain of to what he was committing.

Jacob risked a smile.

Once he was satisfied that Jacob was calm again, Fairfield walked to the door. "Stay in touch," he told Caplain, "you know where I'll be."

Then he waved goodbye to Jacob for the final time.

6

From the sparse and wind-battered treeline of the hill above, Bulmer watched the activity in the hospital car park and grazed on his pipe-stalk. The breeze snatched the smoke as he exhaled.

After Eric White's stark warning, Bulmer was in no doubt that his time at the eye of the storm was ending. He knew that the tempest would now follow him wherever he went, and that the only way to protect those he cared about was to stay away from them.

He had confirmed his suspicions that very morning. The letter he had received, so obviously a configuration document, had almost subdued him. Almost. Fortunately, Bulmer's mind had become inured to its effects long ago. Moreover, he had since developed the skills to understand its instruction without becoming its slave. Evidently whoever sent it had intended that he come here, to the hospital, and rendezvous with Greg Cole.

They were to disrupt Jacob's transfer, and deliver the boy to Rowcroft.

He found himself wondering what resistance Greg Cole might have had to his own half of these orders, if any. He then found himself wondering which poor soul had previously been brainwashed into attempting Susan Cole's kidnap.

Bulmer checked his watch; it would be midday soon.

In the car park, the distant police escort looked almost ready.

He wondered just who else might show up for the main event.

Patiently Bulmer waited for his chance; maybe his final chance. With his foreknowledge, he could strike a blow against Rowcroft's plans. More importantly, he could finally help the Cole family. He could break Greg's configuration, just as he had his own, and seize one last opportunity for redemption.

But he had to do so quickly.

For many years, the hounds of Rowcroft had been nipping at his heels, and he had become well-versed in evading them. Soon, however, the wolves of Pelion would be coming for him.

Fairfield was feeling conspicuous in his own workplace. He could have worn civvies as a disguise, he mused, if only he owned any.

With Jacob's original diary in his hand, still in its evidence bag, he nudged open the door to the Police Station canteen and peered in. Although he trusted Maggie, who had gone to the evidence room for him, Fairfield knew that DCI Hill would learn of his presence eventually. What Fairfield also knew, however, was that the canteen would be deserted at this time of day, the lull before the shift change and after the lunchtime rush. It was also the one place you would never find Laurence Hill.

Sure enough, the canteen's final customers, two civilian admin workers, were just wandering back to their offices. Old Bill, the cook, was the last man standing. Fairfield wandered over to him and, with the traditional exchange of nods, Bill slid a mug of tea and a pre-packaged cheese sandwich over the counter; Fairfield's usual elevenses snack. Fairfield carried them to a far table, removed his coat, and then unpackaged Jacob's diary.

He carefully prised the latch apart, and opened the cover.

The difference was astounding. The book was alive with the character of its author's handwriting, in strange and colourful inks. In comparison to the flat, monochrome reproductions that they had circulated, it was like switching from photographs of long dead friends to being in their living presence. A chill ran across Fairfield's skin. He couldn't explain it.

Fairfield read as swiftly as he could, impatient to understand Jacob's message, but already the experience was making him uncomfortable. Passages that he had read many times before in their photocopied form now came alive to him. His emotions were no longer his own. He felt heartache when Jacob felt heartache, elation when Jacob felt elation. In the text, his harrowing first day back at school was just ending. Fairfield forced himself to break away, flipping the diary over and resting it face-down, splayed, on the canteen table.

Nervously, Fairfield's hand found his tobacco and papers and he began to roll a thin cigarette, his mind turbulent and yet liberated. What the hell had he just experienced? A natural talent of Jacob's, or something created by Pelion and Bulmer? Could the boy somehow communicate empathically through his writing, or was it something more sinister?

He considered Bulmer's warnings about taking care in what one read.

Fairfield lit the completed cigarette with his tarnished brass Zippo and savoured the experience. His senses seemed suddenly sharper. He glanced guiltily over at Old Bill, expecting disapproval, but instead he saw Old Bill's dentures grinning back at him. The cook then showed off the cigarette he himself was puffing on while he swept the kitchen floor.

Fairfield centred himself for another session, and continued reading.

This time he found himself becoming calmer. Jacob was now describing his growing closeness to Sam Wilcox, the older man's enthusiasm for the Good Book, and the moral compass that it brought to his life. Fairfield then experienced the joy that Jacob had felt, with the realisation that Susan Cole was his saviour, and that deliverance from the inequities of the world, as described in the New Testament, were indeed possible.

Fairfield read on.

After a while, his cigarette went untouched. It flared and then dwindled, turning to ash, ignored. The canteen faded away, and Fairfield became completely absorbed, tears silently tumbling down his face when his trust in Susan Cole and Sam Wilcox was shattered. When the arguments had started. The loneliness and isolation as Jacob drifted further from his adopted parents, and pared down his life to almost that of a hermit in his empty room, with only his Bible, his constant, left for solace. And then, eventually, even Susan herself had rejected him. He'd begged her; he'd pleaded with her to absolve him of his sins, to take him away from this benighted world but she said no, she said it was too late, that she should never have come here.

Panic and despair.

With a ragged gasp, Fairfield forced himself to break away from the diary. His heart was pounding, and he was disoriented. A cold crescent of ash was dangling from his ochre fingertips. How long had he been immersed in this diary? It might have been thirty minutes — it felt like six months. He took a paper napkin from the table dispenser and mopped his brow.

Suddenly, the sound of the heavy doors made him jump. Self-consciously, Fairfield looked on as a WPC walked in and used the vending machines by the entrance. Fairfield hunkered down and waited until she had gone, his shoulders tense.

The diary called to him.

As soon as the coast was clear again, he turned the page to the next entry.

Saturday, 13th July 2002.

The day Susan Cole had disappeared.

The eloquent, careful handwriting suddenly stopped. Deep, wandering scrawls cut brutal scars across the paper, an outpouring of fury and frustration, for page after page. These sections of seemingly random lines had never been photocopied, originally considered to be artefacts of Jacob's angst, nothing more. Fairfield stared at them, transfixed, enthralled by their savagery.

And then, in front of his eyes, the tangle of ink began to swirl and spin, creating a vortex that drew Fairfield's mind ever closer.

He felt a rising terror as he descended. Why, when he needed her the most, was she leaving? Leaving him here on his own, helpless and floundering. His grip on reality collapsing. He had to see her, one last time. He'd make her understand. Save me… heal me… or else take me with you to Paradise.

There is nothing left for me here.

Then the maelstrom subsided, into symmetry. Lines coalesced with other lines. Form became shape; then shape became reality. Fairfield's mind descended into a borderless mist and soon there was no more canteen, no more police station, no more colour, only shifting shades of grey and spectres in the fog.

A tall, imposing silhouette rose up in front of him.

It had a new front door.

Calmly, and with the certainty of acceptance, Fairfield and Jacob entered Susan Cole's house together.

7

You are there to witness the end.

It stands there, at the top of the stairs.

Always the stairs.

The laboured, ragged, howling of The Devil is all that you can hear. It fills the stinking air; it echoes through your bones; it forces the breath back down your throat. In its hands The Devil holds her, trapping her in its claws. Her body is insignificant against that of her captor, and she is powerless to break free. The Devil's baleful eyes stare down at you through its long, dirty hair and dare you to intervene.

Your courage fails you.

Then, through the low, mocking rumble of The Devil's laughter, you hear her mournful scream. She cries out once, twice, each breath in between taking a lifetime to renew itself. The hopelessness of her lament burns you like poison.

The eyes of The Devil flare.

It pushes her head backwards over the windowsill. The landing window hurtles down like a guillotine. The thick, heavy wood slams into her neck, and her song is abruptly silenced.

Then the mist thickens, and the triumphant, terrifying roar of the Beast grows louder. Soon only its cacophony fills your mind and you long for death to release you.

Then, just as suddenly as it appeared, The Devil is gone, and you are alone with your fallen Saviour. Her broken body lies before you at the bottom of the stairs. Never before have you felt more wretched. The light that once burned so fiercely within you is gone, extinguished by the horror you have just witnessed.

But it is not the end.

Soon you realise; this is the moment as it was written. This is the moment of her becoming. You know instinctively what must be done. You understand now. This is why they have passed the knowledge on to you, so that you alone could be here at this time. So that you can save Her. It has happened before, and it can happen again.

Then, after She returns, you will both take up arms and you will battle The Devil together.

In just three days' time.

Fairfield's eyes snapped open, and he was suddenly awake.

He was not where he was expecting to be.

Blinking away his confusion, he rubbed his tousled head and looked around. He was in the top corridor of the station, next to his grandfather's photograph. His whole body was shaking with nervous energy, and footfalls, conversations, and distant door-slams were assaulting his senses. He had no recollection of how he got there, and yet his presence was provoking no comment from passers-by.

He looked down and saw that Jacob's diary was still in his hand.

Was this reality? Somehow it felt false; maybe even more so than the nightmarish experience he had just undergone. Had he really just witnessed Susan Cole's murder, through Jacob's eyes?

He steadied himself against the wall.

Through the fanlight windows above him, Fairfield heard the rumble of vehicles, no doubt the support team for Jacob's escort convoy preparing to leave.

His eyes drifted along the old photographs as he composed himself. They were the same images as they had always been; crowd shots of the old market; landscapes from a less developed suburbia; the High Street, with what passed for heavy traffic in those days. Something drew his attention to one photograph in particular, however: a sepia tableau of proud workers, cultivating Harkham Common in Edwardian times.

And then he saw it.

His heart skipped a beat, and suddenly everything was clear.

Without thinking, Fairfield grabbed hold of the photograph, ripping it from the wall and dislodging the plaster behind it. Two uniformed officers, making their way down the corridor, gave him a puzzled look as they passed. Fervently, Fairfield turned the cracked walnut frame one way and then the next, at each turn closely examining the image within. There could be no mistaking what it showed. He slowly raised his head, a horrified understanding etched into his face.

"Jesus Christ...," he whispered.

Inspector Menzies had originally been looking forward to a well-deserved afternoon off, but now he found himself being accosted in the locker room by Duncan Fairfield.

"Brian! There you are!"

Menzies smiled patronizingly as he closed his locker door. "Take it easy now, poppet," he teased. "We wouldn't want you keeling over and going on sick leave, would we?"

Fairfield, the photograph still in his hand, charged forward and clasped Menzies by the shoulders. "I need your help," he said, earnestly.

Menzies' eyes narrowed. "Are you on duty or not?"

"Depends who you ask. This is important, Brian. I need as many hands as you can spare, and we'll probably need some sort of lifting equipment..."

"Hang on mate," protested Menzies, "I was supposed to have finished at two, and I've got a coffee addiction to feed..."

"Shut up and listen!" snapped Fairfield. Menzies did so, but grudgingly. "Can you get lifting equipment?" continued Fairfield. "Hoists, hydraulic jacks, anything?"

Menzies scratched his head. "Well, I could have a word with Phil over at the fire station, I suppose... but what the hell for?"

"Just get whatever you can, and as many strong arms as possible."

"You do realise I actually have a long list of real things to do, don't you Duncan?" preached Menzies sarcastically. "Hill will have my guts for garters if I just drop everything and follow you off on one of your..."

Fairfield gripped Menzies' arms even tighter, and looked straight into his eyes. "I think I've found her, Brian," he said, his voice trembling. "I think I know where she is."

And he handed Menzies the photograph.

8

Caplain pointed towards the far end of the hospital car park.

"We'll be leaving via that service road. It's a little more discreet." The group followed Caplain's finger and saw a narrow tarmac road. Through a border of thick hedges, it snaked down through the fields, and to the base of the hill on which the Hospital lay. "After that," continued Caplain, facing his team again, "it's onto the bypass for about three-quarters of a mile. If anybody's going to try anything, then this is where it's most likely to happen. It's open ground, there are plenty of slip roads on and off the main drag, and the other side drops into a residential bloody rabbit warren. So be on your guard. Once we get past that stretch, we're on to the flyover, the motorway, and relative safety. Any questions?"

Hollander raised a hand. "Can I just ask what sort of threat we're expecting, sir? This all seems a bit excessive for a teenage kid."

Paul Black answered this, before Caplain could speak.

"There is a very real threat of a kidnap attempt," said Black, addressing the whole group and not just Hollander. "But we've got the jump on them, courtesy of some sharp detective work by DI Fairfield."

Caplain could not believe what he was hearing. A few days ago, Black was writing Fairfield off. Now he was singing his praises, and sucking up to Caplain in the process. Then it dawned on Caplain just how ambitious his colleague of less than a week really was, and he found himself wondering how long such loyalty would last.

Black turned round to Caplain, and smiled.

Ken Bulmer's patience had paid off.

Just as his concentration had started to falter, he had spotted it. It was Greg Cole's car, and it was turning into the hospital's southern entrance. Bulmer recognised it from RAF Greenwood.

He tapped out his dwindling pipe on a tree trunk, and moved cautiously down the hill, towards the hospital, keeping to the curve of the landscape. From this distance it was unlikely Cole would spot him, but Bulmer wanted to gauge where Cole was ultimately headed first. He hung back while Cole parked up and paid the meter. Shortly afterwards, Bulmer saw his quarry walk away from the main building and towards a smaller one, further down the hill, that was connected to the hospital by a low, concrete umbilical. Bulmer followed him.

It wasn't long before Bulmer was close enough to see the sign. It read simply: 'Pathology.' Bulmer smiled to himself. Back to his roots, he mused. After scanning the landscape around it, Bulmer began to form an idea as to Cole's plan. The rear of the Pathology building opened onto fields, and then these fields bordered the hospital service road. From here, Cole could co-ordinate an attack on Jacob's transport, or even launch one himself.

Unless he was stopped.

Bulmer waited for Cole to enter the ugly, single-storeyed building, and then followed.

Caplain threw the keys over to DS Black.

"Well volunteered, Blackie," he said. "You're driving the limo."

Black instinctively caught the keys before he realised what was happening, and then stared at the waiting ambulance. His look of disdain spoke volumes. "But Guv," he complained, "it's a heap of old rust."

"That it may be," replied Caplain, "but it's got iron grilles on the rear doors and windows, which is extra security we may end up needing. I also want a qualified police driver behind the wheel, instead of the security firms. I've read your file, Blackie; you were top of your class. This is your reward."

"With the greatest of respect," Black argued, "my advanced driving course was not in a bread van."

"Cobblers, you've driven a police transit, haven't you?"

"Yes, but…"

"Same difference, then."

Clearly seeing this as the final word, Caplain cut the protesting Black off mid-sentence and clapped his hands together, unconsciously emulating Fairfield. "Okay, you lot," he said, glancing at his watch. "Just gone two o'clock, so our guests will be here shortly. Here's the drill." He pointed at the uniformed officers. "Take the traffic cars down the hill now and park up on the hard shoulder of the bypass, one on each side. That way we have the angles covered, and a bit of obvious police presence. You never know, it might deter them if they're just hoping for a lucky opportunity."

PC Hollander and his colleagues nodded in agreement.

"Once Morgan and his medical staff are all loaded up, we'll follow in convoy," continued Caplain. "Harvey, Sally; you'll take the lead in Sally's car. Blackie will follow in the ambulance. Des and I will bring up the rear in my car. That way we're protecting the ambulance from both ends. Keep communications open, and stay in touch. If anything happens, normal procedure. We close ranks, and get out of there as soon as. Any questions?"

Caplain got his answer in the form of silence, and eight determined faces. Not bad for his first few hours as an Inspector, he thought.

As he emerged from darkness, Jacob shielded his eyes.

"Nice day for it, Jacob," remarked Nurse Tomkin, who was pushing his wheel chair. "Bright light's not a problem when the sun's out, eh?"

Two security guards and an orderly were escorting them, and a tardy Dr. Montgomery had just joined them in the lobby. The group turned right, and headed down the side path towards Caplain's staging area. By the time they arrived there, the squad cars had already left and everyone was ready for the off. Two more orderlies were waiting for Jacob by the rear doors of the ambulance.

"Nice day for it," repeated Jacob.

Suddenly he reached up and grabbed Montgomery's hand, startling the large doctor, and making him break his step. Nurse Tomkin frowned as the resistance on the wheel chair she was pushing doubled.

"How many days has it been?" Jacob asked uneasily, as though remembering an important appointment.

"Since what, Jacob?"

Then Jacob just shook his head dismissively, and let go of the doctor's hand. He started to look around himself with suspicion.

They continued their journey in silence.

Caplain felt a small surge of satisfaction as the convoy moved off only two minutes behind schedule.

So that he could better direct his colleagues over the radio, Caplain had elected to be a passenger in his own car and let Des Potts drive. He watched as Sally Fisher's car pulled away and then disappeared through the break in the hedgerow. A few seconds later, the diesel engine of Black's ambulance rumbled into life, and he followed her.

Caplain nodded to Potts..

"Let's get this show on the road, shall we, Des?"

Groaning at Caplain's pun, Potts released the handbrake and they eased forward.

Paul Black hated it already.

For a start, the service road was too narrow and the hedges too high. The ambulance had no power steering, the suspension was woolly, the seat was too low, and the gear-stick felt thin and fragile. The visibility was also poor. The rear view mirror was redundant; there was a steel plate separating the back of the ambulance from the driver's cabin, with only a tiny grille, and Black could see nothing through it. That just left the broad wing mirrors, but they were getting battered by the hedgerows.

And then there was the company. Slumped in the passenger seat was a hospital security guard. He was a big man in his thirties, with one of those hangdog faces that was born to be miserable. He was staring mournfully out of the window. Black considered making conversation, but then thought better of it.

In the back of the ambulance, Jacob studied his travelling companions warily. He was sitting in the top right corner, on the other side of the steel partition to Black. Opposite Jacob, Dr. Montgomery was busy trying to get comfortable in the cramped conditions. The two young orderlies were sitting by the doors, and were happily chatting to Jacob's police escort.

The vehicle gently rocked from side to side.

Montgomery, a good twenty years older and from a different world, found the orderlies' conversation about the upcoming football season somewhat lightweight, and so he turned his attention to Jacob. "What did you mean earlier?" he raised his voice slightly, over the clattering of the engine. "When you asked how many days it had been?"

"Mum's late," Jacob said guardedly. "I thought she'd gone away for good, but Mr Fairfield's going to find her. Bring her back."

Puzzled, Montgomery wondered whether it was Jacob's medication talking. Even with it, Jacob's moods seemed as mercurial as the weather. "She hasn't gone away though, Jacob," he said. "You saw your parents this morning; they gave you your nice new clothes, your trainers…"

"Not them," interrupted Jacob, his voice calm and simple. "They're Imposters. Won't be seeing them again."

He crossed his arms confidently and looked over at the orderlies. They noticed him and glanced quickly back, a fleeting uncertainty in their eyes, before continuing with their conversation. Tales of Jacob's violent misadventures had been widely reported.

Montgomery sighed, and humoured him.

"Don't worry, I'm sure we will," he explained, for both their benefits. "That's where we're going right now. And both your mum and dad will be waiting."

It was then that Jacob began to get anxious.

"No, we're going to see Mum," he protested, an undercurrent of panic in his voice. "That was the plan. Just do as we planned."

Jacob got to his feet.

Hunched over under the low ceiling, he pulled his arms defensively over his chest and began muttering to himself. He circled the same spot, the rubber on his brand new trainers squeaking as he moved. "No, no, no," he murmured, repeatedly. "Not right. Not going here. Have to go there instead. Must go there."

Immediately, everyone else in the ambulance was on edge.

The police officer and the orderlies half stood, ready to move forward, but Montgomery waved them back. "Don't crowd him," he said softly, before turning back to Jacob. "Everything will be fine, Jacob. Please don't be worried. Why don't you sit back down so that we can look after you? We don't want you bumping your head, now do we?"

Ignoring him, Jacob continued to pace anxiously.

Just then, there was a sharp grating noise as the hatch to the driver's cabin slid open. From beyond it came the voice of Paul Black.

"Everything all right back there?"

At this sound Jacob froze.

Slowly facing the front of the compartment, he grasped the iron grille and pulled himself forward. He peered cautiously through the open hatch. At the same time, the moribund Security Guard turned around in its seat and addressed Jacob's terrified face.

"What you want?" the guard grunted.

Jacob let out an anguished cry and pulled, hard.

With a screech of rending metal and shattered fixings, Jacob peeled the iron mesh back to the floor as if he were folding down a bed sheet.

Cramped conditions or not, Montgomery and the others scrambled to their feet and retreated from Jacob, huddling as close to the doors as possible. But Jacob ignored them. His arms shot forward and through the now unprotected hatch.

He grabbed the Security Guard's head, lifted him backwards out of his seat, and began to scream.

9

Sally Fisher saw a flash of movement in her rear-view mirror, and looked up.

"What the hell?"

Behind her, the back end of the ambulance was swaying violently. Then she heard the screech of braking tyres. Immediately she slammed on her own brakes. A split-second later, she heard Potts doing the same in Caplain's car.

From the passenger seat, Gossett spun round and stared out of the back window. "I don't believe it! We've only come a few yards!"

"Quick! Get up their arse! Don't give 'em room to open the doors!"

At Caplain's command, Potts threw their car into first gear and drove it straight forward, with the engine howling in complaint.

The ambulance had come to a halt at an angle, blocking the lane, its front left corner buried in one hedge and the back right skewed into the other. Potts aimed Caplain's car straight at it but, before they could get there, the ambulance's rear doors came flying off their hinges.

"Shit!" yelled Potts.

He stamped his feet down hard as the doors toppled into their path. The brakes kicked in, but then locked into a skid. The car bucked as its front wheels struck the tumbling doors and then pushed them ahead of it like a sparking snowplough, the friction bringing them to a halt only millimetres from impact.

Their engine spluttered and stalled.

Caplain was already reaching for the door when the stationary vehicle suddenly shook, and the roof buckled down towards them.

"It's Morgan!" cried Potts.

Caplain grabbed the radio.

Using Caplain's car as a stepping-stone, Jacob leapt onto the roof of the ambulance. He saw DCs Fisher and Gossett abandon their car and start running towards him. Without delay, he slid himself down the driver's side of the ambulance and into the road.

It was then that DS Black swung the driver's door open with all of his might, and struck Jacob violently on his left side. Jacob, however, seemed to absorb the impact into his forward momentum and spun back round to face the ambulance. With a cry of rage he kicked the door, slamming it shut again and crumpling it inwards. Black, who had still been holding on to it, cried out as his arm was bent backwards with the force and showered with glass. He glared at Jacob through the shattered window. Jacob stood for a moment and glared back, his eyes ablaze with unadulterated malice.

Black tugged at the door lever, but it was jammed. He scowled at the Security Guard next to him. "Don't strain yourself, will you?!" he shouted.

"It's the hedge!" whined the Guard. "I can't get out!"

Then Jacob saw that Fisher and Gossett were almost upon him. Swiftly he clambered up the side of the ambulance, and launched himself from the tyres, gaining as much height as he could. The whole hedgerow swayed as he crashed into it. Without looking back, he pulled himself up and over.

He landed at a crouch in the Hospital gardens, and then broke into a run.

He was free.

Harvey Gossett was the first to reach the ambulance, and to see the damage Jacob had caused to it. He peered in through the windscreen and saw Black lying despondently behind the wheel. "Paul? You guys alright in there?"

"We're fine," replied Black tersely, "just get us out!"

From the passenger side, the Guard tapped Black on the shoulder. "Did you need this? It was under my chair," he said, and handed him a first aid kit in a heavy plastic box.

Black looked at it approvingly. "Thanks," he replied. "That looks just the ticket." Then he yelled out, "Mind your eyes, Harvey!"

Gossett ducked for cover as the heavy first aid kit came crashing through the windscreen. Black's head and shoulders quickly followed it, and Gossett began helping his colleague through the window frame.

Behind them, Caplain and Potts were clambering over the bonnet of their own car and into the rear cabin of the ambulance.

Inside they saw unsecured debris covering the floor, and four fully-grown men groaning amongst the mess. While Potts saw to the two orderlies and the police constable, Caplain continued on to the groggy Dr. Montgomery.

"You all right, doctor?" Caplain helped him return to the side bench.

Blinking, Montgomery shook his head and then started to rub the back of it. "No permanent damage done," he growled dopily. "Where's Jacob?"

Before Caplain could answer, Sally Fisher, red faced and short of breath, appeared at the front grille. Green stains now streaked her jeans, and the left sleeve of her blouse was torn. "Morgan's legged it into the hospital grounds. I tried to get through the hedge after him, but I think he's been drinking rocket fuel. I couldn't break through, let alone follow him."

At this, Montgomery tried to get up but dizziness overcame him. He collapsed back onto his seat with a crash.

"Careful, doctor," said Caplain. "Leave this to us."

"You don't understand," gasped Montgomery. "I think he's going somewhere specific. He wants to see his mother..."

"But we were going to Gardener Heritage anyway," argued Potts.

Caplain could feel his skin tighten as he made the connection. "I don't think that's what he meant, Des," he said softly. Leaning into the front cabin, he slapped the immobile Security Guard on the arm. "Why haven't you called for help yet, you useless article?" he snapped. "Earn yer bloody keep!"

Embarrassed, the Guard fumbled for his radio.

It was then that Caplain glanced out through the shattered windscreen.

And couldn't believe what he was seeing.

An enraged Paul Black was doing his best to disassemble the hedgerow by hand.

"I tried that," Sally told him desperately. "It's too bloody thick..."

"That little sod's mine," grunted Black, in between sharp tugs on the hedge trunks. "He can't have gotten far."

"Sergeant Black!" Caplain's voice bellowed from the cockpit of the ambulance. "What the hell are you doing? Get back here and move this bloody ambulance!"

"With all due respect, sir," said Black, before balancing himself precariously on the rear wheel-arch, "the keys are in the ignition." With a primal groan of effort, Black launched himself forwards. He jammed his feet into the bough of a thick branch. "I'll get after him this way," he gasped at his colleagues. "You head him off!"

He rolled out of sight, and into the gardens.

A black cloud descended across Caplain's features.

"Sally, Harvey!" he barked. "You're still mobile. Morgan'll be heading out of the grounds, so use your car to get ahead of him. We'll follow as soon as we shift this flaming scrap heap!" He smacked the side of the ambulance door in frustration. "You'd best hook up with the squad cars on the bypass. And stay in contact!"

Gossett and Fisher turned and sprinted back to their vehicle.

Meanwhile, Caplain angrily turned the key in the ambulance's ignition. The engine coughed and shuddered, but refused to turn over.

"Come on!" he shouted.

Dr Neil Wetherall finished loading the autoclave, sealed it and switched it on. Then, as he turned to leave the sluice room, he stopped short at what he saw through the open door.

Standing in the small reception area of the Pathology department was a man Wetherall had never seen before; sixty-something, balding and clad in tweed; the ghost of Colonel Blimp. He seemed to be getting his bearings, searching for something. Wetherall froze. For a moment there was silence, except for the distant, muffled whine of a surgical drill.

After a while the intruder moved off again, down the long central corridor, and towards the autopsy theatre. At this, Dr Wetherall returned to his senses and spurred himself into action.

"Hey! Stop!" Wetherall cried, hastily dumping his latex gloves in the clinical waste bin, and then hurrying out of the sluice room in pursuit. "Medical staff only through here!"

The Colonel Blimp man was already several yards ahead of Wetherall. "Then you can relax, dear chap," he said without breaking his stride, "I was carving cadavers in a place like this before you were even born."

Dr Wetherall broke into a run and caught up with Bulmer, stumbling into pace with him and clearly flustered over what his next move should be. "I'm really going to have to ask you to leave," Wetherall told him.

"No need," said Bulmer. "Out is the direction I'm headed in anyway. Tell me young man; have you seen anyone else pass through here in the last few minutes?"

Wetherall frowned. "What? No. No, I haven't..."

"Glad to hear it. Focussed on your work. You'll go far. Does this place have a back door?"

"Um... yes, next left."

"Thank you. I'd get back to your autoclave if I were you, my dear fellow; heard the faintest of whistles, your seal might need replacing."

Then, just as they reached the thick, plastic strips of the sterile area, Bulmer swung sharply to his left as instructed.

The bewildered Dr Wetherall came to a halt, and watched him go.

After shutting the fire-escape door behind him, Bulmer took a few paces into the field and stopped to scan the landscape again.

There was still no sign of Greg Cole. The man had disappeared.

Bulmer calculated the distance to the field's opposite edge, and concluded that Cole wouldn't have had time to make it to the border yet, let alone cross into another field or onto the road. Bulmer took a handkerchief from his waistcoat and dabbed at his brow, which had dipped in confusion. Where the hell had the man gone?

Perhaps he should retrace his steps.

As Bulmer turned back to the Pathology building, there was a thunderous rustling from his right, and a hollow thump.

Bulmer looked over and saw that one of the perimeter hedges was swaying in the aftermath of an impact, about a hundred yards down the hill. In front of it, on the grass below, a young man in jeans and a dark t-shirt was crouching; to all intents and purposes a teenage boy. His eyes were wide in panic, his breaths rapid and short. Soon afterwards, the boy unfurled from his crouch, and broke into a sprint across the yellowing grass.

Bulmer slowly smiled in recognition.

It had been years since he had last seen Jacob Morgan.

He had forgotten the otherworldliness of the boy. With pride, Bulmer stood atop the rise and watched the strange figure fly across the field; his drawn features, his thin but formidable frame, powering him at full strength towards the far side of the field. Once Jacob got there, he would be out of the hospital grounds and onto the road.

Then, suddenly, Jacob stopped dead in his tracks. He remained there for several seconds, chest heaving, and staring upwards at Bulmer with a curious expression on his face. A moment later, he was walking briskly up the hill. In a nervous gesture of goodwill, Bulmer walked a few paces down to meet him.

Eventually they came face to face. Bulmer smiled hesitantly, but Jacob's quizzical expression remained, as though he was encountering a new species.

"Hello, my boy," said Bulmer, warmly. He wanted to extend his hand in greeting, but the boy looked only one step away from lunacy and he thought better of it. "Where are you off to in such a hurry, then, eh?"

"I'm going to see my Mum," replied Jacob proudly.

The ache that his answer brought to Bulmer's heart was all consuming. He smiled his way through it. "Good for you, Old Chap, good for you," Bulmer nodded approvingly. "Give her my fondest when you see her, won't you? And tell her that I won't be long. Will you do that for me, Jacob?"

Jacob considered this for a moment.

"Okay," he said, eventually.

Just then, they heard an enraged cry and the heavier thump of a less elegant landing. They saw Paul Black come lumbering through his third hedge. His clothes were torn, and coated in leaves, but his expression was resolute. As he struggled upright again, Black spotted Jacob and Bulmer straight away.

"Bye!" said Jacob cheerfully, and resumed his sprint towards the far hedge.

Immediately Black picked an intercept trajectory, and went for it. Nobody was getting away, not this time. Forcing his lungs to breathe deeper, and his leg muscles to pump harder, Black gradually began to close the space between him and his quarry.

They would both be reaching their goals with only a split second to spare.

10

Fairfield and Menzies were turning onto Harkham Common when they got the call.

Briefly taking one hand away from the steering wheel, Fairfield thrust his mobile at Menzies and concentrated on hurtling down the driveway.

"DI Fairfield's phone, Inspector Menzies speaking."

Menzies listened to the phone but said nothing.

They rolled into the broad car park. Fairfield was pleased to see that some uniforms were already on the scene. To their left, the portacabin that had been their Incident Room during the Cole search was being unlocked and prepared. All they needed now was the damn Fire Brigade. As Fairfield parked up, Menzies ended the call and handed the mobile back, his face glazed with disbelief.

"That was Jed Caplain," he said. "It's Morgan…"

At the sound of those words, Fairfield knew that there was no time to lose.

Sally Fisher's car almost didn't make it round the bollards at the hospital entrance, and swayed dangerously out into the right hand lane.

Fisher struggled to regain control of her steering, while at the same time negotiate the thick traffic of the bypass. Harvey Gossett, desperately trying to monitor the on-going pursuit, could now see two figures charging over the crest of the grounds towards them. "Stay in the inside lane!" he shouted. "Here they come!"

Fisher quickly indicated left, and then wrenched the car over again. A white van behind them honked its disapproval.

"Have you given any thought as to what we're actually going to do when we catch up with them?" demanded Fisher.

"Jesus, that boy can run," exclaimed Gossett. "But Paul's not doing badly either! He's catching him up! Pull over! He's nearly got him!"

"What do you mean, pull over?!" cried Fisher. "There isn't anywhere!"

Gossett glanced down out of his window; the dual carriageway was bordered by only a thin line of kerbstones, and perhaps eighteen inches of grass. "Shit," he said, "you'll just have to…"

Fisher broke hard and flung the car up onto the narrow verge. A thick pall of smoke billowed from her tyres. The white van that was following them, not to mention the next half-dozen cars in the inside lane, slammed their hands down onto their horns and veered sharply around this new obstacle.

"Sorry," Fisher switched on their hazard lights, "it was the only way. I'll sort out the traffic, you help Black."

After a quick check of their wing mirrors, the two detectives leapt out of the car. Gossett made a bee-line for Black and his quarry; Fisher threw open her car boot. Already she was conscious of the rubbernecking drivers around them, and the potential for an accident.

Where were those squad cars?

Black launched himself at Jacob Morgan's fleeing shoulders.

He had intended it to be a carefully timed rugby tackle, but urgency, heat, and adrenaline had eroded all chance of strategy and he found himself just lunging forward.

The two collided at full speed and tumbled forward as one, their momentum sending them crashing into the branches. Jacob cried out in anger and frustration, his limbs thrashing wildly at his captor, but the hedgerow had entangled him and he could not deliver his blows. Black fought to keep as tight a hold on Jacob as he could, grimacing as twigs and sharp fingernails scratched at his face. But then he heard the welcome wail of police sirens, and it bolstered his resolve. Help was on its way.

"Hang on in there!" cried a disembodied voice. "I've got him!"

Two arms dropped down from the top of the hedge, and grabbed hold of Jacob's shoulders. In an instant, Black realised what was happening and panic seized him.

"No! Don't!"

Harvey Gossett pulled with all his might, gasping with effort, and dragged Jacob backwards through the remaining inches of foliage. "Got ya!" exclaimed Gossett.

"Harvey, be careful!" warned Black at the top of his voice, while struggling to release his snagged clothes.

Hollander's patrol car had now pulled up onto the verge behind Fisher's, and switched off its sirens. It kept its blue lights flashing, however, to warn oncoming traffic. Fisher held up her hand in greeting, and began to approach the new arrival. She could also see the second squad car pulling over, on the opposite carriageway.

Gossett, who was holding Morgan in an arm-lock in front of him, looked over at PC Hollander and smiled. "Well, the cavalry's arrived at last. Typical, now that the fun's all over!"

Just then, Jacob jerked into life again. He stamped down hard on his captor's feet, and smashed Gossett's nose with the crown of his skull. Gossett roared in pain, instinctively releasing his hold on the boy and staggering backwards against Fisher's car, hands to his face.

"No!" howled Black in desperation, finally free of the briar. He lunged forward, but missed Jacob by millimetres. The boy ran towards Fisher and the Squad Car.

Thinking quickly, Fisher grabbed a baton from the still open boot. She extended it with a flick of her wrist, and positioned herself directly in the centre of Jacob's only escape route: the gap between the two cars. Her expression dared Jacob to try and get past. In support of this, Hollander began to inch his vehicle forward and hem them both in.

Jacob paused for a split second, assessing the situation. His new clothes were now torn and drenched in sweat. Beads of scarlet welled from the scratches on his face and arms. His eyes, however, remained bright and cold. Fisher stared into them, but saw nothing except her reflection.

And then Jacob smiled.

"You're pretty," he said, before grabbing hold of the two-foot metal sign that Fisher had put there only moments before; it read 'Police Accident'. He flung it hard at Fisher, who had to throw herself to the ground to avoid it. Missing her head by a hair's breadth, it continued towards the windscreen of the squad car. The PCs inside quickly swung their arms up to protect their faces. As the sign smashed into the laminated glass, Jacob turned and dived through the channel formed by Fisher's open boot.

He emerged like a dart from the other side and landed on the inside lane of the dual carriageway, tucking his knees inwards and absorbing the impact into a forward roll. The air was filled with the screech of tyres and the baying of car-horns, as the traffic slewed either side of him. A white hatchback skidded out of control and up into the central reservation. Immediately, Jacob leapt to his feet and ran towards the crashed vehicle, his energy undiminished, and vaulted the stricken car effortlessly. Clearing the crash barrier, he landed on the opposite carriageway.

Without stopping to look back, Jacob ran along the central reservation, his relentless legs pounding. The second Squad Car, who now had the target on their side of the road, wheel-span into life and set off in pursuit. It too activated its sirens and emergency lights, but the traffic was thick. The driver yelled out of his window at the oncoming cars, demanding that they let him out.

All the time Jacob was getting further away.

Fisher ran over to Hollander's squad car. The sign that Jacob had thrown had struck it dead centre, but the toughened screen hadn't broken and a triangular bulge of tessellated glass now separated Hollander from his passenger.

"Are you guys okay?" Fisher asked anxiously.

"Shaken but not stirred," quipped the dazed Hollander.

"See if you can radio through to Caplain and Potts," she ordered. "They may be able to get under the flyover and come back down the other carriageway, head Morgan off." Leaving Hollander to his message, she rushed back to her own car. Harvey Gossett was leaning against the passenger door and prodding his nose gingerly. "Broken?" Fisher had time to ask, before Paul Black slammed a hand onto her shoulder and pushed her angrily aside.

He strode up to Gossett. "What the fuck was that?" he yelled into the other man's face, his voice shaking.

"Jesus, Paul," answered Gossett, remaining calm, "chill out, I was trying to help…"

"I had him! I had him, you stupid bastard!"

Gossett squared up to Black and looked him straight in the eye. "Yeah, well next time you're in a scrape you can get stuffed," he told Black bitterly. "I'm the one who got a broken nose for my troubles."

"You deserve it," declared Black, waving a hand at the shattered police car. "Because this is all your fault. Thanks to you, Harvey, Morgan is still out there!"

Ken Bulmer felt numb.

He had always suspected that a flicker of hope remained in his heart, but his encounter with Jacob had forced him to face it. Deep down, a tiny part of him was screaming and kicking against the hand of fate. Deep down, a tiny part of him had wanted to live. Perhaps that was why he had allowed Eric White to torture him into letting Fairfield down so badly. But now he understood, and he finally realised why. Now that he had stood face to face with Jacob, and touched his spirit, he knew that it had been Jacob's voice in the back of his mind; Jacob telling him to survive.

Because they had needed to see each other, one last time before the end.

The summer breeze gusted.

Bulmer turned his face to the sun, his eyes closed, and savoured the sensations. The sounds of police sirens and panicking traffic reached him, carried on the wind, but he was not concerned. He knew that Jacob was strong. When Bulmer lifted his eyelids again, he saw that a figure was silently approaching him.

"Hello, Old Chap," Bulmer said. "You're a little late, I'm afraid."

Greg Cole came to a halt beside him.

Bulmer cast an eye over Cole; he was dressed strangely, as though he had selected clothes at random. His expression was impassive. There was something in his right hand. It glinted in the sunlight. Eventually Cole answered, flatly: "Late?"

"Yes, late. Jacob's long gone," Bulmer told him. "You see, Old Boy, I know full well why you're here. What your orders are. I'm sorry to report that you've had a bit of a wasted journey."

"Really?," Cole responded, his tone remaining emotionless.

"And you've only yourself to blame," continued Bulmer, turning to face Cole square on. "You should have listened to me," he said, suddenly angry. "Damn it, Greg, you should have come with me to see Rowcroft, not blabbed to Fairfield. With Rowcroft, we could have at least salvaged something, but now they're on the warpath and tying up loose ends! Don't you see, my dear old friend?" Bulmer sighed in frustration. "They were testing your whole family! They wanted to see how their tinkering developed under parallel conditions; Adam was nurture, and your new son was to be nature."

At this Cole flinched, ever so slightly. "Susan lost the baby," he said. "You could have stopped it there and then. But you didn't."

Bulmer slowly shook his head. He glanced down at Cole's hand again, and the metal object in its grasp. Eventually he said:

"There's something you need to know. It's about Jacob Morgan, the young lad you were ordered here for."

There was a pause.

Bulmer looked back up at Cole and noticed that, for the first time since their encounter began, Cole seemed to be displaying emotion. His lips had tightened together, into a narrow but disturbing grin.

"Those weren't my orders," Cole told him, and he lifted up the bone saw. Its steel glimmered as he advanced towards Bulmer. "I was sent here for you."

Bulmer took a deep breath. "I see. Well, I must admit, Old Chap, I didn't think it would be you," he said, a rueful smile lifting his ruddy cheeks, "but now I think about it... I expect it's what she would have wanted."

11

Five miles away on Harkham Common, a breathless Fairfield answered his mobile phone for the third time.

"Jed. What news?" he gasped, wiping his brow with a handkerchief.

They were hurriedly yomping up the lakeside path, with a group of twelve police and fire officers at their side. Menzies was just as short of breath as Fairfield, but the fire fighters seemed unaffected in their heavy coats and boots.

"You're not going to believe this," he heard Caplain say. "We had Morgan cornered, and..."

Fairfield noticed at once. "What do mean, 'had'?"

"Damn boy took a suicidal leap from the top of the Sheerwell flyover, landed in the trees below. He just dropped to the ground and kept running!"

Fairfield turned the phone and spat out an expletive under his breath. Beside him, Inspector Menzies exchanged a worried glance with their colleagues. "Okay," continued Fairfield, calming down and addressing the phone again, "which way's he headed now?"

"He used the line of the flyover for cover for a while," replied Caplain, "and then jumped a fence and turned south. Sheerwell Valley estate. All our bloody cars were up on the flyover, though, weren't they. We're entering the estate now, but Morgan's got a hell of a head start."

Suddenly Fairfield came to a halt, as did the group around him.

"Hang on just one minute...," he said pensively, and then frowned in concentration. He looked around at the hill he and his party were climbing. A few degrees aside, the path they were taking ran due north. If the hill had not been there, and if there had been no limit to Fairfield's vision, he could imagine Jacob on the horizon, running towards them in a cloud of dust. He resumed his phone conversation. "Jed, you mentioned that Morgan's looking for his mother?"

"That's what he said."

Fairfield nodded grimly. "Then if I'm right, he's on his way here, to the common."

"The common? You've found something?"

"Not yet," Fairfield mopped his brow again. "We had to wait for the fire crew, but we're headed up to the woods now. I've got a horrible feeling about it, though."

"Shall we join you there?"

Menzies and the rest of the group looked back at Fairfield impatiently, keen to get on. "No," Fairfield told Caplain, "I've a better idea. Get as many men as you can to Harkham Grammar."

"The school?"

"If Morgan's coming here through Sheerwell Valley then Harkham Grammar lies directly in his path. He'll have to cut through the playing fields and up into the woods. We can be waiting in force, trap him in the grounds. All you need to do is drive him in the right direction."

Caplain sounded uncertain. "I don't know, Duncan. This kid's not natural..."

"Trust me, Jed. This is where he's headed."

On Harkham Grammar's playing fields, eight teenage runners were limbering up for the 1500 metres. Cheers were ringing out from the grandstand. Presiding over it all, the school faculty looked on from the head of the track, as they relaxed in their deck chairs.

Robert Brooks sat back with a sigh of satisfaction, proudly drinking in the spectacle that was their forty-eighth annual End of Term Sports Day.

"I think it's gone very well this year. Don't you?"

Miss Biggs nodded ambivalently; she was just glad that it would soon be over. "Perfect weather," she remarked, "although the grandstand's twice as big as last year's, and twice as expensive. Shame about the Fire Engine having to leave, too; the St. Johns lot look a bit forlorn out there now, all alone."

Brooks greedily swallowed some of his lemonade, crunching a shard of ice with his molars and making Miss Biggs cringe at the noise it made. "Well, when you've got to go, you've got to go," he said philosophically, and from the corner of his mouth. "Perils of the emergency services."

Biggs' eyes narrowed as she peered into the sunlight, and watched a gangly sixth-former negotiating the High Jump. "Knowing our luck, there'll probably be a fire now," she said wistfully.

Brooks chuckled. "Do try and put your pessimism aside, Patience. The sun is in the sky, and the people who pay our wages are having a whale of a time." He plucked a slice of lemon from his glass. After sucking the life from it, he waved the shrunken rind up at the clear blue sky. "Apart from a thunderstorm, what could possibly go wrong?"

It was then, and with perfect timing, that Miss Bellamy the Art mistress came hurrying over to them from the tennis courts. She was skinny and prim, with a quiet, breathy voice that one always had to concentrate to hear. She crouched discreetly down between them, and tapped Brooks on the shoulder. "Headmaster!" she whispered. "Headmaster! I don't know what to say... you need to come quickly."

"Whatever's the matter?" Brooks frowned. "The race is just about to..."

"You really should come now, Headmaster."

With a sigh of intolerance, Brooks rose melodramatically from his deckchair. Turning round to face the quadrant, he squinted through the tennis court fences at the car park, and the driveway beyond. Then, after his initial disbelief had faded, his eyes grew wide and his jaw dropped.

From behind him came a loud report, as the starter fired his pistol. Shouts of encouragement filled the air from the direction of the grandstand. Robert Brooks, however, was paying attention to none of it.

"This," he began, his voice ascending with each syllable, "...is a joke. It has to be... a joke." He staggered forward, tipping over his deckchair in the process, and gripped the tennis court fence with both hands. Like an inmate cursing the world from his prison window, he shrieked in outrage, "It's... Sports Day!"

With the courtly sound of gravel under their wheels, a convoy of police vehicles was rolling into the school car park. At its head was the maroon car of Sally Fisher, followed by two squad cars and a transit van.

After stomping defiantly back to the wreckage of his deckchair, Brooks retrieved his suit jacket, re-fastened the top collar button of his shirt, and straightened his tie. "Right. We'll soon see about this," he declared. "Come along, Miss Biggs."

He looked over to check whether Miss Biggs was also suitably incensed, and saw only an empty deck chair. Brooks' head snapped impatiently around, scanning all directions in a heartbeat.

He turned to Miss Bellamy. "Where is Miss Biggs?" he demanded incredulously. "She was here a second ago!"

Miss Bellamy shrugged helplessly back at him.

As he led his group of officers past the school buildings, Black was speaking to his mobile. With him were DCs Fisher and Gossett — his nose now a vivid purple — and ten uniformed officers. The call was over in seconds, and he pocketed the phone before turning to his colleagues. "That was the Acting DI. Morgan's definitely headed this way."

"He's not the only one," remarked Gossett, with a nod.

They followed Gossett's gaze and saw Robert Brooks marching towards them. The headmaster didn't even wait until he was in earshot before speaking. "What's the meaning of this intrusion?" he yelled indignantly. "We're in the middle of a school event!"

Black walked out to meet him, holding his warrant card open for inspection. "Detective Sergeant Black, Sir, Harkham CID. Sorry for the disruption, but we need to get across your fields."

"We are running a race!" Brooks protested, as though that was the end of the matter. Anxiously, he glanced back and saw what he feared the most; a smattering of curious faces were starting to appear at the gates, including, much to Brooks' horror and embarrassment, one of their most revered governors.

"I quite understand, sir," Black explained, and not certain that he had Brooks' full attention, "but a prisoner has escaped custody and we have reason to believe he may be headed this way. We'd like to form a secure perimeter around your fields."

This prompted a different attitude entirely.

"Escaped prisoner?" repeated Brooks nervously. "Are they... dangerous?"Black made a conscious decision not to reveal Jacob's identity to his Headmaster. "There shouldn't be any danger," he said, "but, to be on the safe side, I would start telling your guests to make their way home, if I were you."

At this, Brooks' mood flipped over into panic. "But... but," he stammered, "the prize-giving, the brass band..."

Sally Fisher took a step forward, and rested a sympathetic hand on Brooks' arm. "I'm afraid they'll have to wait, Mr Brooks," she said reassuringly. "Especially if you want to avoid a scandal."

"S...scandal?"

Gossett understood Sally's tactic immediately, and ran with it. "Hopefully not," he said, with just the right amount of uncertainty in his voice, "not if you let us handle the situation now. We don't want another Harkham Grammar headline in the papers so soon, do we, sir?"

"Everything all right, Bob?"

Brooks jumped out of his skin as a large, stately looking man appeared behind him. "Oh, fine, fine, Sir Geoffrey, nothing we can't handle. I hope you and the other governors are enjoying the day?"

"Fine?" repeated Sir Geoffrey sceptically. "What do you need half the police force for, then?"

"Oh, nothing," replied Brooks immediately. "Just a trifling matter. We may, however, need to, um…"

"Yes?" barked Sir Geoffrey impatiently.

"…evacuate the playing fields," concluded Brooks, his voice small and pathetic.

Sir Geoffrey raised an eyebrow.

Back on Harkham Common, work at the cliff-top was progressing slowly. The team were already mopping their ruddy faces and having to catch their breath. Menzies and the Fire Chief were deep in conversation, discussing their next move, when Fairfield joined them from across the clearing.

"That was Jed on the phone. We've got people at the school now, so Morgan can't be far behind. How are we doing?"

"We've had to give up on the jacks," said Menzies despondently. "They just sink into the ground. We'll probably need some sort of harness, and a powered winch."

Fairfield nodded. "Let's get one up here, then."

"It's not as simple as that, Inspector," interjected the Fire Chief. "Even if we managed to get a winch up here, we'd still need to power it. That means a portable generator, cabling…"

"Fine," answered Fairfield brusquely, "the generator can power some arc lights, too. I don't care if we have to work on into the night. I'll authorise the overtime."

There was a pause as both men considered his response. Menzies spoke first. "Look, Duncan; are you sure about this? If your theory is right, it would mean that someone would have had to lift the top off the Coffee Table themselves in the first place. Just look at the trouble the professionals are having. It's solid granite. And then, where would the suspect have put it once it was off? There are no marks on the surrounding rocks, no impressions in the ground…"

Looking around, Fairfield was aware that it wasn't just Menzies and the Fire Chief who were now looking at him expectantly. He saw one set of tired eyes after another, each as determined to stop work as he was to proceed.

"You've been to Stonehenge, haven't you?" Fairfield said eventually, his features resolute. "We go on."

Ignoring the groans of dismay from the rest of the team, Fairfield singled out four uniformed officers and then pointed to the trees behind them. "You lot. Go through those woods and get yourselves down to the school playing fields; give Jed and Blackie a hand."

He then turned back to the remaining officers.

"And you lot; get this rock lifted. It's coming up if it kills us."

12

He was nearly at the meeting place. He could feel it.

The excitement focussed Jacob's adrenaline as the houses flashed past him. He would show the Imposters. He would show the Doubters. He'd prove Montgomery wrong. Soon they would all be together again, side-by-side and powerful; and then The Devil had better run.

Jacob heard the roar of approaching police cars.

He quickened his pace.

The residential streets around him dwindled into old, low buildings; what looked like a small commercial estate. The concrete buildings were weathered and worn. They obscured Jacob's view ahead, but that didn't matter. He knew he was close. Eagerly, he turned the next corner.

It was a dead end. He had expected wide, open fields.

For the first time, his way was blocked.

Jacob slowed down to a stumbling walk, uncertain of what to do next. The police were almost on him, two streets away at the most.

He saw there was a builder's merchant at the end of the cul-de-sac. Its yard was stacked high with any number of obstacles. Jacob's mind raced as he cautiously approached it, studying the layout, absorbing every detail of his surroundings. And then, just as Caplain's car rounded the corner and accelerated towards him, Jacob heard a sound that reignited his courage. From beyond the builders' yard, the breeze brought to his ears the crack of a starting pistol, and the roar of an excited crowd.

He had arrived after all.

The exhilaration within him returned, more powerful than ever. Jacob ran into the yard at full speed, heading straight for the back fence.

Near the entrance, a young man was stacking palettes of bricks with a forklift truck. As Jacob flew past him, the man scowled and shouted out a warning. His mood was then not improved when two cars, one of them a marked police car, came screeching to a halt in his forecourt, enveloping them all in a thick cloud of dust. It wasn't long before four coppers came running up to him.

"What's your game?!" shouted the man, while lowering his forklift load to the ground.

"Sorry, mate," Caplain called up to him. "Won't keep you long. Did you see where he went?"

Forklift Man frowned at them, and then pointed behind him, straight down the centre of the yard. There was a single-storey office building to the left of the plot, but the right hand side was dense with supplies. Stacks of tiles, bricks and breezeblocks formed an avenue all the way to back. Suddenly, from the direction he was pointing, there came a succession of ear-splitting impacts. The officers ran forward to investigate. Forklift Man switched off his truck, and followed them.

Jacob Morgan was winding his way through the material stacks, grabbing hold of the twine that held each of them in balance as he went, and pulling on it sharply. Like domino bones they tumbled. Some fell as one column, their contents shattering within their mesh, while others splintered into thousands of pieces, the debris rendering the yard behind them impassable.

Jacob was walling himself in.

Forklift Man looked on in desperate silence, his jaw agape.

"Somehow I don't think he wants to be followed," remarked Des Potts.

Urgently, Caplain turned to their overall-clad host.

"Is there another way round?"

Forklift came hurtling back to reality. "What? Oh... er... yes. Sort of. There's a gap behind the office..."

Without waiting for the end of the sentence, Caplain rushed over to the concrete building, giving orders as he went. "Des, you and me will go round. Hollander, you and Spence see if you can get over that bloody rubble. And don't let him backtrack on us!"

The group of officers split up. The anxious forklift driver scurried after Caplain and Potts. "Wait!" he called out. "It's only a two foot gap, if that! It's all overgrown..." He caught up with them just as Caplain was squeezing his way between the mouldy wall and the rusty wire fence behind it. Des Potts had already gone in ahead of him. It was a tight fit, and there was an uneven carpet of old rubbish. It turned and twisted their feet. Before disappearing completely, Caplain smiled reassuringly at the forklift man.

"Relax," he said. "We'll give you a crime number." The man then looked so despondent and helpless that Caplain felt compelled to add, "You are insured, aren't you?"

Jacob had reached the final barrier.

A row of palettes containing roofing tiles, stacked at least eight feet high, stood in front of an even taller wire fence. The owners had taken no chances with security, and crested it with curls of razor wire.

Beyond it, however, he could see the rolling green playing fields of Harkham Grammar. He saw his classmates running the athletics track. It was agonising to be so close. There was little time. She would be waiting for him.

Jacob hurled himself at the nearest stack, slid his hands and feet between the rows of tiles, and started to climb. The thin clay slates cracked and sagged under his weight. For each foot higher that he scrambled, he sank back two. Quickly changing his approach, Jacob grasped the thick twine that bound the stack instead. The metal threads dug into his palms, but he made better progress. Soon he made it to the summit of the stack, and staggered uneasily to his feet.

This left only the fence and the razor wire to conquer.

"Jacob! Wait!"

His head snapped round. Des Potts was emerging from the far side of the office building, perhaps ten yards away at the most. Soon he would be all the way out. With a cry of frustration, Jacob grasped the fence and tried to tear it down, but the concrete posts stopped it folding, and all it did was deform beneath his hands.

So instead, Jacob bent down, and picked something up.

Potts only just ducked in time.

The spinning tile, travelling at the velocity of a rifle round, struck the corner where his head had been only an instant before. Clay shrapnel peppered the side of his face. Potts gingerly patted his cheek and found spots of red. He called out to Caplain, who was still a few feet behind him, telling him to stay back. Then there were four more blows in quick succession, four more tiles disintegrating at the speed of sound. Potts backed away from the open corner as fast as the uneven ground would allow.

Atop his terracotta battlement, Jacob was about to select another tile when suddenly his left kneecap flared with pain.

Enraged, he looked down to see PC Spence, balancing precariously from the side of the tile stack. For a second time, Spence hacked at Jacob's legs with his baton. Jacob spun and kicked out at his attacker. Spence threw himself backwards to avoid the blow, and dropped back to ground level.

Nevertheless, the split-second distraction had been enough.

PC Hollander appeared at the other side of the stack, extending his baton with a dour determination, hoping that Morgan couldn't deflect two attackers at once. Des Potts had now also emerged from his cramped alley, and was running forward, Caplain hot on his heels.

Jacob desperately hurled himself at the back fence, straddled one of the concrete posts, and used the wire mesh either side of it as the rungs of a ladder. He quickly began to pull himself upwards.

"Oh no you bloody don't," cried Hollander, and gestured at Spence to give him a leg up.

"Careful," warned Caplain as he and Potts finally reached them, "it's not stable…"

With a roar of effort, Spence lifted his colleague up onto another tile stack, to the left of the one Jacob had just abandoned. Reluctantly following their lead, Caplain crouched down and propelled Potts onto the stack on the right. While struggling to keep their balance, Hollander and Potts then took up flanking positions.

Jacob screamed like a trapped animal as they grasped each of his legs and began to pull him away from the fence. The boy pulled himself in, closer in to the links, supporting his weight using his arms alone, and thrashed his legs like a demon to release their hold. Hollander's grip lapsed briefly, but was soon re-established. Potts clenched his features tight with the effort, the blood on his face mixing with rivulets of sweat.

It was then that Jacob changed.

The anxiety faded. First with one hand, and then the other, Jacob reached up and grabbed hold of the razor wire. With a slow and deliberate power he lifted himself up until his chin was level with his hands, bending his legs and curling them up into a crouching position. Hollander and Potts found themselves being dragged helplessly upwards, their hands slipping down to Jacob's ankles. They tried to steady themselves on the stacks below, but their trashing feet served only to scatter the tiles, like cards from a dealer's shoe. With a shout of alarm, Caplain and Spence backed away from the falling debris.

Soon Hollander and Potts were dangling in mid-air.

As though he was meditating, Jacob silently held his position. His fists tightened on the razor wire. Warm scarlet began to trickle down his forearms. Supporting the weight of three seemed not to trouble him at all, whereas his two passengers were gasping with the exertion of supporting only themselves.

"Christ…," murmured Caplain. He and Spence began to scramble up what was left of the stacks, arms reaching out to support their colleagues' weight. But then Jacob lifted himself higher still, straightening his elbows and pushing downwards onto the wire.

Hollander was the first to fall, collapsing backwards onto the remains of the stack below, his stab-vest softening the impact but shattering the top layer of tiles. He lay there, winded and dazed.

Grimly, Des Potts clung on.

His left leg now free, Jacob began to stamp remorselessly down on Potts' fingers, still entwined around his right ankle.

Once, twice.

Potts cried out in pain with each strike, but did not yield.

Three times. Four times.

There was a sickening crack. Potts screamed and fell, with not only his grip broken. Caplain and Spence did their best to catch him, but he landed hard on his side in the dust, howling in pain and cursing Jacob Morgan's name. The fingers of Potts' right hand were hanging from his palm at an unnatural angle.

Without looking back, Jacob swung himself over the top of the fence, landed deftly on the playing fields beyond, and was gone.

13

Oblivious to the situation unfolding around him, Mr Blanchard the sports master was doing his best to instil some drama into the closing moments of the 1500 metres. Relishing his hour of glory, Blanchard held the cheap microphone to his lips and imagined himself in the media box at the Olympic Games.

"The last two hundred metres, Ladies and Gents," he enthused. "And it's still too close to call! Carstairs is holding onto his early lead, but only just! Walsh is hot on his heels, and we all know how well he did last year. But wait! Who's this coming up on the outside? It's… it's…"

Blanchard paused for a second, and did a double take.

The runners were in their traditional all-white kit, but now a boy clad in jeans and a t-shirt seemed to be being rapidly overtaking them. Blanchard reached for his binoculars and rammed them into his eyes. "Good grief," he said, to himself but amplified by the microphone regardless. "Is that… Jacob Morgan out there?"

Blanchard looked on in amazement as Edward Carstairs, bright young star of Harkham Grammar's athletics team, received an elbow in his face and tumbled to the grass. Unable to avoid him, his seven opponents found their legs cut away and they too fell like skittles. Jacob Morgan leapt calmly over them all, and kept going.

The excited cheers of the crowd died back into a confused silence.

In the school car park, the heads of Black and his colleagues whirled round at the mention of Morgan's name.

"Did you hear what I just heard?" asked Sally Fisher.

At the far side of the field, the four officers that Fairfield had despatched from the common emerged from the tree line. The first sight that greeted them was the fracas on the track, and the heap of groaning sixth-formers that it had left behind.

After spotting Morgan's fleeing form, two of the officers ran down the bank to intercept him, while the others stayed put as ordered.

Black ran across the tennis courts at top speed, with Fisher, Gossett and a dozen officers at his heels.

Nonplussed, Robert Brooks looked on from the gate and waited for the ground to swallow him.

"Please don't be alarmed, Ladies and Gents," boomed Blanchard's voice from the announcer's tent. "Every great sporting event has its streakers, after all!"

Blanchard lowered his microphone, and looked on in bewilderment as police officers invaded his beloved pitch from both sides. In addition, there was now a commotion in the grandstand. More and more spectators were now standing up for a better view, or hurrying down the steps to the exit, with panic on their faces.

Jacob soon noticed the two groups of Imposters heading for him. He veered sharply to his left, and maintained his break-neck pace.

The grandstand had emptied.

Dozens of gawping faces now cluttered the touchlines, three rows deep, milling and chattering amongst themselves. As Jacob turned, and began to run straight towards them, the speculative babble descended into cries of alarm. Clearly enough people within the crowd had heard about Jacob from the local news. As one, the crowd began to back away from the field's edge.

DS Black and his party had also seen Jacob's manoeuvre. They turned right, along the verge of the bank and towards the anxious crowd. "Get out of the way!" yelled Black. "Don't approach him!"

Some people started to flee to the car park, but the majority stayed put in morbid fascination. Those that had decided discretion was the better part of valour hastened across the tennis courts, only to find Robert Brooks blocking their exit. "Don't go!" he pleaded. "The day's not over yet! Let the police handle it, it's what we pay our taxes for…"

But Brooks was shoved roughly out of the way.

Jacob reached the crowd. A second later, so did Black and his group.

But whereas the detectives had to fight their way through, Jacob was afforded a clean run as people backed away from him. Some even cried out in shock.

"Let… us… through!" roared Black, struggling to part the spectators with his arms. He tried to keep his eyes on Jacob, tracking his path. He can't have been more than ten feet away. Frantically, Black waved an arm at some of the uniformed officers behind him "Get round the back!" he shouted, smiling a brief apology to the woman that he had just deafened. He pointed wildly at the empty grandstand. The officers understood immediately, and began to swarm down the back of the tents, running parallel to the crowd.

Black looked forward again but Jacob was gone. "Damn it!"

"Sarge!" Harvey Gossett tapped him on the shoulder. "I think I saw Morgan go under the tarpaulin. Over there." Gossett pointed at the grandstand's far corner, where a flap was now open, its ropes lying loose on the grass.

"He's trying to hide inside," said Black, with a grin of satisfaction. "Uniform should be round the back by now. Sally; go and let them know what's happening. Harvey, see if you can't get this crowd moved back."

Fisher nodded briskly and started pushing her way back out of the crowd. Gossett raised his hands above head level, and shouted out to his captive audience. "Ladies and Gentlemen, please can I ask you all to move back down the bank and onto the field…"

As Black reached the torn corner of the grandstand, two uniformed officers he didn't recognise joined him from the direction of the field. They were flushed, and out of breath.

"Sir," gulped one, "PCs Craig and Tallamy. DI Fairfield sent us to assist. Did we get Morgan?"

Black did a double take and frowned. "Fairfield?"

"The man himself," PC Craig confirmed, waving a hand at the nearby woods. "He's over there on the common, excavating the rocks."

Black looked intrigued.

"Is he, indeed?"

In the gloom of the empty grandstand, Jacob paused in his journey. He crouched in the crook of the scaffolding, staring down at the carpet of litter, and listened. He could hear hushed voices from beyond the tarpaulin. He could see the slim, dancing shadows disturbing the sunlight at its base.

The thick, heavy boots of police officers were now patrolling all four walls.

This left him only one option.

Undaunted, Jacob begin to climb upwards.

There was a narrow alley between the back of the grandstand and the side of the gymnasium building, and it was into this that Sally Fisher and six Constables now crowded. They crouched down, and began untying the knotted ropes.

"Quickly," said Fisher in hushed tones, "the DS is driving him to us." Nervously, her fingers slipped and fumbled in their task. Morgan was unpredictable and violent, and could appear at any moment. Although Fisher normally thrived in tense situations, this one was testing her limits.

Just then, the tension increased.

"What was that?" hissed one of the Constables, getting to his feet abruptly and scanning the wall with anxious eyes. His colleagues soon followed suit. A single, sharp movement had rippled the canvas. They began to slowly back away.

"Stand ready," warned Sally quietly.

Three of the six Constables extended their batons. Another carefully slid a pair of handcuffs from his belt. They waited for what seemed like an eternity.

Then the canvas flap lifted, and the head and shoulders of PC Tallamy emerged. "Did you get him?" he asked, squinting in the sun.

There was a collective sigh of frustration and the officers lowered their batons.Sally Fisher felt the anxiety in her chest rising yet again.

"Didn't you?"

And not one of them noticed the swift flash of movement, far above their heads.

14

It had taken several minutes for Jed Caplain to reach the Grammar School entrance.

The queue of vehicles leaving the grounds had spilled over into both lanes of the short driveway, vying for position, and leaving common courtesy behind them. In the end, Caplain had blocked everybody in with his own vehicle, and taken to waving his warrant card at them.

"Back you go, please!" cried Caplain over the din of outraged car horns. "Everyone back! You will all need to re-park, and wait for an officer to speak with you." Several drivers leant out of their windows and shouted at him, possibly sceptical of whether the dishevelled, dust covered man before them really was a police officer. "Thank you for your co-operation!" Caplain concluded.

He made his way to the car park through the stationery vehicles. As he strode into the gravel courtyard, Robert Brooks hurried over to meet him.

"Sergeant Caplain!" exclaimed the Headmaster. "At last a familiar face."

Caplain kept walking, forcing Brooks to turn round and trot along beside him as they spoke. "That's 'Acting Inspector' today, Mr Brooks," Caplain told him. "Special offer. See that pile of metal over by your gates?"

Brooks couldn't miss the noisome gridlock. He nodded nervously. "Yes, some of our guests have taken exception to this afternoon's abrupt climax."

"Well, I take exception to them leaving," said Caplain. "They could have an extra passenger they hadn't bargained for. Get someone down there and close the gates. Nobody goes until I say otherwise."

Caplain increased his pace and strode off in the direction of the tennis courts, leaving Brooks standing in his wake. "Close the gates?" The Headmaster repeated incredulously, as if he'd just been asked to fly an aircraft blindfold. "Where's Wilcox when you need him?" he tutted.

Moreover, where was Miss Biggs, he added in his mind. From the moment the first police car had entered the premises, she had been conspicuous by her absence.

Caplain reached the tennis court gate just as Black, Fisher, and Gossett emerged from it. "Well?" demanded Caplain.

Black obviously hesitated too long before answering, because Caplain's face had sagged into disbelief before he'd finished his first word. "He's...," began Black. "We've got him cornered, Sir."

"Cornered where, Blackie?"

Black took a deep breath. Behind him, Fisher and Gossett shifted uneasily on their feet. "He's definitely still in the grounds."

"How do you know that?" exploded Caplain angrily. "I've just strolled in here unchallenged, what if he just strolled out the same way? What if he's in the boot of one of those cars?"

"We've started a search..."

"I suggest you do more than that. I want statements from everyone who was here. I want every vehicle searched before it leaves, understand?"

"Sir," replied Black sheepishly.

"I want bodies all round the perimeter," continued Caplain. "Secure it. There are more uniforms and dogs on the way. Search the grounds, search the outbuildings, and search the school. Other than Brooks and his staff, I want the place evacuated. Get them to help with access, and then get them out of harm's way. Got that?"

"Got it," said Black.

Gossett sighed remorsefully.

"We almost had him Jed," he told Caplain. "We were so bloody close."

Caplain nodded grimly. "Aye," he growled. "And if I had a fiver for every time I'd almost caught Jacob Morgan this afternoon, I could retire and not worry about it."

Fisher looked down at Caplain's torn and dust-stained clothes. "Are you okay? You look like you've been through the mill yourself."

Caplain's demeanour softened. "We had a run in with Morgan. I'm all right, but Des didn't come off too well; some bones broken in his hand, and cuts to his face. Carl Hollander's taken him up to casualty."

Sally shivered. That could easily have been any one of them. She thought of the rusty accident sign, embedded in Hollander's windscreen.

Caplain turned to Black. "Blackie; I'm relying on you to flush this bugger out. And quickly, too; the sun'll be setting before long. Stay in touch," He turned to go. "I'm going to report in to the boss in ten minutes' time. I'd like it to be good news, so let's get cracking."

Caplain had only walked four paces when Black called after him.

"The boss? Would that be DCI Hill or DI Fairfield?"

Caplain swivelled round in the gravel to face him.

"What's that supposed to mean?"

"Nothing," lied Black, "it's just that we were told Fairfield's on sick leave."

"He is."

"Then what's he doing digging up Harkham Common?"

Fisher and Gossett exchanged glances.

Caplain smiled thinly. "Just as Fairfield was going on leave," he explained, thinking on his feet, "there was a breakthrough on the Cole case. We think Morgan was headed back there for something."

Black was clearly not convinced.

Fisher, however, was more hopeful. "Perhaps we didn't do so badly after all," she said. "We may not have Morgan in custody yet, but we've stopped him getting to the common. Fairfield should be free to finish up now."

"But have we?" argued Black.

Caplain sighed impatiently. "Meaning what?"

His expression grim, Black addressed each of his colleagues in turn as he spoke. "Morgan changed course at the last minute. There were only two officers guarding the woods, but dozens in the school grounds, and he changed course. He ran straight to the superior numbers, even though for him it would have been a matter of seconds to overpower the smaller force, and gain access to the woods. Why?" Black let the question hang for a moment, and then continued. "What if we haven't given Fairfield the time he needs, but Morgan himself? What if his objective has been the school all along?"

Above them, a curtain fell back into place on the second storey of the school building.

Patience Biggs stepped away from the window, and silently crossed to the rear of the office. Upon reaching a wardrobe, she opened the door and reached inside.

Moments later, she was walking purposefully out of the room.

A bundle of dark, heavy material was in her arms.

With only half an hour to go before the end of her shift, Janice Pollard was busy clearing the sluice room and humming to herself. She was going out to dinner with her friends that evening, and couldn't wait for the working day to end.

As she reached into the sink for the final kidney bowl, Dr Neil Wetherall ran through the door and pushed her away from it.

Janice opened her mouth to protest, but then she saw that Wetherall's face was ashen, and beaded with sweat. His white lab coat was streaked with what looked like coffee stains. She stepped aside. Wetherall gripped the sides of the unit and was violently sick, his shoulders heaving, and with the deep chamber of the sink providing excellent acoustics.

So taken aback was she, that Janice took longer than usual to come up with a sarcastic remark. "Well," she quipped, "if you still want to be a pathologist, Neil, then you're going to need a stronger stomach than that!"

Wetherall spat out a strand of bilious saliva, and wiped his mouth on his coat sleeve. He look desperately up at her. "Call... the police," he said between heavy gasps, his voice flat in the sink. "Now."

Janice frowned. "Police? What on earth..."

"Just call them. Please."

"But..."

"Now, Janice!" Wetherall rolled over and slid downwards, his back to the cold metal doors. He ended up sat on the floor, his mouth dry, and his pallor deathly.

Janice crouched down next to him. "Neil, what's going on?" she asked. "Why the police? Is it to do with that intruder from earlier?"

Wetherall swallowed hard, and nodded.

"He's back," he said. "In the theatre this time."

Janice's jaw tightened. "Right. Wait here, I'll call security."

She started to stand up, but Wetherall's clammy hand restrained her.

"There's no rush," he said.

So far that Tuesday, PC Carl Hollander had skipped breakfast, attended a dawn raid, dealt with a runaway goods lorry on the A40, stood smoking in a car park for two hours — that was a good bit — had a sign thrown at him, gotten his squad car trashed, chased a teenager for miles in a different squad car, gone climbing in a builder's yard, and then rushed an injured colleague to hospital.

Sitting in casualty with Des Potts had seemed like a blessed relief. But then the emergency call had come in from Harkham General, in a bizarre reversal of roles from the norm. After leaving Potts with the nursing staff, Hollander called himself in as attending and rushed across to Pathology.

By the time he entered the small reception area, three of his colleagues had already arrived. To his left a WPC was interviewing a young man and a young woman, both of whom were in white laboratory coats and nursing a vending-machine tea. Hollander nodded at the WPC in greeting. The two other officers had gathered further down the corridor, outside the autopsy theatre. They were muttering anxiously amongst themselves. As Hollander approached, they fell silent and stepped away from the doorway, which he now noticed was surrounded by a pool of water. Hollander peered through into the theatre.

The room contained two men. Neither moved nor looked up at Hollander's arrival.

One of the men was sitting on the stainless steel operating table, with his hands folded neatly in his lap. He was staring at the flooded floor. Next to him, in the gutters of the operating table, there lay a bone saw. The water of the still-running sluice tap was swirling around its blade, before tumbling over the edge of the table. A wad of blood-soaked paper was blocking the drain.

Hollander frowned and turned to the nearest Constable. "Chris, hasn't anyone disarmed him yet?" he whispered.

"After you," answered Chris nervously.

"Has he said anything?"

"Hasn't so much as blinked since we got here."

Hollander produced a set of sterile gloves from his belt, and began rolling them down onto his hands. "Right you are, then" he said fatalistically. "I suppose today can't get any worse." He took a hesitant step into the theatre. Water squelched around his boots. The man on the table didn't react, even when Hollander crept right up to him and waved a tentative hand in front of the man's face. Prompting sharp intakes of breath from his colleagues at the door, Hollander then gently reached into the man's jacket and plucked out his wallet. He then picked up the bone saw and dragged it out of harm's way. Still no reaction.

Hollander then risked a glance downwards, to the second man.

The water on that part of the floor was darker.

Crimson eddies wandered lazily around Kenneth Bulmer. His ruddy cheeks were now pale, his tweed now thick and sodden. Two halves of a bow tie now flanked his wide-open throat.

Hollander sighed, and prepared his handcuffs. After glancing at the name in the wallet, he gathered the table man's limp hands into his own and said, "Gregory Cole, I am arresting you on suspicion of murder. You are not obliged to say anything…"

"Good," remarked Constable Chris from the doorway, "we'll never get him to shut up if he starts."

Hollander turned and scowled at him before continuing.

"...but anything you do say may be recorded and given in evidence."

The handcuffs snapped shut.

15

The police teams at Harkham Grammar raced to complete their tasks by sundown, unaware that Jacob Morgan was watching their every move.

His escape had been relatively easy. Swiftly and silently, he had jumped across to a window just below the roof of the gymnasium, swung across the rafters inside and then up through an open skylight. From there he had crossed the roof to the school's crowning glass dome, unseen.

From beside the bell tower, Jacob could covertly observe the entire grounds, despite the failing light. He kept low, creeping around the base of the tower in a crouching position. He could see them gathered at the gates; they were confirming the identity of staff members as they left through the checkpoint.

Jacob waited patiently.

Soon the school and its grounds would be empty.

Soon she would be here.

The school buildings were dark and silent now, a sinister silhouette in the twilight, broken only by reflections of the setting sun in the science lab windows.

In the car park, Robert Brooks sighed as he handed Black the densely packed ring of master keys. A battered leather fob hung from it, sporting a Harley Davidson logo. "It's all yours, Sergeant. No-one's due back here until September, so take your time."

Black took the keys and smiled graciously. "If we haven't finished by then, Mr Brooks, then I'll be out of a job." He knew that, prior to Sports Day, the staff had already locked most of the school buildings for the summer. Logic dictated, therefore, that Jacob still had to be somewhere in the sprawling grounds. Since their initial arrival, the police presence at Harkham Grammar had doubled. It was only a matter of time before Black's officers and the dog teams smoked him out.

Black glanced down at the Harley Davidson key ring and wondered whether anybody had told Brooks that his caretaker was dead yet. "Can I get someone to give you a lift home?" he asked Brooks.

"That would be most kind, but can't I hang on here?" replied Brooks hopefully. "I've a few choice words I'd like to say to Mr Morgan."

Black smiled. Didn't they all. "We have your contact details, so we'll be in touch as soon as there's any news. We'll get your keys back to you later tonight."

Brooks reluctantly acquiesced, taking one last glance around the grounds. He hated to end the year like this. "Oh, very well," he said miserably. "I shall leave you to it. Thank you for the offer, but it's only fifteen minutes' walk up the road. I'll go out the back gate."

"You'll need to be escorted, though," Black told him. "At least until you're off the premises." He gestured at a nearby Constable, who broke off their conversation with DC Gossett and walked over to join them.

"If I must," said Brooks dismissively.

The Constable smiled convivially at Brooks, and extended a courteous arm to say 'after you'.

The Fire Chief approached Fairfield and Menzies, his face grimy from the construction work. Behind him, the thick metal A-Frame of the powered winch was now straddling the rocks at the cliff edge.

"We're ready," he said.

Fairfield nodded. "Then what are we waiting for?"

The Chief signalled to the two men that were operating the generator. One held it steady while the other pulled the ripcord. The mechanism chugged into life on the third attempt. Power surged through the winch, and the thick steel cable began to lift its hook up and away from the rocks. After halting it in mid-air, the operators gave the Chief a thumbs-up signal.

"Right," ordered the Chief. "Let's get the harness on."

A mixture of fire fighters and police officers began threading the straps of a blue canvas harness around the edges of the Coffee Table, and the horizontal slab of granite at its peak. They then gathered the three central straps together, in readiness for the winch hook.

Menzies leaned over to Fairfield. "Shouldn't SOCO be here for this?"

"If we need them, we'll call them."

"You just don't want everyone standing around here for hours and hours, and then you turning out to be wrong, do you?" remarked Menzies ominously.

Fairfield glowered at him.

"It's dusk. Now we've got the generator, why don't you make yourself useful and sort those bloody arc lamps out? Get some proper light on the subject?"

Jacob could hear voices and footsteps approaching.

Happier now to risk bolder moves with the coming darkness, he scurried to the gutter and peered down through a drainage hole. Through the twilight, he could see two figures walking briskly along the path below him, both male, one in a police uniform and one in an ill-fitting suit.

With a small thrill of amusement, Jacob recognised his Headmaster. Here he was, Robert Brooks, at Jacob's mercy. It must have been from heaven sent.

Quickly, Jacob played it out in his mind. There was only one protector to get past. Jacob could immobilise him easily, within seconds of landing. Then he would lift Brooks from the ground, and make him suffer. He would demonstrate how helpless and feeble Brooks really was, just like every time that Brooks had poured humiliation upon Jacob. He would teach Brooks the terror of not being in control of his own fate; and then Brooks would meet that fate.

Yes, that is what would be done.

Just then, Jacob heard more voices in the distance, and remembered that other officers were still patrolling the rear of the building.

He had to do it now, while they were still far away.

Jacob stepped onto the parapet. Soon Brooks and his guardian would be directly underneath him.

He prepared to jump.

— No, Jacob.

The boy froze at the mention of his name. His heartbeat wavered at the sound of her voice. It had come from behind him.

His assault on Brooks forgotten, Jacob stumbled back across the dark rooftop in bewilderment and awe. He immediately relaxed into a childish innocence, his eyes rapidly scanning the shadows.

— Come to me Jacob.

Where was she? Her gentle voice was filling his mind, and for a fleeting second, Jacob felt that she was speaking to him from within. As he wandered nearer to the dome, she spoke again.

— I am beneath you.

Jacob crouched and peered into the gloom below. He wiped the summer dust from the glass with the end of his t-shirt. The atrium was dark, but enough light still reached within for him to see outlines, if not detail. Directly below he could see the edge of the balcony, and the sweep of the staircase down which he had threatened to push Andrew Knight. Then Jacob looked further, to the smooth, tiled floor of the main hallway.

A cloaked figure was standing there.

It waited at the centre of a dark crucifix, a long cross of shadow cast through the window bars by the light of the dying day. The figure remained perfectly still, and did not look up. It was then that her voice echoed inside him once more.

— I promised I would come back for you, Jacob.

Jacob's heart soared with delight. He yearned to gaze upon her kind face again but her cowl was deep, and her features were obscured. He could see enough, however, to know that her jaw did not move when she spoke.

In fact, no part of her moved at all.

"Where did you go?" muttered Jacob, almost inaudibly.

— You know the answer to that. I'm back now, that's all that matters.

"Why were you gone so long?"

Her reply was not an answer.

— None of that is important now.

Suddenly, a twinge of panic gripped Jacob's stomach.

— You must trust me. I know a special place where we can hide, but we must be quick. You must come to me now, Jacob.

It was then that disappointment overwhelmed Jacob's tired mind. He leant against the curved wooden struts of the dome, his strength ebbing. Tears began to form in his eyes. It felt different. He was only a few feet away from her, but somehow it felt different. Then he realised: so confident had he been that she would come back, so absolutely certain of her return, that he had not stopped to think of how the process of her death might affect her; or corrupt her. That maybe she would not return the same person.

The fire had not re-kindled. He was in her presence, but still the chill winds echoed in his soul.

Now, at the last, he doubted.

"Who are you?" he whispered sadly, his breath shallow.

— You know who I am.

"I...I...don't believe...," he stammered. His tears began to run down the glass like rain. The figure below him remained unmoved in the darkness, its voice still soft, but with a hint of pleading in its tone.

— I have enough faith for both of us. Let me reward you.

Jacob closed his swollen eyelids, not wishing to look at her anymore. He longed to banish her voice from his mind.

— Believe in me Jacob. I am risen.

With the coarse grating of stone on stone, the huge slab of the Coffee Table shifted on its axis.

The firemen backed away from it, fearing it would fall. "The load's uneven!" shouted the Chief over the chatter of the generator. "Shorten the harness at the far end!" Warily, his team ducked underneath the block and began hasty adjustments.

While this was happening, Fairfield stomped impatiently over to the generator. "For Christ's sake, it's pitch-black over here!"

Crouching down, he picked up the disconnected end of a power cable and plugged it in to one of the generator's auxiliary ports. The revolutions of the winch gears dipped briefly, as the distribution of power caught up, but within a few seconds four powerful arc lamps had flickered into life.

The entire clearing now shone with an intense white light.

As the winch team worked, stark shadows now mirrored their movements.

Fairfield nodded in satisfaction.

"...and there was light," added Menzies sarcastically.

Jacob's bloodshot eyes grew wide, and he slowly rose to his feet.

Sniffing back his tears, he gazed in wonder at the western horizon. There, against the perfect backdrop of the dusk, against the russets and purples of the setting sun, and beyond the rolling silhouettes of the distant trees, a shaft of divine light was rising from Her Tomb.

The doubt melted away.

Jacob burst out laughing with inexpressible joy.

He had questioned Her, and She had answered.

She had truly risen.

16

From above them came the crash of breaking glass.

They were at Sally Fisher's car, about to contact Caplain for an update, when they heard it. A split second later, they heard the echoing sound of glass shards raining down onto the floor inside.

The detectives immediately started to sprint towards the school, leaving the door of Fisher's car wide open. Black shouted out to his colleagues. "I'll check the main building. Sally, go left, and check the gym. Harvey, you check the science block."

"Everything's locked up!" protested Gossett.

"Then I'll open up the main entrance, and make my way towards you from inside," Black's answer was swift. "I'll check each room as I go, and lock it again."

"I'll muster some of the uniforms here for backup," suggested Fisher.

"Good idea. But check the gym first, just in case."

Fisher and Gossett had the same thought, and looked at each other. Black's tactic of charging into a dark, empty building without backup, to confront a preternaturally strong psycho, seemed somewhat reckless. Did they really want to put themselves at risk, just so that Black could get himself noticed?

"Come on, come on, let's go!" urged Black, and continued to the main doors without giving his colleagues a second glance. With a final look of resignation, Fisher and Gossett ran off to their assigned tasks.

It was now almost completely dark, and Black was grateful for the security light as he struggled to find the correct master key. He hadn't yet had a chance to familiarise himself with them. Flicking through the bunch quickly, he tried each one in turn, trying not to drop them in his haste.

He could hear voices on the other side of the door.

Jacob had landed in a perfect crouch, directly in front of the cloaked figure and in a ring of shattered glass. Motes of splintered wood and paint came fluttering down after him. Slowly he stood upright, face to face with the woman he now knew was Susan Cole.

For the next few moments they stood in silence, as if enthralled by simply being in each other's presence. Jacob's breath was halting, as though from fear, but his expression remained composed.

"So what happens now?" he asked.

From beneath her robe appeared a long, emaciated arm. She held out her hand to him. "Come with me, Jacob," she pleaded, this time no longer in his head. "There is a place I'd like to show you. Then we shall both be free, and no Imposter will ever trouble us again."

Jacob smiled and took her hand.

Caplain finally made it to the clearing.

He hadn't needed his torch for the last hundred yards, so strong was the light from the arc lamps. They had been a beacon to him, guiding him up the hill. As he approached Fairfield and Menzies, Caplain cast his eye over the rumbling machinery. "So," he said. "This is where it's all happening, eh?"

Fairfield was watching the harness and its monolithic load intently, and didn't look over as he spoke. "You're just in time, Jed," he told him. "If you pardon the expression, I think we're about to lift the lid on the mystery of Susan Cole."

At a signal from the Fire Chief, the winch roared into overdrive.

The stony summit of the Coffee Table began to rise slowly towards the heavens. Under the deafening noise of the winch motor, and the urgent shouts of the firemen, nobody heard the sigh of escaping stale air.

At last, he found a key that turned in the lock.

Black pushed hard at the broad oak doors, stumbling as he hurried over the threshold and almost falling flat on his face. After taking three or four steps into the gloom he stopped, and peered around him. Glass crunched under the soles of his shoes. He looked upwards at the damage Jacob had inflicted on one of the dome's curving panes; large, pointed shards still dangled there precariously.

Black's eyes quickly adjusted, and he was about to continue into the bowels of the school when something made him look up again, this time to his right. He saw the shadows change at the top of the staircase; a burst of movement. Two pale squares of light flashed across the back of the balcony, as the doors to the first floor opened and closed.

With any thoughts of stealth forgotten, Black bounded up the stairs two at a time, pushing hard against the banister to power himself onwards, and then slammed through the double-doors in pursuit.

The huge granite block was now dangling in mid-air, albeit not that far from the ground, and pulling the canvas straps so taught that at first no one approached it. It cast a solid, rectangular shadow over the rock formations like a dungeon pendulum.

Beneath it lay what could be considered the legs of the Coffee Table, its true nature now exposed; a deep granite trough, some eight feet in length and two feet deep, scarred by centuries of moss, lichen and ancient rainfall.

Fairfield had walked past the water-trough's photo every day for years, but never understood it until today. The last vestige of a centuries-old waypoint, it was where travellers and their horses would refresh themselves during the long trek along the River Cout. The water within it, however, had long since gone.

Darkness shrouded its current contents.

Nobody spoke.

For the first time since Caplain's arrival, Fairfield turned to him and looked him straight in the eye. "Torch please, Jed."

Caplain handed the large, rubber-clad torch to Fairfield, who switched it on and walked slowly forwards with it. The remainder of the group fell in behind him. When he reached the narrow end of the trough, Fairfield shone the torch downwards. The gazes of twelve apprehensive faces followed the beam and peered over the edge, their features cast into those of grotesque gargoyles.

"Jesus..." whispered the Fire Chief in awe.

Keeping the torch shining down into the trough, Fairfield looked up at him and scowled. "That wasn't funny, even when I said it."

Black was about to run around the next corner when something told him to stop. He skidded to a halt. Warily, he walked around the corner instead.

Before him stretched a long, typical school corridor. On the right was a bare wall and a notice board, on the left a row of half-glazed classrooms. Apart from the glow of the external lights beyond them, the rest of the corridor was in shadow. At the far end of the corridor, another set of double-doors stood tantalisingly open.

For some reason, this made Black feel uneasy. He decided to test the water. "Jacob?" he called out, as though summoning a child for their dinner. His voice echoed in the empty halls. "We have unfinished business, you and I. Don't you think it's time we stopped all this?" Slowly Black crept forward, step by step, and continued his one-sided conversation with the darkness. "Aren't you tired by now? I certainly am. All you need to do is just show yourself, and then we can all go home."

His appeal produced results sooner than he expected.

At the other end of the corridor, still several metres away, two figures stepped into view in the open doorway. Black frowned; one of them was Jacob Morgan, the other was unknown to him. It wore a dark cloak, like the grim reaper itself. The three of them stared at each other for a moment, and then Jacob said:

"I am home."

Taking a handle each, they began to close the doors.

Black leapt forward and raced down the murky corridor towards them. The master keys he was still holding jingled and rattled with every footfall. He ran as fast as he could, desperate to get there before the doors sealed between them. But then, at the last possible second, and just as the faintest spark of hope crossed Black's mind, they slammed the doors shut. From the other side came a metallic clank; a locking bar slotting into place.

Black came to a sudden and ungainly halt, his shoulder slamming into the fire doors. He pushed desperately against them but they would not yield, the bar on the opposite side holding them solid, and he quickly saw that there was no keyhole for his master keys to work their magic on.

He cursed under his breath.

Black pressed his face up against the small square of toughened glass in the left hand door, peering through into the gloom beyond. He saw three shallow steps leading to a higher level. The corridor was of a different design, and he guessed that Jacob and his strange companion had now crossed into the New Wing.

Suddenly a face appeared in the glass, opposite his own.

Startled, Black cried out and stepped backwards.

It was the head of the cloaked figure.

Black realised that his heart was pounding. Beneath the figure's hood, all he could see of its face was a pair of thin, dry lips. But then two gaunt hands reached up, and threw the hood back.

— You must not interfere.

The voice resonated inside Black's head, and he heard it clearly.

But the mouth of Patience Biggs did not open once.

"So," said Caplain. "Is it her then, you reckon?"

Fairfield shot him a withering look. "Well it would be a remarkable coincidence if it wasn't."

"Shall I call SOCO?" asked Menzies, hopeful of a chance to go elsewhere.

"Thanks, Brian," sighed Fairfield, his voice now calm. "Make the call. This should be documented as soon as possible." Fairfield slowly swept the torch beam across the trough once more, as though this time he might see something different.

Susan Cole was asleep, curled up onto her right side.

The baggy caftan shirt she had worn to the airport was wrapped around her like a blanket. A blossom of dried blood had decorated its folds, and stained the stone floor around her with the same, dark colour. The skin on her hands and feet was mottled, purple and loose, her complexion the colour of ash. Her eyes were half closed, the corneas beneath them dull and dry, and her mouth was slightly ajar as if expecting a sneeze. Finally the torch beam arrived at what used to be a glorious ramble of auburn curls, but was now clotted into a grisly tangle.

Around her forehead hung a crown of barbed wire.

17

It was then that inspiration struck Paul Black.

He rushed over to the nearest classroom. Although Black didn't realise, it was the geography room of Mr Greaves. There was a verdigris-encrusted Yale lock on the door. Holding them inches away from his face, Black ran through the master keys in the half dark, searching for one with the same clammy green pigment. It didn't take him long.

Black made his way past the ranks of empty desks, and to the teacher's dais at the front of the room. A quick search yielded just the thing he needed; a hardwood metre rule, its drawing edge capped with solid brass. Seizing it eagerly, Black hurried back to the fire doors, thrust the rule through the central seal, and slammed it up hard into the underside of the locking bar.

He felt the bar lift as the rule struck, and threw himself into the doors with his full weight, barging them apart with his shoulder. Without looking back, Black discarded the rule and bounded up the steps.

As he entered the New Wing he saw yet more pitch-black corridors, and no sign of Biggs or Jacob. For a moment he stood silently at the top of the stairs, getting his breath back and straining to hear a sound, any sound, that might tell him which way to turn next.

Then, as if on cue, the boom of a slamming door echoed upwards from the nearby stairwell.

Upon reaching the final flight of stairs, Black found himself returning to ground level. The smell of chemicals, stale splints and old gas reached him; he was entering the Science Block.

Below him he could see a small entrance hall, glass fronted and dimly illuminated by the ambient light. Through the windows he could see the lawns of the courtyard, but no sign of Harvey Gossett. Cautiously he turned around and began to walk backwards down the stairs, keeping an eye on the blind spot behind him, wary of ambush. Eventually, and without incident, he set foot in the hallway.

At the far end, beyond a row of lockers, there was a door with a plastic sign bolted to it: 'Laboratory A'.

The door was ajar.

Puzzled, Black looked down at his master keys; supposedly the only set.

It had to be a trap. The sensible thing to do was to just close the door again and lock it. He could then rendezvous with his colleagues in the courtyard, and leave his quarry incarcerated in the New Wing until reinforcements arrived.

However, Paul Black had long ago abandoned sensibility.

He headed for the open door.

The laboratory reminded Black of a church.

As with the hallway, the ambient light from outside was enough to see the room clearly. The lone tutor's bench at the front of the room, complete with its own Bunsen burner and bank of electrical sockets, was the altar to which the students' benches faced. It even had a central aisle.

This was where Jacob Morgan was waiting for him.

Hanging back in the doorway for a moment, Black quickly scanned the room for Miss Biggs. After satisfying himself that the area around the tutor's bench was clear, he walked cautiously over to it.

Jacob seemed unconcerned by his approach.

"She is risen," he said. "I no longer fear you."

Black snorted humourlessly. "Go on, then, say it: you'll tell your Mum on me?"

"Together, we will cast you down."

Black slowly shook his head. "Okay, enough. Stop deluding yourself. She's not Susan Cole; she's the school secretary in fancy dress." He secretly hoped that Biggs was concealed somewhere and could hear this too; maybe if he baited her enough, she'd reveal herself. Black risked another step forward.

Jacob remained defiant.

"You cannot hurt us any longer. She is all-powerful."

"Really? So where is she now, then?"

"Clearing a path."

"And leaving you unprotected?"

Just then, an acrid odour reached Black's senses, and he came to an abrupt halt. He sniffed the air experimentally.

Suddenly he became painfully aware of a soft hissing. The aroma of gas here was definitely stronger. It was then that Black realised just how foolish he had been in focussing on Jacob, despite his earlier caution. The trap had still been sprung.

At that same instant, the door slammed shut, and a key turned in its lock.

Miss Biggs, the hood of her cloak now gathered back around her neck, marched purposefully through the front doors of the New Wing. After producing a separate set of keys from beneath her robes, she then locked them behind her.

From the lawn at the centre of the courtyard, the lone figure of a man looked on silently. Once Miss Biggs had tested the locked door handles, she walked over to join him.

Hearing the front doors crashing shut made Black run over to the window. He could see Biggs striding across the lawn. There was someone else there with her, a man. Black hammered at the glass frantically, and screamed at them. Maybe Biggs had thought Jacob was alone in the lab.

If they heard him, they did not respond.

The bitter, tainted air was thickening rapidly. Black knew it would not be long before the gas became overwhelming. He shouted across to Jacob, who was in a dream world of his own, apparently unperturbed. "Climb to the clean air!" yelled Black. "Get on the benches! Get above it!"

Jacob just stared at him. "She will protect me," he said, but soon afterwards he started to splutter and cough.

Abandoning his attempts to get Biggs' attention, Black rushed up to the door and slammed desperately into it with his shoulder. His senses were already drowning, and his lungs becoming raw. He focussed his mind on controlling his breath.

Then he spotted the pipe next to the door.

From its embossed metal tags, Black recognised it as being the main gas line. He scoured it for the shut-off valve, but then saw that someone had sheared it clean off at the handle. "Bastards!" gasped Black.

He glanced back at Jacob, who was now making his way feebly down the aisle towards him, rasping and coughing into his hand. Black looked around the room desperately. "Jacob!" he shouted. "You've got to help me! We have to turn all the burners off at the wall!" But Jacob didn't hear him. Dazed, he collapsed against the tutor's bench.

As he hurried over to help the boy, Black noticed that the impact had dislodged the electrical socket bank. Through the gap he saw a crude device hidden within it, into which someone had deliberately re-routed the wires from their normal paths. In alarm, Black looked out of the window. The unknown man had now turned to face the lab.

Black immediately spotted the detonation control in the man's hand and, at the same second, recognised his face.

In a deliberate taunt, Philip Knight held the switch aloft to give Black a better view. Knight smiled, a dark, delicious smile of revenge, and started to back quickly away from the building. Miss Biggs followed him.

Trying hard not to panic, Black lunged forward and grabbed Jacob's prone body. He wrapped the semi-conscious boy's arm around his own shoulder and began to stumble towards the window, swaying under their combined weight. There was no time to take care, and when Black deposited Jacob on the bench beneath the window the boy dropped awkwardly. With his arms now free again, Black picked up a tall, metal stool and began to smash it against the windowpane repeatedly, each impact accompanied by a groan of effort. Soon tiny fractures began to appear, and Black redoubled his efforts, concentrating his assault on their centre.

The glass shattered, and the entire window sagged away from its frame.

Quickly Black clambered onto the bench, eager to get his head into the fresh air. In the distance, he could see Biggs and Knight retreating to the far side of the car park. Suddenly a shout went up from their right, and Black saw Harvey Gossett and a dozen officers running at them from the main building, torch beams swaying back and forth in the night. Black's eyes then darted back to Philip Knight. His heart froze when he saw the panic in Knight's face.

It was a matter of seconds.

He had to move now, or not at all.

Frantically, Black reached back in for Jacob and tried to drag the boy straight out by his t-shirt. He slid a few inches forward, but nowhere near far enough. Black gripped the boy's arms at the elbows and pulled again. Suddenly, as Jacob's head reached the window frame, his bleary eyes shot open. Then Jacob's hands jerked upwards. They grasped Black firmly by the temples, and dragged his head down until their faces were only inches apart. Black instinctively tried to pull away, but the boy's grip was like iron.

Their eyes locked, and time stood still.

"I forgive you," whispered Jacob.

Philip Knight's thumb pressed down onto the switch.

By the time the thunderous crack of the explosion reached Harkham Common, the fireball had risen fifty feet into the sky.

As one, the faces of the late Susan Cole's liberators turned to the east, and watched the blossoming flames in dismay. Their own discovery momentarily forgotten, Fairfield staggered to the tree line, his expression blank, his features illuminated softly by the distant inferno.

Inspector Menzies was the first to recover his faculties.

"What the hell was that?"

Caplain hurried across the clearing, and followed Fairfield's gaze.

"It's the school! It must be!"

Somehow, Fairfield knew immediately what had happened. He felt it deep inside; an anguished cry; the lone voice screaming in the darkness, and then suddenly silenced. He watched the flames flutter away into nothing, until the bleak woods were in shadow once more. Only then did he speak, a single word.

"Jacob…"

Wednesday
24th July, 2002

1

The new day brought rainclouds.

For the first time in almost a month, sharp, northerly winds were blowing. No rain had fallen yet, but it was only matter of time. Fairfield pulled his overcoat tighter as he crossed the exposed car park of Harkham General. The coat kept out the wind, but did nothing for his cold heart.

So much tragedy in one day.

When they had returned to the station the previous evening, DCI Hill had taken him quietly to one side. At first, Fairfield had thought that he was in for a roasting, for not starting his sick leave. Then Hill had broken the news about Ken Bulmer's death. The DCI had stayed back for three hours just so he could tell Fairfield in person, a gesture which surprised Fairfield in its sentimentality, but was appreciated nonetheless. The successful discovery of Susan Cole had seemed something of a side issue to him after that.

Hill had gone one to insist that Fairfield continue his sick leave, and avoid the station until further notice. Fairfield suspected that this was just to keep him away from Philip Knight and Greg Cole, who were on remand there pending their transfer to divisional headquarters in Mareswood. Fairfield knew, however, that any act of vengeance against them would be pointless. The real culprits behind Bulmer and Jacob Morgan's murders weren't in the cells.

One day, Fairfield vowed, he would repay those responsible in their own currency.

Perhaps today.

As he entered Paul Black's hospital room, Fairfield could see that the man of the hour already had lots of company. He was holding court from his bed, surrounded by two nurses, Jed Caplain, and a young woman that Fairfield didn't immediately recognise. She had a small wad of cotton wool on her cheek, held there with surgical tape.

"Not interrupting the hero worship, am I?" Fairfield half joked.

The other visitors greeted him with a mixture of smiles and sympathy. Now that he had a better view of the woman, Fairfield remembered her as Kate Berridge, the supply teacher that Jacob had attacked. Her presence was surprising to him, but he let it go for now and approached Black's bedside with a smile.

Black smiled back, or at least as much as the superficial burns on his face would allow. His legs were in bandages too, due to numerous shrapnel cuts. That he had been thrown clear, and had escaped the explosion with such minor injuries, was nothing short of a miracle, they'd said. Black had told them that he remembered nothing after climbing out of the laboratory window, but the doctors had put that down to shock and concussion.

"You daft sod," Fairfield said warmly. "You thick-headed, wilful, daft young sod. So daft, in fact, that there's talk of a commendation. I think you've just about managed to dispel your status as the New Boy. Good work, Paul."

Black frowned. "Thanks, Guv," he answered, with a small wince of pain. "But I don't deserve it. I got Morgan killed."

"Knight and Biggs did that," interjected Caplain. "You were doing your best to stop them, despite the risk to yourself. That's what a hero does, and a commendation is what a hero gets for it, whether you like it or not."

"There you are, Paul," remarked Kate, "I said you're a hero."

"I'm bloody not," Black protested. "The whole thing was a shambles."

"Well I think you are," Kate insisted.

Fairfield looked across the bed at her.

"Miss… Berridge, isn't it?" he said. "I'm sorry to interrupt things like this, but I'm going to have to ask you to wait outside. Police business."

"That's all right," she lied, "I'd best be going anyway." She blew a kiss at Black. "When you return to the land of the living you must let me cook you dinner again; properly this time. We can compare scars received in the line of duty. And, as you've been so brave, I'll even cook you some cherry pie."

Black nodded weakly back at her. "Sounds nice."

Kate waved goodbye one last time, and then disappeared out of the door. The two nurses left shortly after her. Once the detectives were alone in the room, a grin spread across Caplain's face. "Blimey, Blackie, you're a fast worker!"

Fairfield was not as jovial about it.

"Not really the issue, Jed. Am I missing something here?"

"Don't be too hard on her," frowned Black. "She called my mobile this morning and the nurse answered; thought she was my wife. She was straight round here. She seems to have developed a crush on me, but there's nothing to it, honest."

"I should hope not," Fairfield cautioned him.

Caplain decided to mediate. "Let us worry about all that, Duncan," he said, his tone just the wrong side of patronising. "Why don't you go and make the best of your sabbatical? We'll clear the rest of this bloody mess up."

"I'm not an invalid, Jed!" snapped Fairfield. "And sick leave wasn't my flaming idea!"

An awkward silence descended on the room. The wind rattled the window in its frame. Eventually Black broke the silence, sitting upright in his bed as he spoke. "Sir," he said quietly, "I'm sorry about Dr. Bulmer. I know you two went way back."

Fairfield decided to take Black's condolences at face value. "Thank you," he said. "In fact, that's the other reason I'm here. After I'm done with you lot, I need to go downstairs, and formally identify the —," he stopped short, and corrected himself. "And identify him."

Black shook his head in disbelief.

"Greg Cole, eh?" he said. "I know he was going through it, but I never saw the Morgan connection coming. What's wrong with that family's gene pool?"

"Who knows," sighed Caplain. "After yesterday we probably have a snowball's chance in hell of finding out what really happened."

"Convenient that, wasn't it?" Fairfield's brow furrowed. "And all within one twenty-four period. I'm not buying it. Somebody was behind it all, and I think it was Rowcroft."

"Pelion," Caplain corrected him.

Fairfield waved a hand at him dismissively. "Whatever. Would you put it past them? Just look at the evidence."

Black's curiosity was piqued. "Evidence?" he repeated.

"I bet they were all coerced," continued Fairfield, ignoring Black's question. "Knight, Biggs, even Cole. Rowcroft programmed them, and now that they've served their purpose, they're throwing them to the wolves. Just like Susan Cole and her bogus holiday. Rowcroft used them to take Jacob out of the equation."

Black was glancing from Fairfield to Caplain and back again, like a man who had just woken up in an asylum. "Programmed?"

Caplain smiled politely at Fairfield's rant, and tried to play it down. "I know Hamilton's stories are seductive, Duncan," countered Caplain, "but it's a bit of a leap to suggest yesterday's events were planned. Okay, maybe Biggs and Knight were in league with each other, but nobody could have known that Jacob was going to leg it from the ambulance like that."

"Except Jacob himself," Fairfield replied. "If they can control others, why not him? In fact, he's probably easier to control. They designed him. They must have got to him somehow, conditioned him."

Black held up a confused finger. "Er... guys, did you want to explain..."

"Just think about it, Jed," urged Fairfield. "Rowcroft have been one step ahead of us all the way. They even tricked their way out of our raid. And nobody outside of the nick, or Montgomery's staff, knew about Jacob's transfer. Nobody. Somehow they were ahead of us."

It was then that Black's confusion ended. As Fairfield's last sentence sank in, so did the truth that had been staring him in the face. Black's eyes drifted over to the nightstand, and the newly acquired passenger on his key ring. Something had made him take it from Kate Berridge's flat; a subconscious suspicion. Now he understood why.

"Sorry, Blackie, did you say something?"

Suddenly realising that Caplain was talking to him, Black slowly replied, "Er... yes, as it happens. I didn't say anything earlier, in case Kate cottoned on, but I'm not actually feeling too bad. The burns are a bit sore, but they're not serious, more like friction burns really, and I thought I might discharge myself later on. It's all a bit dull lying here. I can help back at the nick."

Caplain huffed in surprise. "You're joking, aren't you?" he exclaimed. "You've just been blown up, lad! You're not coming anywhere near work until you're one hundred per cent!"

"I'll be fine, honest."

"I think you'd better let the doctors make that decision," admonished Caplain. "Don't you think, Duncan...?" Caplain turned to Fairfield for some moral support, but he was no longer there.

Caplain frowned. "Now where's he got to?"

2

Fairfield nodded, once, and then looked away.

The morgue attendant replaced the sheet, and then wheeled the remains of Kenneth Bulmer back into its locker. As the door slammed shut, so Bulmer's friendship with Fairfield finally ended.

Distractedly, Fairfield wandered towards the morgue entrance. After a few paces, however, he stopped and looked back. Ultimately, he mused, those cold chambers all looked the same. He thought of Kenneth Bulmer, his friend. He thought of Susan Cole, the tragic victim of so-called scientists. He thought of Samuel Wilcox, the gentle giant, who apparently could not live with what he had done. And finally, he thought of Ian and Barbara Morgan, and the pilgrimage they would soon be making to this very room. In a brutal irony, they would be mourning Jacob just metres away from the man and the woman who had borne him.

"All done, then?" asked a familiar Huddersfield burr behind him. The question was posed softly, and with respect.

"Yes," with a sigh Fairfield glanced round at Caplain, "all done. For these poor buggers, at least."

Caplain followed Fairfield's stare. "I still can't get over the common," he said at last, to himself more than to Fairfield. "Mind you, with the stuff we've seen and heard this last week, I wouldn't have been that shocked if Jacob's re-staging of Calvary had actually worked. Not sure about moving Easter to the middle of summer, though," his final quip was an attempt at gallows humour.

"Golgotha," corrected Fairfield. "Calvary was where he was crucified. Golgotha was the tomb he was resurrected from."

"Aye," Caplain nodded, "only this time round, the spear and crown came from an allotment, not a legionary." He was silent for a moment, uncertain whether to venture further. Eventually he took a breath and said, "So, Duncan, this...vision you had reading Morgan's diary." Fairfield didn't react, and so Caplain pressed on. "How much detail was there? Could you make out any faces?"

"It makes no odds," growled Fairfield. "There's no way it'll stand up in court."

"True," Caplain remarked, "but at the same time the brass upstairs are going to want to know how you knew where to look. How are you going to explain that it was all in a mental message from Jacob?"

"That's just it," said Fairfield, after a pause. "I'm not even sure what the hell it was. It was terrifying. A jumble of different senses. Could Jacob even pull something that powerful together on his own? Maybe it didn't even come from him originally. I don't know."

Caplain frowned. "Well who else, then? Any ideas?"

Immediately Fairfield found himself thinking of the Elderly Gentleman, and his mysterious appearance at St. Andrew's church. "One or two," he said at last.

"Well," said Caplain philosophically, "rather you write the report than me."

"Let's just say Jacob told me where to find Susan," suggested Fairfield, "and leave it at that. It's the truth, as far as we know. Jacob was just... showing her his last respects. She was already dead, after all."

Caplain's dark humour resurfaced. "I don't suppose he pointed the finger at Sam Wilcox for the original murder too, did he?"

"All I saw in the vision was a man with long hair. It wasn't clear."

Caplain nodded, and decided to let it drop for now.

After taking a faltering breath, Fairfield then stepped forward and rested his hand on a particular locker door. Caplain joined him there. "He was the last, you know," Fairfield told him, his voice hollow. "Or, rather, I'm the last now."

"The last?" Caplain enquired gently.

"Of the old team. Bulmer was my last link to them. My father, my sister...now it's just me." Fairfield's hand slowly drifted down the steel door, as though his arm was losing the energy to keep it there. "Did I ever tell you about Bulmer and my sister, Jed?"

Caplain's throat moved in discomfort. "Aye, you've mentioned it over a pint once or twice. Best not drag it all up again at a time like this, though, eh? Focus on the happier memories."

At this Fairfield broke into an ironic smile.

"I never forgave him, you know. For the longest time. For surviving."

"Surviving the cancer?"

"No. For surviving instead of my sister."

Caplain frowned at the bitterness in Fairfield's voice. For the first time in their fifteen years together, Caplain had seen a spark of genuine hatred in Fairfield, and was now unsure how to react.

"They chose to end things on their own terms, you see," Fairfield continued. "So...deliriously happy were they. They knew that Deborah couldn't have kids, and Ken was on his way out with bowel cancer... I mean, who wouldn't?" he concluded sarcastically.

Caplain's blood ran cold with realisation.

"She didn't survive the attempt, and he did?"

Fairfield uttered a harsh laugh. "Oh no, they both died. It just took Bulmer twenty years longer to do it." Angrily, he slammed his palm into the locker door, startling everyone in the morgue, and making Jed Caplain take a wary step back.

Duncan Fairfield then marched out of the room, his eyes distant, and his expression cold. He didn't give Caplain a second glance. The Yorkshireman hurried after him, matching his pace once he had caught up. "Take it easy, Duncan. I thought you'd come down here to pay your respects…"

"I've done that," replied Fairfield callously, "and now I'm going to pay my respects to Pelion."

The glass doors at the front of the Hospital only just parted in time. Fairfield maintained his strident pace as he walked across the car-park, with Jed Caplain at his side.

"Duncan, I don't think you're thinking straight."

"Oh, I'm on top of the world, Jeremy," said Fairfield, sarcasm through clenched teeth. "Fan-bastard-tastic, why wouldn't I be?"

They reached Fairfield's piebald car. Fairfield climbed into it and turned the keys in the ignition, after shutting the door emphatically. It was clear he did not intend Caplain to join him. Before he could drive off without another word, however, Caplain hammered on his window and tore Fairfield's door open again.

"Duncan, I don't know what you think you're doing, but whatever it is this is definitely not the time. Your emotions are all over the place. Bound to be. I understand that. But you need to let things settle for a bit. And before you go charging in anywhere like a bull elephant, you need to remember that officially you're not a copper at the moment, either; you're on suspension."

Fairfield looked angrily up at Caplain.

"That's probably for the best."

Caplain's hands barely escaped injury as the door slammed shut.

The car roared away, at twice the revolutions it needed, and drove at full speed towards the hospital exit.

"Shit!" Caplain quickly located his own car, and ran to it.

3

"Now you're just showing off, mate."

Paul Black broke off from packing his bag and looked up. DC Des Potts, with his right arm in a sling, had invited himself into Black's hospital room and was now beaming at him in camaraderie.

"You see," continued Potts light-heartedly, "up until last night I thought that I was the big man; running Morgan down and cornering him, and getting crippled in the course of duty." Potts lifted his damaged hand as far as the sling would allow. "And there I was, with all these lovely nurses at my disposal, thinking what a brave bloke I was, and then... bam! You have to go and upstage me!"

Black smiled stiffly. "Sorry, Des. Either you have it or you don't, I suppose. Your injuries can't have been that trivial, though, if they kept you in overnight."

Potts sucked at his teeth in mock disgust. "Concussion, they said. But I reckon they just wanted me around for entertainment, what with you being all unconscious and everything. Second best, aren't I? Homeward bound now, though."

"Lucky man. I'm trying to negotiate time off for good behaviour myself," replied Black. He sat up on the edge of his bed, and tried to pull on a shoe. Potts darted forward with his one good hand, and between them they managed to lever on both of them. "It's all superficial," Black continued, "and I feel fine in myself."

Potts laughed.

"Says the superhero! Listen, mate, if I've had to stay in here overnight, then you bloody well have to. Besides, I've got important stuff to do." Playfully, Potts tapped his nose and then got back on his feet.

Black considered this reaction while he buttoned his shirt.

"I can always pull rank, you know, get you to spill the beans."

Potts shook his head complacently.

"Not this one, mate. It's divisional."

Black let this information sink in for a moment, and then smiled. "Well, I'd best let you get on, then. See you back at the nick."

Potts walked over to the door. "Yeah, nice one. Make sure you get lots of rest first, though, eh?" With one last beaming smile, he was gone.

Alone with his thoughts once again, Paul Black finished getting dressed quietly and methodically. Once he'd finished, he reached over to the grapes that Kate Berridge had brought him, plucked one deftly from its truss, and popped it into his mouth. His expression remained thoughtful as he chewed.

Then he wiped his lips and hands with a tissue, and pressed the red button that brought Nurses. Almost immediately, a dour-faced Ward Sister arrived to reward his efforts. She stared at him with an expectant look.

Black smiled his widest smile.

"Hello. I'd like to speak to someone about being discharged, please."

"Ladies and Gentlemen, members of the Press, I would like to apologise for this morning's rather inclement weather, and assure you all of a much warmer welcome. Welcome to the future, and welcome to Pelion!"

Eric White spread his arms wide in greeting, and bathed in the ensuing applause. From his podium, he could see that every face in the two hundred strong audience was smiling back at him as they clapped: reporters, regional dignitaries, and selected individuals from local business. They sat in what was once the car park of Rowcroft Medical, in row after row of comfortable, expensive seating, having been lured to Pelion's inaugural press conference by the promise of free drinks and preferential contracts.

One person, however, wasn't clapping.

In stark contrast to his visit twenty-four hours ago, Fairfield had found the entrance barriers wide open, the security office unmanned, and a large, colourful sign declaring the presence of Pelion. Anybody who had a mind to could just walk in off the street, and pick from Rowcroft Medical's bones whatever meat had been left behind. He had slipped onto one of the back rows just as the conference had started, and it was from there that he now looked on in mute indignation.

In his embittered state, Fairfield was reminded of Nuremburg newsreels.

"Budge up!" The unkempt pile of second-hand designer clothes that was Terry Digger, ace reporter, collapsed heavily into the chair next to Fairfield. "I'm a bit late," Digger bared his yellowing teeth lasciviously. "Up all night, if you get my drift…" His risqué wink made Fairfield's skin crawl. "So," continued Digger, resuming an air of professionalism. "What've I missed?"

Fairfield took a deep breath, and replied under sufferance. "Nothing. Just a load of marketing-speak from our bleach-toothed friend up there."

Digger narrowed his eyes and squinted in the direction of the podium.

"Bugger. I'll never get a decent recording from this distance…"

"Should have set your alarm, then, shouldn't you?" remarked Fairfield sharply. "Didn't you have to get up anyway? To walk your date?"

Digger winced melodramatically.

"That's not very nice, Mr. Fairfield…"

"I imagine it wasn't, no."

"All right, all right!" protested Digger. "Who pushed over your pile of pennies this morning, then? If anything it's me who should be knarky with you; you banged up three of my closest friends last night! Who am I going to drink with now?" Shrugging his shoulders and frowning in mock offence, Digger turned back to the conference.

Fairfield folded his arms and said nothing.

The latest round of applause had died down and Eric White, as though he had been speaking in public since childhood, chose precisely the correct moment to continue his address. "Ladies and gentlemen, we all have one thing in common. We are blessed with this wonderful community of ours, and in the opportunity to live and work in it. Together, we can make it the best we possibly can…"

"Get me a bucket," muttered Fairfield.

"And so, it is with great pleasure that I would like to announce our brand new initiative: the Community Integration Project! We want to wash away the insular attitudes of our predecessors, and to open our doors to new faces and new ideas; new blood and new minds; and especially the young school leavers amongst us, to whom we can offer unique challenges, and unique rewards. We would like to take this opportunity to reach out to our Community, and invite you all to join us… in building the future!"

The walls of Pelion's new Harkham laboratories echoed with thunderous applause. A cynical Fairfield looked over to see whether Digger was buying the propaganda, and found the reporter frowning.

"You know," said Digger. "I'm sure I've seen that bloke somewhere before…"

"I don't doubt it, Terry," replied Fairfield. "I suspect more people have encountered Mr. White than they realise. The question is, like you, do they remember it afterwards?"

This did nothing to alleviate Digger's confusion, so he changed the subject instead. "So... you here in a professional capacity, then?"

But Fairfield didn't answer him. His expression grim and determined, he turned back instead to the virtuous Eric White.

Jed Caplain's car flew out of the bypass slip road, and onto the Barton Industrial Estate at last.

Heading for the old Rowcroft premises, its driver hung up his mobile phone in frustration, and tossed it onto the passenger seat. Four unsuccessful contact attempts were more than enough for the message to get through.

Fairfield wasn't going to listen to anybody.

With the conference now over, the audience began to file slowly away. A few dozen remained, however, and were now queuing up at the Community Integration Project tent for application forms. Ushers, sporting brand new Pelion t-shirts, were beginning to stack the empty chairs.

Eric White, having descended from his podium, milled happily among the stragglers, shaking hands and cracking jokes like a presidential candidate, his bodyguards never far away and ever vigilant.

As he was shaking the hand of the Chairman of Harkham Grammar's Board of Governors, White happened to glance over the man's shoulder and beheld a curious sight. Beyond the diminishing rows of vacant chairs, far at the back, a solitary figure remained seated, its arms folded, and its gaze fixed intently upon him. As their eyes met, the figure rose from its seat, expressionless, and began to walk down the central aisle. It was a middle-aged man in a long, grey overcoat.

Intrigued, White made his excuses and walked up to meet him. This sudden change of plan caught his security personnel off guard, and they hurried after him.

High above them, through the broad glass walls of what used to be Vanessa Daniels' office, another pair of eyes looked on with interest as Fairfield and White approached each other.

White, flanked by his bodyguards, thrust out his hand in greeting.

"Good morning! And thank you for coming," he enthused. "Eric White, CEO of Pelion UK."

Fairfield kept his hands firmly in his coat pockets. "I know," he answered dryly. "I fell asleep through most of your presentation, but that much I did get."

White's smile lost none of its intensity. "Well, if your memory needs jogging, I'll be more than happy to help. Or perhaps you have a question?"

"As a matter of fact I do. I'd like to ask about your Community Integration programme. I'm interested in which way round its intended to operate."

"How do you mean?"

Fairfield watched White's face for a reaction as he spoke. "Well, are you offering to integrate your company into the community, or the community into your company? Let's be honest; isn't it just another recruitment drive for kids you can brainwash and murder like Jacob Morgan?"

The security man to Fairfield's left stepped forward aggressively, but White restrained him. White's face was no longer smiling, and his brow was settling into the ghost of a frown.

"I'm afraid you have me at a disadvantage, Mr....?"

"Come off it, White," chided Fairfield, "it's only been a week, and I know you remember me. And I know that it's only the name of this company that's changed; your activities will go on as they always have."

White folded his arms. "You seem to have a somewhat jaundiced opinion of us," he said. "And as for your rather ambiguous allegations, I've no idea how you think you can prove any of it. We accept that Rowcroft had a less than stellar reputation, but we're committed to improving that. A new broom sweeps clean, as they say."

Fairfield took a step closer to White. His voice carried a cold menace.

"Convenient, though, isn't it?" he said. "A chap of your age suddenly getting control of an organisation like this? Bit of a step up from selling insurance to old codgers, isn't it?"

White's infuriating smile returned. "I'm sure that, at one time or another, we've all had to make ends meet while we waited for the really big breaks to come along, haven't we?"

Fairfield laughed humourlessly.

"And what a smashing break you seem to have had. You must be feeling pretty pleased with yourself. I wonder, how many lives did you trample over to get it?"

"Yes, well; it's no bed of roses inheriting a company of this size," countered White, his face briefly becoming grave. "And, of course, the many problems that go with it. But I relish a challenge, and I'm confident that we'll be ironing out those wrinkles before you can say 'customer satisfaction'."

"Great," said Fairfield. "It'll leave the way clear for you to make a whole load of new mistakes."

The smile again. "Most amusing. Yes, on the whole I think I'm going to enjoy my new role immensely. There are, however, one or two logistical issues still to address. We seem to be having a spot of trouble tracking down all of our employees. There's one fellow in particular, a Mr..." White paused theatrically, trying to remember the name that eluded him. Finally, he clicked his fingers and his face lit up again. "Kenneth Bulmer! He seems to have gone to ground, I'm sorry to say. If he doesn't turn up for work soon, he'll be for the chop!"

At this, Fairfield's repressed grief burst free and he surged suddenly forwards, grabbing White violently by the lapels. He pushed him backwards over the edge of the nearest row of chairs, and pinned White down with an arm across his throat.

The bodyguards grabbed at Fairfield's flailing coat but White gestured to them to stay where they were, even though his face was now turning red. "Wait!" he rasped. "Wait, wait..."

Fairfield eased the pressure, but kept him held down. White took a shuddering, grateful intake of breath. Even now, however, he couldn't resist looking up into Fairfield's tear-streaked features and teasing him. "You should control that temper of yours, Inspector," he said, his voice hoarse. "Wasn't one nervous breakdown enough for you?"

Fairfield deliberately banged White's head against a chair arm. "You think you're so clever, don't you?" he hissed. "But I know things about you as well. I know the things that your company has done, and I'm holding you responsible."

White leaned away from his attacker's breath.

"The only thing you're holding is my thousand pound suit, Duncan," he remarked from the corner of his mouth. "And you're creasing it!"

It was then that a hand gripped each of Fairfield's shoulders, and pulled him away. Fairfield rounded angrily on his assailant, but found himself face to face with an exhausted Jed Caplain.

"Duncan!" Caplain said, his chest heaving. "Stop. This isn't the way."

White got to his feet, and rubbed his bruised neck tenderly. "Oh look. Your ex-colleague has come to arrest you for assault," he quipped, gradually getting his breath back. "Isn't that sweet?" He straightened his suit.

Fairfield turned his back on Caplain, and stood face to face with White once more. His voice was low and threatening. It trembled with repressed emotion. "Remember this day, Mr. White, and savour your new reign while it lasts. Because from now on, I'm going to be watching everything you do. This company rapes people's lives, so I'm going to bring it down. You take pleasure in letting it, so I'm going to bring you down. Even if it takes me until I'm old and grey, I will bring you down. Depend on it."

Fairfield turned and walked away. Caplain took a last, wary look at the fuming bodyguards, and then followed him.

White spent a few moments adjusting his tie, before shouting after them:

"But Duncan… you already are old and grey!"

A gentle amusement drifted across his features, but soon it was replaced by a scowl as dark as the clouds above them. Then White glared at his bodyguards. "And where the hell were you two?" he snapped.

It was then that a thin, electronic beeping rang out. White tutted with impatience, and answered the call. He swallowed hard as he heard the voice on the other end of the phone.

"Was that Fairfield?" it said. The voice was deep and smooth, like poison. It had the subtle rhythms and melody of a South American accent. Instinctively, White turned around and looked up at the window of Vanessa Daniels' old office.

"It was."

"Interesting. Still so… sanctimonious. He never changes, does he?

"No Sir, he doesn't"

The phone call came to an abrupt end, and White saw the caller walk away from the frosted glass. After putting the phone back in his pocket, White turned to look again at the receding figures of Fairfield and Caplain, who were now just two more additions to the crowd leaving the main gates.

"More's the pity," he added, ruefully.

4

DCI Hill abhorred overcast days; they turned his attic office into a dismal, dark cupboard. Reluctantly he walked over to the switch, and flicked on the strip lights. He abhorred those too, but that morning they were an unfortunate necessity.

Just as he was sitting back at his desk, there was a knock at his door and DC Des Potts entered, tentatively. He was carrying a beige folder in his unslung hand. "Sorry to disturb you, sir. You wanted this toxicological report?"

"That's quite all right, Mr Potts," replied Hill, smiling benevolently and holding out his open hand. "I'm just glad you're feeling well enough to come back to duty, after yesterday's shenanigans."

Potts walked the rest of the way in, and handed over the report. "Nothing else for it," he said sheepishly. "The Acting DI told me to rest up for a couple of days, but I've never been one for daytime telly, sir."

Hill smiled patiently, but didn't look up. He was busy perusing the folder's contents. After a while, he frowned. "Somewhat disappointing," he said, and then read part of the report aloud, "'Acted like a massive dose of barbiturates'. Hmm. I was hoping for something a bit more concrete to offer Wilcox's lawyers; they're baying for our blood."

Potts nodded in sympathy. "The guy at the lab said he'd never seen anything like it. Reckoned it was a designer drug, made to order."

Hill closed the folder and slowly laid it on his desk.

"They're going to have a field day with this," he said reluctantly. "How can we have such a thing lying willy-nilly around a police station? That's what they'll say."

"Didn't Fairfield say that Dr Hamilton brought it here?" suggested Potts.

At this Hill scowled and said nothing. He handed the report back to Potts, before removing his spectacles and rubbing the bridge of his nose. "Ah, yes," Hill sighed, "my favourite subject. I trust the arrangements were all satisfactory, Mr Potts?"

"Yes, sir. The Mareswood boys collected her yesterday, and I signed the last of the paperwork not half an hour ago. That's me out of the loop now."

"Good man," commended Hill. "The less any one person knows about these things, the better." He replaced his spectacles and then tutted scornfully. "A new identity indeed! I happen to think that young Miss Hamilton got a much better outcome from this than she deserved. Courtesy of the taxpayer, of course."

Potts nodded wistfully.

"I wonder where she'll end up?"

Beneath wheeling and screeching seagulls, they struggled up the cobbled hill in first gear.

From the back seat of the old Cortina, Elspeth Hamilton hadn't needed any extraordinary abilities to sense that they were by the sea. Her nose and taste buds had recognised the distinctive tang of ozone; and the sounds of lapping water and sea birds were soothing to her ears. She had never forgotten them from her childhood. And earlier, as they'd left the main road and began what felt like a steep descent, her failing eyes had briefly flared into life. She had seen a blurred strip of shimmering azure that could only have been the ocean, disappearing over the horizon.

But now they were climbing again. The noise of the engine was close and confined; moving between buildings, perhaps, and stone walls?

In the end, Elspeth mused, perhaps it didn't matter. These were the last few moments of her old life. Soon they would be irrelevant.

Before long, she would wake up to perpetual darkness.

As the local Health Worker, Caroline Fenton had readily volunteered to welcome a new resident to the village, and to help the poor, partially-sighted lady to settle in to her new home. Now that she'd encountered the newcomer's cantankerous attitude, however, she was beginning to regret it.

"I'm not a cripple!"

The woman brushed Caroline's helping hands angrily away, and brandished her cane.

"I'm sorry, Rose," said Caroline, and took a step back. She looked on patiently as the lady she knew as Rose Llewellyn got comfortable in the sun chair. They were on the small balcony of Rose's new cottage, which was perched right at the top of the high street. Below them, the rest of the village clung to the hillside in a haphazard jumble, all the way down to the harbour.

Caroline watched as Rose sat back in her chair, and enjoyed the wind on her face. It was blowing in gently from the bay. For a woman so young, reflected Caroline, Rose had the bitterness and short temper of an octogenarian spinster. So far, she had criticised Caroline's punctuality, her precious Cortina, and nearly everything Caroline said or did to help.

Now she had lapsed into silence. The buxom Health Worker wasn't sure of what to do next, and so fell back on an old favourite.

"Can I get you anything?" she asked brightly.

"A time machine," answered Rose immediately, without opening her eyes.

"Oh, I see," Caroline joked, her full features blossoming into a grin. "You want to return to the twenty-first century already? I admit we're a bit off the beaten track down here, but you'll soon find…"

"Look. I'll make you a deal," interrupted Rose. Her level voice was a perfect contrast to Caroline's jolly demeanour. "If you leave me in peace and quiet for the rest of today, I promise not to hit you with my stick at all tomorrow. What do you say?"

Caroline refused to get offended. "Right you are, Rose," she agreed. "I've programmed my number into your telephone, just in case. Just press the big Memory Dial button at the top, and then the number one button below it. I'll come running."

Rose cracked a momentary smile, perhaps mentally picturing Caroline's ample frame in the act of running. "That's very kind," remarked Rose bitterly. "Now all I need to do is find the telephone. I could always wait until it rings, I suppose, that would make it a bit easier."

Caroline sighed and looked out to sea. The views over the Mawr bay were spectacular, and despite her impolite treatment she felt sympathy for Rose, who would probably never get to enjoy them. It must be so hard, thought Caroline, especially while in the prime of life, to be trapped inside your own head with only your resentment for company. She rested a hand on Rose's shoulder and smiled, even though it would go unseen.

"You're a card, you are. I'll go put the kettle on, shall I?"

Caroline stepped through the patio door and back into the cottage.

She left Rose Llewellyn sitting silently in the sun, who in turn left Elspeth Hamilton behind forever.

5

A large London taxi was occupying his usual space.

Fairfield cursed under his breath. He couldn't park outside his flat. He was about to speed past, and give the taxi a piece of his mind, when he noticed who was climbing into it. Feet slamming down hard in an emergency stop, and blocking the cab in, Fairfield wound down his window and called out:

"David! Wait!"

Half in, half out of his cab the tall, lean form of David Fairfield rolled his eyes to the heavens and started to unload his luggage onto the pavement again. Meanwhile, Fairfield moved his car forward. When David had finished he apologised to the taxi-driver, who pulled away, shaking his head. Fairfield quickly parked his car in the freed space and then walked over to his son, smiling apologetically.

"David…"

"You forgot I was coming, didn't you?"

Fairfield looked his son up and down. He'd filled out considerably over the last few months, no doubt because of the physical training regime at Hendon. His thick, brown hair made Fairfield jealous and the boy's flat stomach made him long for his youth. Fleetingly David also reminded him of Jacob, but that was a thought that Fairfield quickly dismissed. "Of course not!" he replied, not entirely convincingly. "Sorry… we've had a murder case, and it's been… hectic. Here, let me get your bags."

David had two bulging sports bags but he picked them up, one in each hand, before his father could get to them. "You're okay, Dad," David said. "But you got here just in time. I was about to give up on you and go."

"Yes, I saw. Sorry about that. It's good to see you. Please, come on in," Fairfield dragged the gate open and began to lead them down to his basement flat. "Mind the steps, they're a bit worn."

David turned sideways on the narrow stairway, to accommodate the bulky luggage. He looked at his father's faded overcoat in front of him and smiled. Despite his lack of punctuality, it was nice that some things didn't change. When all was said and done, he enjoyed seeing his Dad.

Which made what he was about to tell him even harder.

As Fairfield's front door swung open it struck an envelope lying on the mat below it, snagging its up-turned corner and making it tumble over onto the carpet.

Fairfield crouched to pick it up.

David struggled past him into the hallway, and gratefully dumped his bags. He closed the door behind him. His father, however, was staring fixedly at the envelope in his hand and hadn't moved. Now he was nearer, David noticed the older man's reddened, tired eyes. "Are you all right, Dad?" he asked, hanging up his leather jacket on the peg behind the door.

Fairfield glanced up absent-mindedly. "Hmm? Yes, yes, I'm fine. It's been a…hard week. Your…um," he cleared his throat theatrically. "Well, Ken Bulmer passed away yesterday."

David's face fell. He had only met Bulmer as a small boy and barely remembered him; the smell of pipe tobacco, that was about all. Nevertheless, he knew what an impact it would have had on his father. "Shit. Dad, I'm so sorry," he put a comforting hand on Fairfield's shoulder. "You should have phoned, I could have come another time…"

Fairfield gently shook his head, and rested his own hand on that of his son. "No. It's better that you're here. In fact…" His face brightening with inspiration, Fairfield reached into his back trouser pocket and then handed over a twenty pound note. "Why don't you pop down to the corner-shop? You remember where it is, don't you? I need some baccy, and you can pick up some beers for us, too."

David took the note and narrowed his eyes suspiciously, troubled by memories of being given pocket money to disappear.

"The fridge is empty, son," urged Fairfield. "We need to get the beers in, and I need a smoke like you wouldn't believe!"

David shook his head in mock confusion. "So what's this, then? Lovely to see you, and oh, by the way, here's some errands that need doing?"

"Don't be daft, David," said Fairfield, opening the front door again. "Go on, son; I'm gasping."

Frowning, David disappeared reluctantly out of the flat and up the stone steps. After slowly pushing the front door to, Fairfield waited a few moments. Then, when he was sure that David had covered some distance, he resumed his examination of the envelope.

It had a distinctive rising sun emblem in the top left corner, like the one he'd seen in Hamilton's folder, and it was postmarked with Tuesday's date. Yesterday.

Fairfield was about to open it when he hesitated. A scene came to mind: the arrival of Susan Cole's competition letter. He imagined how excited she would have been, unaware that it would send her down a path from which she would never return.

He only had a small window until David returned. A window in which to either open the envelope, or in which to rip it to shreds and forget it had ever existed.

Before he had the chance to change his mind, he took a deep breath, gripped the sealed flap at the back of the envelope, and tore it open.

Two items fell into Fairfield's hand.

One was a brown envelope, folded closed and unsealed. The second was a Rowcroft Medical compliment slip. On it was a handwritten message in graceful, flowing script.

My dear Mr Fairfield,

Please find enclosed a curiosity that I discovered while clearing out my office. I thought that it might be of some small interest to your good self, now that the dust has settled. Perhaps one day we can discuss it in person.

Your servant,

Vanessa Daniels

P.S. My thanks for opening the envelope. It shows you still have faith.

His astonished mind racing to catch up, Fairfield quickly turned over the outer envelope and double-checked the postmark. It was definitely yesterday's date. How had she, this woman that fate had never allowed him to meet, known in advance to send it?

Fairfield put Vanessa Daniels' note to the back of the pile and walked through into the lounge. After choosing the armchair nearest the door, to maintain a lookout for the returning David, he sat down and flipped open the smaller brown envelope.

Reaching inside with his thumb and forefinger, he found a folded piece of paper and pulled. The paper had a translucent, glossy quality that he didn't immediately recognise but, as he unfolded it, the format became familiar. Red piping edged the block of copperplate script at its centre, and the crest of the British Government dominated its top.

Then Fairfield read the names on the Birth Certificate.

6

Kate Berridge was beginning to wish she had never mentioned Cherry Pie.

Her normally tidy kitchen was now littered with dirty mixing bowls, spilt tapioca and half-open slabs of butter. Flour covered her huge oak dining table. The only thing that had gone right so far was the cherry mixture, which was waiting patiently in its bowl. At present, she was trying to roll out some pastry without it crumbling into jigsaw pieces, her second attempt.

Paul Black had better bloody appreciate it.

Just then, her mobile phone began to bleat mournfully from a shelf across the room. After putting down the rolling pin, she wiped her hands on her apron and hurried over. She answered cautiously.

"Hello?" It wasn't long before her face glowed with relief. "Vanessa! Where the hell have you been? I've been trying to get hold of you for two days! There's a report in the paper that Rowcroft have gone down the tubes!"

When she answered, Vanessa Daniels' voice lacked its normal self-assurance. She spoke in short, nervous bursts. "It's not what you think. Sorry to keep you in the dark until now, but the stakes have just got a hell of a lot higher and I need your help."

Kate frowned. "Well, yeah, sure," she agreed. "What do you need?"

"Rowcroft as you knew it is no more. It's been stolen it from me. But you can help me to get it back. Do you still have some of the Compound? You can tell me, this is a secure call."

Keeping the phone to her ear, Kate passed through the string door into her hallway. "Hold on a minute, I'm just looking..." She opened the airing cupboard door and stood on tiptoe. Her fingers scrabbled blindly in the darkness until they found a small metal box.

"One box left," she reported, closing the cupboard.

"Good. Tomorrow morning, bring it to the footbridge. Usual time."

"Can't we meet at your flat?" asked Kate, concern creeping into her voice.

"That's no longer an option. Make no mistake, Kate, we are running out of allies and I am gambling everything. Everything. But...when we get back what is rightfully ours, those that helped me will be richly rewarded."

Kate's mood brightened, but only slightly.

"Richly?" she repeated hopefully.

"Augmentations will only be the beginning. Tomorrow. Don't be late."

The phone went silent. Kate held on to it for a moment, while the conversation sunk in. Slipping the metal box into her apron pocket, she slowly walked back down the hallway, considering Vanessa's words. Although she had only just started to dabble in the murky world of Rowcroft and their associates, Kate realised enough to know that, if Vanessa Daniels was afraid, they would be up against some serious players.

Deep in thought, she walked back through the string door into the kitchen.

And screamed.

Paul Black was now standing by her sink.

Kate grabbed at her chest in shock, and then disintegrated into nervous laughter. "Jesus, Paul! You scared seven types of shit out of me!"

"Sorry," Black said flatly.

Kate crossed the kitchen and joined him at the far side, carefully taking his bandaged hands and kissing him on his un-scarred cheek. "How are you?" she smiled, nodding bashfully towards the pastry chaos. "I wasn't expecting you out so early! You've spoiled your own surprise, you know." Kate's eyes drifted past him, and to her front door. The bolt was in place from the inside. "Hold on," she said, hesitantly. "How did you get in, Paul?"

Paul reached tenderly into his trouser pocket and held up her spare key. Kate's eyes darted over to the empty hook where it should have been hanging, and realisation dawned, as well as the disbelief that she hadn't noticed it earlier. "Why... why have you got that?" she asked, a faint anxiety in her voice.

"I discharged myself," explained Black, addressing her first question instead. "Couldn't laze about all day. Had things to do, and the burns aren't too bad. Could be worse; at least I don't have to worry about getting a tan this year."

Kate smiled nervously, feeling somehow compelled to join in with Black's joke. "Or hair loss," she half-chuckled, gesturing at Black's red-raw scalp, "if that had been me, I'd have gotten blown up the day after I'd been to the salon."

Black smiled thinly. "Yes, that was lucky. I got mine cut for my new job, you see. Number two, all over. Nice and tidy."

"Really? Sounds practical, but I don't think it would suit me."

"Yeah. This time last week, you probably wouldn't have recognised me. Up until then my hair was longer. Much, much longer," Black held her gaze with his own. "But then you knew that already, didn't you? Couldn't keep your hands off my pictures."

It was then that Kate's anxiety blossomed into fear. Her muscles tensed, and she repeated her question.

"Paul, why have you got my key?"

"I had to take precautions."

"Against what?"

"Against you."

Black put the key back in his pocket, his face remaining strangely emotionless. The effect was made even more disturbing by his scalded features. A cold automaton had replaced the shy, awkward man that Kate had first met, and she slowly backed away from him.

"W...why would you need protecting against me?" Kate stammered.

Black took a step forward, and nonchalantly ran his finger across the flour-covered table. "Who were you on the phone to?" he asked, casually.

Kate's mind tried to produce a convincing answer. "Nobody, really," she replied quickly. "Just my teaching agency. They wanted to know when I'd be back..."

"Ah, yes," interrupted Black. "Your health seems much improved today. As I recall, we were supposed to be comparing scars, but you don't seem to have any?"

Kate's hand shot up to her smooth, unblemished cheek and she remembered that she was not wearing her bandage.

"It's... they healed...," she stuttered.

"Don't insult me. Accelerated metabolism; standard Level One augmentation, isn't it? But you made a schoolboy mistake. If you heal your outsides too quickly, you only draw attention to yourself. Concentrate on your insides first; take that as a tip from an old hand."

"I don't know what you're talking about..."

"Yes, you do. Your ineptitude gives it away. You're with Rowcroft."

"Please, I don't know what you mean..."

Black shook his head in theatrical disappointment, and leant on the dining table with both hands. "Kate," he sighed. "I hope you can appreciate the position you've put me in now. Legally I'm obliged to report you."

In a sudden burst of indignation, Kate marched angrily up to him. "Yeah?!" she snapped. "Well I can report you, mate! Some copper you are! You stole my key and then trespassed on my property!"

Black shook his head again, and smiled.

"I think your memory is playing tricks. We're having a relationship, and you gave me the spare key to your flat."

Kate stood back in disbelief, her hands defiantly on her hips.

"You're really a piece of work, aren't you? All designer stubble and butter wouldn't melt, but really you're just as screwed up as all the other bastards out there. And to think I actually fancied you!"

"How unfortunate," remarked Black indifferently. "Did it complicate your challenge from Vanessa Daniels?"

"Who?" Kate attempted a bluff.

"The woman you were just talking to on the phone. Unless there's someone else called Vanessa, who happens to work at your employment agency? I can have that checked in a matter of minutes, you know."

Kate's eyes narrowed. She glared at him, but said nothing.

Black stood straight again, and flashed her a condescending look. "It makes no odds to me," he told her. "She's nothing I can't handle. What you should be mindful of though, Kate, is that her methods are no longer in favour. Without Rowcroft around, your augmentations are just going to fade away. There's no-one to maintain them any longer. That is something I can help you with."

Kate swore under her breath, and sagged despondently down against the edge of the dining table. She anxiously rubbed at her eyes with a floury hand.

"Okay," she said quietly. "So what happens now?"

"Well," began Black, turning round to sit down behind her. "There are a couple of solutions before us, each quite straightforward, but each requiring us to do something difficult first." He began to run his fingers through the back of her brown bobbed hair.

She shivered nervously at his touch.

"What's the first solution?" she asked quietly.

"I arrest you for conspiracy to pervert the course of justice, not to mention any sundry crimes we can dig up that occurred as a result of your dishonest tale-telling, and I take you down the nick. Goodbye dignity, goodbye liberty, goodbye augmentations."

Kate tried to swallow but her throat had become dry.

"And the other one?"

"You come clean to me, here and now, about everything you know, and in return I help you get out of this."

"Out?" queried Kate.

"Right out," said Black. "For good."

"I won't have any backlash from Daniels?"

"None at all."

"And I won't have any of your fellow officers coming round to arrest me two years down the line?"

"Absolutely. I guarantee it. But I'll need to know everything."

Kate began to chew worriedly on the end of her apron strings, as she considered Black's offer. It didn't take her long.

"The second," she said eventually.

Behind her, Black smiled broadly.

"Sensible decision. Just a few questions, then, and it'll all be over."

Kate nodded.

"First question," announced Black. "Was it you that gave away Jacob Morgan's location to Elspeth Hamilton?"

The word left Kate Berridge's lips like a heavy weight.

"Yes."

Black continued.

"Second question. Did you attempt to seduce me for information?"

Tears began to form in Kate's eyes.

"Y-yes…"

"Well done. Almost finished. And, for the star prize…," said Black, his fingers curling quietly around the handle of the rolling pin. "Was it you that gave Rowcroft the timings of Jacob's transport yesterday?"

Kate nodded, a pathetic whimper the only sound.

Black smiled and stood up behind her.

"Thank you, Kate. I mean that. Thank you very much indeed."

He hefted the rolling pin in his hand.

"And now comes the difficult part."

The solid wooden cylinder flashed out. There was a sickening crack, like walnuts at Christmas, and Black felt the resistance drop away from his arm. The life wilted from Kate's body in an instant and it slumped back, rolling through her unfinished pastry, before falling from the dining table and striking the kitchen floor. The bowl of pulped cherries shattered as it landed beside her.

There was a beat as Black composed himself.

Intrigued, he watched the cherry mixture swirl into the sluggish blood, and admired the delicate patterns it created on the tiles. Taking care not to interrupt its artistry with his step, he put down the rolling pin and then bent down over her silent corpse. "I think you handled that decision very well," he told her.

He slid the metal box from her apron.

Then, after plucking a tea towel from its hook, he glared at the mess on the dining table. "Dear, dear," he said reproachfully. "Look what you've done to this beautiful wood."

And he began to clean.

7

Tears were flooding down Fairfield's cheeks.

He screwed up the birth certificate and hurled it across the room. Again, the words of Kenneth Bulmer echoed in his head.

…the bond is especially strong among family members.

Then, from the hallway, came the sound of the front door slamming and the rustle of carrier bags. Shortly afterwards David bounded eagerly into the lounge. "I'm afraid they didn't have much in the way of beer…" he began, before he caught sight of his father in the armchair, his head cradled in his hands. David dropped the bags and rushed over. "Dad? What's wrong?"

Fairfield sat back upright, and wiped his eyes. "It's nothing," he said, deliberately composing himself. "Stress, probably. Everything's gotten on top of me recently. Don't worry about it. Just get the beers in the fridge."

"I don't believe you," declared a suspicious David. "You don't want to make yourself ill again, now do you?"

Fairfield sniffed, and smiled ironically.

"You're the second person to say that to me today."

With a sigh he rose from his chair, and began collecting the discarded envelopes and scrunched up paper balls from the carpet. When he had finished, he deposited them all in the waste-paper basket. He then walked over to David's abandoned carrier bags, picking them up one at a time and peering inside.

"Which one's got my baccy in?"

"Dad, stop changing the subject," admonished David.

"Well then, if you won't tell me," Fairfield picked up the bags defiantly, "I shall go and stock up the fridge myself. Back in a tick." Still wearing his overcoat, Fairfield trotted out of the lounge like an overgrown bag lady. "Make yourself at home," said his voice from the kitchen.

David waited for a moment, and then walked quietly to the waste paper basket.

Just now, as he had been coming back down the stairs, David was sure he had looked through the window and seen Fairfield fling something across the lounge in anger. David rooted around in the bin. It was not long until he found the crumpled Birth Certificate.

He heard the din of aluminium cans being stacked together. Acting quickly, and making as little noise as possible, David smoothed out the creases and read the certificate. It seemed to be for a man called Jacob Bulmer. David frowned. His eyes automatically dropped further down the certificate and found what they were expecting; the father's name was Kenneth Charles Bulmer. Nevertheless, it was when David read the mother's maiden name that his heart skipped a beat.

Beauchamp.

David instinctively looked up at the photograph of his Aunt Deborah, stood as always in pride of place on his father's writing desk. He had never known her — she had died not long after he was born — but he had always enjoyed looking at her picture, and her funny French writing. His father spoke of her with great affection, and David imagined that he would have liked her, his Auntie Deb. By all accounts, her students always did. The students in her French classes. She would get them to call her Miss Beauchamp; a joke to break the ice at the start of term, and to kick-start their vocabulary.

Puzzled, David considered the implications.

If this certificate was correct, it would mean that David had a cousin about which nobody had ever told him; his father's nephew. He would be at least twenty-one by now.

Just then, he heard footsteps from down the hall.

Hurriedly, David screwed the certificate back into a ball and put it in the bin. He made it back to the sofa just as Fairfield, now bereft of overcoat, wandered in carrying two cans of beer. He passed one to David.

"There you go," Fairfield said. "Let's get the warm ones out of the way quickly, eh?" Fairfield collapsed back into his armchair and guzzled half of his can in one go.

David watched him, a perplexed expression on his face.

"Dad... should you be drinking? Don't you have to be at work at some point?"

Fairfield chuckled and shook his head. "Not today, my lad, not today. And not for a while. I've decided that the whole experience is just too damned complicated. Cheers." He raised his can in a toast, and this time David joined him. "So," continued Fairfield. "What's this big news of yours?"

David waved his hand dismissively.

"It's nothing. It can wait."

"No, go on. You came all this way to tell me in person."

"It's not that far, Dad. Anyway, now's probably not the right time."

"Don't be daft."

"No, honestly. You're feeling low, and you're probably going to flip…"

Fairfield's eyes narrowed. "Why, what have you done?" he asked suspiciously.

David put his beer can down on the low coffee table between them, and sat forward in his seat. For a second his expression was so serious that Fairfield thought the boy was going to propose to him.

"Promise me you won't get angry," said David.

"Out with it, for God's sake!" cried Fairfield, light-heartedly.

"Okay…"

David took a deep breath.

"I'm sorry, Dad, but… it's the police thing. I don't think it's for me. I'm quitting Hendon." He watched his father's face for a reaction, and braced himself for the inevitable onslaught.

Instead, Duncan Fairfield considered his words for a moment, after which he nodded, seemingly in approval, and rose from his chair. He rested his own beer can next to David's, and held open his arms.

"I understand, son," he said. "And you should do what you feel is right."

Utterly astonished, David's face broke into a broad grin.

"I thought you'd be so mad…"

He walked into his father's arms and they embraced warmly. Never before, in all the awkward years of their stilted relationship, not through David's troublesome childhood, and not even through the acrimonious divorce of Fairfield and his mother, had they come together so closely, and without inhibition. Fairfield's hold grew tighter around his son, and he patted him lovingly on his back.

"I'm not mad," he said, his voice cracked with emotion. "At least, not because of that. But if you have an opportunity to be happy, son, you should grab it. Life is far, far too short."

They parted their embrace and, as though choreographed, leant down to pick up their beers at precisely the same moment.

"But what about the infamous Fairfield legacy?" asked David.

"Well," Fairfield sighed. "The world of law enforcement is just going to have to muddle along without you, I suppose. The one, simple condition I must enforce, however, is that you start a brand new legacy, and dominate your chosen profession for hundreds of years to come."

"It's a deal!" chuckled David, raising his can.

They sipped a toast together, and sat back down.

"So," said Fairfield. "Have you thought about what you're going to do?"

"Well, I had a hankering for journalism…"

Fairfield roared out loud with laughter, heartily, spontaneously, for what felt like the only time he could remember. The thought of his son mixing with the likes of Terry Digger tickled his sense of humour. "In that case, son, my only word of advice is to stay on top of your personal hygiene, and don't be tempted to start buying your clothes from car boot sales!"

David also found this amusing.

"You can talk!" he laughed. "Mr Columbo Coat!"

And for the first time in either of their lives, father and son spent the afternoon together as friends, old differences forgotten, and looking to the future.

8

That evening the downpours came, under the cover of darkness.

Paul Black turned in the front door of his maisonette, removed his jacket and then shook it dry in the porch. Once he had finished he hung it up, closed the front door behind him, and then reached up to switch on the hall light.

Nothing happened.

His senses immediately sharpening, he stood still and focussed. To his right he could hear the gentle hum of his refrigerator, and the rumble of the gas boiler. From outside, he heard the windswept rustle of the trees and hedges. Above him, the upstairs landing was silent. From ahead he heard a soft, metallic clicking as the carriage clock on the lounge mantelpiece ticked away the seconds. And then, barely perceptible, the creak of leather. Black recognised the sound immediately; the winged, leather reading chair in his lounge was occupied.

Somebody was waiting for him in the darkness.

Black cursed his weakened state. He was in no shape for a full-on confrontation. Slowly he crept forward, through the archway and into the lounge area, his head immediately turning left towards the bay window. There he could see the high back of the chair silhouetted against the street lights. Then he saw another, fiery point of light bloom at its centre, and he smelt cigarette smoke.

As he stepped forward to confront the intruder, however, he heard a voice from behind him instead. "You're a difficult man to find." Black whirled round as a man emerged from the gloom of the dining area. The rainfall had stained the linen suit that the man wore. In his hand he carried the photograph that Kate Berridge had broken. "A bit careless leaving this lying around, isn't it?"

Black's jaw tightened in recognition. "I shouldn't be that difficult to find, Mr White," he said, scathingly, "not to someone with your resources. Actually, not to anyone. My name's on the lease for this place, and I'm already paying council tax."

White smiled at this. "Ah," he said conspiratorially, "in the physical sense, yes, you are quite obvious. I meant in the sense of a noise in the night time, or the lost piece of a jigsaw puzzle. Imagine my surprise when I realised that there was a hole in my picture. The shape of the hole was obvious, but not the pattern that should go in it. Now that we have tracked you down, however, the picture is complete."

Black's head darted over to the shadowy figure in the chair, but it had not moved. It had yet to speak. He turned to address White again. "Are you going to talk rubbish all night, or are you just going to get on with what you came here to do?"

White feigned surprise at Black's inference, and clutched his chest to demonstrate his purity. "Kill you? Not at all! Why would I do a thing like that?" He began to circle the room around Black, who in turn ensured he remained facing White as he moved, a defensive posture. "If anything," continued Eric White, "I'm here to give you some positive feedback. Your efforts were courageous, under the circumstances."

"I'm flattered," remarked Black acerbically.

White tutted, and wagged a finger. "Alas, no, Mr Black, I cannot give you any credit for it. Your success was merely a side effect of my failure. So focussed was I on resolving the Jacob Morgan situation, so intent was I on putting Vanessa Daniels and her band of upstarts in their place... that I completely overlooked the possibility of a third party taking Susan Cole. Nevertheless, once everything was resolved, and I had time to reflect, it seemed the only explanation. The jigsaw's missing piece."

"So you came looking for me?"

White laughed out loud.

"We couldn't very well miss you, my friend! Surviving the gas explosion like that wasn't a very bright thing to do."

Black smiled ruefully. "You'd have preferred I died?"

"Win-win for us," shrugged White. "By surviving you singled yourself out; in death you would have been one less competitor to worry about. But that's easy to say in hindsight. Our key interest here... is your interest. Your interest in Susan Cole," White crossed over to the bay window, and rested his hand on the back of the reading chair. Its occupant continued to smoke in silence. "Which is why my Employer wanted to meet you," declared White.

Black stepped closer to them.

"Well," he said brusquely. "Now he has."

A throaty chuckle emerged from the figure in the chair.

"The man has spirit," said a resonant, Latin voice.

"Glad you approve," replied Black dryly. He looked up at White. "Aren't you going to introduce us?"

The smoking figure ignored his request, and continued to speak. "Mr. Black, it is clear to me that when you saw us in your home you expected to die. This is good. It demonstrates you have accepted responsibility, and show remorse for what you have done, and that perhaps there is some potential left in you after all."

"Remorse?"

"For the mess you made of Susan Cole's kidnap," interjected White, his voice sharp and accusatory. "The mess that I had to clear up, while you hid behind your policeman's helmet. Don't you realise how close we all came to being blown wide open?"

Black scoffed at this. "And if you had left things well alone, Eric, I could have had Morgan in custody by now! Alive!"

"Doubtful," countered White. "You're an amateur. Out of control. You need either taking in hand, or stepping on."

"I don't think you have the balls to do either!"

"Gentlemen, gentlemen," from the chair the velvet voice cut in to their argument, "what is done is done. Luckily, and largely due to the good efforts of Mr. White, the situation was resolved. If anything, Pelion is in a better position publicly."

The room fell into silence.

Eventually Black looked at the seated man and said, "So, where does this leave us?"

The cigarette light flared again. Then, with the creak of old leather, the man in the chair stood up and stepped into the light. He was shorter than Black, fuller in stature, and wearing what looked to be an aubergine coloured suit with a collarless white shirt. All of it had been tailored to fit. On the left lapel of his jacket was pinned a small, wooden broach, of an intricate design. His hair was a blend of different greys, long and greased back. The face below it gave the impression of a man in his fifties, although the healthy, olive skin, inherited from his Latin American origins, could have disguised considerably more years. His eyes were as dark as ebony, and a heavy brow veiled their intent. Black also noticed that the carvings on his lapel pin were the same as those on his wooden cigarette holder.

The man stepped right up to Black, almost touching. Black smelt stale tobacco on his breath as he spoke. "We think you have potential, Paulito, and are prepared to assist you in clearing up this other... little mess that you have made."

Black frowned unconvincingly. "I don't know what..."

"Yes you do," said the man patiently, and then he sighed. "You simply must stop killing all the school-teachers, mi amigo, or nobody will learn their lessons."

Black's eyes moved back and forth, trying to read those of the other men, but he saw nothing. They were obviously skilled, and far more than he; the Latin man especially so. It was like staring into a pitch-black mirror and seeing only your own reflection.

"Paulito," said the man eventually, "I shall be direct. There is but one question I mean to ask you. One question, and then we can all go our separate ways."

On cue, Eric White concluded his Employer's sentence.

"Who do you work for?"

Black considered his answer for almost a minute, with the ticking of his carriage clock serenading the countdown. Eventually he realised that there was only one way he could respond. He risked a gentle smile.

"You?" he said hopefully.

"Good!" exclaimed the mysterious individual that White had referred to as his Employer. "Then we are in accord." For a moment the man held his thumb and forefinger either side of his cigarette, and he stared into the glowing embers at its end.

Eventually he pinched them shut, and restored the darkness.

Saturday
27th July, 2002

Tom Sullivan clapped his hands together in glee. There was a pile of strong, fresh timber leaning against his allotment fence, next to the beginnings of a freshly turned over vegetable plot.

"Mr Fairfield," he said. "I really don't know what to say."

Fairfield smiled magnanimously and shook the old man's proffered hand.

"Not at all, Tom. I promised we'd sort this mess out, and so we have."

Sullivan's lined old face beamed at him. "Yes, but to take care of it personally like this! Thank you! Thank you all!"

He waved at the toiling figures of Harvey Gossett and Sally Fisher, both clad in mud-streaked t-shirts, jeans, and Wellingtons. They paused to lean on their garden forks and return his gesture, Sally even mustering a feeble smile, before resuming their dig.

"Shame the weather isn't a bit better," said Sullivan, casting his eyes up to the unbroken clouds that had dogged the area for the last few days. "British summer, eh? How about I go and sort out a flask of tea?"

"That sounds smashing, Tom," answered Fairfield.

Then the old man strolled off, down the alleyway to Waterleat Drive.

Once he was out of sight, Fairfield crossed over to where Gossett and Fisher were doing battle with the overgrown soil. Like them, he was wearing a plain white t-shirt, stained with mud and sweat, but had even dug out his old khaki shorts in case of fine weather. Helping to restore Tom Sullivan's shattered allotment was proving to be a strangely satisfying experience. It had gone some way to alleviating the loneliness and the boredom that Fairfield had been feeling while still on his 'sick leave'. It was good to work on something with his colleagues.

With his friends.

"Okay you two," he said to Fisher and Gossett, "time for a breather."

Harvey Gossett gratefully threw down his fork and collapsed into a sitting position by the side of his plot, out of breath and his hands on his knees.

"Cheers, Guv," he said sarcastically, "you're all heart."

"Not at all, Harvey. Thank you both for volunteering. And knock it off with the 'Guv'; we're not in the office now. Call me Duncan, it'll add to the fun."

"Oh yeah, of course," moaned Sally, wiping the sweat from her brow with the back of her arm. "The fun. Three cheers for the fun.

And while we're on the subject, where are those other two scroungers?"

"You called?"

They turned to see Jed Caplain and Paul Black emerging from the alleyway, each man dressed in the oldest, dirtiest clothes they could find.

Harvey looked theatrically at his watch. "And what time do you call this?" he joked. "We've all got better things to do with our weekends as well, you know!"

Fairfield hushed him. "Blimey, don't let Sullivan hear you saying that…"

"We just saw Sullivan in the alley," said Caplain. "Where's he off to?"

"Getting the brews in," answered Fairfield.

Caplain rubbed his hands together. "Lovely! That's a good start!"

Sally Fisher eyed him suspiciously. "Oh no you don't! You have to do some actual work before you qualify for some tea. Harvey and me have been at it for two hours!"

"Blimey!" quipped Caplain. "It's no wonder you're both walking funny…"

Ignoring Jed's double entendre, Fairfield turned to Paul Black. "You didn't have to come along to this, you know," he told him. "We'd have understood. How are you feeling now?"

Black turned his bandaged hands around experimentally. "Not too bad, thanks," he answered. "I couldn't let you lot have all the fun, could I? I'd like to do my bit if I can."

"Okay then," Fairfield searched around for a moment, and then his eyes found the stack of timber. "We'll get the greenhouse frame up and you can start painting it. We've still got a few hours before the glaziers arrive, it should dry in time."

Black seemed satisfied with this. "No problem."

Fairfield fished his tobacco-rolling paraphernalia from his shorts pocket, and lowered himself to the ground beside Harvey. As he rolled a cigarette, he looked up at Caplain. "So, what took you guys so long to get here, anyway?"

"Sorry about that, Duncan," smiled Caplain bashfully. "I stopped by Blackie's place to pick him up, and we got nattering. He showed me around. You should see the place! A Victorian conversion in Barton Pines, if you please. Lots of nice stuff in it, too."

This prompted raised eyebrows from all present.

"Get me a transfer to Warwick CID immediately," remarked Sally. "They obviously pay better!"

Black shuffled his feet with embarrassment. "Come off it, Jed, it's just a few nick-knacks I've picked up over the years…"

"Nick-knacks?" exclaimed Caplain. "It's a bachelor pad extraordinaire! I mean; that farmhouse dining table of yours, the lovely big oak one, that must have cost a packet. Where did you get that?"

Without missing a beat, Black smiled and looked him straight in the eye.

"House clearance."

Three rollups and two flasks of hot, sweet tea later, the refreshed workforce began their endeavours anew. Despite the overcast, muggy weather and the close sweaty working conditions, it was rewarding to see the constant joy on Tom Sullivan's face. In the parts of the plot they had finished tilling, the old man had already begun stringing out his seeding lines, and muttering about radishes.

To the rear of the allotment, they had managed between them to get the new greenhouse frame assembled, sturdily if somewhat inelegantly, and Black was now starting his second coat of white gloss.

The top of the roughly dug-over plot was being hoed into finer soil by Gossett and Fisher, who were at the same time taking care to remove any debris or broken glass left behind from Jacob Morgan's visit.

Further down the plot, Fairfield and Caplain were now driving their spades into the solid, sun-baked earth, breaking it into smaller pieces, and turning it over for Gossett and Fisher to follow them. Just then, the sky darkened for the briefest of moments and Fairfield stopped digging to look upwards. Leaning on his spade, he began scanning the heavens. Caplain glanced over, his world-worn features flushed and beaded with sweat.

"You can't be having another fag break, surely?"

Fairfield shook his head.

"I think it's going to rain," he said, wistfully.

"That's all we need," huffed Caplain, resuming his work. "Mud."

Eventually Fairfield cast his eyes downwards again, and sighed deeply.

"I meant what I said, you know."

Caplain had only dug two spade-fulls of soil before Fairfield's non-sequitur brought him to another halt. Admitting defeat, he stood upright and began flexing some life back into his shoulder muscles.

"What do you mean?"

"You know what I mean."

Caplain stepped closer to his friend, and lowered his voice. "You don't seriously think you can take on a multi-national like Pelion and win do you?" he said. "We've seen their true colours. Their lawyers could wipe you off the face of the earth without even breaking a sweat!"

Fairfield's expression took on a grim determination.

"Jed, that's precisely why somebody needs to stand up to them. They ride rough-shod over us and nobody lifts a finger."

Caplain shook his head in despair.

"You're mad. Those guys are everywhere. Global. You're just a middle-aged copper, waiting for retirement in a nothing town in middle-England. You wouldn't even make a dent."

A wry smile appeared across Fairfield's face.

"That almost sounds like a dare," he said.

With the morning drawing to an end, and the weather closing in, the volunteer gardeners began to pack up their tools and secure their materials. They threw a tarpaulin over the newly painted greenhouse, and Tom Sullivan, infused with pride over his rejuvenated allotment, invited everyone back to his house for a late lunch. It would be ham sandwiches and, Sullivan had threatened mischievously, perhaps the odd tot of whiskey.

Only Duncan Fairfield worked on, going beyond the original boundary of Sullivan's vegetable plot and methodically clearing away the undergrowth there, right up to the ditch that marked the start of the woodlands and the common. He had not rested or spoken a word for over an hour, and seemed oblivious to his colleague's calls to stop and join them for lunch.

Finally they shouted out that they would see him there, and left him to it.

Fairfield's concentration was broken as a spot of rain struck his face.

Once again, he stopped digging and looked up at the dark, pregnant clouds that were looming ominously over the rooftops. They stretched as far as he could see. Another raindrop splashed down onto the back of his bare hand, streaking a clean path in the dirt there; then another, and another.

Fairfield smiled at the irony.

"Should have brought my coat, I suppose," he muttered.

And he returned to work, paying no heed to the gathering storm.

Deconstruction

Victory is not achieved without sacrifice.

The cost of Duncan Fairfield's growing obsession becomes clear as those closest to him start to pay the price.

When Fairfield himself is implicated in murder, an unstoppable chain of events begins that will lead him to a dramatic confrontation with not only the terrifying power at the heart of Pelion, but also with his own past.

The author and publisher would like to thank the following people:

Wendy Allchin
Judith Andrews
Kelly Austin
Christina Baker
Selena Bartley
Martin Black
Victoria Burney
Lisa Carroll
Mike Cook
Helen Coupe
Alix Cox
Anthony Cox
Paul Cresser
Mike Dyne
Trevor French
Trevor Godfrey
Katherine Hunt
Andrew Jarvis
Declan Kennedy
Brenda Leach
Karen Leighton
Suzanne Lindsey
Linda Little
Kim McKay
Lisa Mooney
Sophie Mortimer
George Rawlinson
Chris Reid
Donna Maria Rice
Lisa Sale
Chris Sanders
Sarah Sloan
Mellony Taper
Kiernan Wagstaff
Ben Weller
Allan Wenham
Stephen Wood
Vicci Wynne

Match Day
By Darren Floyd

A comic thriller about three people having three different days, on the same match day in Cardiff.

Cathy is a woman disappointed in life when her dream turns into a nightmare, and mires her with debt which she doesn't have a hope of paying off. Suddenly she is offered a chance of a new life in Australia, but first she must take a desperate gamble...

Martin is a bitter policeman with decades on the job, and a shameful secret in his past. He finds himself wrapped up in events that he could never have anticipated.

Leigh is a supporter; he just wants to get into see the match. Unfortunately he gets split up from his mate who has his ticket. He finds himself alone in a city full of sports fans. Now if he can only find a ticket...

Gradually these three people's paths collide, and none of their lives will be the same again...

The Ancient nodded. "The book will explain this to you. One day the Seeker shall appear, and with my blood in your veins you will know him..."

Meet Willem Townsend: London-based entrepreneur; loving friend; loyal uncle. He seems to have everything going for him, but deep down Will is trapped by work, family and the sheer mundanity of daily routine. Stepping outside his comfort zone he begins an internet romance, and, despite the reservations of his best friend Jake, Will arranges to meet his lover for a weekend getaway. The weekend passes, and not a word is heard from Will. Jake organises a search for his friend, fearing the worst, and as the frenetic hunt progresses, he begins to realise that Will may have meant more to him than he was willing to believe. In Southend, a naked man is found in a garden, suffering from a trauma that he cannot recall. And when the memories come flooding back, they are borne by blood. He holds the key to a secret world, where the price of entry is death...

Diary of a Parallel Man
By David Elham

Imagine a world where God is a proven reality. Adam and Eve have passed the test of obedience and have been granted everlasting life for themselves and their offspring. In time the borders of Eden are extended until the whole earth is a paradise populated by sinless people who enjoy perfect health and never age. What if a man born in that world suddenly found himself in ours? This is the story of Mahershalalhashbaz, told in his own words. It is the story of a massive clash of cultures, of ethics, of truths; the story of a man who deals only in absolutes having to live in a world where nothing is certain, where people struggle with conflicting beliefs, and live only to die. Surviving on Manchester's streets, he relies on the one person to have shown him kindness in this bewildering reality, a young woman named Kirsty. She is a staunch atheist – he knows that God exists for sure. But as their friendship grows, both of them begin to see life from fresh perspectives. This is a love story like no other. After reading it, you may never see things the same way again.

www.hirstbooks.com

Follow us on Facebook and Twitter for special offers, new3s and chats
with our authors